NO SMALL THING

A NOVEL OF THE AMERICAN REVOLUTION

Also by COYLE:

Team Yankee	1987
Sword Point	1988
Bright Star	1990
Trial by Fire	1992
The Ten Thousand	1993
Code of Honor	1994
Look Away	1995
Until the End	1996
Savage Wilderness	1997
God's Children	2000
Dead Hand	2001
Against All Enemies	2002
More than Courage	2003
They are Soldiers	2003
Cat 'n Mouse	2007
No Warriors, No Glory	2009
The Eighth Day	2017
A Savage War of Empire	2025
No Small Thing	2025

'Cyber Knights' **- Combat, Volume 3: Combat** 2002

'Breakthrough on Bloody Ridge' **- Victory, Volume 2: Into the Fire** 2004

NO SMALL THING

A NOVEL OF THE AMERICAN REVOLUTION

HAROLD COYLE

Master Wings Publishing
104 S. Michigan Ave, Suite 1000
Chicago, Illinois, 60603
312-374-9455
masterwingspublishing.com

No Small Thing by Harold Coyle

ISBN: 979-8985788648

Maps by Daniel Huffman

Cover design by Richard Ljoenes LLC
Cover artwork: The Redoubt, Battle of Bunker Hill, June 17, 1775 by Don Troiani. All Rights Reserved 2025 / Bridgeman Images

1775

"I am satisfied that one active campaign… burning two or three of their towns, will set everything to rights."

Major John Pitcairn, Royal Marines

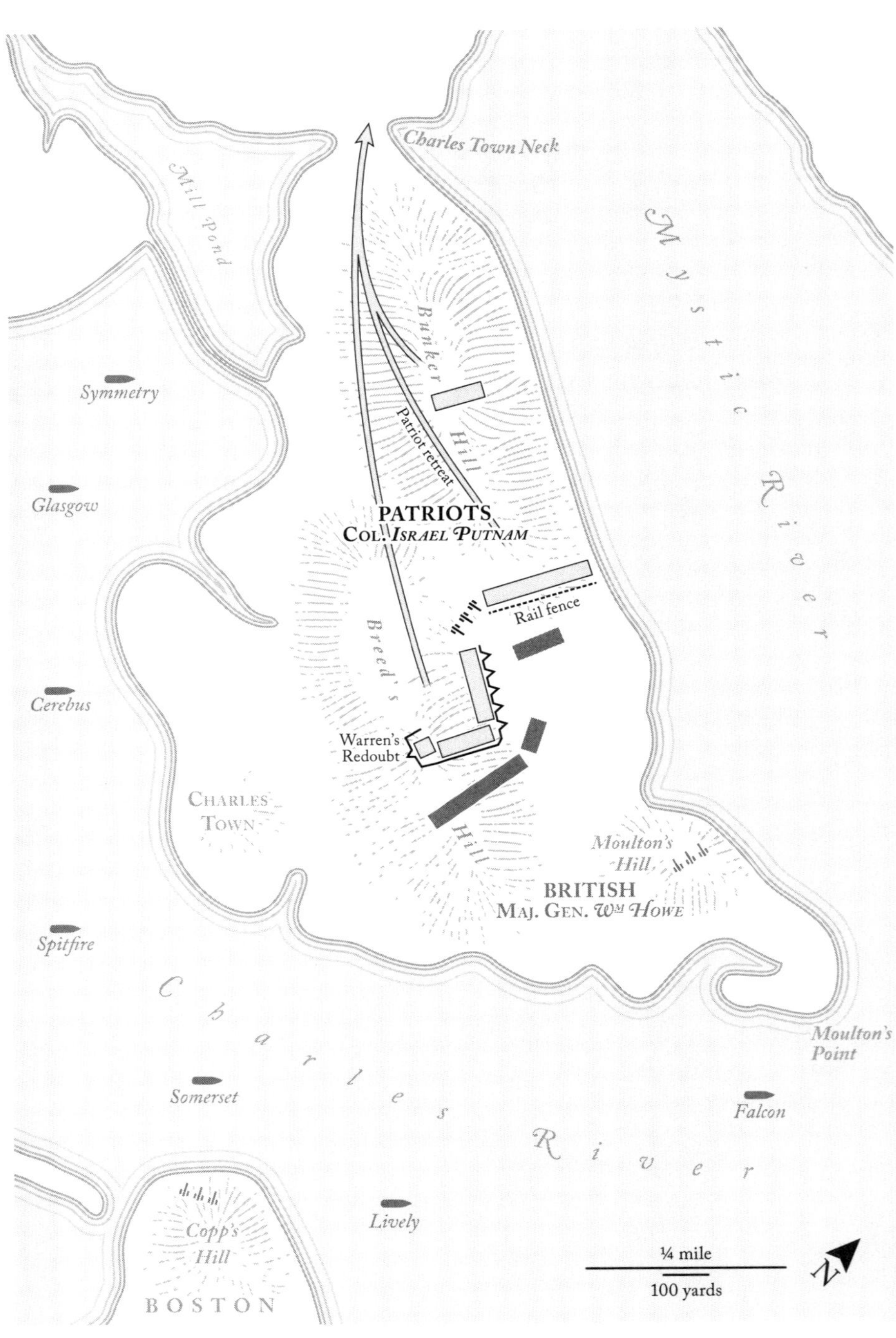
Charles Town Neck
Mill Pond
Mystic River
Bunker Hill
Patriot retreat
Symmetry
Glasgow
PATRIOTS
Col. Israel Putnam
Rail fence
Breed's Hill
Cerebus
Warren's Redoubt
Charles Town
Moulton's Hill
BRITISH
Maj. Gen. Wm Howe
Spitfire
Charles River
Moulton's Point
Somerset
Falcon
Lively
Copp's Hill
Boston
¼ mile
100 yards
N

ONE

"The Rebels are determined to go through with it . . ."
Brigadier General Hugh, Lord Percy

Breeds Hill, Massachusetts
Dawn, 17 June 1775

LONG BEFORE DAWN, the nervous excitement that had driven Anthony Carter on through the night began to ebb away like the outgoing tide. Exhausted, thirsty, and more than a little disappointed the entire night had been wasted digging in the dirt, the sixteen-year-old Framingham militiaman paused. With a quick downward thrust of his shovel, he sank its blade into the ground at his feet. Slowly and gingerly, like a man well past his prime suffering from a severe bout of rheumatism, he drew himself up fully erect for the first time in hours. In doing so, he became keenly aware of every aching muscle in his body, causing him to let out a low, mournful grunt no one, save him, heard as the men to either side, lost in their own thoughts and labors, continued to beaver away at the ground in front of them in silence.

Closing his eyes, Anthony reached behind and pressed the palms of his hands flat against the small of his back before arching over backwards, relishing the relief such a trivial change in his posture could bring. For the briefest of moments, he found he was able to ignore the sound other members of his company made as they tossed more dirt onto the earthworks they had spent the night throwing up on the crest of a hill overlooking Boston Harbor. Though no stranger to hard work, his efforts over the past few hours left every muscle in Anthony's body sore and aching. Opening his eyes, he took a moment to stare up at the clear predawn sky before straightening up and gripping the handle of his shovel. But instead of taking it up to continue his work, he leaned over it, using it as a rest.

Casting a quick glance over the lip of the earthworks that were now more than chest high, he could clearly see the sleeping city just across the bay. In the gathering light of a new day, he found he was able to make out some of Boston's more distinct landmarks. Most notable was the spire of the North Church, sitting just back from the town's north shore, piercing the dim skyline like a lone sentinel keeping watch over a city that had yet to awaken. It was said that it was from there Robert Newman, the sexton of the church, had hung two lanterns, the signal which sent fellow patriots on a predawn ride, stirring a sleeping colony to arms.

Now that had been a day, Anthony thought as he once more stood upright, stirred by the memory of his first taste of battle. It was one he would never forget. Like this day, it had begun long before dawn on that chilly April day when he had mustered on the village green with the other members of his militia company. By the time the sun had set, they had marched close to twenty miles and fought side by side with neighbors and strangers alike. United in a common cause, they had scurried along the road that wound its way from Concord to Boston, firing on the King's soldiers every chance that came their way. In doing so, they had started a war.

As dramatic as those events had been, they paled in comparison to what had happened within Anthony. Somewhere along that road, littered with discarded kit tossed aside by British soldiers struggling to reach the safety of Boston, he had ceased being a mere blacksmith's apprentice, condemned to endless hours feeding coal into the forge and pumping the smithy's bellow. He did not know where exactly it had occurred; all he could be sure of was, at the end of that day, he was no longer the boy who had kissed his worried mother's cheek before setting out to muster on the town's common. Having stood shoulder to shoulder with men who were his community's leading citizens in the face of enemy fire, he could not help but appreciate he had finally found the courage to sever the last bonds tethering him to a loving, but overly protective mother. What he could not answer with any degree of surety in the days that followed as his militia company joined the army besieging the British in Boston, was just *what* he was.

To fancy himself a soldier was an illusion Anthony's captain wasted little time in dismissing. *"Going toe-to-toe with a well-handled regiment determined to stand their ground isn't the same as sniping at a gaggle of harried men eager to beat a hasty retreat back to the safety of Boston,"* he had cautioned Anthony after joining him and several of his friends as they sat about a campfire one night. *"The red coats and the officers who command them aren't like us. They have nothing but their regiment. That's their home, one they'll fight for with the same stubborn doggedness we'd fight with to defend ours."* Then, with an expression he often wore when he wanted it to be known he would brook no argument from any of the men he commanded, the captain took to looking across the fire into the faces of each and every one of the men gathered about it. *"We've crossed the Rubicon, lads. There's no way back. As I see it, we have but two choices: We either slink away back to our homes and live the rest of our lives under the English yoke, or use what time we have to become the best soldiers we can be. With a little luck, hard work, and God's blessing, we might be able to hold our own against the lobster backs when their generals get tired with their whoring and drinking and decide the time has come to put us back in our place."*

Coming to his feet, the captain had drawn himself up. *"The choice is yours,"* he had declared crisply. *"I'll not think ill of any man here who decides he's not up the hardships and dangers we'll be facing in the days ahead. But be warned," he concluded in a low, almost menacing voice. "If you do stay, I'll cut you no slack. Nor will I take any of your guff. You're soldiers now. The time has come to start behaving like one."*

At that very moment, leaning on the handle of his shovel, peering off into the predawn gloom, Anthony did not much feel like a soldier. Lowering his gaze from the distant horizon, he eyed the other men with whom he had spent the night digging. Though they considered themselves to be part of an army, not one of his companions had a uniform. They still wore the same clothing as they had on the day they were called to arms by the roll of the drums and the clamoring of church bells, and a stench of stale sweat and cookfire smoke followed them wherever they went like an invisible haze. Despite his best efforts to maintain some personal cleanliness—a state his mother had always told him was the mark of a proper gentlemen—Anthony found he was unable to rid himself of the filth that seemed to be as much a part of being a soldier as shouldering a musket.

The muskets he and his companions were expected to defend these earthworks with were not in much better shape. Though all guns were kept fully functional and ready for use at a moment's notice, they were as varied as the clothing worn by the men who carried them. Some, like Anthony, were fortunate enough to possess an English-made Short Land pattern, affectionately known as a Brown Bess. It was a weapon made for no other purpose but war, firing a ball of lead three quarters of an inch in diameter and a full ounce in weight. Most of the weapons haphazardly stacked off to the side waiting while the soldiers busied themselves digging earthworks had been designed for hunting game, not men. Almost no one had a bayonet. Even though Anthony had managed to secure one of those beastly instruments, he quickly found that it was a weapon he knew nothing about. Like so many other skills that were second nature to the British soldiers, close-quarters combat—the sort where you can feel the breath of your foe upon your face—was still a mystery to young Anthony and his fellow rebels.

"Best get your back into it, lad," the captain called out as he made his way along the rear of his company. "There'll be plenty of time to worry and fret as we wait for those lobster backs to sort out what to do about us once they've seen what we've done here."

Doing his best to be as blasé as the situation would permit, Anthony turned to face his captain.

"Oh, I'm not worried."

Coming to a stop, the captain looked into Anthony's eyes. He seemed to be wondering if the boy before him was as foolish as his words or if he was just trying to put up as brave a front as so many of the others entrusted to his care had done. Giving him the benefit of the doubt, the captain managed to hint at a smile as he placed a reassuring hand on Anthony's shoulder.

"Be a good lad and get back to work," he intoned in a fatherly way. "We'll need all the dirt we can pile up in front of us when the sailors on those ships out there in the harbor finally get around to turning their guns on us."

Mention of the British warships anchored in the harbor cut a chill through Anthony, stripping away some of the foolish confidence young men possess in abundance. During the fighting in April, they had not faced anything like the heavy ship-borne cannon that would be brought to bear upon their hilltop fortifications once the enemy below discovered what they were up to. On the road between Concord and Boston, Anthony and his companions had been exposed only to musket fire. In the beginning, he had been concerned a great deal by the well-disciplined volleys loosed by the retreating British from time to time but had quickly learned he could avoid any real danger so long as he listened closely to the orders shouted by British officers and ducked behind something solid just before the command to fire was given. Even when British light infantry threatened their position by breaking their column to clear the woods of rebels, the officers around Anthony had the wisdom to move his company out of harm's way before the agile soldiers of the British flank companies could close with them.

The captain had no need to tell Anthony, or anyone else in his company, this day would be different. The earthworks they had spent hours digging were to be held, come what may. There would be no precipitous withdrawals to another, less hotly contested spot when the British drew too near. This would be a stand-up fight, with the Americans exposed while their foes unleashed whatever force they chose to bring to bear against them. With that thought in mind, Anthony took one long, hard look at the silent warships peacefully riding at anchor in the harbor before he once more threw himself into the task at hand. He would add as much dirt as time permitted to the earthen barrier that would, in a few short hours, be all that stood between him and the best trained army in the world.

Boston, Massachusetts
11:30 AM, 17 June 1775

Word they would move against the rebels who occupied the heights above Charlestown had shaken the troops encamped on the Commons out of their lethargy after the affair at Concord and Lexington and into a flurry of activity. Grenadier Lieutenant James Keating of the 23rd Regiment of Foot, who had taken part in that debacle, was especially keen to avenge the humiliating drubbing they had endured on that day. So too were his men, each eager to have a go at the treasonous curs who had sniped at them from the woods and behind stonewalls during their long, tortuous retreat from Concord. When James's captain had informed him and his fellow officers of the earthworks the rebels had thrown up overnight on the heights above Charlestown indicating they intended to hold their ground, James could not have been more pleased.

"Good!" he snapped by way of response. "Maybe today we'll have a chance to give them a taste of good English steel."

The enthusiasm that greeted the orders they would be moving on the enemy waned somewhat as the morning wore on and noon found James and his company still in Boston. The word *immediate* did not have quite the same meaning when applied to a military operation as it did for civilians. It took time for General Gage and his fellow general officers to decide what needed to be done and how they would go about doing it. Even after a plan had been devised and the orders had been drafted, it was hours before those orders made their way down the chain of command, going from general to colonel, colonel to captain, captain to sergeant, sergeant to private. And while it was true the soldiers James and his peers would soon be leading into battle had not been sitting about idle, the myriad of chores they needed to tend to in order to prepare for battle were no less tedious. Rations they would need for the balance of the day had to be issued, cooked, and stowed. Worn musket flints had to be replaced with fresh ones. Cartridge boxes and canteens needed filling. And since there was no telling how long they would be gone from an encampment that had been their home for months, every soldier took to rummaging through their tents, sorting out what they would leave behind while neatly stowing those personal items they would be taking with them in their knapsacks.

Even when the troops selected to retake Charlestown Heights finally did step off onto Tremont Street at eleven thirty, there was still the matter of moving them across the bay, which was never an easy feat even in the best of times. Not having any boats of his own, General William Howe, the officer selected by General Thomas Gage to command the actual assault, had to rely on the Royal Navy. Being as unprepared as the Army was for this sudden turn of events, Admiral Samuel Graves faced the task of mustering up a small fleet of tenders, launches, yawls, and dinghies belonging to his ships and from their civilian owners. These were gathered at the Long Wharf and other docks along the harbor where James Keating, 2,300 grenadiers, light infantrymen, and soldiers who would carry out the assault on the newly dug rebel earthworks headed off to when all was ready.

Breeds Hill, Massachusetts
Noon, 17 June 1775

It was not long before the British let it be known they had no intention of allowing the Americans to remain on Breeds Hill unmolested. Just after dawn, the HMS *Lively*, a twenty-gun post ship, began pelting the newly dug earthworks with a steady barrage of nine-pound solid shot. Even men like Anthony Carter who had taken part in the fight the previous April were, at first, unnerved by the experience. Being fired on by warships they had no way of answering caused a number of the rebel soldiers to question the wisdom of occupying such an exposed position. Some, believing they had been sent on a fool's errand bound to end badly, began to drift away as other warships in the harbor moved into positions from which they could join the *Lively's* incessant, unchallenged bombardment.

It was some time before the initial shock of being fired on by cannons wore off. When it did, Anthony could not help but be fascinated by the way solid shot plowing into the face of the redoubt protecting him and his fellow militiamen tossed great pillars of earth into the air before raining clods of dirt down on them without doing any real damage. Unlike musket balls that were noticeable only when they smacked into a nearby tree or zinged by harmlessly, he was surprised he was able to catch sight of cannon balls in mid-flight. This led him to look up from his labors and glance over the lip of the earthworks and out over the harbor whenever his captain wasn't near at hand. When he did manage to catch sight of a cannon ball in flight, he'd straighten up and watch in utter fascination as it arched its way through the still morning air toward them. Those that hit the forward face of the redoubt buried themselves into the ground. Every so often one would fall short and either burrow into the dirt or skip along the ground, leaving Anthony to look upon them as being little more than harmless distractions, no more dangerous than a child's toy ball.

This near mesmerizing curiosity changed with a suddenness when one of the four-inch spheres sheared off the head of a militiaman not more than ten yards from the very spot where Anthony was standing, showering those around the poor soul with blood, brains, and bits of shredded flesh. Those who were not struck dumb by the grisly demise of their companion drew back in shock amid cries of terror and piteous howls. Were it not for the actions of their commander, William Prescott, Anthony was convinced the trickle of men making their way back home would have turned into a torrent. Prescott, a veteran of both King George's War and the French and Indian War, kept this from happening by clambering up onto the top of the earthwork his men had thrown up and slowly strutting along it, muttering words of encouragement to those who were on the verge of giving way to their panic.

Anthony watched and listened as best he could to what Prescott was saying even as he eyed the warships that continued to rain shot down upon them. While the evil black spheres belched from the enemy cannons were causing little real harm, he came to realize their true value lay in the fear they inspired. A bullet killed, but left the body whole. A cannonball, he realized, had the power to eviscerate a man in the blink of an eye. It was a lesson in warfare he found himself dwelling on as he went back to digging with renewed vigor.

Charlestown Peninsula
2:00 PM, 17 June 1777

James was not at all sure what was worse, the heat that was causing sweat to trickle down his face from under his bearskin cap, the agonizingly slow pace with which things were progressing, or his inability to do nothing more than be swept along like a piece of driftwood as the force General Howe had assembled made its way through the streets of Boston. The men were loaded into a motley collection of boats Admiral Graves had assembled and rowed sedately across the bay to the Charlestown Peninsula. As he and the forty grenadiers of the 23rd Foot waited for the other companies belonging to the converged battalion they were part of to disembark and assemble, the only thing James was able to take comfort in was that the rebels perched on the hill above them had made no effort to oppose their landing.

A sudden uptick in the intensity of cannon fire being directed at the rebel redoubt from both ship and batteries located on Boston's north shore, accompanied by the flurry of fife and drum, alerted James that all was finally ready. Now, as the order came to move off the beach they had landed on and advance up the hill where the rebels were entrenched, James wondered if he was ready.

Breeds Hill, Massachusetts
2:00 PM, 17 June 1775

"Will ya look at that," Tommy Smith muttered under his breath as he, Anthony, and the others in their company watched ranks of British grenadiers wheel into line well beyond musket range as if they were on parade.

Back in April, when many of them had fired on the British retreating from Concord, the closed nature of the terrain, broken up by small fields surrounded by stone walls, woodlots, and homes had permitted only glimpses of their red-coated quarry. Few had been able to see more than a few dozen English soldiers at any given moment. Now, however, standing on the firing step of the earthworks they had thrown up on the crest of Breeds Hill, they could see the vast majority of the more than 2,000 soldiers General Howe was preparing to throw against them. It was a sight that inspired both awe and fear.

Across the bay in Boston, the good citizens of that city were also watching the spectacle. Gathered on rooftops or crowded on the wharfs lining the city's north shore, they watched, waiting for the battle to unfold. In the bay, warships had inched their way as close as they dared in order to pound the freshly dug position with shot from all points. On the Charlestown Peninsula itself, atop a modest piece of high ground named Morton's Hill, blue-clad British gunners could be seen fussing about their guns, preparing to join the bombardment. To the right, lay the village of Charlestown, or what was left of it, for British warships had set it ablaze as a prelude to the storm General Howe was preparing to unleash.

It was to their front, however, that held the full attention of the 1,600 men who stood ready to defend the imposing rebel earthworks atop Breeds Hill they had erected in the span of a single night. Like the others in his company, Anthony watched in silence as British officers trooped the line of soldiers they would soon lead against them, adjusting the alignment of their companies or correcting the dress of a soldier's kit. The calm deliberateness with which they went about preparing to assault betrayed a confidence that was, to Anthony, alarming.

"They mean to attack us," he muttered louder than he meant to.

Taken aback, Tommy Smith turned toward the young apprentice and eyed him up and down as if trying to ascertain if the boy was in his right mind. Coming to the conclusion he was, Smith spat over his shoulder before pinning Anthony with a glacial stare.

"Of course they mean to attack, ya wee eejit," he snapped. "You think they rowed all the way across the bay and are parading about down there for the sheer hell of it?"

Wincing, Anthony tried to think of something to say, something that would allow him to recover a modicum of respectability in the eyes of his fellow militiaman. But no words came to mind. Embarrassed by the very idea a man like Smith, someone he greatly admired, thought him a fool, caused Anthony to turn away, going back to eyeing the silent ranks of red-coated soldiers massed at the foot of the hill.

This fight would be far different than the one in April. There was no denying that, though Anthony was canny enough to keep it to himself this time. He would not be free to scurry about, seeking another concealed spot from which to fire on the English column winding its way through the New England countryside whenever an officer who was part of that column threw out skirmishers to chase away the rebels who were tormenting them. On this day, he and the men to his left and right would be expected to stand their ground. It was a daunting proposition, one that caused Anthony to glance over his shoulder toward the narrow break at the rear of the redoubt that served as both entrance and exit, wondering if anyone would notice if he joined those who had already given in to their fears and left the redoubt.

Doing his best to keep others from seeing any sign of his own mounting fear, Anthony studied the faces of his companions in an effort to divine their thoughts, their feelings, their intentions. To a man, they betrayed little of their inner worlds. All were peering ahead over the top of the earthworks, watching the unfolding drama just as he had been, with taut, enigmatic, and unflinching expressions. Perhaps those who would have run when the British finally would march up the gentle grass covering the slope were already gone, leaving only those who had the strength of will to see this thing through, come what may. If that was so, and Anthony was still there among such men, the sixteen-year-old youth figured he could find the will to remain too.

As if reading Anthony's thoughts, his captain came up behind him and laid a gentling hand upon his shoulder.

"You'll be fine, lad," the officer murmured softly in his ear. "Just remember what I told you. Wait for the order to fire."

Unable to speak for fear of letting on just how nervous he was, the best Anthony could do by way of acknowledgement was to offer his captain a quick nod.

After a light pat on Anthony's shoulder, the captain moved on. The captain repeated the same directive to the other men, making his presence known and reassuring men who were his friends and neighbors as best he could that they would not be facing the coming ordeal alone.

Breeds Hill, Massachusetts
Shortly after 3:00 PM, 17 June 1775

The plan, as James understood it, was simple enough. While a sizable force commanded by Brigadier Robert Pigot threatened to move against the rebel position on the hill towering above them, the main assault would strike along the northern shore of the peninsula. This effort, made by the light companies drawn from their parent regiments and grouped into a converged battalion, would bypass the earthworks on the heights in order to take the redoubt by the flank and rear. Supporting this attack to their left would be another converged battalion made up entirely of grenadier companies, each with forty or so men who were considered to be the army's elite. Given they were going up against militia, James, like his fellow officers, was confident they would have little difficulty in reaching the freshly erected earthworks and putting any rebel foolish enough to stand his ground to the sword.

This confidence eroded somewhat not long after they stepped off and began their assent toward the rebel redoubt. Unlike the Common where they had practiced their evolutions until every man in the company moved as one, the ground they were advancing over was broken up by stout rail fences, countless rocks hidden by tall grass, and pockmarked by unseen holes and burrows. Even moving at a measured seventy-five paces per minute, maintaining alignment was proving difficult. Pushing bodily over the crude fences they encountered without pausing was impossible. All of this conspired to turn their assault into a series of disjointed starts and stops during which noncommissioned officers yelled, cursed, and shoved their charges about in an effort to maintain both pace and formation. When they found themselves confronted by a particularly well-built fence that could not be climbed over, the grenadiers of James's company and those to either side had no choice but to ground arms and disassemble it by hand.

"Where the bloody hell are the pioneers," James muttered as he and Captain Blakeney, his commanding officer, found themselves reduced to mere spectators as they stood watching their men labor to clear the way.

"Back in Boston," Blakeney snipped bitterly as he wiped a drop off from the tip of his nose. "Damn them and whoever forgot to send them along."

It was during one of these unforeseen pauses that somewhere along the line some of the grenadiers began to fire. Upon seeing they were still well beyond effective range, officers and sergeants ordered them to hold their fire. While most did, others, frustrated and unnerved by the manner with which things were unfolding, ignored that order. This resulted in even more confusion as the massed battalion of grenadiers lurched forward in fits and starts.

James was in the midst of doing what he could to keep the men to his immediate front aligned and moving forward when, off to their right, a single distinct voice shouted out, "*FIRE*!"

The thunderous volley, though ragged in comparison to his company's full capabilities, was no less devastating, cutting through the light companies advancing along the beach like an invisible scythe. After a brief pause, during which the rebels reloaded, another volley was unleashed. Then another. Then another. And while these subsequent volleys were even more disjointed than the first had been, they were no less deadly.

Already keyed up, more and more grenadiers took to ignoring the orders of their officers and began to fire at the rebels to their front.

"Hold your fire," James yelled for all he was worth. "*HOLD! YOUR! FIRE!*"

If anyone heard him, they did not listen, though they did continue to slowly advance, tripping and stumbling as they went until, to their front, a rebel officer raised his arm and shouted out the order for the men along his portion of the redoubt to mount the firing step.

-⋘•⋙-

"Aim low, lads, and wait for the order to fire," Anthony's captain repeated as he slowly made his way along the rear of his company.

Exhaustion, thirst, and hunger were forgotten as Anthony stood before the firing step of the redoubt, nervously flicking the hammer of his musket with his thumb as he waited to step up and take his position on the firing step. The feelings coursing through his body were odd, a strange, indecipherable mix of fear, excitement, and impatience. All conspired to ratchet up an already heightened sense of awareness unlike anything he had ever felt. That he was about to kill other men, and possibly be killed himself, never entered his mind. There simply was not enough time to dwell on that as he continued to lightly rub his musket's hammer with the tip of his thumb.

"UP!"

Without the need to think, without a hint of hesitation, Anthony boosted himself up onto the firing step, jerking the musket's hammer back to full cock as he did so. Once there, he leveled his weapon, tucked its stock into his right shoulder, and cocked his head to the side, sighting along its long barrel. Ever so slightly he adjusted his aim, picking out a single British soldier from amongst the solid mass that was now less than fifty yards away.

"FIRE!"

-⋘•⋙-

Shock gave way to anger as James and the pitifully few grenadiers belonging to the 23rd who had survived the first assault paused to gather themselves and await new orders. It had not been a retreat, not in the sense of the word as he understood it. It had been more like recoiling from a body blow delivered with overwhelming force: not a brutal, irresistible impact that had thrown them back down the hill to where they had started their advance.

Panting, as much as from the rapidity with which his heart was pounding as from his exertions, James struggled to catch his breath and wipe the sweat from his brow. It was only then that he discovered he was no longer wearing his bearskin cap. When and how he had lost it did not much matter. What did was that it and the bulk of his company were gone. This thought caused him to look about. Through the drifting smoke of musket fire he caught sight of General Howe, alone and, at the moment, looking as befuddled as he felt.

Slowly, as if awakening from a terrible nightmare, grenadiers, officers, and rankers alike began to shake off the shock of their failed attack. After regaining the full use of their senses, they set about pulling themselves back into a semblance of order.

"All right, settle down and fall in," James called out to no one in particular.

Upon hearing the sound of a familiar voice, those grenadiers belonging to the 23rd who could still do so began to fall in. While their numbers were pitifully reduced, there was not a man among them who was not ready to go forward again, if for no other reason than to redeem themselves by extracting vengeance upon the rebels.

"They're going to try it again!" an astonished voice cried out after a second assault had been thrown back. "The bastards are going to try it again!"

Unable to help himself, Anthony peeked over the lip of the earthworks. At a distance of a couple hundred yards, he could clearly see British officers and sergeants going back and forth, ordering their remaining soldiers to drop their packs and dressing the ranks. Unable to do anything but wait until they were once more in range, while holding his musket in his left hand by the swell of its stock, he stuck his right hand into the cartridge box resting on his hip. After fumbling about a second, the tips of his fingers finally touched upon his last cartridge.

There had to be more, he told himself as he turned to look down into the open box. It was empty. Looking up, he caught sight of Tommy Smith who had been doing the same. When their eyes met, Tommy grunted.

"Looks like we're jiggered."

Unable to think of a suitable reply, Anthony looked about, noticing others had come to the same conclusion Tommy and he had. This thought caused Anthony to once more glance over his shoulder toward the narrow break at the rear of the redoubt. He wondered if, in the rush to escape that would come once everyone had fired their last rounds, he would be able to reach the break before the British reached him.

There was but one thought on James's mind as he advanced up the hill a third time with the remaining four grenadiers who had thus far survived the awful execution that had struck down their fellows. He ignored the pitiful cries of the wounded strewn about in the tamped grass stained bright red with their blood as he stepped over them and their dead comrades. Like every man to his left and right, his eyes were firmly fixed on the rebel earthworks before them, determined to kill every damned rebel he came across. It was not pride that drove him on, nor was it a dedication to his sworn duty as an officer. There was nothing at all noble or high-minded behind his determination to reach those earthworks and lay into the damnable rebels defending them. It was nothing more than pure, animalistic fury and a desire to exact vengeance.

A single stray shot fired during the last frantic moments of the assault as he clambered up the front slope of the redoubt kept Lieutenant James Keating from laying into the bastards scrambling about like frightened children before him. As it was, he took what little comfort he could in having made it as far as the lip of the earthworks. There, no longer able to go on, he dropped to his knees and watched as others rushed past him. With bayonets leveled, James's soldiers tore into the midst of the treasonous rebels who had not been fast enough to make good on their escape.

-⋘⋘•⋙⋙-

Having stood his ground until he had fired off his last round, Anthony felt no shame in fleeing. There was no point in remaining in the redoubt now that it was swarming with bloody-minded British soldiers. He had done all that anyone could expect of him and, if the opportunity to do so again came his way, he would take it.

TWO

"From the east to the west, blow the trumpet to arms."

Thomas Paine, July 1775

Winchester, Virginia
July 1775

WITH EVENING FAST approaching, the small inn owned by Ian and Megan McPherson began to fill with settlers, drovers, and teamsters traveling along the Great Wagon Road. They were seeking nothing more than a meal and, if they could afford it, a place to spend the night before continuing their journey. The residents of Winchester who had already set aside their daily labors and joined them were interested in something far more valuable, something every traveler seemed to have an abundance of that summer: news.

Situated near the northern end of the Shenandoah Valley, the inn and the surrounding community were considered the gateway to the rich farmlands, both settled and yet to be claimed, that lay to the south. It was a fact Megan had become keenly aware of during the closing days of the French and Indian War. A peddler from Philadelphia who was seeking to ply his trade in the settlements along that road claimed it would soon be the most heavily traveled in all the colonies.

"Once the Indians have been dealt with properly, there'll be no end to the folks who'll be making their way down from Pennsylvania," he had proclaimed loudly to anyone willing to listen. "In no time, no time at all, they'll be shipping their produce back north. Settlers seeking land of their own, and merchants eager to sell them the goods they'll need, will stop here to enjoy a good meal and a good night's rest in a warm bed before continuing on into the wilderness beyond," he added with a smile and a wink at Megan as she was refilling his mug with ale.

With this in mind, when Ian had been mustered out of Colonel Washington's regiment, Megan convinced him to stay on and help the old widow she had been working for at the time. In truth, it had taken little to convince Ian to give up his dreams of laying claim to a parcel of land they could call their own. Neither one of them was a farmer. Ian had been but sixteen when, in the wake of the Glorious '45, he had been transported to the colonies with countless other Scots who had rallied to Charles Stuart's banner.

Megan had come to Virginia as an indentured servant from Ireland. The two had met in Alexandria, Virginia, quite by accident in 1754 when Ian, newly recruited by Colonel Washington, was encamped there with a regiment raised to chase the French from the Forks of the Ohio. That he had continued to soldier on despite having been an apprentice to a wheelwright was not difficult for Megan to understand. Ian was a Scot, born and bred to be a soldier by his clan's chieftain. What was astonishing, even to her, was she had followed him in 1756 as soon as she learned he was serving at Fort Louden, which at the time was one of several forts built to protect the western frontier of Virginia from Indians who were being spurred on by the French to raid the English colonists. There Megan had worked as a cook and serving girl for the former owner of the inn until she died in 1759. For reasons the man's widow never fully explained, she kept Megan on and, when the woman passed, left the inn to her and Ian.

As the peddler had predicted, once peace came to the colonies, a flood of Scot-Irish immigrants fresh from Europe and Germans from Pennsylvania began to make their way up the valley. Some stayed in Virginia. Many went on to find their place in the backcountry of North Carolina. All, it seemed to Megan, stopped at her inn, if only for a pint of ale or a nip of fresh apple cider.

That she considered it her inn was only natural, for Ian tended to be very outspoken and combative whenever the subject of the King or politics came up. This naturally made for a bad combination when it came to dealing with patrons whose diverse opinions all too often conflicted with his. Whether Ian argued with them due to his convictions or simply because he was a Scot who was not happy unless he was fighting with someone did not matter to Megan, which is why she had encouraged him to take up his old trade.

"The number of wagons going past our door increases every day," she murmured as if thinking out loud to herself one night as they were preparing for bed after a long and tiring day. "No doubt a good many of them are in need of repair."

"Aye, I expect so," Ian replied as he sat on the opposite side of their bed, holding up a stocking and carefully inspecting a fresh hole in it as if trying to decide if it was worth the effort to mend it.

"Well, I was thinking," Megan mused as she finished pulling her nightshirt over her head before crawling up onto the bed and making her way over to where Ian sat. Coming to rest on her knees behind him, she reached out, placing her hands on his shoulders and gently began to work out the kinks in his tired, sore muscles. "If you were to set up a small shop in the shed where some of the travelers put their horses, you could tend to their wagons and carts while Gretchen and I look after their other needs," she cooed sweetly in his ear.

"Other needs?" he asked while giving her a questioning glance over his shoulder.

Taking a hand away from his shoulder, she gave her husband a playful slap on the back of his head.

"Ian McPherson, you know very well what I mean."

"Aye, I know what you meant," he chuckled. "I was just making sure there weren't any other mad schemes running about in that head of yours."

"It's not a mad scheme," she countered, taking care to keep her temper in check. "It makes perfect sense. I mean, while you and Boy are fixing their wagons, taking great care to make sure you've done a good job of it by checking twice, maybe three times, the poor teamsters will have naught to do but sit around, partaking of our hospitality and sharing stories with other teamsters waiting for you to look at their wagons."

Ian chuckled, "You're a clever one, you are."

"I know," she murmured seductively as she went back to gently kneading his sore muscles. "After all, I married you, didn't I?"

In time, what had started out as nothing more than a sideline that provided Megan and Ian with extra hard currency and trade goods teamsters often used to pay became a thriving business. It kept Ian and a young man they had taken in when he was just a boy busy from sunup to sundown and, from time to time, well into the night if the owner of the wagon was in a hurry and was willing to pay extra.

The young man, who everyone including Ian called Boy, was not related to Ian or Megan, at least not by blood. Who he was had always been something of a mystery, one the regular patrons of the inn often speculated on, but never in the presence of Ian, Megan, or Boy. How he had come to be taken in by the McPhersons was about all that was known with any degree of certainty: During the waning days of the French and Indian War, a patrol Ian was leading had come across Boy wandering through the woods, naked and in a daze. The boy was but four or five then. After sending him back to Fort Louden with two of his men, Ian had continued on until he came across a farmstead that had been attacked several days before by an Indian raiding party. A body had been found burned beyond recognition in the charred remains of the crude cabin. If there had been others, there was no sign of them, leading Ian to assume they had either been taken away as captives or, like Boy, had run off into the woods. A thorough search of the ruins and the surrounding area turned up nothing, not even a scrap of paper that gave Ian a clue as to who the boy or who his parents had been. When no one came forward to claim him, Megan had informed Ian they would keep him. "It's the Christian thing to do," she had declared in the tone of voice she used when she was in no mood to argue.

Ian had not argued, but not because he was a good Christian. Having seen what men were able to do in the name of God, he had all but given up belief in that one, all powerful being. Instead, he put his faith in his own two hands, the love of his wife and family, and a few trusted friends, one of whom had paid a visit to the inn that July day for the first time in many years.

-<<<<•>>>>-

When Megan saw Ezra Shaw standing in the open doorway of the inn, she drew in a deep breath. He was waiting for his eyes to become accustomed to an interior lit by whatever light managed to pass through windows Gretchen had not yet had time to clean. Megan had had no need to ask why Shaw had come.

When he finally noticed Megan standing on the other side of the room, Shaw smiled. It quickly disappeared, however, when he took note of her expression. It was same look that other wives and mothers had greeted him with as he sought out men he knew and could trust.

Megan did not wait to hear what he had to say nor did she make any effort to welcome a man who shared a terrible secret with her and Ian, one that led, in a most unfortunate way, to their owning the inn. As calmly as she could, she told Ian's former captain her husband was in the wheelwright's shop next to the inn.

With a tip of his hat and a quickly muttered "thank you," Shaw withdrew.

-⋘•⋙-

A tap on his shoulder caused Ian to look up from the wheel he and Boy had just finished resetting on its spindle. With a nod, Boy indicated someone was coming up behind them. When he saw who it was, Ian grunted. He too knew why Ezra Shaw, a man he still called Captain even though neither of them had worn a uniform in years, was here.

"Finish up here," Ian instructed the quiet young man who seldom spoke. "Then check with the women and see if they have need of you."

Pausing, Ian wiped axle grease off his hands with a rag as he watched Shaw approach, wondering what he would say, what he would do. He had been expecting someone to come, to ask him to go take up arms and march off to war with them. That Dan Morgan had not bothered to did not much surprise Ian. Morgan had been recruiting men who were crack shots and used to living rough. The last time Ian had lived under the stars for more than a night or two had been in 1758, when he had marched north with Colonel Washington, whose regiment was part of an expedition mounted by Brigadier General John Forbes against the French at Fort Duquesne. It had been a dismal experience, conducted in the fall when anyone with any sense had stacked arms and settled in for the winter.

Shaw, who like Megan was Irish, was more than a friend. Having lost his father and just about every male relative he could lay claim to at Culloden or during the Clearance, Ian had latched onto the man when he had joined the Virginia Militia. In turn, Shaw took it upon himself to fill that void, just as Ian had with Boy. So rather than ask why Shaw had journeyed all the way from Fredericksburg to see him, after exchanging heartfelt greetings, Ian motioned for Shaw to join him, and the men took a seat on a bench set against the front of the shop.

"I see the boy is still with you," Shaw began as he watched the young man as he finished hammering the wheel's lynchpin into place. Boy then gave the wheel a good shake and spin it to make sure all was in order.

"Aye, he is. And mighty glad I am of it. He's a good worker," Ian replied with a touch of pride in his voice.

"Did he ever tell you his name?"

Ian gave his head a slow, sad shake. "No."

"What did you name him then?"

"We didn't. Well, I didn't," Ian corrected himself. "Megan took to calling him Patrick at first, after that saint of yours, but somehow it didn't seem to take. So we let the matter drop."

Dumbfounded, Shaw drew back. "That was a damned foolish thing to do. A man's got to have a name."

Again, Ian hesitated before answering. When he did, he dropped his gaze a moment before glancing over at Shaw out of the corner of his eyes.

"For the longest time both Megan and I thought the lad would come around, would remember something, or tell us who he was. So rather than saddle him another name he might not like, or think we were trying to impose our will on him, we simply took to calling him Boy."

Ian's sad tale was interrupted when a young girl with honey blond hair, Delft blue eyes, and a fetching smile emerged from the inn bearing tankards of ale for them. After thanking her, Shaw watched her leave before turning to Ian and cocking a brow.

"One of yours?"

"No, the daughter of a family Megan buys her cider from. She works at the inn."

"She's a pretty thing," Shaw muttered as the girl paused in the doorway of the inn to look back at them and give Shaw a sly smile that told him she was well aware he had been following her every move.

"She's German," Ian intoned flatly before taking a sip of his ale. Like most Highlanders, he had no use for anyone who was not a Scot, leaving Shaw no need to ask what he had meant by that last comment.

"So, what do other people call the boy?" Shaw asked after enjoying a sip of ale.

"Boy," Ian replied as he stared down at the tankard he held clutched tightly to his chest. "A few of the local wags call him McPherson-son, making a show of pretending to stutter." Eager to move onto another, less awkward subject, he took to telling Shaw of his other children, those he had sired. This included Kyle, age fourteen; Rose, age twelve; and Caitlin, age ten. "They're all wee little devils, especially Rose," Ian declared. "She takes after her mam."

"That's not a bad thing, you know," Shaw pointed out.

"No, it's not," Ian agreed.

The two took a moment to enjoy their ale as each dwelt on their own memories of how Megan had made her way west at a time when traveling to Winchester was a hazardous undertaking to find Ian and inform him she intended to marry him. It was the thought of the journey she had made that caused Ian to look over at Shaw. "Well, are you going to ask me?"

Returning Ian's gaze, Shaw sighed. "Do I have to?"

"Oh, I dare say I'm entitled to that."

"You want me to tell you why I came here when you know damned well why?"

"I would think you would at least have the courtesy to tell me why I should follow another damned fool who's taken up arms against the British," Ian replied sharply.

"Colonel Washington is no fool," Shaw countered.

"Aye, he's not, or he wasn't last I served under him. But that was a long time ago, and we were fighting *with* the English, not against them."

Rather than argue with a man who was never shy about fighting, Shaw leaned forward, planted his elbows on his knees, and stared down into the tankard he held.

"Tell me, why did you follow Prince Charlie back in '45?"

"The same reason my grandfather did: Our chieftains called on us to fight for him and our rightful King."

"Is that really why you took up arms against George II?" Shaw asked as he peeked over the rim of his tankard at Ian.

Ian didn't answer. He had no need to. Like so many others, his reasons for following the foppish boy who was no more a leader than his own young Rose was more than simply answering the call of his chieftain. Having seen how the English had lorded over them, he was determined to rid his ancestors' land of people who were, and to many would always be, foreign intruders.

When Ian did not answer, Shaw glanced about at the inn and the wheelwright's shop.

"You've done well for yourself here," he stated admiringly. "Better than most of our kinsmen had a right to hope for when the English ran us off our land, land that had belonged to our fathers, their fathers, and their father's fathers. The English have no claim to it other than that which they conjured up out of thin air." He let that thought hang in the air as he drained his tankard. Then, coming to his feet, Shaw turned to face Ian. "How long do you suppose it will be before someone back in London gets it in his head they need this patch of ground, land that we fought and bled for, sending you and yours packing at the point of a bayonet?"

Ian did not answer that question. Instead, he finished what was left in his tankard, rose to his feet, and placed a hand on Shaw's shoulder.

"Dinner should be ready soon. I expect you'll be wanting to shake some road dust off before we eat. I know Herself will not let me anywhere near the table until after I've washed. We'll talk later."

A small, knowing smile brightened Shaw's face, brought on by the knowledge that the man he was counting on to help him whip farmers, shopkeepers, and boys into soldiers would be making the trip back east to Williamsburg where the regiment Patrick Henry was forming would be mustering.

-⋘•⋙-

"You're going, aren't you?" Megan blurted when, later that night, Ian slipped into the room after ensuring the last of the inn's patrons had either retired to their rooms, returned to their homes, or headed back to wherever they had left their wagon.

Stopping just inside the door, he wondered whether he should stand his ground and attempt to reason with his wife, or flee while he still had the chance.

Standing on the far side of the room in her shift with her tightly crossed arms pressed against her bosom, Megan glared at Ian as she waited for him to reply. When he didn't, she shook her head.

"You're a fool, Ian Hamish McPherson. A damned, thick-headed, bloody Scottish fool."

Deciding it would be pointless to try to explain to her why he was going, not with the mood Megan was in, Ian closed the door and made his way over to his side of their bed. He pulled off his shirt as he went, watching her as a man approaching a dangerous animal poised to strike would.

"I do not wish to fight with you."

"Oh, you'll fight the English, but not me, your own wife."

"Aye, I'll fight them," he admitted in a low, almost resigned tone of voice.

In the dim light provided by a single candle set on a nightstand next to her, Megan could not help but see the deep shadows of her husband's careworn expression. As much as she wanted to hang onto the anger she felt over his decision to march off with Ezra Shaw without so much as discussing the matter with her, if for no other reason than to extract a modicum of vengeance, Megan found herself unable to do so. After heaving a great sigh, she dropped her arms to her side and lowered her chin, causing her long, auburn hair to cascade down along the side of her face.

"I don't understand," she whispered in a tone of voice that reminded Ian of the way Rose did whenever she came to him with a question concerning all the great mysteries of life her older brother was unable to explain to her.

"I think you do," he replied softly while slipping into a clean nightshirt Megan had laid out for him on his side of the bed.

Peeking up, she drew in a deep breath. She did. The man standing across from her was no innkeeper. He was a Highlander, through and through. While there were more than a few aspects of his nature that still caused her to question her own sanity for following him to Winchester during the last war, when that town was but a cluster of crude homes perched on the very edge of civilization, she could not deny the fact had he not agreed to go with Shaw, she probably would have lost all respect for him.

She stood thinking as she watched him pull back the thin coverlet she spread over the bed during the day and crawl into bed, never once taking his eyes off hers. Had he turned his back on Shaw, and by extension what he saw as his responsibilities, she would have.

Thus resigned, she shoved aside the last of her anger and joined him. Sliding across the down-filled mattress until her head lay on the same pillow as Ian's, she placed a gentle hand on his cheek.

"Fool that you are, I love you, Ian Hamish McPherson."

The relief he felt over this simple declaration was clear on Ian's face, as it lit up with a mischievous little smile.

"How much do you love me?" he asked in a deep, husky voice.

Megan did not answer, not at first. Instead, she rose up on one elbow, reached behind her, and snuffed out the lone candle that had been lighting the room before snuggling up to him and giving him a quick kiss.

"Must I show you?" she whispered in his ear even as she was placing a hand on his side.

"Aye, you must."

With that, she ever so slowly began to run the tips of her fingers down along his side and across his stomach as she prepared to do just that.

THREE

"That the King can do no wrong is a necessary and fundamental principle of the English constitution."
Sir William Blackstone,
Commentaries on the Laws of England, 1765

New York City
July 1775

WITH THE ROYAL Governor reduced to near impotence by the provincial rabble who sought to replace him with one of their own, and honest citizens of means living in fear for their very lives, Katherine Shields dreaded the thought of spending time in a city her Dutch ancestors had helped found. Not that she had much of a choice. Her factor held strong opinions concerning the obligations the people of the colony owed to their sovereign lord and had been unable to keep those opinions to himself. Like other men loyal to the Crown, he had not hesitated to make it known he had no intention of submitting to the yoke of mob rule. And like them, he had found it prudent to follow countless others who shared his views to take ship for England where he would wait until the King's soldiers put things right.

Arriving at her townhouse located across from Bowling Green just before the noon bell, Katherine was greeted by Elizabeth van

Deventer, her housekeeper. After a perfunctory bob of the head, the woman held out a small envelope.

"This arrived but an hour ago, ma'am."

Having told no one save those who were part of her household staff who had a need to know of her intention to travel down from her estates just north of Albany, Katherine's curiosity was piqued.

"Who is it from?" she asked as she studied the envelope her housekeeper held out to her as she peeled off her riding gloves.

"The boy who brought it said it was from Lady Katherine Trent."

With nothing more than a frown, Katherine took the envelope from her housekeeper with one hand while passing her gloves off with the other. The ability of a woman who seemed to take singular delight in defying social convention to discover what people she viewed as rivals were up to came as no great surprise to Katherine. Nor did the content of the enclosed note astonish her in the least bit. The first thought that crossed her mind was to send a note of her own, turning down Kat Trent's invitation to tea later that afternoon, if for no other reason than to allow herself an opportunity to find out just how much of a muddle her former factor had left in the wake of his precipitous departure.

"Is the Major about?" she asked as she made her way to the study, staring down at the note she held at arm's length as if trying to divine Kat Trent's intentions from it.

"No, ma'am. He set out to see the governor early this morning. He's not yet returned."

It took every bit of willpower Katherine could muster to keep from giving voice to the uncharitable thoughts running through her head. It had been a foolish idea that her husband, whom even she now referred to as *the Major*, would help her salvage what they could during the crisis that threatened to engulf the American colonies. Thomas Shields had made it quite clear in recent years he was her husband in name only.

In the waning days of the French and Indian War, when it had finally become clear the British and their interests in the Americas were going to be triumphant, their marriage had made perfect sense. As an only child, she was the sole heir to vast tracks of land north of Albany as well as a number of business concerns in New York City. Her Dutch ancestors established themselves long before New York became an English colony. Over the years it had become a matter of faith each generation would do its utmost to build upon the influence and wealth of one of the colony's most powerful mercantile empires. To do so, Katherine needed a son. While it was not entirely unheard of, a woman who engaged in commerce was considered by all who mattered to be a social pariah, looked down upon with distain by Katherine and her ilk as no different than a fish monger's wife.

That she had succeed in fulfilling her duty to the Van der Hoff dynasty by giving birth to Edward Xavier Shields, her first and only child, proved to be a blessing. It allowed her to forego the dubious pleasure of her husband's company and concentrate, instead, on the task of expanding her already considerable holdings. For his part, Thomas was more than satisfied with this arrangement, for it left him free to divide his time with his mistress in London and New York City, where he played at being a country gentleman and confidant to the Royal Governor. Even more important to Katherine was his lack of interest in the day-to-day management of the mercantile empire that underpinned his position within society. He proudly proclaimed he was a soldier, not a shopkeeper, to anyone who foolishly attempted to discuss matters of commerce and trade in his presence.

Were it not for events in Boston, Katherine imagined this arrangement would have continued unabated until her son was ready to take up the burden of overseeing the commercial empire he would one day inherit. Prevailing circumstances, however, and the machinations of her husband who did not waste a single opportunity to ingratiate himself to Governor Tyron, put her and her interests in a most awkward position. Even before blood had been shed, Thomas, with his keen nose for predicting which way the political winds were blowing, had taken to petitioning the Royal Governor in the hope he would be granted a charter to either raise a provincial regiment loyal to the King or, failing that, be given a letter of introduction to General Gage, the military governor of Massachusetts and commander of the King's forces in the American colonies. Of the two, Katherine hoped Tyron would avail himself of the opportunity to rid himself of Thomas by shipping him off to Boston. That she might have to spend several thousand pounds to purchase a commission Thomas would consider suitable did not bother her in the least. If anything, it would be to her advantage to have a husband who, in the time of crisis, took up arms in the defense of their King and tamped down a rebellion that threatened the precious status quo her business concerns relied upon in order to thrive.

Like many, Katherine never even entertained the idea that the King would not prevail. What did concern her was finding a way of protecting her interests from competitors who were members to the Committee of Sixty and using the current crisis to wreak havoc on their rivals by labeling them as Tories. It was a matter she needed to address, the sooner, the better.

Upon entering the study, she paused, taking a moment to once more hold up the invitation and study it. As much as she despised Kat Trent, she could not help but think, given the circumstances in which they both now found themselves, spending time with that woman could prove useful. If nothing else, she just might be able to learn how a slip of a girl like Kat Trent, a most unconventional member of the peerage, had thus far avoided running afoul of the rabble that all but exiled the Royal Governor to a man-of-war riding at anchor in the bay little more than a mile from where she stood. If a girl raised in Jamaica could manage to keep the provincial wolves at bay, Katherine Shields had no doubt she, the daughter of a shrewd Dutch patroon and native New Yorker, could do better.

Aboard the HMS Asia, New York Harbor

Believing he was finished for the day, Governor William Tyron eased back in his seat before calling out to his secretary.

"Is there anything else that needs my immediate attention?" he asked plaintively in the hope the answer would be a resounding no.

The young man sitting at a small field desk next to the door of the HMS *Asia*'s great cabin looked up from the letter he had been copying.

"I believe Major Thomas Shields is still waiting to see you, sir."

Frowning, Tyron considered having his secretary send the man away, but stopped as an idea began to take shape. If the reports concerning the recent battle fought across the bay from Boston were to be believed, there would be a need for officers to replace those who had been killed or invalided during an engagement that had sent shockwaves throughout the colonies and across the sea to London. Perhaps General Howe, who had lost all twelve of his aides and staff officers in that action, would be able to find a use for someone like Shields. As annoying as the man often was, there was no denying his credentials were impeccable. Not only was the man a veteran of the war, married into an old Dutch family, and now a permanent resident in New York after that war, he was intimately familiar with the colony's people and their politics. Such a man, Tyron reasoned, would be useful to any general saddled with the odious task of putting down a rebellion fast getting out of hand.

"Is my latest letter to General Gage informing him of our need for additional troops here in New York ready?" Tyron asked.

Setting aside his quill, the harried secretary took to leafing through the sheaf of correspondence he'd not yet had time to copy.

"No, sir," the secretary muttered despondently when he found the letter.

Tyron's frown upended upon hearing this.

"Excellent. Set it aside, for I wish to amend it. Then, would you be so kind as to show Major Shields in?"

New York City

Long before New England militiamen stood their ground on Lexington Green, Edward Shields had been engaged in open rebellion, though it had nothing to do with taxation or a lack of colonial representation in Parliament. His struggle was far more domestic, but no less important to a young man whose father sought to instill that service to King and country was the noblest pursuit for a man, and whose strong-willed mother was determined to steer him into a vocation in which he had little interest.

As a child, Edward's rebellious nature had manifested in the sort of behavior one expected of a boy who spent a great deal of time in a city such as New York. Thomas saw his son's habit of slipping away from his tutor every chance that came his way as nothing more than the natural manifestations of a spirited young boy eager to be out and about with his friends rather than confined to a stuffy, lifeless classroom. For her part, Katherine all but encouraged Edward's habit of wandering along the wharfs of the city, listening to the sailors freely share their tall tales of life on the high seas, then she would ask him when he was caught doing so what he had learned about the world of commerce and trade. It was not until he had started attending meetings with David Gray, the son of a prosperous merchant with whom Katherine often did business, and listening to Isaac Sears, Alexander McDougall, and other rabble-rousers who openly preached sedition and treason that Katherine and Thomas became concerned, though for entirely different reasons.

Edward's parents had good reason to be troubled by their son's latest act of defiance. Not satisfied with merely listening to the inflammatory rhetoric espoused by men determined to stand against a King they considered a tyrant, Edward had taken to tagging along with his fellow students at King's College whenever they joined a group of Liberty Boys. The Liberty Boys had a mind to take matters into their own hands and show the Royal Governor that they, the citizens of New York, would no longer tolerate arbitrary dictates handed down by him or any king who had no regard for the American colonies other than to milk them for all they were worth. The night he had joined the Liberty Boys who had boarded the *Nancy* anchored at Sandy Hook to dump tea the merchantman was carrying into the harbor was, to a young man like Edward, beyond thrilling. So too was the day the Virginian who had been appointed by Continental Congress to command the troops gathered around Boston had passed through the city. It was the thought of joining those of his friends who were determined to set aside their studies and follow George Washington to Boston that gave Shields pause.

Voicing their opposition to policies of the King, his advisors, and Parliament they thought to be onerous or oppressive took no great courage. As Englishmen, it was their right to do so, a privilege enshrined in the Magna Carta and guaranteed by the English constitution. Even participating in acts of civil disobedience could be justified. Taking up arms against the King, however, was another matter altogether. Citizens in England and in the colonies were reminded of the consequences of doing so every fifth of November when they gathered to celebrate the execution of Guy Fawkes, a notorious Papist traitor who had been caught planting gunpowder beneath the House of Lords. That an entire population could be punished in a manner no less heinously had been amply demonstrated by the King's own uncle who, in the wake of the Jacobean Rebellion, had laid waste to the Scottish Highlands.

The bloody battle fought in June provided all the proof Edward needed that the King had every intention of imposing his will on those colonists who defied his edicts, leaving Edward to wonder if the repression Butcher Cumberland had metered out after the '45 would be repeated here, in New York, before his very eyes. Yet, the idea of doing nothing, waiting to see if this would be the case in this war—his war—was not an attractive option, for it would be too late to do anything by then.

This stark reality left Edward with only one of two choices: join Gray and his other classmates determined to fight for rights bestowed upon them by the English constitution or stand with the King and, by extension, his father. Hanging back, looking after the family's business as his Dutch grandfather had done during the French and Indian War and as his mother wished him to do was dismissed out of hand. Edward knew far too many Scots who had been imprisoned or transported to the colonies whose only crime in 1746 had been being born a Scot. This led Edward to wonder where, if the British army did prevail, the King would transport those who had opposed him. Canada, most likely, he expected. Since he did not care for the cold, Edward concluded they—those Americans who had taken to calling themselves patriots—would have to win. But before he could turn his full attention to doing what he could to see to that, Edward would need to muster up the courage needed to tell his mother the truth. He would be throwing his lot in with people she looked down upon as being little more than an unruly mob whose leaders deserved to be hung, drawn, and quartered.

Neither Katherine Shields nor Lady Katherine Trent bothered with the sort of small talk, social chitchat, or gossip women of their standing tended to engage in while sipping tea. Not even the events compelling Katherine Shields to set aside her pride and accept Kat Trent's invitation were touched upon. Determined to spend as little time in the presence of a woman she considered to be a lady in name only, following a perfunctory greeting bereft of even a hint of cordiality, Katherine opened their conversation by asking Kat

Trent how she managed to keep the merchants, sea captains, and tradesmen with whom she did business on a daily basis from taking advantage of her.

Never having learned, much less understood, the art of cordial tête-à-tête in which women of means took such delight, Kat was relieved Katherine Shields was quick to make clear her presence was purely mercenary. It also confirmed Kat's suspicion that Katherine Shields intended to try her hand at managing her own business affairs. At the thought, Kat hid a knowing smirk by bringing her teacup up to her lips with one hand without bothering to hold its matching saucer to catch any stray drops that might speckle her simple, yet well-fitting day dress.

"No doubt you are well aware there's really no great secret when it comes to dealing with merchants, shopkeepers, and speculators," Kat stated matter-of-factly. "Once you let it be known you will not be cowed or bullied into accepting terms not to your liking, they will see their way clear to ignore the fact you are a woman."

"I expect that is far easier said than done," Katherine Shields muttered dismissively in response.

"To the contrary, it is," Kat countered crisply. "All you need to do is make an example of one or two men of note. Once word spreads you're not to be trifled with, the others tend to fall in line."

Katherine cocked a brow.

"May I ask just what sort of example?"

Before she answered, Lady Katherine Trent canted her head to one side. A coy little smile graced her lips as she recalled an incident that was still a topic of discussion among the city's merchants whenever they gathered in their coffee houses to exchange news of the day and discuss their affairs.

"You are no doubt familiar with Hiram Copper, a merchant who deals in imported wools. Not long after I'd taken over the dry goods shop my uncle had bequeathed to me in accordance with my grandfather's will, I discovered I needed to secure a reliable source of that commodity. I went to Mr. Copper and made an offer that was quite generous. As you can well imagine, he took one look at me and decided I was an easy mark."

Kat Trent paused to refill her teacup, asking Katherine if she wished to have her tea freshened. Having no wish to spend any more time with her hostess than was necessary, Katherine demurred.

"Thank you, but no."

Taking her time, Kat Trent added what Katherine Shields considered to be far too much sugar and a touch of cream, before stirring her tea with an irritating deliberateness Katherine assumed was intentional. Such antics, when used while negotiating with men, very often had the same effect they were having on Katherine Shields. Kat had found it caused self-important men who considered their time to be far more precious than that of a woman's, even one they were doing business with, to become so impatient to be rid of her that they agreed to terms and conditions they ordinarily would not have otherwise simply to be finished with the matter at hand and see her off.

"What did cause Mr. Cooper to finally see things your away?" Katherine asked with a slight, but noticeable edge in her voice.

"We never did come to terms," Kat Trent informed her guest as she took up her teacup and its saucer. "I simply smiled, thanked him for his time, and took my leave."

"Without securing the wool you needed?"

"Oh, I secured the wool, but from a young agent from Dublin. Having just arrived in this colony, he was quite eager to establish himself here. When I informed him of my needs, he was more than willing to do business with me for considerably less than I had offered Mr. Cooper."

"I have always been of the opinion men enjoyed the back and forth bickering when conducting business," Katherine pointed out. "They seem to derive a certain pleasure from verbally jousting with each other."

Setting aside her teacup, Kat folded her hands in her lap, and leaned forward. Narrowing her eyes, she fixed Katherine in a steady, unflinching gaze.

"I don't."

Both the tone of the young, red-haired daughter whose grandfather had been an earl and the look in her eyes caused Katherine to recoil ever so slightly.

After managing to catch on, Katherine drew herself up. Tilting her head back ever so slightly, she looked down the bridge of her nose at her hostess.

"I would like to hear more, but unfortunately I must run along," Katherine murmured airily. "I expect my husband will be returning from his meeting with the governor soon."

In addition to mastering the art of dealing with hardnosed merchants and sea captains, Kat had learned how to put women who assumed airs in their place.

"Oh, I quite understand," she declared politely. "I too must be running along if I hope to be on time for dinner with the governor this evening. I expect the poor man will be exhausted after spending the entire day dealing with self-important men seeking favors from him."

With a tight nod and a pasted-on smile lacking sincerity, Katherine Shields ignored the slight leveled at her husband as she came to her feet and took her leave.

The door to the formal parlor had no sooner closed behind Katherine Shields than Kat Trent let her guard down. With slumped shoulders and a sour look on her face, she took up her tea before throwing herself against the back of her chair in a petulant manner her sister had often affected whenever she was displeased. Ignoring the way the tea in her cup splattered on the skirt of her work-a-day attire, Kat took to trying to figure out what just what Katherine Shields wanted from her. The woman was clearly up to something. That much was certain. Kat took a sip of tea while continuing to glare at the door. No doubt Katherine, too, appreciated the coming storm about to upend their world in ways no one could predict and was determined to take advantage of the resulting crisis. As much as Kat detested having anything to do with Katherine and women of her ilk, it could not be dismissed out of hand that the two of them might very well have to do business with each other to survive. Regardless, Kat Trent was not about to embrace the ever pretentious and ambitious Katherine Shields.

Grunting in a most unladylike manner, Kat set aside her teacup, came to her feet, and took a moment to consider how she would deal with Katherine.

"Well," she muttered to herself as she readied to sally forth on that day's errands, "I'll not discover what that snooty Dutch cow is up to by sitting about sipping tea."

With that, she stepped off with a determined briskness that characterized the way she went about all her affairs.

Thomas Shields waited until dinner to inform his wife and son he would be off to Boston in a few days.

"In addition to personally delivering several important dispatches to General Gage, the governor wishes me to describe the current situation he is facing here in New York. Though, I doubt it will do any good."

In an effort to allow his wife and son an opportunity to ponder why he thought his report on conditions in New York would do little good, Thomas took up a spoonful of soup and made something of a show of enjoying it.

Only, when it became clear neither his son nor his wife was going to ask that he enumerate his reasons for holding such an opinion, did he continue.

"If even half of the stories concerning Howe's assault against the rebel earthworks above Charlestown are true, I imagine General Gage doesn't have a single soldier to spare."

Again he paused, and again, Katherine and Edward chose not to indulge him by asking him questions or joining in on a discussion on which he was so keen. Having failed to elicit the kind of response he had been expecting, Thomas settled into finishing his soup. It was not until they were well into the main course of the meal that he revealed the real cause of his excitement for his pending trip.

"While there, I intend to petition the general for a position, if not on his staff, then with one of the regiments under his command. Failing that, I shall call in a favor or two from acquaintances of mine who are close to the King."

As he had anticipated, this bit of news caught Katherine's attention. Looking down the length of the table, she took a moment to regard her husband who, pleased that he had finally managed to arouse her interest in what he was saying, popped a morsel of meat in his mouth and began to slowly chew it.

"Do you think they will take you?" she asked, doing her best to keep her voice from betraying the hopefulness she felt over the prospect of ridding herself of him.

"Not only have I heard losses among the officers were dreadful, but I have it on good authority the King will be sending substantial reinforcements from England and Ireland come spring. In order to be of any use to Howe, those regiments will have to be brought up to their full wartime strength."

"Would not the colonels of those regiments wish to fill their ranks with officers of their own choosing, men who are able and willing to pay for whatever vacancies there may be?" Katherine asked, hoping that if he was able to secure a position that would keep him away from New York, the cost would not prove too costly for her.

Satisfied his wife had decided to join in on the conversation, Thomas set aside his knife and fork, folded his hands on the table before him, and shook his head.

"Most regiments here in the colonies are commanded by their, lieutenant colonel, allowing their colonels to remain in England where they can tend to other, more important matters."

Never having taken any interest in her husband's affairs in much the same way he did not bother himself with hers, Katherine had never been able to understand how a man could be the colonel of a regiment and not take the field when his company went to war.

"Will they be able to make decisions regarding who replaces the officers who were lost?" she asked.

"Ordinarily, they would have a great deal to say. I expect, at the moment, however, they'll have little choice but to fill the vacancies with whomever they can find with the wherewithal and the appropriate standing. The regiments in Boston need officers now. Those in England and Ireland, almost as quickly, for they will need to start recruiting as soon as they are informed they will be going and will need to train before they take ship. Which brings me to my next point," he continued as he cast his gaze to his son who had been listening to this exchange. "I wish to take you with me."

Taken aback, Edward was unable to ask why before his mother did so. "Whatever for?"

Thomas grinned, giving his son a wink. "No doubt they'll be needing lieutenants as well as majors."

In a manner any mother would have been in sympathy with, Katherine protested, though her reasons for doing so were not strictly maternal.

"That's not possible. He's only seventeen."

"I was only sixteen when I went north with Cumberland to put down the Scottish rebels in '46."

"Does he not have a say in this?"

"I've never known a young gentleman worth his salt who would pass up the opportunity to follow the drums and march off to war," Thomas countered without feeling the need to solicit his son's opinion on the matter. "Besides, it will make a man of him," he added as he took up his wine glass. "He's a Shield, a breed of men who are not cut out to be a ribbon clerk."

"Better a live ribbon clerk than a dead soldier," Katherine snapped.

"That's your father speaking," Thomas muttered with a casual airiness that irritated Katherine.

"Yes, it is. But it is also *his mother*."

Having no wish to debate the matter any further, Thomas turned instead to Edward.

"A post ship will be leaving for Boston in two days. You're to be ready to accompany me when it does."

The indecision Edward had been tormented by earlier in the day evaporated in the twinkling of an eye. He nodded as he returned his father's gaze. He would go to Boston, but not at his father's side.

FOUR

"The human heart is the starting point in all matters pertaining to war."

Maurice de Saxe, 1732

Versailles, France September 1775

IT WAS NOT so much the way the petitioners sitting about in the stuffy antechamber of the Foreign Minister's office took to staring at him when he entered the room that gave Anton de Chevalier pause. Not that he could blame them. The sight of an officer with unpowdered hair in an unadorned uniform more befitting a lowly gunner than an officer holding the King's commission often caused people to stare. What maddened Anton was the way self-important men such as those awaiting an audience with the Minister gazed down their long, aristocratic noses at him with the same contempt he imagined they afforded a particularly odious Parisian beggar. Few, if any, had ever done more than travel between Paris, where they spent their time attending fashionable saloons, squandering away their fortunes gambling or whoring, and here at court, seeking to secure favors and titles they had done nothing to earn.

Rather than take a seat, Anton marched boldly up to the young man seated at a desk just off to one side of the door leading to the Minister's office. Anton left his name before informing the clerk he would be outside in a garden that was visible just below the room they were in. With that, he smartly pivoted about on his heels, threw his head back, and swept the room with a critical, contemptuous eye before making his way out.

In comparison to the other gardens at Versailles, the one he entered was small and, like the Captain of Artillery himself, quite modest. The one feature it had in its favor were tall hedges lining the path. Though trimmed with a precision that rivaled the way women at court tended to their hair, Anton reveled in the garden's near seclusion and the crisp, natural scent of the air. Closing his eyes, he could almost imagine he was once again in America, slowly making his way along a beaten trail meandering its way through a virgin forest.

Opening his eyes, he took to gazing up at the clouds drifting lazily across the sky. The time he had spent in North America during a war his peers had come to know as the Seven Years' War but he could only think of as the French and Indian War continued to cast a long shadow on his life. He had arrived in New France a bright-eyed young officer with no other thought than to prove himself, both as a soldier and as a man. What he had discovered in the savage wilderness for which he had been sent to fight was a world as different from the one he had known as a boy as could be imagined. The endless, unspoiled forests, wide, raging rivers, and stunning vistas he had beheld made an impression on him that had lost none of its awe-inspiring wonder with the passage of time.

"Ah, there you are," a voice from behind him called out.

Turning, Anton was momentarily taken aback by the sight of Charles Gravier, the Comte de Vergennes and Foreign Minister to King Louis XVI, quickly making his way toward him. Coming to a halt, Anton waited for Vergennes.

"I was told you were out here, taking a turn through the garden," Vergennes stated as he drew a frilly handkerchief from his sleeve. "Can't blame you for wishing to wait out here rather than back there," he added with a quick nod of his head back toward the palace as he mopped sweat from his brow. "If I knew they wouldn't find me, I'd hide out here as well."

The Comte had no need to elaborate as to whom he was referring. Anton's father, who had served as a minister to the old King, still spoke contemptuously of the sycophants and petitioners who followed him about like a pack of stray dogs begging for a bone wherever he went.

"You would think they believed the King's coffers were bottomless," Vergennes muttered in disgust.

Anton all but bit his tongue in an effort to keep from pointing out such beliefs were not all that difficult to fall prey to given the lavishness with which the Queen threw money about on frivolities and entertainment. Instead, he gave Vergennes a belated bow. It was an obligatory gesture expected of an officer of Anton's rank but also bought him time to banish his scurrilous thoughts concerning the queen.

"My father informed me you wished to speak to me," Anton declared as he straightened up.

Before responding, Vergennes lowered the handkerchief from his brow and glanced over his shoulder. Only when he was sure they were alone did he place a hand on Anton's upper arm and, with a tug, indicated he wished to walk as he talked.

"I have often heard your father speak of your love for the American wilderness and your longing to one day return to it. No doubt you are well aware of what is going on there," the minister continued without pause. "It seems everyone is speaking of nothing else these days."

That the topic Vergennes broached concerned the events playing out in the American colonies came as no surprise to Anton. Like his fellow officers, he had been following them with keen interest, not all of which was professional. This allowed him to simply nod in acknowledgement without looking over at Vergennes as the two slowly made their way along. He had never kept it a secret that he longed to go back. On the contrary, those fascinated by Rousseau's philosophy on nature unspoiled by the hand of civilization and its superiority often sought Anton out, if for no other reason than to discover if what Rousseau had said had any merit. In relating his experiences in the American wilderness, he often spoke of his wish to return, though he never shared with anyone, not even his closest friends, why he never had.

"There are some at court who believe recent events unfolding around the port city of Boston have created a number of tempting opportunities for us," Vergennes continued guardedly.

"I have heard such talk myself."

"Tell me, does it surprise you the Americans have been able accomplish all that they have?" Vergennes asked carefully.

Anton shook his head ever so slightly. "Not in the least, monsieur. What surprises me is that the English are surprised. While the colonists are considered to be Englishmen by their King, they are not."

As if finding the captain's assessment in agreement with his own, Vergennes nodded.

"Yes, I expect they are not," he muttered as if to himself before lapsing into silence.

When he did speak again, the Foreign Minister peppered Anton with a rapid-fire series of questions, ranging from the nature of the American character to the land that had played a role in molding it. With an ease that would have led someone to believe Anton had just returned from the Americas, he told of his experiences. Only when Anton was sure the minister had exhausted his litany of questions, did he put a question to Vergennes he had been asking himself from the very moment he had received the minister's summons.

"Outside of soliciting my opinions on this matter, I am assuming there is a reason you have sent for me. May I ask what it is?"

Looking over the captain from head to toe as they continued to slowly make their way along, Vergennes could not help but smile.

"Your father told me you were not one to idly dawdle like those insufferable fools I find myself surrounded by."

"I am a soldier, monsieur. We are a species not given to prevarication."

"Oh, but I wish that were true of all soldiers," Vergennes moaned regretfully as he rolled his eyes.

"Yes, well, be that as it may..."

"Are you acquainted with Pierre de Beaumarchais?" the minister asked without waiting for Anton to finish his thought.

"Not personally, no, but I am well aware of who he is. The scandals and lawsuits involving Beaumarchais and Madame Goezman are still a topic of discussion by those who take an interest in such things."

"Hmm, yes. Well, at present, Beaumarchais is in London and in contact with a number of important people, some working on behalf of the American colonists who have taken up arms against their King. He sends me information of interest to France and, from time to time, undertakes certain delicate chores on my behalf."

Anton thought this meant spying as he cast a leery gaze over toward the minister out of the corner of his eye.

"Recently he has been sending me reports concerning the strength and ability of the American army besieging Boston that I personally find difficult to believe. Along with these reports are strongly worded suggestions that it would be in our best interest to provide that army with weapons, munitions, and, above all else, funds."

Having anticipated as much, given the tenor of their discussion so far, Anton merely nodded as the two took another turn through the small garden. During the last war between France and England, French agents had provided native tribes as far south as Virginia and the Carolinas with arms to draw English and provincial troops away from the heart of New France. He would have been surprised if there were not men close to the King looking to take advantage of the current crisis in the American colonies for no other reason than to discomfit France's traditional enemy and extract a modicum of revenge for peace terms that stripped France of its Canadian colonies.

"May I ask why you distrust Monsieur Beaumarchais's reports?" Anton ventured cautiously.

"I have come to believe he is too much in sympathy with the American cause, which leads me to believe he might be exaggerating the size and abilities of the American army in Massachusetts."

By now, it was clear to Anton where this conversation was going. Still, he wished to have Vergennes spell out exactly what he wanted.

"How I may be of service to you in this matter, monsieur?"

Tugging at the arm he was holding, the Foreign Minister pulled Anton closer, bowing his head slightly as he presented the captain of artillery with his proposal in a hushed, secretive voice.

Without giving the matter the amount of consideration such an undertaking required, Anton knew he would accept de Vergennes's charter even before he had relieved himself of the man's presence. Anton did, however, ask the minister if he could give him some time to consider his proposal. His reason for agreeing to go to America and to essentially spy on the colonists had nothing to do with his sense of duty or the hope that, by taking on this task, he would be rewarded upon returning to France. It was Sarah Carter.

During one long and memorable winter, when the bitter cold rendered active campaigning by large bodies of troops impossible, Anton had wintered in Quebec. There, he met Sarah. Sarah had been taken from her western Massachusetts farm by the Indians during a raid and sold to a Canadian priest. He, in turn, passed her on to the French colonial authorities who held her until she could be exchanged for French-Canadian captives being held by the English.

It had not been love that brought them together that winter. Anton had no illusions about that. She had lost her family, her home, and, as often happened when a person is overwhelmed by such calamities, the very will to live. He, a professional soldier, had come to the sad conclusion that nothing he could do would stave off the defeat he and his fellow officers knew was but a matter of time. There had been nothing untoward about what they had done. Far from regretting it, each took comfort in the time they had spent together. Like many men, Anton was able to find solace in the arms of a lover and she, a fleeting feeling of security. The only regret Anton had was that their union had resulted in a child—a boy—who he discovered later, upon returning to Quebec to find Sarah, was gone.

Whether he would be able to find her, if for no other reason than to reassure himself that she finally did find a place where she could feel safe was, in Anton's mind, questionable at best. He had no guarantee she would return to Massachusetts. Were he in her position, having experienced nothing but sorrow and loss there, that would have been the last place on earth he would have gone. Still, the idea of not trying to find her, of passing up this opportunity to fill a terrible void that haunted him would have been foolish. And, if by some chance, he was afforded an opportunity to make amends with Sarah, he would gladly take it, if for no other reason than to allow his soul some peace. For while Anton was a professional soldier, well-schooled in the cruel science of war, he was still the same young dreamer who had beheld the wondrous beauty of an unspoiled land, one that was alive with possibilities as boundless as its vistas.

FIVE

"If my soldiers were to think,
not one would remain in the ranks."
Frederick the Great, 1712-1786

Williamsburg, Virginia
October 1775

EXHAUSTED AND near voiceless, Ian tossed aside the flap of the tent he and Ezra Shaw shared. Taking care to avoid bumping into the small folding table that served as both field desk and dinner table at which Shaw was seated, Ian maneuvered himself around to his side of the tent. He was proud of the table. He had fashioned it himself before setting out from Winchester. He laid his musket against the side of his cot before throwing himself onto it.

Looking up from the duty roster he had been laboriously penning, Shaw brought his hands up to his face and gently rubbed his tired eyes with the tips of his fingers.

"How goes it, lad? Are they ready to take on our kinsmen?"

Ian shot his captain a dirty look. "They're no kinsmen of mine, at least none my granddad was ever willing to lay claim to."

"Well, you've got me there," Shaw chuckled. "Me, I'm tied to the bastards by blood on my mother's side, or so I'm told."

"Unless you're eager to share a tree branch with that effigy of the governor the lads strung up in front of the Royal Palace, then I'd keep that to myself," Ian muttered.

"Still there, is it?"

"Aye, but he's beginning to look a wee bit sad. Some of the lads who are spoiling for a fight have taken to knocking the stuffing out of Lord of Dunmore."

"And how are you doing with preparing them for the day they come face to face with the real Lord Dunmore?" Shaw asked, returning to his original question.

"I'd have a better chance of turning lead into gold than this lot into soldiers," Ian groused.

Shaw eased back on the small collapsible campstool that had been cobbled together at the same time the table had been built and flexed the fingers of his writing hand to work out the cramps.

"They're not that bad. Better, I dare say, than we were when we first marched off to Ohio with Colonel Washington. If you recall, there wasn't a man amongst us who could keep in step with the one to his left or his right."

Lowering his hands, Ian shot his captain and friend a quick, sideways glance. "It takes more than marching to and fro like a Prussian grenadier to make a soldier. Long before either of us went off to fight, then or when I took up arms against the English during the '45, you, me, and McPike not only knew how to fight, but we were used to living rough. Any one of us could march for days with nocht but a mouthful of stale bread to keep us going and go straight off into battle without needing to stop and rest."

"Aye, and we still lost," Shaw grunted as he paused to reflect upon his own sad memories. "We lost everything we had, save our pride."

In a flash, Ian sat up, swung his legs over the side of the cot, and stared at Shaw. "That's the point I'm trying to make, you wee gork. Those men out there, they're not soldiers," he blurted as he thrust his am out and pointed toward the open tent flap. "They never will be."

Rather than argue the point, one that had more merit than Shaw was willing to admit, he stared at Ian for the longest time before speaking.

"Why did you follow Prince Charlie in '45?" he finally asked.

Taken aback by this sudden change in tact, Ian placed his hands on his knees, leaned forward, and returned Shaw's stare.

"For the same reason you and your lot took on your English overseers. Our laird called on us to fulfill our oaths to him."

"And?" Shaw asked pointedly, cocking a brow.

Ian knew what he was asking. He could still recall the thrill he felt at the age of fourteen when he was told he was old enough to march off to war. Dropping his chin a smidge, as if embarrassed by the thought, he hesitated.

"You've told me many a time how your granddad, upon hearing the call, stirred himself from his deathbed, shuffled over to the hearth, took down his broadsword, and handed it to you."

Dropping his gaze down to the trodden grass that served as the floor of their tent, Ian could remember everything that had passed between him and his grandfather that day. *"I'm dyin' lad, and cannot heed the call. You're a man now and must go in my stead."* The pride he felt as he stood there before his grandfather, accepting the broadsword his father had passed down to him still caused his heart to flutter.

Still, he told himself as he struggled to return to the matter at hand, that had nothing to do with the point he had been trying to make. Drawing himself up, he once more looked over at Shaw who watched him like a hawk eyeing a dormouse in the grass below.

"Yes, I went," Ian admitted grudgingly. "Like the rest of the poor bloody damned fools who'd grown up believing in a cause that was doomed before Charlie raised his banner at Glenaladale."

"Why do ya say 'doomed'?" Shaw asked as he leaned forward as if challenging Ian.

Ian was able to answer that without hesitation. "The man was a fool, and we the more so for following him."

"Do ya think Colonel Washington is a fool?"

The temptation to remind his friend that Washington was now a general was set aside for a moment as he took to countering Shaw's assertions.

"Who was it who led us into the wilderness in 1754, started a war with the French, and then sat around in a wretched excuse of a fort waiting for the French to come and whip us like dogs?"

"The same man who kept his head at the Monongahela while those gentleman soldiers from England flopped about like fresh caught fish thrown on dry land," Shaw countered sharply. "The same man who kept the natives at bay with nothing more than sheer grit, determination, and one understrength regiment of half trained provincials who were no different than the lads we're responsible for."

Chastised, but not cowed, Ian took a moment as he scrambled to pull together a suitable counter argument in his head.

Shaw did not wait for him to put words to it. "Those men out there are no fools," he declared, pointing to the open flap of their tent. "They didn't come here because someone said I'm your liege and you must. They're here because they believe in what they're being called on to fight for."

After letting that thought sink in, Shaw straightened up and gave Ian a sly little grin before he continued.

"I expect half of 'em will be regretting they've forsaken the warmth of their hearth and the tenderness of their wives long before their first pair of shoes wear out. Those who were swayed by the fiery words with which Colonel Henry is so fond of showering upon us will wake up one morning, set aside their muskets, and turn for home. But those who stay," Shaw exclaimed with passion that set his eyes ablaze, "those who stay with us—determined to see this thing through—they'll be fighters, able to stand toe-to-toe with the best the English can send against us."

The conviction in his commander's voice and the determined, unflinching gaze with which he held him stifled any thought on

Ian's part of trying to counter the man's argument. Instead, Ian turned to another matter that was troubling him.

"That's all well and good. But will you answer me this? What in God's name possessed you to make me your lieutenant?" Ian asked plaintively. "McPike is not only older, but he has more experience when it comes to leading men. He should be the lieutenant and me the sergeant."

Chuckling, Shaw reached over onto the desk, picked up the quill with which he had been writing, and twirled it between his fingers.

"Because, laddie, you can use one of these. The most McPike is able to do is make his mark."

"Do ya not think that's a pretty weak argument for making a man an officer? You know as well as I do there's many a fine gentlemen officer who can read and write but couldn't lead a thirsty horse to water."

"That's true. But they're not here. You are. And since you are, you can finish this roster the colonel wants while I take a stroll about the company to allow the men to see I'm still alive and breathing," Shaw added as he rose to his feet and held the quill out toward Ian.

"Well, I expect that's as good a reason as any," Ian muttered as he took the pen. "Just don't go fussing like Megan does whenever I misspell a word or two."

Stopping at the entrance to their tent, Shaw looked over his shoulder at Ian. "Oh, you can be sure I'll never do that, lad. Seeing the way you invent new ways of misspelling words is quite entertaining."

Before he could inform his commanding officer where he could go, Shaw had put on his hat and was gone, leaving Ian no choice but to take his captain's place and, with a deliberateness that often gave him headaches, took to scratching out the names of men the two of them would one day lead into battle.

Winchester, Virginia
October 1775

The child Ian McPherson had found wandering in the woods naked and alone not far from a burned farmstead did not utter a single word for weeks. Megan, who took him in, did her best to coax a name from the child, but did not push.

"The wee lad is in shock," she had informed Ian every time he pressed her to find out who he was. *"When he's ready, he'll tell us."* But he never had.

Only after two months had passed did Ian decide to take matters in hand and give the child a name; though, he did not have one in mind when he informed Megan of his decision. Never at a loss as to what to do, she had not wasted a second in rendering her thoughts on the matter.

"Patrick, after our blessed Saint Patrick who wandered alone in the wilderness after escaping from captivity," she had exclaimed. Finding no reason to object, Ian had readily agreed.

The boy went by that name for nearly a year until one morning, during breakfast, Ian asked the child— who was then six by their reckoning—if he would be interested helping him mend a wagon wheel. Upon hearing the name he had been given, the boy had looked across the table at Ian and informed his name was not Patrick. It was not so much the words he uttered that caused both Megan and Ian to start. It was not even the way he had delivered the words in a clear, crisp voice that told them there was nothing at all wrong with his ability to speak. Rather, it was the haunted gaze with which the boy had held them. Megan, who was the first to recover her wits, and believing the boy was finally ready to speak, asked him what this name was then. Rather than answering, the boy continued to stare at her for the longest time as if wondering if he should tell her. For reasons he never shared with them, he did not, choosing instead to turn his attention back to eating his breakfast in silence.

From that day onward, whenever speaking to him or of him, Megan, Ian, and anyone else who had the need to referred to him as either Boy or the McPhersons' boy. And though he did begin to speak, he did so sparingly and only when there was a need to in a clear, unfaltering voice that betrayed an accent. Upon hearing the boy, a traveler who had been staying at the inn informed Megan that the boy's parents had, undoubtedly, been Welsh.

While the boy's taciturn nature led some people to think he was a simpleton, he proved to be quite bright, causing Megan to engage a wandering scholar who was seeking a position to teach herself and the boy to read and write in exchange for two meals a day and a place to sleep. Even when Ian decided the boy was old enough to learn the trade of wheelwright, Megan insisted he be allowed to continue with his studies.

"The boy has a knack for learning," she had pointed out. *"He should be given a chance to decide for himself what he'll be when he's of an age to do so, which is more than you or I ever had."*

Unable to find fault with this, Ian had agreed. Not that he had much of a choice in the matter. Megan was, as Ian often pointed out when on the verge of losing an argument, very Irish, and a woman who, once she had made up her mind, could not be persuaded to change it.

What Ian did take exception to was the boy's habit of sneaking off whenever the opportunity arose to read a book he had managed to borrow from people who were staying at the inn. It did not matter what the subject of the book was. Even newspapers that were weeks old were eagerly scarfed up, front to back, beginning to end. When the boy could find nothing new to read, he spent his time with Gretchen Richter learning German, a language he was soon speaking with greater frequency than English. While this puzzled Ian, Megan understood there was more to his predilection for spoken German than a simple desire to add to his ever-expanding store of knowledge.

By the age of ten, the boy had managed to put his skills with the written word and a smooth, flowing hand to good use, penning letters for illiterate travelers and local patrons of the inn. Since people paid a fee for the boy's services and his services brought them to the inn where they drank or ate while conducting their business with the boy, Ian turned a blind eye to his frequent absences from the wheelwright shop.

The coming of their own children did nothing to lessen either the love Ian and Megan had for the boy, or the pride they felt in his abilities. The attachment Megan felt for him was especially strong, for in her eyes, he was her first. This led to a closeness and understanding between the two Ian was never able to quite match. So, when the boy came into the inn's kitchen where Megan was kneading dough and stood at the table across from her, she stopped what she was doing, looked up, and sighed.

"Aye, I miss him too," she murmured without having to ask the reason for the boy's somber expression.

"I am going to Williamsburg," he declared bluntly.

Megan had no need to ask him why. She had seen the way the boy scanned the *Virginia Gazette* whenever a copy made its way to the inn, searching for any news concerning the politics that had led Ian and like-minded men to take up arms. Despite never having discussed the issues that had led to rebellion against the Crown, Megan had no doubt where the boy's sympathies lay. So, rather than wasting any time asking him to justify his decision, she felt the urge to respond as most mothers did when a child of theirs expressed a desire to go off to war.

Unfortunately, she found she was unable to do so, for she was a prisoner of her own convictions. If they had guessed right when they had taken him in, the boy was now twenty-two, capable by any measure to make his own decisions and intelligent enough to understand the consequences. Nor could she use the argument she needed him to help with the inn. Between Gretchen Richter and her own children, who ranged from ages fifteen to eleven, Megan had all the help she needed. Even the wheelwright shop could continue to operate to a degree, for Ian had taken on another apprentice who, with his oldest natural son, was more than able to handle rudimentary repairs. Besides, Megan had no desire to argue with the boy. Though he was not of their blood, the boy took after them in all the ways that were important, some of which were, at times, infuriating. This included a stubborn streak both she and Ian claimed was the fault of the other.

Resigning herself to the sad fact she was about to see another of her men go off to war, Megan set aside the bread dough, wiped her hands on her apron, and made her way around the table to the boy. Wrapping her arms about him, she lay her head against his chest, as much to keep him from seeing the tears welling in her eyes as to hold onto him for as long as she could.

The boy said nothing as he wrapped his arms tightly about her. He had no need to, for Megan knew, as all mothers worthy of the title do, that the love she had for him was matched only by the love he had for her.

SIX

"I shall endeavor to discharge my duty to society, considering myself only as the citizen, moved by the melancholy necessity of taking up arms for the public safety."

Richard Montgomery
Letter to James Duane, 1775

Fort Saint-Jean, Canada
November 1775

"HONORS OF WAR, the colonel calls it," Kevin Farrell growled contemptuously before bending over and spitting on the ground in the path of a British soldier passing before him. When the Englishman turned toward Farrell and glared at him, the gruff farmer who had given up the plow to fight for a cause he believed in with all his heart met the man's eyes and scowled. "That's all the honors you'll get from me."

A sharp rebuke from an English sergeant was sufficient to keep the offended soldier from breaking ranks and laying into Farrell, leaving him free to nudge Edward Shields with his elbow.

"If there's one thing I know for sure, laddie, it's that if we were the ones who were doin' the surrenderin' instead of them, we'd be runnin' the gauntlet straight to the nearest tree where'd they'd hang the lot of us."

Living with a father who had expressed that very sentiment on more occasions than he wished to recall whenever he spoke of men like Alexander McDougall and Isaac Sears, Edward knew what Farrell was saying was all too true. With nothing to add to the gruff farmer's sentiment, he tightened his hold on his musket and watched the British soldiers march as if on parade out of the earthworks they had gamely held against ever mounting odds for close to two months. Were it not for the threat of starvation and the increasing weight of the bombardment leveled against them, he imagined the British commander would have laughed off the terms Brigadier General Richard Montgomery, the commander of the American forces the Congress in Philadelphia had sent to invade Canada, had tendered.

Two thoughts came to mind as Edward studied the British soldiers and Canadian militiamen passing before him to where they would lay down their weapons. The first was their attitudes. Though their commander had been compelled by circumstances to accept Montgomery's terms, the English were behaving as if things had been the other way around. Those who were not able to hide their feelings bore an expression that betrayed their disgust over the realization they had been humbled by a pathetic ragtag collection of half trained provincials unworthy of the name *soldier*. In truth, now that he was able to see for himself just what kind of men they had been up against, Edward found it a little difficult to believe they had prevailed over the fort's garrison.

This unwelcomed observation led to the second and by far more troubling concern Edward found himself dwelling on with ever-increasing frequency. After glancing to his left at Farrell and silently nodding in agreement, he turned his attention to a gangly boy by the name of David Gardner. Racked by fever and barely able to stand, Gardner was paying no attention to what was going on around him as he leaned half bent over, clutching his musket as if it were a cane in an effort to keep from toppling over. The very sight of him was, for Edward, a perfect analogy for the army of which he was a part. What made their general think that a bedraggled army such as theirs could conquer a province as vast as Quebec, one stoutly defended by soldiers no different than those before him, and with winter coming on? Even if a majority of Canadians were as eager to throw off English rule as some of the regiment's officers seemed to think, he doubted there would be enough willing to join their ranks to make up for those who had been killed, wounded, or were, like Gardner, all but laid low by a fever that had already claimed over half the men with which New York's 1st Regiment had started out.

A chill caused Edward to look away from an English drummer boy dressed in a bright yellow coat, the reverse colors of his regiment's facings, and down at the ground at his feet which were awash in a shallow puddle of muddy water. Glancing around, he wondered if there was some way he could shift about in the loosely packed ranks to a spot that was not so wet. Having no wish to bother Gardner who was struggling to keep from falling over, Edward leaned over and whispered to Farrell, asking if he could move over just a bit. The Irishman who had not hesitated to join Alexander McDougall's regiment saw right off what Edward wanted to do. Having taken a liking to him, Farrell was about to shuffle over a bit and allow Edward to share the small patch of dry ground upon which he was perched. Before he could, an officer prowling behind them to ensure the soldiers maintained an appropriate degree of decorum during the ceremony snarled.

"Steady in the ranks. You wouldn't want the English thinking we're an undisciplined rabble, now would you?"

"Too bloody late for that," Farrell groused under his breath as he and Edward ceased their jostling.

The two men turned their attention back to the watching a company belonging to the Royal Highland Regiment of Émigrés march by. With a shiver, as much from the damp coldness racking his body as from his untimely reflections, Edward attempted to take his mind off his discomfort by recounting the erroneous assumptions concerning the nature of war that had led him to this place. Inevitably this gave rise to two questions. The first was one he and his companions often mulled over as they stood their watch or sat about the cookfire. Given the chance to do it again, would they have signed on to fight the British? Some chose to answer that question simply by walking away when an opportune moment to desert came their way, preferring to face the scorn of their friends and neighbors rather than spend another day enduring the hardships few had bargained for when they had sighed up.

Edward dwelt on the second question with an annoying regularity as it was more personal, a question only he could answer. Of all the paths he could have followed in his quest to assert his independence from two people who saw him not as their son, but as an extension of themselves, had this been the wisest? At the time he had decided to defy his father and ignore his mother's advice, it had all made sense. But now?

"Too bloody late for that," Edward grumbled under his breath as he shifted his weight from one foot numbed by cold and wetness to the other.

"What's that, lad?" Farrell asked.

Realizing he had unconsciously voiced his thoughts, Edward gave his head a quick shake before glancing over at Farrell out of the corner of his eye. "Nothing."

"in the ranks."

-⋘•⋙-

The path that took Edward Shields from his ancestral Dutch homestead—established when Broadway was nothing more than a footpath—to a muddy field on the banks of the Richelieu River where he and his comrades in Alexander McDougal's regiment witnessed English soldiers silently surrendering their arms had been long and trying. Along the way he had fought several battles, none of which had played out the way he had imagined they would as a boy raised among the colony's privileged class.

The first had taken place in the parlor of the house across from Bowling Green where he had grown up in the shadows of a woman determined to make him something he was not and a man loyal to a King who was as foreign to Edward as the first Van der Hoff to arrive in New Netherlands had been to the Manhattoes Indians. Having no wish to allow his father to bully him into complying with his wishes, Edward waited to inform his father he would not be accompanying him until the very morning the post ship they were to take to Boston was due to leave. He chose to make his druthers known following a hearty breakfast, during which his father once again regaled his son with stories of campaigning.

"Don't expect to be treated to fare like this while on the march," his father had declared in a tone of voice that reminded Edward of a teacher preparing his charges for a particularly grueling exercise. "Though officers with the means to supplement the meager rations doled out by the quartermaster and an enterprising orderly seldom go wanting, there will be days when you'll find yourself savoring a stale crust of bread as if it were a feast."

With an indifference his father chose not to note, both his mother and Edward sat with their heads bowed in mute silence, staring down at the food before them as each dwelt on what his father's imminent departure would mean to each of them. For her part, Edward's mother found herself having to suppress the joy she felt over the prospect that she would soon be rid of the man. With him gone, she would be free to follow Lady Katherine Trent's example and take her business affairs in hand without having to listen to him lecture her on how unseemly it was for a woman of her pedigree to dabble in commerce. *"You are my wife, not that of a peasant,"* Thomas had reminded her time and time again whenever an associate of his mocked him for her habit of dabbling in commercial activities. *"Nor are you a common serving maid in a dockside alehouse."*

Her rejoinder to that and similar remarks was always the same. *"If you took an interest in the family's business affairs, I wouldn't have to."* It was a rebuke delivered with a sharpness that would have caused a lesser man to forget Katherine was a woman.

Thomas never did raise his hand to her, though Edward often suspected his father was sorely tempted to. Edward was never quite able to determine if his father kept his temper in check because he still held the King's commission and considered himself a gentleman or out of fear of what Katherine would do if he did. Instead of physically lashing out at her, his father would draw himself up, throw his head back, and sniff as he glared at Katherine, reminding her brusquely he was a soldier. Having done so, he would promptly pivot about on his heels and march out of the room before she had a chance to respond.

Knowing his father might not show similar restraint when Edward told him he would not be going to Boston with him and accepting the King's shilling, Edward steeled himself for the coming confrontation. He was by no means a coward nor was he a stranger to being on the wrong end of a sound thrashing. As a child growing up in the rough and tumble world of a seaport founded by his Dutch ancestors and still dominated by their descendants, he often found himself compelled to fight the sons of men who felt their fathers had been cheated by Katherine's factor. As the rift between radical elements led by men like McDougall and the Crown grew, children whose fathers openly defied the unpopular laws handed down by Parliament were added to the lists. Edward's father made no secret of his unflinching support of the King.

When these altercations came to the attention of Edward's parents, each would use the incident to make a point. His father saw such altercations as proof his son understood the need to defend the family's good name. *"The disparaging of a man's honor cannot go unchallenged,"* he would stress to his bruised and battered son. *"Regardless of the cost, you must stand up to those who seek to bully and impugn that which you hold dear, whether it be your family's good name or the principles by which you live."*

Edward's mother took a different, very practical stance on this issue. "*You cannot fight everyone who crosses you, for everyone has their own particular views and beliefs,*" she advised. "*Besides, people who oppose you one day can easily become an important ally the next, and vice versa,*" she had quickly added. "*You must, therefore, choose your battles carefully, weighing what might be lost if you do nothing against what you could lose if you commit yourself. For even in victory, the cost can easily outweigh the gain.*"

Having determined going with his father was counter to what he considered his best interest, Edward had looked up from his breakfast, first eyeing his father, then his mother, wondering as he did so what the price of his pending defiance would be. That there would be a most hideous row when he informed his father he would not be accompanying him was a given. His father would view his defiance as a rejection of him and all he stood for, a grievous insult to a man who viewed service to King and country as the only honorable profession worthy of a gentleman such as he.

It was what would follow when his father was gone and what his mother would say that Edward was unsure of. His mother, like most women he knew, was an unfathomable creature. She could hide her thoughts behind a demure smile and cover all traces of activities she wished to keep secret with the same ease she erased her own footsteps along a dusty path with the hem of her gown. What Edward did know and what she had never made a secret of was her determination to see him take over the commercial empire her father had bequeathed to her. When he had been younger, his mother's efforts toward this end had amounted to little more than ensuring Edward was raised in the company of children she considered to be his peers, boys belonging the colony's most prominent families who would, in time, become the political and commercial elite of the colony. She also gave him seemingly minor tasks well within his capabilities that she imagined would appeal to a bright young boy his age. Edward seldom made any objections to these less than subtle nudges, for he enjoyed most of them. After all, spending his day dockside and perched upon a crate of newly arrived crockery while keeping a tally of what was being unloaded from a ship was far more enjoyable to a boy of ten than being lorded over by a pasty-faced tutor learning Latin and Greek. His mother's errands allowed him to mingle with rough-hewn sailors and dock hands—men so very different from the pompous, self-assured fops with which his father associated.

Had Katherine been more attuned to her son's nature and dreams and had the presence of mind to accommodate them, his mother would have been able to come as close to enjoying as normal a mother-son relationship as a Van der Hoff female could. But she was first and always a Van der Hoff, as dedicated to her family's commercial interests as Thomas Shields was to serving his King. Neither appreciated that their son, growing up amid political and social upheaval that threatened to pit colonists against a distant and, to many, tyrannical King, had not only adopted the views of boys he considered peers but found himself in agreement with them.

Relying on the advantage of a well-timed ambush, as taught to him by the sons of dockhands and common laborers when confronting a rival gang, Edward waited until his small family gathered in the parlor as his father told him it was time to bid his mother farewell. Rather than going to his mother perched upon a chair as if she were Marie Antoinette, Edward turned to face his father, drawing himself up to his full height and locking eyes with him.

"I shall not be going with you, Father."

Taken aback, Thomas gave his head a quick shake before returning his son's steady, unflinching gaze. "You most certainly are," his father snapped as soon as he found his voice.

"No, I am not."

It was not so much the shock of his son's declaration that shook Thomas. Rather, it was the calmness he saw in the boy's eyes that caused him to blanch. This decision was no spur of the moment hesitation caused by fear or a reluctance to leave home and hearth. Thomas had seen men who, at the last minute, had found any number of reasons to keep from stepping up and doing what was expected of them, whether in battle or when faced with the need to carry out a particularly distasteful order. Such loathsome creatures tended to cringe, drawing back half a step as they averted their gaze. Edward was doing neither.

Several seconds passed in silence before Thomas was able to again collect himself. When he was ready, he stepped forward, meeting his son's steady gaze.

"You dare defy me?" Thomas growled menacingly.

Having anticipated such petty theatrics, Edward countered with an easy smirk and a line attributed to Marcus Junius Brutus.

"Sic semper tyrannis."

Shock gave way to rage. Making no effort to hold back, Thomas backhanded his son across his face with all the force he could muster, sending Edward reeling and bringing Katherine to her feet.

"Thomas!" Katherine shouted.

Distracted by his wife's cry, Thomas glanced over to where she stood, clutching her fists at her sides as her eyes darted between father and son. Only when he was sure Katherine had no intention of stepping between them did Thomas return his attention to Edward who had, in the interim, recovered from the blow.

Once more, Edward drew himself up to his full height as he wiped a trickle of blood from the corner of mouth.

"You need to hurry, Father," Edward stated with a calmness surprising even himself. "It wouldn't do to keep *your King* waiting."

It was not his son's cool, unflinching demeanor that struck Thomas with all the force of a body blow. It was the words "your King" and the disparaging manner with which Edward uttered them that caused Thomas to step back in horror, wondering how it had come to pass that his son could turn against him and everything he held dear. Unable to come to grips with this conundrum, Thomas did as he had so often did in the past when dealing with his wife. Without another word, he turned his back on Edward and left the room.

Only when Thomas was gone did Katherine rush over to Edward, who stood staring at the open doorway through which his father had disappeared. She placed a comforting hand on his arm but was clearly at a loss as to what to say.

Edward was not. With his father gone, Edward rounded on his mother.

"I know what you would have me do," he asserted with a coolness that matched his eyes.

Made of sterner stuff than many gave her credit for, Katherine pulled her hand away and sniffed.

"And what would that be?"

"You would have me stand off to the side, watching and waiting to determine how best to take advantage of the crisis that will soon be upon us."

It was now Edward's turn to be surprised as his mother gave her head a quick shake. With a sly little smile, Katherine reached up and placed a gentle hand on the cheek his father had struck.

"Like your father, you do not know me as well as you think."

As proof of this assertion, when Edward informed his mother he intended to go with his friends and join one of the militia regiments being formed, she made no effort to dissuade him. She did not even object to his decision to decline a commission as an officer in the 2nd New York, a regiment that drew heavily from the Dutch portion of the colony's population, and to instead enlist as a private in McDougall's regiment. If anything, Katherine saw this as something of an advantage. It would be the officers who would be hung when the rebellion was crushed and not those who had foolishly believed the rubbish those officers had spewed. At most, her son would serve time as a prisoner. She could use that time to encourage a corruptible official to see to it Edward was well looked after and, in time, pardoned. After that, Edward would have little choice but to follow the path she had prepared for her son.

"I expect, by the time this unfortunate fuss is over and you have completed your studies, you'll be ready to settle down and assume your rightful place," she told him later that day when he was taking his leave of her.

What neither of them had any way of knowing was how long that "unfortunate fuss" would last.

Just how difficult bringing an end to the "fuss" would be became painfully clear to Edward when, in the first week of September, a force of some 1,200 men led by General Montgomery was set upon by Indians shortly after they had crossed the Richelieu River south of Fort Saint-Jean. Had Kevin Farrell not reached from behind the fallen tree where he had taken cover and grabbed hold of Edward's shirttail, pulling him down on top of him and out of harm's way, Edward imagined his military career would have ended then and there.

"Don't make it easy for 'em, boy," Farrell advised Edward calmly as he peeked up over the log and searched for a target while ignoring officers issuing orders that made no sense to him. "In this kind of fight, you don't wanna take a shot unless you're sure of your target. The moment one of them natives realizes you've fired, he'll be on you like a horsefly on a lame broodmare, whoopin' and a hollerin' like a fiend."

In the close confines of the forest, the choking, dirty white smoke lingering from discharged weapons stung Edward's eyes and caused him to cough. The screamed war cries of their assailants mingled with the pitiful moans from the wounded and the frantic efforts of officers trying to assert themselves made it all but impossible for Edward to make sense of what was going on. Were it not for Farrell beside him, cannily peeking up every few seconds to take a well-aimed shot at an Indian, Edward had no doubt he would have taken to his heels and fled for the boats as so many others had.

Still, it took a sharp rebuke from the grizzled farmer to galvanize him into action. This was delivered just after Farrell had fired before sinking back down behind the safety of the log.

Looking over at Edward, he snorted. "Well, are you gonna join this fight, or just sit there with your thumb up your arse and wait for one of them Indians to come along and kill ya?"

Blinking, Edward peered wide-eyed at Farrell for a second before concluding the man was right. Doing nothing was a death warrant. Taking up the musket he was gripping for all he was worth and killing the bastards who were hell-bent on killing him was the only way he would be able to see this through. As he had on the day he had informed his father he would not be going with him to Boston, Edward took a deep breath as he mustered up the courage to join the chaotic fight swirling around him. Only when he was ready—when he was sure he could do what needed to be done—did Edward prop himself up, rest his gun on the log just as he had seen Farrell do, take aim at a particularly fearsome warrior no more than twenty paces away, and fire.

Pleased he had been wrong about a boy he had taken a liking to, Farrell grinned, nodding his approval at Edward's determination.

"We take turns," Farrell advised after Edward had dropped back down behind the log to reload. "I'll be holdin' my shot until you're reloaded, and you do the same. That way one of us is always ready to take out any devil who tries to catch us with nothin' more dangerous in our hands than our pricks."

Despite the desperateness of the situation, Edward was pleased he had managed to win the approval of a man to which neither of his parents would have given a second thought, save how they could make use of him to their own ends. It was at that moment, in a place so very different than where he had been as he had stood up to his parents, that Edward realized he had won the greatest battle he would ever face, a battle he had entered as a boy, but would emerge from as a man, God willing.

-⋘◆⋙-

By the time the last of the British soldiers had marched out of their battered fort and laid down their arms, David Gardner was near collapse. Without seeking permission or waiting until the sickly classmate with whom he had once studied Latin at King's College passed out, Edward gave Farrell a nudge. Edward nodded his head in Gardner's direction when he had Farrell's attention.

"Come on. Let's get him back to camp," Edward said.

With a snort, Farrell took up his musket, slung it over his shoulder as Edward had, and grabbed one of Gardner's arms.

"Come on, laddie," Farrell murmured in a gruff, but reassuring voice. "Let's get ya where ya can lay down for a while. You're gonna need your rest if ya hope to make it all the way to Quebec."

That Gardener might succumb to his illness long before they reached Quebec was something both Edward and Farrell appreciated. That did not stop them from trying to ease the man's suffering as best they could for as long as they could. To have done otherwise was inconceivable. But what drove Edward was not patriotism nor was it a sense of obligation—either to a family tradition that measured a man's worth by his service to them or to a King who ruled a country Edward never even seen. David Gardner, like Farrell and every other man in his company, was Edward's friend and comrade. They shared whatever food they had between them. They slept cheek to cheek under the same blanket to keep warm at night. And they kept each other going when the very idea of taking another step seemed impossible. Forgotten were the reasons Edward had so carefully enumerated to himself as he was preparing to stand up to his father and to reject the path his mother had in mind for his future. On this cold, wet November day, the only cause in which Edward was interested was to see David Gardner safely back to camp. The cause for which he was fighting had been discovered in the swirling chaos of his first true battle. It involved nothing more complicated than simply being there for the men by his side, just as they would be for him when he was in need.

SEVEN

"An aide-de-camp is to his general is what Mercury was to Jupiter, and what the jackal is to the lion."

Francis Grose,
Advice to the Officers of
the British Army, 1782

Boston
November 1775

JAMES KEATING paused mid-sentence, setting aside the quill he had been using to record the woman's woeful tale, and looked up at her.

"I thought you said three soldiers broke into your house," he muttered, making no effort to check the irritation he felt at the disjointed manner of the woman's story.

"There were, your lordship," she declared wide-eyed.

He stared at her, waiting for her to continue, but when she did not and simply returned his steady gaze, James glanced down at what he had recorded.

"Previously you said two men pushed you aside, made for your kitchen, and took to rummaging about looking for food."

"Yes, yes. That's the truth of it, your lordship. They were quite rude, they were. Called me all sorts of names a good Christian woman like me ought not be called."

Drawing in a deep breath, James once more looked up at the woman, clasped his hands together on the desk before him, and leaned forward.

"Madam, I am a captain, not a lord."

"I can see that, your lordship," the woman sniffed indignantly as she drew herself up.

Averting his gaze, James gave his head a quick shake. "Yes, of course," he muttered under his breath. "Now, concerning the soldiers, were there two or three?"

"Three, your lordship."

"All right, fine. What, may I ask, was the third man doing while the other two were rummaging about in your kitchen?"

"Layin' in the doorway, your lordship. Passed out stone cold he was."

"Was he drunk?"

The woman frowned. "They were all drunk. I told ya that, I did."

She had not told him that, or at least as far as James could remember she had not. At this point, he no longer knew what the woman had told him as she had skipped about in a most confusing and incoherent manner. Deciding he was not going to be able to sort out her story, James asked if she would be able to identify the soldiers.

"Of course I can," she huffed indignantly. "I'm not blind, you know."

"No, madam. I am sure you are not."

She suddenly hesitated, looking off to one side as a thought occurred to her.

"Well, I did see the faces of the two who made it to the kitchen," she informed James when she finally looked back at him. "The other one who passed out in the doorway fell flat on his face before I could get a good look at him."

"Yes, well, I imagine once we find the first two, we'll be able to discover who the third man was. Now, what else can you tell me about these men? What color were the facings and buttons of their uniforms?"

"The same as yours, your lordship," the woman declared crisply without a whit of hesitation.

Upon hearing this, it took all of James's remaining willpower to keep from groaning. Based on nothing more than that and the location of the woman's home, James concluded the miscreants in question were members of his regiment. He imagined he had passed the woman's home any number of times as he made his way from their encampment to the part of the city where most of the taverns and inns his soldiers frequented were located. He had made that journey either in response to a report of a fight in which his men had been involved or in the hopes of preventing one.

Deciding there was little more to be gained by listening to the woman's disjointed account of the incident, James added a note to his regimental adjutant at the bottom of the page. When he was finished, he leaned forward and handed the paper to her.

"Take this to the adjutant of the 23rd Regiment of Foot. He'll arrange to have you go down the line when the regiment is on parade and see if you can identify the men in question."

"And then?" she asked, taking the paper.

"If it can be proven they are guilty of breaking into your home, they will be punished."

"What about the food they took? What they didn't steal, they scattered all about on the floor and trampled on it. It was all I had for me and the children."

Informing her he could do nothing about that was dismissed without a second thought. As annoying as the woman was, she was a fellow countryman who, through no fault of her own, was the victim of a crime becoming all too common place in the besieged city. James snatched the paper from her, took up his quill, and penned an addendum.

"I've added a request that the regimental adjutant compensate you for your loss. Will that be sufficient?" he asked as he handed the paper back.

The woman smiled before bobbing with what he imagined she thought was a proper curtsy.

"Thank you, your lordship. You've been most kind, your lordship," she said before turning in a whirl of skirts and leaving.

When she was gone, James rested his elbows on the table and lowered his face into the open palms of his upturned hands.

"Corporal Halleck!" he called.

James's orderly, doubling as his clerk, appeared in the open door of the small room where James worked. "Yes, sir?" Halleck asked.

"Is there anyone else waiting?" James asked without lifting his head from his hands.

"Yes, sir. That gentleman who says he can't print anything if he can't get paper is here again. Says he wants to see the general."

Sitting bolt upright, James slammed a fist on the table as he glared at his orderly.

"PAPER!" he yelled. "The bloody city is on the verge of starvation, and that man is worried about paper?"

James realized the printer had taken heed of his outburst and fled as the sound of someone scurrying across the floor followed by the opening and closing of a door met James's ears. After a quick check over his shoulder, Halleck looked back at his officer.

"Well, sir, it seems the gentleman decided he could come back tomorrow."

This brought a weary smile to James's face, the first he had been able to scrounge up all day. With a sweep of his hand, he pushed aside the stack of requests, complaints, and petitions he had yet to review and answer. Coming to his feet, he looked over at Halleck.

"I need a drink."

This caused the young corporal to chuckle. "After handlin' the lot that came through today, I dare say you could use a few more than one."

"Right you are," James beamed as he reached into a pocket of his vest, fished out a coin, and flipped it to his orderly who caught it deftly. "Enjoy a pint yourself. You've earned it."

"I will, sir," Halleck replied as he held the coin up by way of acknowledgement before tucking it securely in the pocket of his own vest.

"Oh, and Corporal, do me a favor and don't go breaking into anyone's home on your way to the tavern. I have enough dealing with the pathetic lot that comes begging without having to sort you out as well."

Having something of a reputation as being cheeky, a quality that rankled his sergeant major but James found endearing, Halleck grinned.

"I'll do my best to keep that in mind, sir," he said before taking off to find his mates and share his reward for a day's work well done.

Alone for the moment, James prepared to sally forth into the cold night in search of a warm hearth, a bowl of hot stew, and something strong to drink. Any illusions James had had that being on the staff of a general officer would be glamorous and exciting had died quite quickly. In large part, this was due to the lingering shock as a result of the bloody assault on the rebel works above Charlestown last June. Even those who had not been there that day had found it difficult to come to terms with what had happened. It was more than the terrible toll the rebels had inflicted on the force Howe had led up that hill. What concerned every officer who gave the matter the thought it deserved was the simple fact the rebels had stood their ground. While the rebels had retreated in the end as predicted, the motley collection of famers and shopkeepers had done so only because many had run out of ammunition. One did not need to be a military genius to appreciate what would have happened had the rebels defending the redoubt been better supplied.

As terrible as the consequences of that day had been, what followed was proving to be far worse. Securing the heights above Charlestown had denied the rebels positions that dominated the northern end of harbor but did nothing to break the stranglehold the rebel army had on Boston. Without access to the farms and country markets that ordinarily fed the city, the besieged army and the city's civilian population depended entirely upon whatever supplies the Royal Navy was able to provide. Matters became even worse as summer gave way to the wet, chilling windswept rains of autumn. Wood needed for cook fires and hearths could only be obtained by chopping down whatever trees there were within the city. When this source was exhausted, homes abandoned by citizens sympathetic to the rebel cause were demolished to meet this most elementary and indispensable need.

The bone chilling New England cold and idleness imposed by the tight siege the rebels maintained could be tolerated. Sustaining body and spirit on a diet that consisted primarily of salt pork and hard bread could not. Lack of fresh fruits and vegetables inevitably led to scurvy and other assorted diseases associated with a poor diet and malnourishment. When smallpox added to the death toll that had reached as high as thirty men a day, some of James's more cynical friends began to speculate that come spring, the Royal Navy would not need more than a handful of ships to evacuate what was left of the garrison and those citizens still loyal to the King.

As grim as conditions were within the besieged city, James's duties as a member of General Howe's staff proved to be the coup de grâce to any romantic notions he had held when he had asked his cousin for help to secure a captaincy and uniforms befitting an aide to the newly appointed commander in chief of his Majesty's forces in America. As James was one of the few officers born in America, Howe's chief of staff decided he was the ideal officer to deal with the civilians who remained in the city. Most were staunch loyalists, Americans who refused to forsake their allegiance to the King. Others, like the widow who owned the house where James was quartered, were simply victims of circumstance, people who wanted nothing more than to protect their property and livelihoods. *"I've nothing else in this world but this house,"* the widow had explained to James one night when he had asked why she did not flee the city as many were doing and had done. *"The minute I leave here it will be pulled down, piece by piece, and tossed into someone else's hearth."*

James let the matter drop as he was unable to deny the sad truth of that statement and knew any pledge he had made to safeguard the woman's property in her absence was a promise he suspected he would be unable to keep.

With his head slightly bowed, James made his way to the foyer where his cloak hung. With his thoughts focused on hoping the widow had saved a bit of the savory stew she somehow managed to cook up despite the scarcity of fresh meat and vegetables, James did not notice Thomas Shields until he spoke.

"Captain Keating, I'm glad I caught you."

Looking up, James forced himself to greet Major Shields in a manner he hoped did not betray his true feelings for the man.

"Major Shields. How may I be of service to you, sir?"

With a smile that struck James as being far too cheerful given the wretchedness of their current day-to-day plight, Thomas informed James he would be departing in the morning.

"General Howe has charged me with the responsibility of reporting to Lord North, delivering his personal summation of the situation we are having to deal with here and answering any questions he might have."

Of all the self-promoters and schemers James encountered, Thomas Shields was, by far, the most insufferable of the lot. It was not so much the way with which he had gone about securing his posting that James found to be unpalatable. James had, after all, seized the opportunity to purchase a captaincy for himself in the wake of the bloody debacle last June. What made Shields so irritating to James was his habit of flaunting his good fortune to everyone. Not even the rumors that Shields's only son had joined the rebel army were enough to mollify Shields's braggadocio.

For his part, Shields ignored the manner with which he was treated by the likes of Keating. He could not chide the man even when he felt he was not being treated with the respect due him. Shields understood how even the most junior officer on Howe's staff could greatly harm his reputation by simply repeating stories regarding his son's treasonous behavior. It was far better to extend his hand to Keating in a gesture of camaraderie than slap the other man's hand away.

"Since I'll be in London before heading off to Ireland to join Lord Cornwallis's regiment, I thought I'd see if you had any messages you wished me to pass along to your father," Thomas proffered in an offhand manner.

James needed little time to consider the offer. Even if he did have something he wished to share with his father, James had no intention of giving Shields the pleasure of doing him a favor, one he expected the major would expect to be repaid.

"It's very kind of you to ask, but thank you, no," James sniffed. "At present, my father and I are not on the best of terms."

"I am so sorry to hear that. Hopefully you and Lady Trent have been able to keep in touch."

The mention of his cousin's name raised alarm bells in the back of James's mind. In the last letter he had received from her, spirited through the siege lines via a courier he suspected was more than a simple messenger boy, Kat Trent had told him of the friendship Shields's wife was attempting with her. *"What the woman hopes to gain from doing so is something I have yet to discern,"* Kat had written. *"Whatever it is, you can be sure it is to her advantage and her advantage alone."* The same thought had occurred to James when Shields, who had paid little attention to him before his arrival in Boston, now took every opportunity to strike up conversation.

"I heard from my cousin just this past week," James replied.

"Is all well with her?"

"Tolerably well, yes. And your wife? Have you heard from her lately?"

Whether Shields took mention of his wife as a swipe—everyone knew the man had a mistress in London who campaigned shamelessly on his behalf—was impossible to tell. Shields was one of those characters that had mastered the fine art of keeping his thoughts from showing.

"Katherine is managing, though I do not know how with the way thing are going in New York. I'm told Governor Tyron is still a virtual prisoner aboard a warship anchored in the harbor."

"I've heard the same. And your son?" James asked doing his best to make his inquiry as innocuous as he could.

In the twinkling of an eye, Shields's affected smile disappeared.

"I've not heard from my son in some time," he all but growled.

"I am sorry to hear that."

"Yes, well," Shields muttered as he dropped his gaze and fumbled with his hat. "I must be off. I've things to tend to before I leave. Good day to you, sir."

James stepped aside to allow the major to pass, chuckling under his breath before taking down his cloak, pulling it around his shoulders, and steeling himself as he prepared to step out into the cold night in search of food, warmth, and something strong to put that day's trials and tribulations behind him. The fear that there might not be enough alcohol in all of Boston to achieve that last goal was set aside for the moment.

EIGHT

"I hope in sixteen or seventeen days to be able to present to your Excellency a noble train of artillery."

Henry Knox
6 December 1775

Cambridge, Massachusetts, November 1775

IT TOOK ANTON de Chevalier just one day wandering through and carefully examining the defenses of the American army camps surrounding Boston to realize the reports Pierre de Beaumarchais had sent to the Comte de Vergennes were even more flawed than the minister had suspected. Having served with Canadian provincials during the Seven Years' War, Anton was not surprised in the least by the familiarity with which officers and their men conducted affairs while in camp. Not even their relaxed, almost causal, manner was enough to trouble an officer who chafed under the ridged formalities of European armies. What did shock Anton was the collective indifference the rebel army exhibited toward even the most basic principles of good order and discipline.

To an officer schooled in the art of war by men who had learned their trade from Seigneur de Vauban and Maurice de Saxe, Anton knew the collection of ill-trained regiments drawn from various colonies had but one thing in common. They all lacked the wherewithal to have any hope of holding their own against an army as great as the one the British would soon set against them. Even more troubling than the shortage of musket flints, munitions, uniforms, and shelter was the absence of a trained staff and a military bureaucracy capable of securing said wherewithal that an army needed when on campaign. As bad this was, in Anton's eyes, it was the appalling lack of effective leadership at all levels that most shocked him.

Everywhere he turned, Anton saw soldiers coming and going as they pleased. Drunkenness among the common soldiers was rife, as was their lack of respect for their officers. It was more than a failure to salute or their habit of using first names even when in ranks. It was the familiarity soldier and officer alike held for each other and their unwillingness to set it aside making imposing military discipline all but impossible. While Anton knew this companionable familiarity bonded the soldiers and their officers in the communities from which they hailed, to his way of thinking, it had no place in an army at war.

"We're not like you, you know," the officer on General Washington's staff serving as his escort informed Anton when he made mention of this in passing. "We don't hold to the same ridged boundaries that separate one class from another."

On seeing this did little to ease Anton's concern, his American escort tried a different tact.

"We may be rich in land, but we here in the colonies lack just about everything else—everything from hard currency to a network of roads worthy of that name. Most villages and farmsteads in New England and elsewhere are small, self-sufficient worlds unto themselves, much like the colonies. The people who live on them depend on their neighbors in good times and bad. Most of the time this is a good thing," the staff officer said as he and Anton passed a group of men seated around a fire, spooning their share of a meal out of a small pot. "Other times it's a curse," he muttered half under his breath as he looked away and stared up at the gray, autumnal sky as if attempting to gauge the weather.

Then, with a quick snap of his head, he eyed Anton as they slowly continued through the camp. "It is not easy for men who, by necessity, have come to depend on themselves and their neighbors to set aside the only way of life they've ever known simply because they're soldiers. Personally, I have no wish to see them abandon the values that have served them so well by submitting to the sort of tyranny on which the English rely to keep their men in the ranks."

Taken aback, Anton returned the American's gaze with a look of astonishment. "But you must, monsieur."

As shocking as the New Englander's statement had been, it was the man's response that left Anton speechless. With a straight face, he regarded Anton as if he was not sure whether the Frenchman was being serious before looking away. Finally, when he concluded there wasn't a simple way of explaining the realities of a world so different from the Frenchman's, the American shrugged.

"Why should I?"

Anton was still reeling over the absurdity of the American's question when they came to the end of the company street along which they had been walking and out onto the small clearing that served as a parade ground and drill field. Stopping, the two men took to watching a captain take his unit through a series of rudimentary drills in a manner that would have earned an aspirant in France's Armée de Terre a severe dressing down.

As difficult as this was for Anton to watch without comment, it was what happened when they were finished and the officer dismissed his men that left him utterly speechless. Two of the soldiers promptly sat down on the ground, lay aside their muskets, and took to removing their shoes. Without a word, their company commander walked over to each of them and collected the shoes.

With mouth agape, Anton turned toward his escort who explained without waiting to be asked. "Their captain is also the village cobbler."

Realizing there was little to be gained in pointing out the absurdity of such an arrangement, Anton could do little more than shake his head and turn away. As he walked back to the house in Cambridge where he was quartered, Anton wondered how, in June, such men had come within a hair's breadth of inflicting a devastating defeat on the British.

-⋘•⋙-

Determining the size and weaknesses of the American army was simple for a veteran soldier such as Anton. The latter was painfully obvious. Everywhere he looked he struggled to keep his expression from betraying his alarm at the manner with which the Americans went about maintaining their tight siege on Boston. Discerning the strengths of the American army, as well as the reason its men continued to stay despite conditions that rivaled the meanest Parisian arrondissement, was not as simple for Anton. He soon realized he would have to pay closer attention to what the Americans said as they sat about their campfires sharing stories of their families, passing judgment on the events of the day, listening attentively to the latest rumor making its way through the ranks, or paying rapt attention as one of their compatriots read aloud from a broadsheet illuminated by the glow of the fire. The latter impressed Anton, for few of the soldiers he had commanded in France were literate. Even fewer had wives. Those who did were more often than not married to camp followers, women who, in France's well-ordered society, barely ranked above a common sex worker.

Ever so slowly it dawned upon Anton that most of the deficiencies were superficial shortcomings that could be addressed with an infusion of weapons, munitions, and training. As real and detrimental as those faults were to an army, the reason these men were here and the bonds that kept them together were what struck Anton as being more than novel. They were this army's strength. In France, the soldiers he commanded were drawn from the dregs of society, men with few prospects or criminals given a choice between serving or rotting in prison. The Americans gathered about the campfires he passed or stood watch with through the night were, with few exceptions, men with families who held an established and respectable place within their communities. Each and every one of them could stand up and walk away, as some did, and return to their livelihoods. Why so many stayed, enduring the chill of a late New England autumn, poor food, and conditions as trying as any he had experienced in war, was a question to which Anton felt he needed an answer if he was to render a complete report to the Comte de Vergennes.

-«««•»»»-

The opportunity to better understand these American rebels and their cause presented itself when a pudgy Bostonian on Washington's staff who had been a bookseller, Henry Knox, came to ask Anton what he knew about Fort Ticonderoga. Having served there when it had gone by the name Carillon and seeing no harm in obliging the American's request, Anton did not hesitate to share every detail he was able to recall of the fort and the region it had been built to defend. In the course of this exchange, Knox revealed his plan to transport to Boston the guns another group of American rebels had secured when they had seized the fort, intending to use them to break the siege. With no need to give the matter a whit of thought, Anton informed Knox he would happily accompany the colonel, if for no other reason than to see how the American intended to accomplish such a feat.

From a professional standpoint, the sheer audacity of Knox's plan was reason enough for Anton to accompany the young bookseller to see if he and the small detachment of men he would take to Ticonderoga could actually haul sixty tons of cannon and munitions three hundred miles through near trackless forests, over the Berkshire Mountains, and across the length of Massachusetts to Boston in the dead of winter. Had he proposed such an undertaking to his own colonel in France, Anton had no doubt he would have been cashiered on the spot.

Henry Knox, however, was not a French colonel of artillery, men who viewed the teachings and traditions of the Marquis de Vauban as all but immutable and sacrosanct. Knox was an American and a young man of twenty-five whose ambitions and dreams impressed Anton as being as boundless as the vast, uncharted North American continent itself. To Knox, the forests, lakes, rivers, and mountains were mere obstructions that needed to be mastered, not feared. Helping Knox overcome the myriad of hurdles they would encounter just as he had as a young lieutenant would be a professional challenge Anton eagerly anticipated. Anton used this to justify his decision to set aside his role to be nothing more than an observer so he could become an active participant in a rebellion in which a growing number of influential men in France had taken an interest. In a letter to Vergennes, Anton indicated that if men like Knox could accomplish such a feat, they could do anything, including defeating the British. He made no mention of the other reasons he chose to participate in the young American colonel's Herculean undertaking. Not only did they have nothing to do with the charter given to him by his King's Foreign Minister or with professional curiosity, but they were of such a personal nature that, if shared with Vergennes, he would undoubtedly entertain second thoughts over his decision to send Anton to America.

Foremost, but not solely, was Anton's desire to fulfill a deep-seated yearning: a longing to discover if he could rekindle the passion and wonderment he had once felt exploring the American wilderness as a naïve young man, alone and tasting freedom for the first time in his life. As bitter as the loss of Canada had been for those who had fought to hold it for France, Anton eventually realized he would not have traded a single moment spent trekking through virgin forests, sailing upon vast, unspoiled lakes, and crossing wide, untamed rivers that two Kings—who had never even seen them—claimed as their own. No written accounts were able to capture the raw beauty he had beheld or the sense of awe it had evoked in him. He was compelled to discover whether he would feel the same now. His other reason for wishing to linger in the Americas, one that was no less compelling that the first, was even more personal.

-⋘•⋙-

In the days before their departure, Colonel Knox concluded that, while Anton's command of the English language was sufficient to allow him to move about independently, it would be woefully inadequate for giving the detailed, technical advice they would soon need when the time came to transport Ticonderoga's heavy guns. For that, a more precise and clear translation from French to English would be required. To that end, Knox informed Anton he would find a man who could serve as both translator and orderly. Anton's insistence that he had no need of an orderly and was more than able to tend to his own needs was ignored. "*It is the least we can do for you, Captain*," Knox had responded. Unable to dissuade the determined young American colonel, Anton had settled on an alternate strategy, a bargain he intended to present to the unfortunate lad who would be pulled from other duties to look after his personal needs. It was a bargain Anton quickly forgot when he met the man Knox had picked.

To Anthony Carter, fortune seemed to smile upon him at every turn in the wake of the bloody battle on Breed's Hill. The English cannonade on that day had so impressed him that Anthony wasted little time in requesting to join Gridley's Continental Artillery Regiment which was undergoing a much needed reorganization. Assigned to a newly formed gun crew, Anthony managed to secure the position he had coveted: handling the ram and sponge. "*It's a most important position*," he had informed his mother in a letter, using French to maintain his proficiency in a language he dreamed of using one day in France itself. "*After each firing, I will swab a wet sponge through the six pounder to which I am assigned to extinguish any burning embers that might remain before a fresh powder charge is inserted and rammed home by me. It is then loaded by Simon Cottrell, another member of the crew who handles the worm—a coil of metal on the end of a long pole shaped like a pig's tail. Once the charge has been rammed home, Simon inserts the shot, which can be a solid ball weighting six pounds or canister, a fiendish round similar to birdshot but that is made up of much larger iron balls."* That his mother might not share the enthusiasm he had for being in such an exposed position and carrying out duties that were dangerous, even under ideal conditions, never crossed Anthony's mind. To a young man of sixteen off on his own for the first time in his life, it was an honor to be charged with such responsibilities.

It was Anthony's command of the French language that brought him to the attention of Henry Knox. Knox had recalled the boy's habit of visiting bookshops whenever the opportunity to travel from Framingham to Boston had come Anthony's way. When asked if he would join a handpicked party Knox would lead to the shores of Lake Champlain to serve as an orderly to a French officer, the young man, who had never traveled more than twenty-five miles from the place where he had been raised, all but leapt at the opportunity. *"I am not quite sure what is required of an orderly,"* he had informed his mother in a letter written the same day he had accepted Knox's offer. *"I expect it will be no different than what I did at the inn whenever you were too busy in the kitchen to look after a guest's needs. Regardless, I shall endeavor to do all I can to be of use to the French captain, for I would not wish to disappoint Colonel Knox, a man I hold in high esteem."*

While her son did not know what was expected of a French officer's orderly, his mother did. Having been traded to the French by the Indians who had taken her in a raid during the previous war, she had spent two years in Quebec. There she had met a young officer who had given her something she had lost: a child. The idea that her son would meet an officer who, in all likelihood, was little different from the one she had known never occurred to her. She thought this as she rushed to finish the letter she would send along with a pair of wool stockings she had been knitting for her son.

-≪≪•≫≫-

Eager to make a good impression on the Frenchman, Anthony had traded a new pair of shoes his mother had sent for a uniform coat. His gun captain's wife had made it using a blue wool blanket she had obtained from another woman who had followed her husband to war.

"You're a bloody fool, Anthony Carter," Simon Cottrell muttered when he heard what Anthony had given away for the coat. "You'll be regrettin' givin' up those shoes in a month when the snow's up to your arse and your toes are turning blue."

Ignoring his friend's admonishments, Anthony admired the coat, brushing an invisible speck of dirt from one sleeve before reaching up with both hands to tug the broad red lapels running down the length of its front. With a self-satisfied grin, he looked up at Simon.

"How do I look?"

"As pretty as a corpse at a wake," Simon chuckled as he stepped closer, reached up, and adjusted Anthony's black neck stock. "What'd ya have to give away for the new shirt?"

"Not a thing," he replied smugly. "My mother sent it along with the shoes and stockings."

With his full attention focused on the coat, Simon had not noticed Anthony's clean stockings. Stepping back, he glanced down at his friend's legs for a second, then back up to his face.

"What'd you do with your old ones?" Simon asked hesitantly.

Reaching out, Anthony placed a hand on his friend's shoulder. "Saved them for you, if you want them."

"Of course I want them," Simon replied in mock surprise. "What do you take me for—some damned fool macaroni who goes about trading a good pair of shoes just so he can look all pretty and military-like for some damned Frog dandy?" Then, dropping his chin a smidge, he peeked up at Anthony, reminding him of a girl who had suddenly gone shy. "And your old shirt? Could I, ah, have that too if you'll not be needing it?"

Giving his friend's shoulder a gentle shake, Anthony shook his head. "Sorry, mate. I'll be needing something to put on my back when I'm washing this one. It simply wouldn't do for me to go about half naked while this one dried."

With a jerk, Simon threw his head back, peering down his nose at Anthony in an affected manner as he returned to chiding his friend with lighthearted mockery.

"Of course not. That would not do, not at all. It would be most barbaric."

Rather than being peeved, Anthony took the hand he had on Simon's shoulder, reached up, and gave his friend a playful slap on his cheek.

"Quite right. Now," Anthony continued as he drew himself up. "I must be off. It wouldn't do to keep Monsieur waiting."

Anthony waited just inside the entryway of the Cambridge home where the French officer was quartered while the mistress of the house went to fetch him. Anthony took the opportunity to again admire his new uniform coat and the fresh, clean shirt in a mirror hanging next to a row of hooks for cloaks and hats. Anthony was especially fond of the brass buttons his gun captain's wife had used. Where she had managed to find them, did not matter. What mattered to Anthony was they were far more martial in appearance than the dull pewter buttons his company commander wore on his coat. That there were other minor differences in the cut of Anthony's coat and that of his captain would be ignored by officers who had served in the last war. Overwhelmed by the serious business of making good on deficiencies such as a lack of gunpowder, flints, tents, shoes, breeches, and blankets, no one paid much attention to what the soldiers wore. Ensuring the men who had built the siege around Boston did not abandon their posts, despite the miserable conditions they endured, trumped such trivial concerns.

The sound of a door opening at the far end of the hall followed by footfalls behind him caused Anthony to glance over his shoulder. Having conjured up a fanciful image of what Captain Anton de Chevalier would look like, he found himself somewhat disappointed by the actual man. Rather than wearing a uniform or the finely tailored coat, ruffled shirt, silk waistcoat, and well-fitting breeches more befitting a European gentleman, the man Anthony assumed was the French captain was dressed in modest attire with unpowdered hair pulled back. Nothing about him was in any way exceptional. Dressed as he was, Anthony imagined the Frenchman would have been able to freely pass among the merchants, professional sorts, and shopkeepers of any fair-sized New England town, unnoticed and unremarked upon. In fact, were it not for the gobsmacked expression with which the man was regarding him, Anthony would have found himself wondering if the man really was a French officer.

Anton found himself unable to do anything but stare. One had to know Sarah Carter to appreciate just how much the boy took after her. The boy was taller than his mother, as tall as he was, and well-proportioned. Both were traits Anton had inherited from his own father, the Marque de Chevalier. Everything else about this boy, however, was a clear and distinct echo of the woman who had borne him, from the milky white skin and rich, chestnut-red hair to the faint constellation of translucent freckles that fell away on either side of his nose. It was the boy's eyes, however, that caused Anton to shudder involuntarily. The eyes with which this young man was studying Anton so intently were no different than those that haunted Anton's dreams, eyes as blue as a late winter day's sky.

Never having met a Frenchman before, let alone one who was an officer, Anthony assumed he had offended the man as the French captain stood rooted to the spot and stared at Anthony as if in shock. Anthony had been told Europeans were very often appalled by the manners of American colonists, which was why he had taken his time as he washed his face and hands, brushed the dried mud off his coat, and carefully clubbed his hair with the new ribbon he had managed to obtain from his captain. As he stood there waiting for the French captain to say something, Anthony hoped he would set aside his reservations and allow him an opportunity to prove he was worthy to serve as his orderly. Anthony was eager to learn all he could from someone who had actually seen and traveled a world about which he had only read in books.

When it became clear the Frenchman was not going to come any closer, Anthony reverted to the habits his mother had instilled in him whenever he had had the time to help the owner of the inn where she worked as a cook. *"Don't stand about waiting for someone to tell you what to do. Step up and do something—anything that strikes you as something that might be helpful or that might need tending to. Even if you're wrong, people will often times forgive you so long as they know your heart was in the right place."* With that thought in mind, Anthony assumed as correct a military posture as he could, raised his chin, and cleared his throat.

"Private Anthony Carter. I am reporting for duty as orderly to a Captain Chevalier. Would you be him, sir?"

Rather than answering and without moving from where he stood, the Frenchman frowned and cocked his head to one side.

"In what year were you born?" Anton asked in a tone of voice barely above that of a whisper.

Like the man's appearance, the question was not at all what Anthony had been expecting. Now wearing a quizzical frown of his own, he canted his head to one side in a manner that mirrored the Frenchman's, as he wondered what his birth year had to do with his suitability as an orderly. Deciding it just might have some bearing on the issue at hand and since he had heard the French were a very peculiar people, Anthony drew himself up and answered.

"1759, sir."

What little doubt had lingered in Anton's mind evaporated like morning mist kissed by the sun. The boy was Sarah Carter's son. His son. Closing his eyes, Anton allowed his head to droop as he brought a hand to his face and gently massaged his forehead. The idea of telling the boy he was his father was discounted out of hand. Though there existed the possibility he might not be the boy's father, Anton had known the boy's mother well enough to appreciate she would not have shared her bed with another man while the two of them had kept each other company during a long, lonely winter in Quebec. He had no doubt of that. The mother superior at the convent where Sarah had been living while waiting to be exchanged for a French captive being held by the English had told him as much when he had returned to inquire after the only woman he had ever loved. *"You, monsieur, are solely responsible for corrupting that poor girl and leading her astray. You and no one else,"* the imperious mother superior had declared in an accusatory tone. It was made all the more damning by the way she had glared at him.

"Are you alright, sir?" Anthony asked in French.

The boy's question caused Anton to jerk his head back and blink. "Umm, yes. Yes, I am. Thank you," he replied in a tone unconvincing even to his own ears.

With the awkwardness of the situation becoming more pronounced with each passing second and eager to either get on with his duties or beat a hasty retreat back to camp and to his friends should the Frenchman find him to be an unsuitable candidate, Anthony decided to press the man for an answer.

"If you would prefer that I leave, I will," he ventured tentatively using the French his mother had taught him.

Once he had recovered from the shock of beholding his son for the first time, Anton found he had no need to give the matter another thought.

"I prefer that you stay."

⁂

With little idea of what was expected of him and even less what was appropriate, Anthony assumed the way Captain Chevalier treated him was the way all French officers dealt their orderlies. This included the wariness with which Anton behaved toward him during the first leg of their journey as they traveled from Cambridge to New York City. Having met only one other Frenchman in his life, and then only in passing, Anthony mistook the French captain's demeanor as Gallic haughtiness. Not that it made any difference to him. The joy he felt about the opportunity to spend time in the company of an educated gentleman who was also a professional soldier was matched only by the elation he derived from traveling to far off places, meeting new people, and seeing things about which he had only read.

"I have you to thank for my good fortune," Anthony wrote his mother shortly after Colonel Knox's small party arrived in New York City. "*Were it not for your insistence that I learn to read and write, I would still be in camp, listening to Simon bemoan his pitiful lot in life or standing guard at one of the redoubts ringing Boston, struggling to stay awake while fighting off the cold, damp chill that sweeps in from the bay.*" It never occurred to a boy of sixteen, unburdened by the responsibilities children levy upon their parents, that his mother would have preferred he remain in Cambridge rather than venture into the vast, savage wilderness that had once claimed her husband, first son, and newborn daughter.

The guarded demeanor Anton endeavored to maintain in the presence of the young American had little to do with established protocols defining interactions between master and servant but from his inability to see Anthony Carter as anything but the child of his beloved Sarah and his own son. This, combined with Anton's uncertainty about revealing himself as the boy's father, kept him from getting too close to Anthony—especially since American colonists did not share his fellow countrymen's lenient sentiments toward bastard children. As the illegitimate son of a French nobleman, Anton had been afforded many of the same opportunities and privileges to which the Marque de Chevalier's legitimate heirs were entitled. Such courtesies, Anton realized, were not extended to the children born out of wedlock in the American colonies. Illegitimate children and their mothers were shunned and shamed by their neighbors and the clergy and were subjected to social condemnation while their fathers were seldom troubled. If what the boy said was true, and Anton had no reason to doubt it was, Sarah Carter had dodged the righteous ostracism she would have endured upon returning to Massachusetts as a woman in her position by instead settling in a different part of the colony and claiming she had been widowed after Anthony had been born.

This exacerbated the dilemma with which Anton struggled as they made their way from Cambridge to New York in the company of Henry Knox and his men. Anton reasoned that if he informed the young man he was his father, Anthony and his mother would become outcasts overnight once word got back to Framingham. This pitted Anton's sense of honor, his fatherly pride, and his obligation to see to the boy's well-being against his wishes not to harm either the boy on the cusp of becoming an admirable young man or the simple, plainspoken, and modest woman who still held a place in his heart. Until he could find a solution allowing him to fulfill his responsibilities as his own father had and without jeopardizing their family's status in their community, Anton resolved to limit his interaction to little more than acquainting himself with his son as best he could by spending as much time with him as was feasible.

This turned out to be far easier than he had expected. It quickly became clear that while Anton was treated with respect, most of the Americans were suspicious of him and his reason for being in America. Not that he could blame them. The majority of the colonists with which he dealt were of English descent and were inheritors of all the traditions, habits, attitudes, and prejudices of their ancestors. This included a loathing of the French and all things Gallic—a bête noire passed down through the generations from their Saxon, Welsh, Scottish, and Irish ancestors, tracing all the way back to the time of the Norman Conquests. The polite, yet ambivalent attitude with which Anton was treated was manifested in many small, but undeniable ways. At Fort George, on the southern shores of Lake George, Anton could not help but note the way Colonel Knox preferred to spend time in the company of an English prisoner by the name of John Andrés who had been captured at Fort Saint-Jean and was, at the moment, awaiting exchange.

Politely excluded from the American officers' company when his professional expertise was not required, Anton was left to his own devices while the boats needed to transport the guns down Lake George from Fort Ticonderoga were gathered. Eager to spend as much time with Anthony as he could, Anton gave into the boy's pleas that he recount the siege of Fort William Henry in August of 1757.

"This was where our first parallel was," he said as he and Anthony walked the ground still baring the scars of that battle. "You can see the way we went forward from here, digging mostly at night," he said, as they trudged through the snow, pointing at the shallow ditches that had been filled but were still clearly visible. "It was grueling work, made all the more difficult due to the sporadic but accurate fire we were pelted with from the fort's heavier guns."

"How long did it take you?" Anthony asked in a pensive timbre Anton did notice as the two followed the zigzagging trace of the filled entrenchments French sappers had dug a full eighteen years before.

"We began work on the first parallel on the 4th of August and the second, which was here, on the 7th." Stopping, Anton gazed across the ground to where the tumbled down, charred remains of the old English fort were barely discernible. "On that day, Maréchal de camp Marquis de Montcalm sent Captain Bougainville, his aide-de-camp, with terms to the English. When they refused, we resumed our bombardment and our digging."

For the longest time, the two simply stood there as Anthony tried to imagine what it had been like. Anton, oblivious to the cold wind that swept across the lake numbing his nose and cheeks, had no difficulty recalling how it had been that day. His mind's eye dredged up long forgotten images of dark shadows laboring away under the cover of darkness. He could almost smell the pungent stench of the freshly turned dirt they tossed like moles crawling their way into a burrow as it mingled with the acrid reek of burned gunpowder. The smell of the sappers' sweat as they stood hunched over and huddled together while laboring away was as strong in Anton's memory as it had been when he had been sent forward to inspect their progress. He remembered how he had had to fight the urge to peek over the lip of the new stretch of trench to see just how close they were to the fort. Only the knowledge that to do so was a death warrant kept him bent over, staring at the backsides of the men who were inching their way forward, one shovel full of dirt at a time.

"They didn't give in when called to surrender, not at first, did they?" Anthony asked.

Jarred from his reminiscing, Anton shook his head. "No, they did not. So we kept digging," he replied as he stepped off, easily reaching a spot that had taken the French sappers two days to dig to. "By the time we had reached this point here, the English had but five cannon left. Knowing we would be able to smash the wall of his fort into kindling, under the rules governing a formal siege, Colonel Monro was free to surrender."

Having witnessed the savage manner with which British soldiers had behaved as they overran the earthworks on Breed's Hill, Anthony was unable to check his incredulity at the idea rules could be adhered to in the heat of battle.

"Rules?" he scoffed bitterly. "I don't understand, monsieur. What rules?"

The tone of his son's question reminded Anton just how unschooled the boy was in the art of war, causing him to explain that the commander of a besieged post was free to surrender it once his opponent had reached a point where his cannon would be able to breech the fortress's wall.

"When that point has been reached and the garrison commander persists in resisting, an assault through the resulting breech is carried out by a force known as a 'forlorn hope.' Those chosen to make that assault who survive are permitted to sack the city or fortress and, if their commander wishes, put the garrison to the sword. A garrison commander who surrenders before the breech is forced, on the other hand, is entitled to the honors of war."

"Honors of war?" Anthony shot back without making the slightest effort to check the bitterness he felt over his knowledge of what followed in the wake of Colonel Monro's surrender. "Is setting natives to butcher near defenseless men and women unable to defend themselves part of these rules?"

Both the sharpness of the boy's accusation and the reminder of what followed Monro's capitulation brought other memories to the forefront of Anton's mind—bitter recollections that all too often had the power to catapult him from a sound sleep. Those nightmares had been the chief reason he had kept from returning to the American colonies. Now, standing so close to where his innocence had died, Anton found himself once more reliving that terrible day.

A single incident in particular—one that epitomized the savage nature so much a part of this new land—replayed itself in Anton's head. It involved a British captain who was about to be scalped alive and a drummer boy not much younger than Anthony. The Englishman had given no thought to his own wound, imploring Anton to save the boy. To this day, Anton could not decide if his futile efforts to do so caused the Indian holding the boy to willfully ignore him or if there simply was no salvation for the lad. Both he and the English captain had been unable to save the boy. They helplessly watched as his throat was slit.

Anton cast his gaze out over the narrow lake nestled between peaceful snow-covered mountains. He was unable to reconcile how the mere presence of man could turn such stark beauty into a living hell that defied description.

"It's alright, sir," Anthony murmured softly in an effort to mend the rift the sharpness of his comment had created in a relationship he was fast coming to cherish. "I know such things come part and parcel with war. I've seen for myself that the King's soldiers, men who some still claim are our brethren, are no better."

Jerking his head about, Anton stared at Anthony.

"Aye," the boy nodded. "As I was leaving the redoubt on Breed's Hill, I couldn't keep from glancing over my shoulder. I watched as the lobsters streamed over the earthworks and went about bayoneting men I'd stood shoulder to shoulder with just seconds before. Grinning like fiends, the bloody bastards ignored the pleas of wounded men and murdered them where they lay."

The dry, haunting tone of his son's voice, matched by an expression so at odds with his young age, told Anton the boy already had demons of his own—a sad realization that sent a shiver down his spine and left him shaking. Turning once more to where the silent remains of the old English fort sat, Anton realized any effort to rediscover the innocence he had lost here was impossible, just as he imagined any effort to spare his son from the horrors of war were. If that were so, and there was no hope of undoing that which was already in the past, perhaps Anton could help the boy by preparing him for the challenges of this war. It was not much nor was it conventional for a father seeking to prepare his son for the future, but it was something that he could do for the boy. It was better than doing nothing as he had on that day so many years before when he had watched the life flow from the drummer boy in a torrent of red.

"You have told me you wish to be a gunner," Anton declared as he turned toward Anthony.

"I do," the boy confirmed as he squared his shoulders and returned Anton's steady gaze.

"Good! Let us start then by learning the parts of a gun and their significance."

"I already know that," Anthony sniffed.

Anton cocked a brow. "Do you? Then perhaps you can point them out and tell me what you think you know."

Both the Frenchman's expression and tone of voice caused Anthony to regret the arrogance of his pronouncement. Sighing, he averted his gaze a second.

"Well, I do know some."

Anton's frown upended as he did something he would never have done had Anthony been a French soldier, even one who was his orderly. Clamping one hand on Anthony's shoulder, he gave the boy an amiable shake.

"Well then, shall we find a cannon and see what we can do to add to your knowledge?"

Like a stray puppy tossed a bone by a kindly stranger, Anthony grinned. "I would like that very much, monsieur."

"As would I," Anton replied.

NINE

"There is a time to pray and a time to fight.
This is the time to fight."

John Peter Gabriel Muhlenberg
Sermon at Woodstock, Virginia 1775

Great Bridge, Virginia
9 December 1775

HAVING FINISHED checking the picket soldiers posted on a small island between the village of Great Bridge and the Elizabeth River, Ian McPherson carefully made his way through the predawn darkness over the earthworks built astride the causeway. He slunk toward one of the fires where the men of his company who were not standing watch stood or sat warming themselves. There, he found Ezra Shaw just as he had left him. Ezra still sat as close to the fire as he could, swaddled in a blanket with his drooping head buried deep within its folds, making him look more like a wizened Indian chieftain than a company commander. Nudging his way into the tight circle of men, Ian turned to one of them and asked if Shaw had finally fallen asleep.

Before the man could answer, a hacking cough caused the pile of blankets to quiver. "I'm awake, ya wee gommy," Shaw grumbled. "Are the pickets?"

"Cold, grumbling, and bored, but awake," Ian replied as he took the musket from his shoulder and rested it in the crook of his arm before reaching his hands toward the fire.

"Good, good," Shaw muttered under his breath as he stared into the fire.

On seeing a look of concern on the face of a youth seated near Shaw, Ian chuckled. "A soldier who's not complaining 'bout this or that needs to be watched," he explained without needing to ask the boy for the cause of his concern.

"I don't complain," the youth countered.

By way of response, Shaw snickered derisively then raised his head out from the blankets wrapped around him and turned toward the youth. He met the boy's wide-eyed look of surprise with a cold, steady gaze.

"Give it time, lad. Give it time."

Ian was about to add his own thoughts to this military truism when the sound of someone easing down off the causeway and treading their way toward the fire caused him and the men to his left and right to peer off in the direction of the noise. Instinctively, they all reached out for their muskets, ready to bring them to bear if need be.

"It's only me," a familiar voice called out from the darkness.

Whereas the others relaxed their guard upon hearing the familiar voice, Ian tensed. "What in the bloody hell are you doin' here, Boy?"

Before answering, Ian's adopted son stepped into the firelight and lowered his musket to his side. "Couldn't sleep," he informed Ian flatly.

"Who can, shakin' so from the cold and the damp?" one of the other men around the fire groused. "Makes my teeth rattle so loud it wakes me up when I do manage to doze off."

"What teeth?" another man asked, feigning surprise at his friend's comment.

"The ones I'm gonna sink into your ugly fat bum," the first man shot back, bearing his teeth as if offering them as proof of his intention to follow through with his threat.

This exchange caused everyone who was gathered about the fire, including Ian, to snicker amid a chorus of hacks and coughs.

Eager to avoid another contentious row with his adopted father, Boy glanced down at Shaw.

"Word is the North Carolinians will be here in a few days with cannon," he informed Shaw. "That's what the Colonel's been waiting for. The adjutant told me once they are, the Governor will have no choice but to abandon Norfolk."

"Don't go presuming to know what the enemy will and will not have to do," Shaw snarled before hocking up a great glob of mucus, which he spat into the fire where it evaporated with a sharp hiss. "Dunmore's a Scot and as stubborn as they come. As long as he's got the Royal Navy at his back and a fair number of regulars he can count on, he's not gonna move an inch. Not unless we make him."

"Aye, he may be as stubborn as they come, but he's no fool," Ian countered as he stared into the fire as he spoke. "He's little more than a hundred soldiers worthy of the name with him. The rest are a rabble— Tories more interested in saving their precious homes and hides than dying for King and country. And that fort he's thrown up across the way is nothing but a ramshackle affair, no better than the one we cobbled together in '54 the first time Colonel Washington marched us to the Ohio." Ian paused as he let his comments gain purchase before continuing. "While it may be true the rabble Dunmore's counting on to regain favor with fat Georgie may mess themselves and turn tail the second they hear a cannon fire, the captain's right about assuming too much about what the enemy will do. The English learned that the hard way last June. I, for one, am not in favor of following their example."

Shaw was about to say a fair number of their own would do likewise but instead took to studying the grim expressions of the men gathered about the fire who had yet to hear a shot fired in anger as they mulled over what Ian had said. Having nothing to add, Shaw scrunched lower into his blanket and turned his attention back to the flames before him as drummers of Colonel Woodford's mixed brigade of Virginians beat reveille.

For his part, Ian looked over at his adopted son, wondering what, if anything, he could do or say to see him safely away from the bloodshed sure to come once all the preliminarily maneuvering and jockeying for position was over and the men on both sides got down to the serious business of killing each other.

Ian had been of two minds when the boy had shown up in Williamsburg in the first week of November, determined to join Shaw's company. Whereas Megan had accepted their adopted son's decision as a choice in which she had no say, Ian had stormed into the regimental adjutant's tent, grabbed Boy by his arm, and all but dragged him out just as he was about to sign his enlistment papers. After hustling Boy off to where they could talk to him in private, Ian had rounded on him. *"What in Christ's name do you think you're playing at?"* he had snapped. *"This is no place for you."*

Neither Ian's behavior nor his tone of voice had rattled the boy. Rather than answering Ian right off, Boy took to looking about. He watched the comings and goings of the men belonging to Patrick Henry's regiment as they tended to camp chores, drilled, or chatted companionably among themselves while gathered about a campfire. The boy waited until Ian, impatient for an answer, had given the arm he still held a shake in an effort to get his attention. *"Well?"* Ian had prodded.

With nothing but his eyes, the boy drew Ian's attention to a corporal's guard marching by. *"What makes me any different than them?"* he had asked calmly as he turned his full attention back toward Ian. *"Am I not a Virginian?"*

Unable to ignore the boy's point, Ian had mentally scrambled to piece together a reasonable rebuke. When nothing came, Ian drew himself up and was about to say, *"Because I said it was no place for you,"* but stopped. Instead, Ian had let go of Boy's arm, stepped back, and studied the lad from head to toe. Though not physically imposing, like many Virginians who had been born and raised in the colony, the boy was close to being six foot tall and sinewy. Years of working side by side Ian mending wagon wheels and tending to the more demanding chores of running an inn had given the boy a straight back and strong, well-toned muscles. Those factors, as well as his age, a keen eye, and proficiency with weapons that surpassed Ian's made him an ideal recruit.

For the longest time, Ian did nothing but return the boy's steady, unflinching stare in silence. The boy was right, of course, and Ian knew it. He also knew it would be an exercise in futility to attempt to use his prerogative as a parent to justify sending Boy back to Winchester. Though Ian and Megan had always treated him as if he were one of their own and the boy had accepted them as such, all three knew this was a matter of necessity. When he had been found, the boy had been old enough to have faint recollections of the unfortunate man and woman who had been his parents by birth. And while Megan suspected they were nothing more than images of faces burned into his memory and haunting echoes of voices, she reasoned they were sufficient to remind him not only what he had lost, but how that had come to pass. Besides, by her reckoning, the boy was of an age when a young man was not only expected to be make his way in the world but soon have a family of his own.

Dropping his gaze, Ian had sighed. *"As much as I would like to, I cannot keep you from enlisting."* Slowly, almost reluctantly, he lifted his eyes until they again met his adopted son's determined gaze. *"Besides, you're far too big for me to spin you about and send you home with a good slap on your backside,"* Ian had added in an effort to lighten the mood.

The relief Boy had felt when he realized he was not going to need to argue with his father was short-lived as Ian drew himself up and studied him with hooded eyes.

"Lettin' you stay does not mean you're going to get your way either. You'll be a soldier, expected to follow orders, no matter how distasteful they might be. You understand that, aye?"

The boy had nodded.

"And you'll not be expecting me to show you any favoritism just because you're my son. If anything, I'll have to be harder on you than the others, if for no other reason than to show the others I'm treating you no different from them."

Drawing himself up manfully, the boy had again nodded. *"I expect that's to be the way of things."*

"Good!" Ian had exclaimed as he once more took the boy's arm and led him back before the regimental adjutant.

The way things played out once the two once more had stood before the very bemused regimental adjutant was not how anyone present expected. When the boy went to sign his enlistment papers, he wrote *Morgan Preston* despite not having planned on doing so. In fact, he had intended to enlist as Patrick McPherson as a way of paying homage to the man and woman who had loved him as only a mother and a father who had raised him could.

Ian, who had been peering over the boy's shoulder to see what name he had used, had been taken aback when he saw what he had penned. Baffled, he had glanced between the name on the paper and the boy's face. *"That's you name?"* he had asked in a tone that betrayed his astonishment and anger in equal parts.

Upon hearing this, the adjutant had glanced, in utter confusion, between Ian, the boy, and the name the boy had written on the paper before him.

Ignoring the adjutant, the boy had straightened up and turned to face Ian. *"It is,"* he replied sheepishly.

Bewildered, Ian had stared down at the boy's signature for the longest time before looking back up at him. *"If you knew your name, boy, why did ya never tell me?"*

Having no wish to answer that question in the presence of the adjutant, the boy had simply shrugged.

Ian's astonishment had evolved fully into anger, causing Ian to draw a deep, menacing breath as he glared at the boy, then at the adjutant who, having no idea what he had done to earn Ian's ire, blinked back furiously.

Without giving the adjutant an opportunity to recover, Ian slapped his hand down on the freshly-signed recruitment papers and spun it about on the field desk. *"You've been lookin' for someone with a steady hand,"* Ian had growled without breaking eye contact with the adjutant. *"The boy not only reads and writes as well as any man in the regiment, but he can do so in German."*

In an instant, the adjutant had understood what Ian was suggesting. Turning his attention away from Ezra Shaw's second-in-command, he had eyed the boy as the hint of a smile tugged at the corner of his lips.

"I see," he had murmured as if to himself. *"Take a seat, Morgan, and copy this letter,"* he had said as he handed the order he had just received and a freshly sharpened quill to the boy.

The victory Ian had felt in seeing Morgan selected by the adjutant as a clerk for both him and the regimental quartermaster was fleeting. A strapping, canny young man who could be relied upon to keep his wits about him and relay an officer's message to another was far too valuable an asset to waste sitting about transcribing orders in Williamsburg. Colonel Woodford saw this right off, which was why he took Morgan along with him when he had set out with his own 2nd Virginia and three companies of the 1st for Norfolk where the Royal Governor was attempting to rally those Virginians who remained steadfast and loyal to the Crown.

His advance came to a halt at Great Bridge on the Elizabeth River, just north of Norfolk where John Murray, the Lord Dunmore, had erected a small fort garrisoned by a hundred or so men. Half of those same men were former slaves who had joined the British in exchange for their freedom. As Ian had so succinctly noted, it was not much of a fort. In truth, it was little more than a log palisade the Governor and his troops called Fort Murray. On seeing it, Woodford's Virginians took to calling it 'the hog pen.' It was enough, however, to give Woodford pause, for the true strength of Dunmore's position was in the terrain.

Built on the southern bank of the Elizabeth River and off to one side of the only road that connected Virginia with North Carolina, the patch of ground on which Fort Murray had been erected was surrounded by the Great Dismal Swamp. The road running past it was on a raised causeway. At best, no more than six men abreast could advance along it, making a direct assault all but suicidal. Woodford, knowing it would be pointless to even try, decided instead to throw up earthworks astride the road on the southern edge of the village of Great Bridge and establish a line of pickets on the small island that lay between the village and the Elizabeth River itself. There, they would wait until the cannon the North Carolinians were supposed to be bringing arrived.

Lord Dunmore, a Scot who fancied himself a great warrior, had no intention of following a script written by his opposite number. Relying on a motley force consisting mostly of ill-trained volunteers bolstered by a few companies of the 14th Regiment of Foot, he intended to take the fight to the rebels before the North Carolinians arrived.

Dawn was just breaking when a flurry of fife and drums, followed by a smattering of gunfire, alerted Ezra Shaw they were under attack. He threw off his blankets, took up his musket, and looked about at the circle of men gathered around the fire.

"Well, boys, looks like old John Murray's decided to come calling," he proclaimed with an affected calm meant to keep men new to battle from panicking. "Stand to arms."

There was no rush, no mad scramble by his men to their posts. With grim determination, they followed their commanding officer's example, taking up their weapons and checking their flash pans and flints before moving off with purpose.

Ian was in the midst of doing likewise when he spotted Morgan following as they made their way toward the earthworks.

"And where do you think you're off to, Boy?" he asked in an offhand manner.

Hesitating, Morgan met his father's stare. "Up there," he replied calmly as he tilted his head toward the earthworks.

"You belong to the adjutant, not Captain Shaw," Ian reminded him. "Besides, you need to head back to let him and the Colonel know what's going on here."

"I signed on to fight."

"You signed up to do what you're ordered to do, and I'm ordering you to get back to camp and tell Colonel Woodford we're under attack."

Drawing himself up, Morgan was about to tell his father someone else could do that when he felt a hand on his shoulder. Snapping his head about, he caught sight of Ezra Shaw's face inches from his own. Giving Morgan's shoulder a slight shake, Shaw regarded him with something of a smile.

"Your father's right. I expect we're going to need a bit of help, which is why you need to tell them back there what's goin' on. Now get."

Arguing with his father was one thing. Defying Captain Shaw, a man who had his own way of dealing with those who crossed him, was an entirely different matter. Having no wish to get on the grizzled veteran's bad side, Morgan turned away and headed back.

Coming up next to Ian, Shaw grunted. "Ya know you'll not always be able to keep him out of harm's way."

Ian nodded. "I know that," he muttered as he watched Morgan until he was sure he was gone. Then, turning, Ian met Shaw's gaze. "That doesn't mean I can't try," he added before following the last of the men who making their way to the earthworks they were expected to hold.

As impressive as the sight of British grenadiers advancing up the causeway were, both Ian and Shaw found themselves all but dumbstruck.

"You'd think they'd have learned after what happened up in Boston," Ian muttered as he watched the column of grenadiers, turned out as if on parade, advancing at a steady, unhurried seventy-five paces a minute.

"I suppose we should be grateful they haven't," Shaw replied grimly without taking his eyes off the British as they drew nearer. "Now, off with you to the other end of the line," he commanded as he drew himself up. "Pass word along as you go that the lads are to wait until I give the order."

"How close are you going to let them come?" Ian asked before moving off.

"Until I can almost kiss that big haired bugger in the front rank," Shaw replied evenly.

Ian nodded before stepping down off the firing step and took to making his way along the rear of the company. As he went, he repeated Shaw's order, taking care to do so with a calm, clear voice.

"No one's to fire until you hear the order. When you do, aim low and send 'em to hell."

Upon reaching the left flank of the company, Ian took up his post next to one of the company's corporals. The two men exchanged a quick glance but said nothing as each prepared himself in their own particular way. For Ian, this amounted to watching the British close in on his position and doing his best to keep from allowing his feelings and thoughts show. Oddly, it was not fear or dread he needed to keep in check. Rather, it was nervous anticipation. It was made all the more unbearable by the way time seemed to crawl along at a slow, stately pace no different than the purposeful manner with which the solid ranks of grenadiers drew ever closer. Their footfalls on the roadway mirrored the sound of Ian's own echoing heartbeat pounding in his ears as they advanced step by agonizingly deliberate step.

Then, in the twinkling of an eye, everything changed. For some reason, a British officer who thought they were on the cusp of success raised his sword when the front rank was but twenty-five yards away from the earthworks where Shaw's men were waiting and shouted, "The day is ours!" As if awoken from a slumber, the column of grenadiers made ready to rush forward. It was at this instant that Shaw gave the order to fire.

With a precision that matched the way in which the British had advanced, the seventy or so Virginians manning the earthworks delivered a sharp, deafening volley. The struggle with which Ian now dealt was the need to take his time reloading. With his eyes stinging from the cloud of smoke created by the mass discharge of weapons and his ears ringing from his own musket, he reached into his cartridge box, drew out a fresh round, and brought it up to his lips, never once taking his eyes off the terrible carnage their first volley had wrought on the British column. With an ease and speed borne from repetitive drilling, Ian and all the men around him managed to reload, bring their muskets to bear, and unleash another volley, then another.

Unlike the battle that took place on the Charlestown Peninsula, the British made no effort to reform and renew their attack. They simply did not have the men or the determined leadership needed to do so. Of the 120 regulars who had set out along the causeway less than thirty minutes prior, fifty-six had been struck down and left behind to writhe in agony or sprawled across the roadway seized in the grip of death.

"My God," a man to Ian's right exclaimed as he peered through the lingering gun smoke and surveyed the carnage before them. "My God."

Lowering his musket, its barrel now warm to the touch, Ian grunted, "God's got nothing to do with this."

When it became clear the British were not returning, a young soldier closer to Ian bent over at the waist and looked down the length of the earthworks to where he was.

"Is it over then?" he asked as he went back to surveying the bloody carnage he had had a hand in creating.

Without taking his eyes off the scene before him, Ian slowly shook his head. "No, lad. It's just beginning."

TEN

"I'll sell my rack, I'll sell my reel,
I'll sell my only spinning wheel,
And buy my love a sword of steel,
My Johnny's gone for a soldier."
"Johnny Has Gone for a Soldier," an Irish folk song popular during the American Revolution

New York City
17 December 1775

LADY KATHERINE TRENT had not parlayed the eclectic collection of businesses she had inherited from her maternal uncle under duress into a thriving consortium by passively waiting for opportunities to fall into her lap. That, coupled with her youth and a social awkwardness at odds with her title would have been enough to single Kat Trent out as a most unique and noteworthy woman among the chosen few who jealously guarded New York's patrician class. Her uniqueness was underscored by an uncanny ability to thread a very fine needle that preserved her standing within New York's tight knit, discriminating social order while brazenly engaging in affairs the colony's self-appointed doyennes felt were best left to men. That she had, out of sheer necessity rather than choice, adopted a lifestyle so contrary to conventional wisdom would surprise no one privy to the tortured path that had carried her from her stepfather's sugar plantation in Jamaica to the most important seaport in the American colonies.

Kat's father, Lord Dempsey, had died a solider at the head of his regiment during the Battle of Minden without ever having laid eyes on her. Her mother had followed Lord Dempsey to the grave five years later. And Kat's beloved sister, the only blood relative she had known as a child, was killed when the ship bearing the two of them to New York was attacked by brigands off the Carolina coast. Were it not for her cousin James Keating and his fiancée Sarah Gray, daughter of a prominent New York citizen, Kat would have been condemned to a pitiful existence as her uncle's ward—in much the same way she and her sister had endured after their mother's death, forced to dance to their stepfather's tune, who tolerated their presence for no other reason than to retain his standing within Jamaican society.

James's decision to liberate Kat from the tyrannical rule he had suffered as a child by setting her on a path to prominence, prosperity, and independence was not altogether altruistic. *"As long as I could remember, I had no wish to become a ribbon clerk like my father, or his father before him,"* James had confessed to Kat not long after she had arrived in New York in the late fall of 1773. *"The way my father haggles with the dour Dutch merchants of this city who judge a man's value in the same way he does a cow or a sack of grain has always struck me as being currish and undignified. A soldier is what I was meant to be. I was always sure of that,"* he had declared this with the sort of confidence that never failed to impress Kat. *"No one, not even my father, was going to keep me from following the drum."* James's rebellion had created a rift that never fully healed, which explained why, when Kat arrived destitute and heartbroken by the loss of her sister, James had come to her rescue with all the élan of a knight errant and feeling not a whit of guilt over an act of that was, at its heart, a blatant betrayal of his father's trust.

It did not take long for Kat to repay James's kindness. Using a portion of the inheritance her uncle had tried to cheat her out of, she had purchased a stately, if somewhat rundown Georgian mansion along lower Broadway. The ever practical young woman wasted no time in inviting James and Sarah to share the home she had come to call Minden Hall that was, in her opinion, far too grand to be occupied by her alone. With a place he could call his own, James was finally able to marry Sarah. The bond between the two cousins was further strengthened when, in the wake of the devastating losses suffered by the British Army during its assault on Breed's Hill, Kat provided James with the funds to secure a captaincy, leading to his post on General William Howe's staff.

Just as James's actions had been more than a simple act of familial charity, Kat's decision to support his advancement was a move to demonstrate, in a roundabout way, she had no argument with the King, for there was no guarantee that the men led by Isaac Sears who had usurped power from the colony's Royal Governor would prevail. Even before word reached New York, fighting had broken out in Massachusetts, and prominent citizens like Frederick Gray, Sarah's father, were convinced the King would send an army to sweep away the rebellious rabble who openly defied him.

That a day of reckoning was coming was never in doubt. What Kat and others like her could not predict was who, in the end, would prevail. Even more uncertain, and of greater importance to the city's merchant class, was what the cost of victory would be, even to those who had allied themselves with the winning side. If she relied solely on the same pragmatic, unsentimental logic and tenacity she drew upon when dealing with merchants, ship's captains, and smugglers, Kat would have found herself in full agreement with Frederick Gray. The British Army, after all, was considered by those who understood such things to be second to none. The idea that thirteen separate colonies, each as different as the next and jealous of its prerogative, could withstand the might of the British Empire relying on ill-trained and indifferently led militia bordered on being absurd.

What kept her from prescribing to what passed as conventional wisdom embraced by her uncle was as complex and enigmatic as she was. As a student of Locke, Rousseau, Hume, and Voltaire, Kat found herself in sympathy with the cause that had led to open warfare between the American colonists and their King. Her narrow escape from the tyranny of her uncle's governance to the freedom she now cherished gave wings to the philosophies espoused by men who championed a social contract between the people and their government—a contract empowering citizens to openly rebel when their government ceased to represent their interests.

It was a sentiment David Gray, Sarah's brother, more than shared with Kat. Like James, David had no qualms about defying his father. *"I suppose if a man intends to break the bonds of allegiance we are told we owe the King simply because tradition and history demand it, then merely declaring that intention is not enough to achieve true freedom,"* David had gaily explained to Kat the day he joined his classmates in enlisting in a newly formed militia. *"A man must prove his resolve by taking up the sword and fighting for his beliefs—otherwise his words are empty. Only action, and the willingness to risk everything, give those words their true meaning."*

Whereas James spoke of soldiering as an honorable pursuit offering adventure and respectability, David spoke with a deep-seated conviction that struck a chord with Kat, convincing her that the men like him—men who now called themselves patriots—might prevail against seemingly impossible odds, just as she had. Prevented by convention even she dare not violate, Kat supported the patriot cause by providing the wherewithal for which David's unit was in desperate need. Those who knew of this, as well as her unhesitating support of her cousin's advancement, saw her conduct as a cynical betrayal of both. Even she had to admit her actions were antithetical. Kat was able to act without hesitation because she, like so many Americans that winter, found herself unable to reconcile a conflict that pitted her uncompromising loyalty to those bound to her by blood, marriage, or tradition against principles she held dear. Until she was able to resolve this conflict, Kat Trent did what was necessary to hold on to all that was dear, knowing full well, in the end, she would lose the affections of one of the two men she cherished.

⁂

After bidding her dinner guests goodnight and seeing them off, Kat made her way to Minden Hall's library. It was a room where she spent much of her time, either tending to business or reading the latest acquisition secured from a bookstore she owned. There, she found David Gray as he stood before one of the numerous bookshelves lining the walls. He lightly traced his fingertips along the spines of the books as he struggled to decide which he would take in place of the volume he had returned earlier that evening.

Upon hearing Kat's footfalls as she made her way to a side table where a decanter of Madera sat, without turning from the task at hand, David mused, "I've never known a woman who was as infatuated with books, or had such an eclectic collection of them, as you."

As she poured a glass of wine for each of them, Kat smiled to herself.

"That's because you've never known a woman like me."

Glancing over his shoulder, David studied his English peer's striking, red-haired daughter, who now stood with her back to him, and found himself agreeing with her comment. Those who adhered to the stifling strictures governing New York society viewed Lady Katherine Trent as a most peculiar aberration and something of a disgrace. David Gray found her unconventional behavior and interests intriguing, and more than a little beguiling. When he saw her take up the two wine glasses as she prepared to pivot towards him, he quickly turned his attention back to the book titles he had been perusing.

He was not quick enough, though, and Kat caught sight of his uniform coat swirling around his boots he hastily turned away. Rather than being pleased he had been eyeing her, Kat sighed. Though David's feelings for Kat were obvious—revealed by his unconcealable jealousy whenever she paid attention to his fellow officers, whom she frequently invited to dine with her—she knew they could never be more than friends. The path she had chosen to travel was a lonely one and beset with numerous pitfalls and hazards having nothing to do with the manner with which she conducted her business affairs or her politics. The best she for which she could ever hope would be to enjoy the company of men such as David and her cousin whenever the opportunity arose.

"How goes it with my sister?" he asked as he accepted the glass of wine from Kat.

"As well as can be expected, given the circumstances," Kat replied flatly as she made her way to the wing-backed chair where she spent a portion of each day reading.

Cocking a brow, David paused. "Meaning?"

Before answering, Kat took her time smoothing the folds of her simple yellow gown brocaded with gold silk embroidery. She had worn it but a year ago at a ball held by the officers of the 23rd Regiment of Foot before they had shipped off to join the British forces now besieged in Boston. Only when she was settled and had taken a sip of her wine did she look up over to where David was watching her.

"Her father, and yours, have been forced to hazard an Atlantic crossing due to his allegiance to the King," she stated bluntly as she eyed David with an accusatory stare. "Her husband, who has already been wounded once, is all but imprisoned in Boston with the bulk of the British Army awaiting surrender either by starvation or by force, provided Colonel Knox delivers the cannons he has taken from Ticonderoga to General Washington. And the twins, who have never laid eyes on their uncle, are giving her fits."

"Sarah's decision not to see me is not mine," David replied sharply.

Rather than being put off by his tone, Kat momentarily inspected David's uniform. The way she eyed him, paired with the cynical smirk tugging at her lips, spoke louder than any words she might have used to parry his supposition. Having no wish to spoil an otherwise enjoyable evening by poking an open wound that affected them both, David took a seat in a matching wing-backed chair and focused solely on savoring a long, lingering sip of wine.

When he finally did look back at Kat, he grunted. "Have you heard anything from Boston as of late?" he asked, as casually as he could.

It was an open secret that Kat and her cousin James wrote each other quite frequently using a private courier who had a knack for passing back and forth through the siege lines. With a twinkle in her eye and a mischievous little grin, Kat tilted her head to one side.

"Is your interest professional, or personal, *Lieutenant* Gray?"

David could not help but wince. His commanding officer, a captain of artillery by the name of Alexander Hamilton, never failed to ask David if Kat had shared anything that would be of interest while visiting. Like all of the officers who knew Kat, Hamilton never directly suggested David press her for information that could be of use to their cause. They had no need to do so as David himself struggled to keep from doing so. Looking up at Kat over the rim of his wine glass, he did his best to conjure up a wisp of a smile.

"I am asking you as your... friend, Kat. Nothing more," he replied airily.

Though David's hesitation was momentary, his struggle to find a word to suitably describe his interest in her caused Kat to hastily sip her wine to hide the blush setting her cheeks ablaze. Only when she was sure she could again speak with ironclad control over her emotions did she share with him select passages from James's latest letter.

"He is of the opinion he and his fellow officers will succumb either to boredom or the cold long before spring comes."

Spring would mean the start of a new campaign season, a trial by fire for David and his fellow patriots charged with the defense of New York. He did not share this concern with Kat. Not that he needed to—Kat was just as aware as anyone who understood the inevitable: It was here, in New York, where the English would strike. Seizing the city and its surrounding area would not only give the British a deep-water harbor from which to base future operations but allow them to rally that portion of the citizenry still loyal to their sovereign King. Unlike the New Englanders, who stood at the very heart of the rebellion, most New Yorkers were still very much undecided about where, exactly, their sympathies lay.

Only after sharing all she was willing to concerning news from Boston did Kat turn their conversation to the army Congress had dispatched to win Canada to their cause.

"I have it on good authority that General Montgomery has no intention of waiting for spring to secure the city of Quebec," Kat mused.

David was not in the least bit surprised Kat was so aware of the state of military affairs. Just that evening he had listened—equal parts amused and alarmed—how freely her guests discussed ongoing operations as well as their plans for future undertakings.

"If he's expecting General Carleton to do him the courtesy of marching out onto the Plains of Abraham as the French did in the last war and allow his troops to be slaughtered, General Montgomery will be sorely disappointed," David offered by way of response. "Anyone who possesses an understanding of the geography knows all Carleton needs to do is hold fast and wait until the spring thaw opens up the St. Lawrence. Once it has, there's precious little Montgomery can do to keep the Royal Navy from sailing right up to the gates of the city and breaking the siege."

"For an officer in the Continental Army, you don't seem to have a great deal of confidence in the abilities of your generals," Kat replied flatly.

"On the contrary, my dear Kat. I have complete faith in them. However, regarding of our efforts in Canada, I have greater confidence in the tenacity of the British soldiers and the stoutness of walls they are defending. Montgomery does not have guns capable of breaching those walls, the quality of soldier needed to storm them, or, come spring, the wherewithal required to fend off the Royal Navy. And then, there's the weather," he added before taking a sip of his wine. "Even here, in the city where our troops have warm, comfortable billets, the weather is taking a toll on them. I shudder to think what conditions are like for the poor devils who followed Montgomery and Arnold into that God forsaken wilderness."

Kat shivered at both David's words and the howling of the wind just outside the window behind the chair in which she sat. She agreed that venturing north had been a gamble. It was fraught with more risks than could have been foreseen by anyone who, during the heady days of summer, had set out to conquer land in the hopes of a fourteenth colony. Kat was reminded, though, as she thoughtfully sipped her wine, that long shots had a habit of paying off, provided one was willing to set aside their fears and persevere. Having reached this point by embracing challenges few would have willingly faced, Kat had faith Richard Montgomery and Benedict Arnold would find a way to succeed. Even if they failed, it would do little to weaken their cause—one to which she found herself being inexorably drawn, if for no other reason than her past that had offered few opportunities, little comfort, and no hope. Only the future—and the cause for which David and his fellow patriots fought—held any promise.

ELEVEN

"Had I been ten days sooner, Quebec must have inevitably fallen into our hands, as there was not one man there to oppose us."

Benedict Arnold, 1775

Quebec, Canada
30 December 1775

WERE IT NOT for the hand that grabbed him by the arm, Edward Shields had no doubt he would have tumbled headlong down the side of the ice-covered cliff along which he and other members of the 1st New York had been slowly inching their way for more than an hour.

"Watch your step, lad," Kevin Farrell called over the howling winds pelting them with snow as he gripped Edward until he regained his footing.

A sharp rebuke from an officer just ahead kept Edward from expressing his gratitude at being saved from plunging headlong into the dark, freezing waters of the St. Lawrence that lay unseen below. Before moving on, despite the bitter chill racking him from head to toe, Edward took a moment to draw in a deep breath of crisp, frigid air to steady himself.

The cold night air was not the sole cause of the violent shivering that shook Edward to his core. As he stared up at the imposing edifice atop the cliff, Edward shuddered at the idea of storming the fortress given what it had taken to subdue the British who had held the rudimentary defenses composed of nothing more than earth and timber at St. John. Doing so in the dead of night during a raging nor'easter was, to Edward, utter madness. Still, the thought of breaking ranks and not pressing forward that evening was something he—like the men ahead and behind him—never seriously considered. Members of Alexander McDougall's regiment who had not possessed the needed fortitude or conviction to campaign in the Canadian wilds had long ago given up and returned to New York or, like David Gardner, died along the way. Only those able to endure the hazards and hardships in service to a cause in which they believed—or, like Edward, who stubbornly stood by choices having little to do with the high-minded ideals of men like Thomas Paine—remained.

A less than gentle nudge from behind warned Edward he needed to press on. It was no easy task, as the trail winding down from Wolfe's Cove to what his captain called 'lower town' was blocked by snowdrifts and manmade barriers. Each time the column was confronted by a towering wall of snow they could not clamber over or bull through, they were forced to scale the steep cliffside to bypass it. Were it not for the tenacity and the example of their general who led them, Edward expected none of them would have made it as far as they had. What remained to be seen was whether General Montgomery's sheer force of will and the ragged yet determined men under his command would be enough to overcome the stout defenses ahead and the British troops waiting behind them.

The first of the British garrison's manmade barriers blocking the route from lower town to Quebec was a line of sharpened picket posts that ran from the river's edge right up to the cliff. It was defended by a blockhouse sitting astride the snow-covered path along which they had been struggling. Without hesitation the column's vanguard—aptly dubbed 'a forlorn hope' and led by General Montgomery himself—took to sawing through four of the pickets. Reduced to being little more than a spectator, Edward pressed against the cliff wall to shield himself from the bitter wind whipping down the St. Lawrence. He held his breath as he felt sure that, at any moment, the occupants of the blockhouse would come to their senses and unleash a hail of lead on the soldiers feverishly working to clear a path.

When nothing happened and the time came for the column to continue, the man following Edward grunted. "Maybe they're asleep."

"More likely the buggers are drunk," Farrell replied warily.

"With all the racket the General's making, I expect they'd have to be," the man behind Edward chuckled.

"Perhaps they're just waiting for us to get closer before they fire," Edward ventured, earning a cold, vicious glare from Farrell.

A sharp, whispered rebuke from their captain put an end to the speculation. As he waited for Farrell to carefully navigate the stubs of the freshly sawed-off picket posts before doing likewise, Edward tightened his grip on his musket, silently hoping the powder in the pan was still dry. He had covered it with a piece of canvas before leaving their encampment early that evening to shield it from the elements. Coming face to face with a determined, well-trained foe was frightening enough. Doing so with a weapon unable to produce nothing more lethal than a shower of sparks when he pulled the trigger was terrifying. It was a fear, however, that diminished, then evaporated, as the column passed the silent blockhouse without a shot being fired. The relief Edward felt as he followed Farrell was short-lived when the column once more was forced to halt by a second line of picket posts.

Impatient and just as eager to press on as the men following him, General Montgomery took a saw from the solider behind him and set to work one of the pickets nearest the cliff face. He chose this spot for the breach after spotting a sturdy two-story stone structure just a few yards beyond the line of picket posts. As an officer who had held the King's commission during the war with France, he doubted they would be as fortunate as they had just moments before. Had Montgomery been tasked with defending the narrow defile his column now traversed, he would have stationed a small detachment in that structure, if for no other reason than to give the main garrison an early warning.

Even if the British commander intended for the troops posted there to do nothing more than raise the alarm, Montgomery had no choice but continue on. The three hundred New Yorkers with him were not the only Americans preparing to storm the city. Further to the east, Brigadier General Benedict Arnold of Connecticut led six hundred men commanded through the heart of Sault au Matelot at the northern end of the lower town and into Quebec. A third column of Canadians led by James Livingston—a New York grain merchant—would stage a feint near St. John's Gate in an attempt to divert some of the city's defenders away from the two main assaults.

Even to someone who was as unschooled in the art of war as Edward, the whole scheme came across as desperate. Still, as Farrell pointed out before they had marched out of camp earlier that evening, it was better than sitting around waiting for hunger, cold, or disease to claim them. *"If the good Lord decides the time has come to take me, it's gonna be while I can still stand on my own two feet."* Though he did not quite share his companion's sanguine views, Edward was more than willing to put his faith in God and trust the judgment of a general who had not only served in the very army they now faced while willingly enduring their miserable lot without complaint but who was also at the very head of the column. In Edward's mind, such courage had to count for something.

Perhaps they just might succeed. As he followed Farrell through the freshly sawn breach General Montgomery had cut, Edward reminded himself that battles could not be calculated with the same unerring neatness with which his mother kept her ledgers. He had seen how a single bold, unexpected move in chess could upend a cautious player's game, and so, with these thoughts in mind, Edward pressed on willingly—consequences be damned.

-≪≪•≫≫-

No one in Richard Montgomery's column heard John Coffin—a Boston tory stationed with the small garrison in the reinforced stone house—caution his men to hold their fire until the rebels drew closer. The hollowing storm swallowed nearly all sound, and even Montgomery's voice barely carried as he shouted, "Come on my good soldiers, your general calls you to come on!"

Those proved to be his last words as sailors and loyal militiamen like Coffin opened fire from the quatrain of three pounders that were positioned on the upper floor of the stone dwelling. The volley of grapeshot struck down Montgomery and the men with him when they were but a few paces from the house.

Very few who had been part of the column's vanguard were as lucky as Captain Aaron Burr, Montgomery's aide-de-camp. Those not already dead or dying in the snow recoiled from the shock of the volley. When word of the debacle reached Montgomery's deputy quartermaster at the rear of the column, he made his way forward to assess the situation. Not only was Montgomery and a goodly number of his officers dead, but the men who had been following had struggled in vain to keep the priming powder in the pans of their muskets dry. The very storm they had hoped would conceal their assault had rendered the weapons of the men useless. Faced with a well-fortified enemy armed with cannon, Campbell's decision to retreat was not a difficult one to make. Edward obeyed without hesitation, for even he understood the fine line separating courage and folly—a line he had no wish to cross as the year, like their efforts to seize Quebec by storm, came to an end.

1776

"These are the times that try men's souls."

Thomas Paine, *The American Crisis*

TWELVE

"No one is without difficulties, whether in high or low life, and every person knows best where their own shoe pinches."

Abigail Adams

Massachusetts
January 1776

OTHER THAN THE light from the dying fire in the hearth, there was but a single stubby candle held upright in a congealed pool of its own wax to illuminate the inn's common room as Anton de Chevalier sat at one of the tables, staring down at a blank sheet of paper before him. With Cambridge now two days march and nothing more daunting than muddy roads to hinder them, the time had come to submit a full report on his observations and opinions on the state of affairs in America to the Comte de Vergennes. Doing so was difficult. It was not the snoring of soldiers asleep on the floor all about him that kept him from putting his thoughts down on paper. Primitive conditions and overcrowded billets could be taken in stride. Anton was, after all, a soldier who had before endured conditions not nearly as lavish as those he and Colonel Knox's soldiers enjoyed now they were once more traveling through long-established communities.

The conundrum stumping Anton as he sat there—absent-mindedly twirling his quill pen between the fingers of his writing hand—was how best to put into words all he had witnessed in Cambridge and during the journey from Ticonderoga. The savage wilderness Knox's men had bulled their way through with nary a whimper or complaint would be all but unimaginable to a man who seldom ventured beyond the well-manicured gardens of Versailles. So too were the challenges they had been called upon to overcome. Anton's own accomplishments during the French and Indian War transporting cannons and stores along rivers, across lakes, and over trails that were little more than footpaths had been daunting enough—and feats he still took pride in. Nothing he had done then or since, however, compared to what a twenty-five-year-old Boston bookshop owner and his command of ill-trained volunteers were on the cusp of accomplishing. Perhaps, he could use that achievement to illustrate his conclusions concerning the Americans and their chances of success in their war against the King. With that thought in mind, he bent over the blank page, dipped the tip of his quill into the inkpot, and began to write.

Your Excellency,

Since last I wrote, I have been afforded an opportunity to participate in a most extraordinary expedition. One that has, in my humble opinion, revealed much about the character of the rebel.

Pausing, Anton eased back ever so slightly to read what he had just written. *Rebel* was not the right word. Had these men been Englishmen in the proper sense of the word, it would have been. But they were not he remembered as he took to glancing about the darkened room at the eclectic collection of men he had been traveling with for the past few months. If there was one thing he had learned during a most extraordinary enterprise that was nearing its end, they were no more English than he. With great deliberateness, he struck through the word *rebel* and wrote American in its place.

This correction, Anton expected, was sure to catch the eye of the Comte de Vergennes, leading him to appreciate just how uncertain he was concerning the nature of the men who had taken up arms against the British.

I beg your forgiveness for having exceeded my charter by accepting the commission I have been offered. I do not do so lightly. In part, it is due to a realization that this conflict is far more complex than even Monsieur Beaumarchais and others who have your ear appreciate.

To start, it would be a mistake to think these Americans are all alike. A Virginian has no more in common with a New Englander than does a Gascon has with an Alsatian. Each is as different from the other in manner and outlook as the very nature of the colony from which they hail. If there is one unifying force that drives these men on in the face of seemingly impossible odds and holds them together, it is a supposition that they have earned the right to live and govern themselves as they see fit.

A sudden realization that he was straying from the charter Vergennes had charged him with caused Anton to again pause. The Comte was not interested in his thoughts on the character of the American colonists, or their reasons for taking up arms against their King. Vergennes's rational for sending him to America was to determine if France could take advantage of what, in his mind, was little more than an insurrection to the discomfort France's traditional foe. With this thought in mind, Anton set aside his personal opinions and concentrated, instead, on the questions the Comte would need to have answers for before advising Louis on whether France should become involved in a war that was, at its heart, a rebellion by colonists against their King.

With Cambridge and Boston within sight, there is no doubt Colonel Knox will succeed in delivering the train of artillery secured by the militiamen from the New Hampshire Grants under Ethan Allen when they seized Fort Ticonderoga in May of last year. With these guns, General Washington will be able to conduct a more aggressive siege against the British forces in Boston—provided they can position Knox's guns on defensible terrain within effective range of the city.

And what guns they were. Something of a smile lit Anton's face as he recounted the list of ordnance that lay under guard but a few yards from where he was seated. Unlike the light field pieces the Americans had at Cambridge, Knox's artillery train included heavy twenty-four pounders, mortars, and howitzers—guns Washington needed to pound the besieged British into submission. Had someone told him the American rebels would succeed in hauling fifty-six cannon, tons of gunpowder, and all the equipment a siege train required three hundred miles through the North American wilderness and over the mountains of western Massachusetts in the dead of winter, Anton would have dismissed the claim as fanciful. And yet, they had. It was more than the audacity of the feat that impressed him, one no French officer would have even contemplated, much less undertaken. Rather, it was the stoic tenacity with which Knox's men had dealt with the myriad of hazards, obstacles, and setbacks every step of the way. The stout young American colonel had no need to beg, beat, or goad his men on as Anton had often found himself needing to do during the last war to accomplish tasks that paled in comparison to what the ill-trained soldiers who followed Knox had overcome. Anton was fascinated by the willingness of those men to persevere in the face of adversity and hardships of every sort—more than what they had achieved. Perhaps this extraordinary collection of farmers, shopkeepers, and common laborers—led by officers little different than themselves—might weather the storm that the English king and an army that prided itself on being unequalled would unleash upon them.

That they would need help in overcoming the challenges in the future was something even the resourceful and unflappable young American colonel freely admitted. Determining just what kind of help France could render to the Americans was one of the reasons Anton had accepted the Comte de Vergennes's commission. But it was only one, and perhaps, the least important one. The other had nothing to do with the American's rebellion against laws imposed upon them by the English Parliament in which they had no say or with his own King's desire to embarrass his fellow monarch. Rather, it was a very personal quest, a pilgrimage Anton had put off for far too long.

But before he could tend to that, he had a letter to finish. With this thought in mind, he dipped his quill in the inkwell once more and hurried to finish his report amid the cacophonous chorus sleeping men make and the crackle of a dying hearth fire. Once the letter was finished, he would be free to see if there was still a place in Sarah Carter's heart for him.

Proof that Sarah Carter had survived the French and Indian War and prospered after a fashion was evidenced by the mere existence of a young man who had become, to Anton, so much more than a companion during a journey that was nearing its end. Anthony Carter was everything one would expect of a young man determined to put his childhood behind as he set out to chart his own course in a wider world that was, to him, new, exciting, and brimming with unlimited possibilities that were his to seize. In many ways, the wide-eyed exuberance Anthony exhibited during the trek to and from Ticonderoga reminded Anton of the awe and wonderment he had experienced the first time he had traversed the vast and untamed American wilderness during his passage from Montreal to the Forks of the Ohio in the spring of 1754. What he had no way of knowing—based on what little Anthony shared with him of his mother—was how Sarah would receive him. It had been almost eighteen years since they had last been together. Like the child he had fathered but had never set eyes upon until a few scant months before, those years had been a lifetime ago and a world apart for him and, surely, for her as well. Whereas he had returned to a country and way of life untouched by war, Sarah and a child he had sired had had to start anew without the benefits of family or position.

Anton was lost in thought as he followed his son from the artillery park to the wayside inn where Sarah was employed. What would he say to Sarah? In France, fathering a child out of wedlock was frowned upon, but not at all uncommon. In his case the results of his father's dalliance with Anton's mother had been handled with discretion. Not only had he acknowledged Anton, but the man had seen to it he was well cared for, received a proper education, and, on reaching his majority, granted a commission by the King himself befitting his standing within the strict and well-ordered social order that governed all aspects of French life.

The Americans were far less understanding of such things. Women like Sarah were looked down upon by the men with whom he had been living and assisting the past few months. He had had come to admire those same men for their commitment to a cause they believed in and a tenacity that had allowed them to accomplish what Anton had thought impossible. The same stubborn, stiff-necked pride they took in their simple yet principled way of life stood in stark contrast to the more cultivated attitudes of Anton's fellow countrymen. Despite the cheerful, almost idyllic, description Anthony painted whenever he spoke of the life he and his mother enjoyed in Massachusetts, Anton suspected the ordeals Sarah had quietly endured had left wounds she hid from her son, wounds that might never have healed. As he marched in step at his son's side, Anton wondered if his return would reopen those wounds, causing Sarah to recoil and put a quick, sharp end to a dream he had clung to for years. Maybe she would somehow manage to forgive him for the suffering he had caused her and fall into his embrace as she had when they had both been so much younger and very much in love.

The inn Anthony led him to proved to be a vast improvement over many of the rough-hewn establishments in which Anton had stayed during his travels as an unofficial advisor to Colonel Knox. Modest and clean, it had a charming, informal cordiality that made him feel welcomed the moment he walked through the door despite the trepidations he felt over a reunion he had put off for far too long.

"She'll be in the cookhouse this time of day," Anthony declared brightly even as he nodded his head by way of acknowledging greetings from other members of Knox's command who were already there and a pretty little waitress who was serving them. "Late afternoon is always the busiest time of day as travelers going to and fro from Boston to Springfield stop for the evening."

The temptation to seize on this fact and put off confronting the only woman he had ever loved was almost too compelling to resist. To have done so after coming this far, however, would have been an act of cowardice by which a proud man and officer in the French army could not abide. Thus, drawing upon the same determination he often relied to see him through battle, Anton weaved his way through the crowded common room of the inn and out a backdoor.

Pausing at the entrance of the cookhouse before following Anthony in, Anton once more found himself wondering what he would say to Sarah. Perhaps he should start by apologizing for his behavior in Quebec—an admission of guilt for a failing of character of which he was not in the least bit ashamed. He could rush to her and gather her up in his arms as he had so often done in his dreams, professing his undying love for her as he placed a gentle, tender kiss on her forehead, her cheek, and finally, her lips.

There was no need for Anthony to point out which of the women scurrying about the kitchen was Sarah Carter. Even with her red hair neatly tucked under a plain white muffin cap identical to the ones worn by the other women bustling about the crowded room, and though her back was to the entrance of the cookhouse as she tended to a suckling pig roasting on a spit, Anton recognized the woman who had haunted his dreams right off.

A stout older woman named Mary kneading dough at the table smiled when she looked up and saw Anthony.

"Well look at you," she declared cheerfully as she stopped what she had been doing, wiped her hands on her apron, and quickly made her way Anthony. "Let me see you, lad," she murmured as she took to inspecting him from head to toe. Pleased by what she saw, she looked up and smiled. "All grown up and looking every bit a proper soldier."

Beaming with pride, Anthony straightened up and returned the smile of a woman who had been like a second mother to him.

"I'm a corporal now," he informed Mary. "Colonel Knox himself told my captain that if he didn't promote me, he'd cashier the man before the day was out."

On hearing the sound of her son's voice, a smile lit Sarah's face as she spun about. Her joy, brought on by the realization he had managed to survive the midwinter ordeal, vanished the second she caught sight of Anton standing in the open doorway of the cookhouse. For a moment, she stood frozen staring just beyond her son at the figure hovering uncertainly, wondering if he was simply a figment of her imagination or the ghost of a man who often haunted her dreams. It was a notion that was quickly dispelled when Anthony turned slightly and, with a casual wave of his hand, introduced Anton as if they were perfect strangers.

"Mother, this is Captain Chevalier of the French Army. He's volunteered to serve on Colonel Knox's staff."

It never occurred to Anton to correct an assumption his son shared with many of the men on Knox's expedition to Ticonderoga. He held neither a commission in an army that lacked everything save men and a cause they believed in or a place on Colonel Knox's staff. If truth be told, by assisting the American colonel as he had,

Anton had exceeded the Comte de Vergennes' mandate by a wide margin. That concern, however, was the furthest thing from his mind as he stood in the open doorway of the cookhouse, staring into the eyes of a woman he had never stopped loving. Only now did he appreciate just how little his professional curiosity or his desire to once more revisit the vast, untamed American wilderness had played in his decision to accept the Comte's commission. What remained to be seen as Sarah Carter haltingly made her way around the table to where he stood was whether she shared his feelings neither time nor distance had been able to diminish.

The childlike delight Anthony felt at being the center of attention of women who had known him his entire life kept him from realizing it was not shyness in the way his mother approached the French officer who had befriended him. Without ever taking her eyes from Anton's, Sarah made her way past the cluster of women gathered about her son. It was not until she was but an arm's distance from Anton that she remembered where she was, causing her to start as if awakening from a trance. Hastily, she fixed her gaze to an invisible spot on the floor at her feet, as much to hide the blush that reddened her cheeks as to find somewhere else to look.

"Forgive me for staring so, monsieur," she declared in French with little more than a quick, breathy whisper as she sketched out a perfunctory bob.

Better prepared for this moment than she, Anton was able to resist the temptation to cup her cheek to raise her downcast eyes until they once more met his. Instead, he returned her greeting with a formal, courtly bow that was so at odds with their surroundings but was, in his mind, both proper and fitting in the presence of his son's mother.

"Madam, you have no need to apologize to me. It is I who am at a loss for the words needed to make amends for my regrettable behavior. I have been..." Unsure how to continue, or even if he should, Anton fell silent.

When the Frenchman failed to continue, Sarah found herself unable to keep from peeking back up and into his eyes—eyes she knew so well. She realized he had changed, a little, as she studied his face—one that so often drifted into her dreams like a gentle summer breeze. He was older yes, but no less handsome.

Lost in the awkwardness of the moment, neither noticed that Mary had moved her attention from Anthony to them as she watched out of the corners of her eyes. It took her but a second to see what only another woman could see. There was no need to give the matter much thought. With a certainty borne from years catering to the needs of strangers and friends who passed through an inn alongside one of the busiest roads in the colonies, Mary concluded that the story Sarah Carter had told her when she had first stepped foot in the inn in the wake of the French and Indian War was, in part at least, a fabrication. Not that it mattered to the cook who had, over the years, become more mother than employer to Sarah. Mary had always suspected Sarah's limp was not the only scar she carried after that war. Now, she knew the full story as she made her way over to where Sarah and the Frenchman stood before each other, locked in hopeless indecision.

With so many thoughts, so many feelings tumbling over each other, Sarah was lost to all around her save the wistful glimmer of hope she imagined she saw in Anton's eyes. Were it not for the feeling of a gentle hand upon her forearm, she would have remained standing before the only man she had ever truly loved, unable to decide how best to deal with this most unexpected reunion, or even if she should.

Startled by Mary's touch, Sarah all but jumped, snapping her head to the cook standing beside her. Mary was regarding Sarah with an expression that suddenly made her aware her behavior was betraying more than she wished. Blushing deeply, she met Mary's eyes but for a second before bringing her hands together before her and once more dropping her gaze.

"I, ah… I am sorry," she muttered as she glanced back at Anton out of the corner of her eyes. "I am neglecting my duties. If you will excuse me."

Sarah's efforts to flee back to the hearth where she had been tending a skewered, suckling pig were thwarted by a tightening of the grip Mary had on her arm.

"Never you mind about that, dear. I'll have one of the lads look after the pig, just like your Anthony used to when he was but wee high," Mary declared as she held her free hand out to her side without ever looking away from Sarah. "You go and spend time with your son and, ah, his friend," she added as she gave Anton a quick peek out of the corner of her eye and a knowing smile. "I've no doubt the two of them are just as eager to tell you of their adventures as you are to hear of them."

A quick glance about the room made Sarah painfully aware she had suddenly become the center of attention. It did not matter whether it was the appearance of a boy all the women who worked in the inn's cookhouse had known since he had been but a baby or the way she had behaved at the sight of Anton. Without a second thought, Sarah hastily wiped her hands on her apron, took it off, and led the two men away.

As Mary watched them go, she smiled to herself. She knew full well that she would, in time, learn all that mattered of the role the strikingly handsome French captain had played in Sarah's past.

Uncertain of the Frenchman's intentions—and unsure of her feelings—with her head bowed and hands tightly clasped, Sarah led Anton and her son to a small table as far away as she could manage from the other guests now filling the inn's common room. There, a young serving girl waited on them. She lingered much too long at their table and was far more attentive to their needs than Sarah felt was necessary. Were it not for her son's efforts to flirt with the girl—a beguiling diversion both were enjoying immensely—that allowed her to cast circumspect glances at the Frenchman from time to time, Sarah would have shooed the girl away by reminding her she had other guests to tend to.

For his part, Anton did his best to remain silent throughout the course of the meal that followed. Having been as bold as he dared by accompanying Anthony to the inn in the first place—and well aware of the way Sarah's fellow inn workers were watching them—he felt it was best to let her decide how best to go forward, if she wished to. Neither her expression nor her not-so-furtive glances at him provided Anton with but a hint as to what she would do or say when they were finally alone. It was a prudent course of action on her part—perhaps the only one that made sense. But, it demanded Anton be patient—a virtue he was finding difficult to uphold now he was so close to discovering if the woman seated across from him shared the same dream to which he had stubbornly clung all these years.

When next Sarah ventured to raise her eyes from her plate of food, she found the Frenchman staring at her. With her son otherwise preoccupied with the serving girl who stood at the edge of the table with her hands wrapped about a pitcher as she listened to him regale her with a particularly exciting tale, Sarah did her best to see beyond the Frenchman's well-guarded expression she knew was but a mask. In doing so, she found her resolve to maintain her distance ebbing fast. It had been far too long and the memories of the time they had spent together far too precious to allow this opportunity to pass without discovering if her hope of requited feelings had been little more than foolish fantasy.

She was still in the midst of deciding how to open a conversation with Anton when an orderly on Knox's staff caught Anton's eyes while making his way across the room toward Sarah and him. Realizing she no longer had his full attention, Sarah dropped her gaze and nudged the uneaten piece of meat on her plate with her fork.

"Excuse me, sir," the orderly said apologetically as he took the serving girl's place and turned his attention to Anton. "Sir, Colonel Knox requests the pleasure of your presence."

For an officer holding the King's commission, a request by a superior, even one prefaced with the word request, was tantamount to an order. He therefore removed his napkin, came to his feet, and bowed to Sarah.

"My apologies, Madame Carter, but I must go."

His disappointment at having to leave just as they were about to overcome their shared awkwardness was palpable. Were it not for the frown he noticed as she gazed up at him and the unmistakable disappointment her eyes betrayed, Anton would have been utterly dashed. Instead, his annoyance at being interrupted at such an inopportune moment was quickly replaced by a feeling of euphoria—Sarah's expression was the first sure sign her feelings mirrored his own. He therefore felt emboldened to make an audacious move—one he expected would tear down the last of the barriers between them that had kept them from expressing their true feelings.

Coming around the table to where she was seated, Anton took Sarah's right hand in his own. Without ever taking his eyes off hers, he bowed deeply and kissed the hand she freely yielded to him.

"May I call on you later, Madame?" he asked tentatively as he straightened up without relinquishing the gentle, yet firm grip with which he held her hand.

After a moment of silence, Sarah nodded as she bowed her head ever so slightly.

"Oui, Monsieur." she whispered breathily without looking up. "I would very much like that."

For the first time since entering the inn, the uncertainty that had kept Anton on edge vanished. In place of the well-guarded expression behind which he had kept his feelings hidden, a wisp of a smile lit his face.

Unable to help herself, Sarah peered up at him though her lashes. She too cast aside her reserve to keep her feelings in check as she allowed the hint of a smile to grace her lips, as warm as a summer breeze. She gave Anton's hand a gentle, reassuring squeeze.

"J'attends avec impatience votre retour."

"Oui. Moi aussi, j'ai hâte d'y retourner," Anton said before smartly pivoting about and following Knox's orderly.

Anton found Henry Knox in his room seated at a small table that served him as both a desk and dinner table. It was more out of habit than a rejection of the informality so prevalent throughout the American army that caused Anton to stop within a few paces of the desk, bring his heels together, and execute a quick bow.

"You wished to see me, Colonel?"

Looking up from the letter he had been busily penning, Knox smiled. "Yes, yes indeed. Would you care to take a seat and join me for dinner?"

With his mind still on Sarah and the promise of what their next meeting held, Anton answered without thinking.

"Thank you, but no." When he saw Knox's expression darken with a frown, he realized he had responded a tad too hastily. "Ah, what I meant to say, Monsieur, is that I have already eaten. I will, of course, accept your offer of a seat."

Like many of his fellow Americans, Knox dismissed Anton's odd behavior without a second thought. The man was, after all, French. Besides being a rare creature in the New England colonies, even to a businessman who plied his trade in a seaport town, Knox was unable to forget that the French officer had been a mortal enemy of England and the American colonies just twelve years prior. While the young colonel had not fought then, a number of Knox's men who had could not forget what they and their Indian allies had done during the course of that war.

After setting aside his quill, Knox took to leafing through a stack of letters even as he began to speak without looking over to where Anton had taken a seat.

"I wish to apologize for not taking the time before this to express my gratitude for the advice and assistance you have rendered during our journey from Ticonderoga. I did, however, find the time to write to General Washington of your services. In response, he sent me this, which I received but an hour ago," Knox stated as he pulled a paper from the stack and, leaning forward, held it out to Anton.

Thinking it was nothing more than a letter expressing the American general's appreciation for what was, in Anton's mind, nothing more than common courtesy, he took the paper and set it on his lap without looking at it.

"I can assure you, Monsieur, when compared to what you and your men did, my contribution to your expedition is hardly worth mentioning."

Easing back in his seat, a smile slowly crept Knox's face. "I think not, Monsieur. Neither does General Washington. Please, read the letter."

Confused as to why it was so important to waste both his time and the young colonel's, but unable to do otherwise given that he was but a captain and Knox a colonel, Anton took up the letter and read it. As expected, the missive opened with an expression of gratitude. It was what followed that caused him to blink as he drew back ever so slightly before glancing up at Knox.

Realizing the Frenchman had reached the most important part of the letter, Knox smiled, but said nothing as Anton turned his attention back to the letter. When he had finished, he brought the page up and waved it about.

"As flattered as I am by the offer, I cannot accept it, Monsieur."

"I was hoping you would," Knox replied. "I expect it would be to your advantage and, no doubt, to the people who sent you to report on the military situation here in the colonies."

Anton said nothing as he met Knox's stare with an expression he hoped did not betray the acute sense of guilt he felt over the way he had so far misrepresented his reason for coming to the American colonies—especially at a time when many who were loyal to their King were leaving them. It did not surprise him in the least that Knox knew why he had hazarded a late fall crossing of the Atlantic and the threat of capture by France's traditional foe who would, he expect, brand him as a spy. What did cause him to hesitate were the consequences he would suffer if he did accept the provisional commission as a major in the Continental Army being offered to him. The achievements the ragtag American army had thus far achieved, while impressive, were due in large measure to a woeful lack of preparedness on the part of the British forces in the colonies, the suddenness and ferocity with which the rebellion had erupted, and the extent of their control of the various colonial governments. Having participated in the campaign to suppress Corsican resistance to French occupation, Anton knew what awaited men like General Washington and Colonel Knox once the English had dispatched a larger, better prepared force to deal with their rebellious subjects. He had no doubt, as he stared into Knox's eyes, that he and Washington knew the same. What he had no way of knowing was if his son, and other men like him, understood this reality.

Then, like a thunderclap, Anton realized he had no choice but to accept the commission. Having ignored his responsibilities as a father for so long, to turn his back on the young man he had come to know and abandon him a second time would be an unbearable disgrace. Whether he would be able to save the boy from the hangman's noose when the end finally came was a question Anton could not answer. He could only be sure that he would be there when that day came, even if he, too, followed his son to the gallows.

Thus resolved, Anton drew himself up and, with a weak smile, nodded. "Monsieur, you may inform your general I would be proud to serve him in whatever capacity he deems appropriate."

"Good, good," Knox declared cheerfully. "You will accompany me in the morning when I leave for Cambridge with the lighter pieces. Until such time as we can decided where they will be of greatest benefit to our efforts, the heavier guns will remain here."

The temptation to ask if he could linger in Framingham for a few days longer was dismissed without a second thought. As much as he wished to find out just where he stood with Sarah, his responsibility to his son and the army of which he was now a part both demanded he put duty before all other considerations. Hopefully the woman he had traveled across an ocean to find would understand. And, if she did not, Anton reasoned as stood to accept Knox's outstretched hand then prepared to leave the room, he still had the memory of what was, for him, a long ago affair of the heart no poet or writer could ever describe.

THIRTEEN

"Guard with jealous attention the public liberty. Suspect everyone who approaches that jewel. Unfortunately, nothing will preserve it but downright force. Whenever you give up that force, you are inevitably ruined."

Patrick Henry

New York City
February 1776

WALKING ALONG streets he had trod since he had been old enough to walk felt strangely odd to Edward Shields. Nothing had changed in the few months that had passed since setting off in the company of men he hardly knew to conquer a province he had cared little about then, and even less now. Save for their expressions, even the people he and Kevin Farrell passed were no different. It was the looks they gave him that told Edward something had changed, something he had given little thought to until that moment. He realized that, in fact, he had changed.

No one needed to tell him the changes had to do with something more than the filthy rags he wore or the reek of wood smoke and unwashed flesh that set him apart from the world to which he had once belonged. In the few short months since he had last made his way along Broadway, circumstances had led him to see the world in an entirely new light. They had also remolded him into someone that was still very much a stranger to even himself. Perhaps, when he finally reached his mother's house and made his way up the steps, a few days spent there would allow him the opportunity he so desperately needed to find out more about this new person he was. Only then, he expected, would he be able to chart a course better suited for that person.

The thought of knocking before entering, or announcing himself as he stepped into the entry hall never occurred to Edward. This was, after all, his home, and despite the rift between himself and his parents, his decision to join the rebel cause had not changed that. He belonged here. That this might not be a sentiment shared by all quickly became evident when Elizabeth van Deventer, the housekeeper, emerged from the rear of the house and stopped the second she saw him.

"And who might you two be?" Elizabeth asked in a sharp tone that made Farrell, who had not noticed her, startle and caused Edward to frown.

"Why, it's me, Elizabeth. Edward," he ventured tentatively. "I've come home."

Taken aback by the very idea that one of the two pathetic wretches standing across the entry hall from her could be her mistress's son caused Elizabeth to frown. But rather than voice her doubts, she wisely took to examining the figure who wore a filthy, threadbare blanket draped over his shoulders more closely. Never having seen Edward with anything resembling a beard, it took her a moment to look past it and the tattered remains of his uniform.

With a suddenness that caused her to gasp, the housekeeper finally saw past Edward's deplorable appearance. Appalled, she brought her right hand up to her mouth in a vain effort to hide her shock even as she took a quick step back.

"Dear God in Heaven. It *is* you!"

Wearing a grim expression that was as much out of character for the boy she had known as was his appearance, Edward nodded.

"It is. And this is Kevin Farrell," he added as he vaguely waved a hand off to one side. "He and I are messmates."

It took more effort than such a simple act normally required for Elizabeth to turn her attention to the man standing next to Edward. When he saw the same expression on the housekeeper's face that had betrayed the disbelief and disgust with which she had greeted him, he cleared his throat.

"Is my mother about?"

Unable to take her eyes off of Farrell, she nodded.

"I expect she's in the study. Since that contemptuous cur of a factor she relied on for all these years ran off for England, she's been reduced to going over the ledgers and looking after her affairs like a common shopkeeper."

Without needing to look behind him, Edward guessed his friend was feeling uncomfortable and quite out of place given the way Elizabeth continued to eye Farrell as if he were a mangy stray that had followed him home.

"We've been on the road since early this morning without the benefit of breakfast or libations," he declared offhandedly in an effort to move things along. "Would you be so kind as to have Teresa bring Kevin—I mean Mister Farrell—eggs, bacon, and coffee?"

"Fresh coffee, if you please," Farrell said hopefully as the prospect of a warm meal overcame the nervous shyness roused by his surroundings and the housekeeper's disdain.

Having recovered somewhat from her shock at the physical appearance of her mistress's son, Elizabeth managed to regain the haughtiness she customarily displayed when dealing with those she considered to be beneath her.

"If you will, follow me to the kitchen," she sniffed.

Having also managed to regain his footing, Edward placed a restraining hand on Farrell's sleeve before he could comply as he regarded the housekeeper down the bridge of his nose in a manner little different than his father often used when addressing a servant.

"Have you forgotten your manners?" he asked scornfully. "Do we not entertain guests invited to share a meal with us in the dining room?"

For several long, awkward seconds, Elizabeth and Farrell looked at each other, then at Edward before once more exchanging a quick glance as they waited to see who would speak next. In the end, it was the steady, unflinching glare Edward pinned upon her that caused the housekeeper to capitulate.

"This way, *Mister* Farrell."

Only when Elizabeth and his friend were gone was Edward free to turn his full attention to his next order of business. Taking his time, he pulled off the ragged blanket draped over his shoulders in lieu of a proper cape and carefully hung it next to his mother's as he had always done in the past. Only after he had taken a step back and saw the two of them side by side did he really appreciate just how much he really had changed since last doing so. As he faced the mirror his mother used to inspect her appearance before stepping out the door, he wondered how he would justify to her a decision these past few months had led him to when he couldn't even explain it to himself. Her world revolved around commerce and trade. To her, everything—even human beings—had a set value. The world he had become a part of and the rules and principles that governed it were not so easily quantified.

Eager to get on with a confrontation he had been dreading for days, Edward put aside his efforts to conjure up a rational argument his mother would understand and turned his full attention to making himself as presentable as possible. Drawing himself up before the mirror, he quickly realized achieving that modest goal was an exercise in futility. Still, just as the patriot army he had been part of had done day after day, he did what he could with what he had as he took to straightening the lapels of his coat that no beggar worth his salt would wear.

The thought of what his mother would say when she laid eyes on his sorry appearance brought a hint of a smile that vanished in as quickly as it came. It was what she would insist upon after she had overcome her shock that worried him. The issue was not in his understanding but lay in how he might respond, for anything he said that did not align with her wishes would, to her ears, be no less treasonous than the stand he had taken against the Crown.

"Well, best to be done with it," Edward muttered under his breath to his hideous reflection in a tone of voice with which Farrell greeted him each morning as they set out to face a new day that all too often promised to be no better than the one before.

The sound of the door behind her opening caused Katherine Shields to frown. Without bothering to look up from the ledger entry she was in the midst of jotting down, she all but barked to what she thought was the courier for whom she had sent.

"You're late. Take the letters from the side table and see to it they are delivered to the proper people."

The sharpness of his mother's voice did not surprise Edward in the least. The genteel manners and polished image she carefully cultivated in the presence of her peers quickly dropped when dealing with anyone in her employment.

"It's not the courier, Mother."

Taken aback by the sound of her son's voice, Katherine pushed away from her desk, spun about in her seat, and began to rise. She stopped the moment she caught sight of Edward. Just as it had been with her housekeeper, it took Katherine several excruciatingly long seconds to see past his filthy rags and unruly beard. When she was finally able to accept the bedraggled creature standing just inside the study's doorway was her son, she found she was at a loss as to what to do. Stepping up and greeting him with an embrace was dismissed without a second thought. Even under the best of circumstances, physical displays of affection were, to Katherine, undignified and loutish. Instead, she drew herself up, clasped her hands together level with her waist, tilted her head back ever so slightly, and sniffed.

"This is a surprise," she stated flatly.

His mother's behavior was not at all a surprise to Edward. No one could ever accuse Katherine Shields of not being interested in her only child's education and welfare. It was her inability to go much beyond that, however, that had, as of late, become painfully obvious to Edward. In all the years he had lived with her, he had never heard anyone, even his own father, describe her as affectionate or loving. Since his mother's lack of tenderness had never before bothered him, he found it odd that it was his foremost thought now as he stood across the room from her.

"I have been led to understand Quebec was still under siege by your General Arnold," Katherine stated once she had managed to compose herself.

Edward ignored the way she made a point of calling Benedict Arnold "your general." Instead, he made his way over to one of the wing-backed chairs and settled into it before responding.

"It is."

When her son failed to expand further and instead sat there quietly studying his chapped, calloused hands in the pale winter light streaming in through the study's windows, Katherine asked the obvious.

"Have you deserted?"

To her surprise, Edward chuckled as he let his hands fall into his lap and turned his full attention to her.

"Deserted? No. I would never do that to you. No," he continued after drawing in a deep breath and letting it out slowly. "Our terms of enlistment—Kevin Farrell's and mine—have expired."

"I see," Katherine murmured as she made her way over to a companion chair across from the one her son was seated in. "Then you are home for good."

That simple question—delivered more as a statement than an inquiry—was not so easily answered. Needing time to sort through a jumble thoughts and feelings he had yet to come to terms with, Edward did not respond at first. Instead, he looked out at the leaden gray sky just beyond the window.

"Perhaps."

"What do you mean, 'perhaps'?"

Glancing over at his mother out of the corner of his eye, he repeated his answer. "Perhaps."

"May I ask what you are thinking?"

Edward did not answer her. With so many memories of a campaign that was, for him, over, and the emotions they roiled up within him still raw, he dare not. No one who had gone north to Canada with General Montgomery and endured what they had would understand—a belief he was sure was doubly true in his mother's case.

When it became clear he was not going to share his thoughts and plans, Katherine came to her feet.

"I expect you are eager to bathe and change into something more suitable. We'll discuss this matter after dinner."

With that, she left the study without bothering to inform Edward what she meant by "this matter." Not that it made any difference to him. Her concerns and what she wished to address with him were the furthest things from his mind. He returned to gazing out at the cold winter sky he did not see as his thoughts returned to memories that were still painfully fresh.

"It's all but impossible to know who can be trusted these days," Katherine proclaimed as she cast a wary eye down the table to where Farrell was seated.

If the gruff Irishman was offended by the way his friend's mother went out of her way to make it known he was not welcomed in her house, he did not show it as he continued to attack the food on his plate as if he feared someone might snatch it from him.

Katherine failed to appreciate it would take more than a woman's sharp tongue and wrinkled, upturned nose to send Farrell fleeing from the room and out the front door in search of a tavern. Dressed in ill-fitting suit clothies Edward had lent him and seated at a table the likes of which he had never beheld, much less dined at, the farmer-turned-soldier was determined to enjoy as much of the rich bounty before him as he could.

Edward was seated across from Farrell and was paying even less attention to his mother. Unlike Farrell, a man able to take every turn of good fortune in stride without ruffling a hair, it took Edward until evening to set aside the feeling of being a stranger in a city he knew so well and the home he had grown up in. These had been haunting him since returning to New York City. He, too, was determined to enjoy the first full meal served at a proper table he had eaten since marching off to Canada. Were it not for the way his mother took advantage of every opportunity to make her displeasure known with his decision to invite someone to dine with them without first seeking her permission, he imagined he would have been able to forget, if only for a while, the hardships he had endured in Canada as he took up the last piece of meat on his plate and popped it in his mouth.

"Going about our business these difficult days have been a trial," Katherine prattled on as she kept a wary eye on Farrell, reminding Edward of someone waiting to catch a thief in the act. "The manner in which otherwise rational men, like Simon Lavin, surrendered to panic when General Clinton's man-of-war and its accompanying transport sailed into the harbor was disgraceful, absolutely disgraceful. You would have thought the devil himself was about to step ashore and march up Broadway. Everyone who could lay their hands on a wagon or a cart piled it high with furniture and trunks and either made for the docks or fled north."

"Naturally you didn't," Edward intoned as he half rose out of his chair and reached across the table with his fork, neatly spearing a slice of meat from a platter sitting in front of his mother.

Try as hard as she might, Katherine was unable to ignore her son's churlish behavior.

"Along with your obligations to this family, I see you have managed to forget your manners," she snipped.

To her surprise, rather than grimacing as he had always done in the past whenever she chastised him, Edward planted his elbows on the table with a loud thump and held the forked meat aloft at eye level.

"I've forgotten nothing, mother," he declared in a low, almost menacing tone as he glared across the table at her.

Katherine drew back, not so much at her son's words or tone of voice but at the look in his eye. It was eerily similar to the way his father regarded her whenever he wished to make it clear he had no wish to argue with her.

With no intention of being drawn into the tête-à-tête between mother and son that grew more contentious with each exchange, Farrell kept his head bowed and his eyes on the plate before him. No one—not even an overdressed, sanctimonious shrew—would keep him from sampling the mixed berry and cream cheese turnovers. He had spied the pastries being prepared while poking about the kitchen in search of something to hold him over until dinner.

Katherine, who was a Van der Hoff first and foremost and mistress of this house, found she could not follow Farrell's example. Tolerating her son's boorish behavior was one thing. She knew enough about soldiering to appreciate even the most accomplished gentlemen tended to be corrupted by the hardships endured on campaign. However, she would not allow his mockery to go unchallenged—mockery directed at her decision to resist fleeing so that she could uphold her responsibilities as the inheritor of a business empire her ancestors had built.

"What would you have me do?" she snipped. "Hike up my skirts and run off at the first whiff of trouble? You've not been here…"

In the brief silence that followed, Edward knew his mother would have ended her statement with "where you belong" had she finished her thought.

"A day does not go by that does not bring a new crisis to this very doorstep," Katherine continued as Edward bit back the resentment he felt over his mother's renewed attempt to mold him into something he was not.

Tossing aside all decorum, Katherine paid no heed to the way her son returned her glacial stare or the presence of a most unwelcome stranger at her table. Warming to her subject, she spat out her words, betraying her bitterness that both Thomas and Edward had run off to war and left her to deal with a growing crisis threatening to upend her world.

"The Committee of Public Safety that claims to govern this city is all but powerless. They and the Provincial Congress do nothing but argue and debate, leaving Colonel Heard and his New Jersey militia to go about the countryside, disarming and arresting men suspected of being loyal to the King right under the noses of Governor Tyron and General Clinton. And rather than lifting a finger to rein in the rabble running wild in the streets, both are content to simply sit out in the bay aboard their warships and watch this colony descend into chaos and utter ruin."

Having heard more than enough of his mother's ranting, Edward pushed himself away from the table and came to his feet. Caught off guard by this, and unsure what her son would do next, Katherine stopped talking as she stared up at him. Farrell, likewise, looked up from his plate and took to studying his friend, wondering if he had somehow missed a cue.

Turning to Farrell, Edward gave his messmate a weak smile. "Would you care to join me for a drink in the parlor?"

Feeling disappointed to miss dessert but seeing no graceful way of refusing, Farrell nodded. "Aye, that would be grand."

Without waiting for Farrell to set aside his cutlery and stand to join him, Edward gave his mother a brief, perfunctory bow then sharply turned on his heel and left the room.

The sight of her son turning his back on her and walking away before she'd finish what she had started came as no great surprise to Katherine, for she'd seen such behavior many times before. The only thing that did trouble her was the realization Edward was taking after his father in more ways than she cared for. Whether she'd be able to curb this disturbing tendency would have to wait until the boy had had a chance to come to terms with the reality of his situation and the world to which he belonged. He was, after all, half Van der Hoff—a lineage known for pragmatism and distinguished by their talent for landing on the correct side of affairs, whether in business or, in times of war, aligning themselves with the victor.

-<<<<•>>>>-

Katherine waited to seek Edward out until she had recovered sufficiently from the anger roused by her son's behavior at dinner and felt confident she would be able to talk to him in a more civil tone. When she was finally ready, she found him in the darkened parlor slumped in a wing-backed chair set in front of the hearth. The flickering flames into which he was staring provided the only source of light in the room. The fire bathed his weathered, expressionless features in an unnatural, eerie glow that caused Katherine to shudder. She would have waited until the following morning to confront him were it not for a compelling need to do so now before he fully recovered from the hardships he had experienced in Canada and the bewilderment he felt at returning home to a city even she no longer recognized. Katherine was the kind of woman who could not let a problem bothering her rest until it was fully resolved to her satisfaction.

The rustling of skirts and sound of footfalls on the polished hardwood floors evoked no response from Edward as she made her way to a matching chair set across to his. Once seated, she clasped her hands in her lap and stared at her son, waiting for him to acknowledge her presence before broaching a subject she hoped he was ready listen to.

For the longest time, the two simply sat there with nothing but the crackling of the fire filling the late-night silence. In time, Katherine concluded her son, who continued to stare vacantly at the fire before him, had no intention of acknowledging her presence. In an effort to snap him out of a stupor she assumed had been brought on by too much drink, she drew herself up, cleared her throat, and spoke.

"I have given some thought to what would be best for you," she declared crisply. "Returning to your studies, given the uncertainty of the times, would be a waste of time. Instead, I believe it would be in our best interests if you took over the duties of factor. Perhaps later, when this unfortunate war is over, you can finish your education."

Edward made no effort to respond or even acknowledge he had heard his mother's words for what seemed like an age to Katherine. When he finally did speak, he did so in a low, haunting tone of voice and without looking away from the fire.

"At night, we'd sit huddled about the fire, trying our damnedest to draw every bit of warmth until it was our turn to stand watch or curl up in a blanket and try to sleep despite the cold that chilled us to the core. No one said much of anything, not after General Montgomery was killed. It was like a part of us had died with him."

Pausing, Edward shivered ever so slightly as the memory of seeing his general's lifeless body, shredded by grapeshot, came to the fore. After giving his head a quick shake in an effort to banish that gruesome image, he glanced at his mother, for the briefest of moments, to see if she was paying attention to what he was saying. Satisfied she was, he returned his gaze to the fire.

"I've watched men die in almost every conceivable way imaginable," he whispered in a low, tormented voice. "The lucky ones, like General Montgomery, met their fate in the span of a single heartbeat. Others, too many others, lingered for days, stubbornly clinging to life in the hope that God would hear their prayers and either see them through or bring a quick end to their suffering."

Caught off guard by her son's words, Katherine was speechless as he lapsed back into silence. When he spoke again, she was relieved to hear him address the very subject she had wished to discuss with him. Her delight, however, was short-lived.

"I know what you would have me do, Mother," Edward muttered despairingly. "You have always made that perfectly clear. And while I love you as a son should, and I expect you love me after your own fashion, I cannot not take the path you wish me to follow."

Having finally managed to find the courage to make his intentions clear to his mother, Edward clutched the arms of his chair, drew himself upright, half turned to face her, and continued before she had time to frame a response.

"I am not a Van der Hoff, Mother. Nor am I a Shield, at least not the sort father would have me become."

Taken aback, Katherine also drew herself up and huffed, "And who, exactly, do you think you are?"

Unable to provide his mother with an answer she would understand, Edward slowly eased back into his chair. Turning his attention back toward the fire, he slowly took to shaking his head.

"I don't rightly know," he whispered.

Katherine's bewilderment morphed into anger. She was determined not to drop the matter lest her son had had more time to put aside the hardships he had endured with the rebel army.

"May I ask how you propose to go about resolving this riddle of yours?"

Edward hesitated but for a second. He had no need to review his decision, for it had come to him instinctively, without the laborious weighing of deficits against gains as one might keep a ledger. Nor did he need to brace himself for his mother's inevitable wrath when he informed her of his decision. If truth be known, he no longer gave a damn what she thought. With a deliberateness that matched his resolve, he once more turned to face her.

"There are new regiments being raised here in the city to replace those no longer worthy of that title. In the morning, Kevin and I will head out and join one."

FOURTEEN

"My God, these fellows have done more work in one night than I could make my army do in three months."

General William Howe
on seeing the rebel earthworks
at Dorchester Heights

Dorchester Heights
5 March 1776

ACROSS THE BAY from where Anton stood, Boston endured its third night of bombardment as Knox's lighter guns and mortars at Lechmere Point, Cobble Hill, and Roxbury continued their assault. Satisfied the British were still blissfully unaware of their fate once the heavy guns were in place, Anton slowly lowered his telescope. To be as surprised as they had been the previous June by the Americans' swift fortification of commanding terrain was forgivable; for the British, like he, had been schooled in the fine art of war in which the Americans put little stock. What was unforgivable, to Anton, was having witnessed the Americans' capabilities only to awaken and discover their besiegers had again, in a single night, erected a pair of formidable earthen forts on an undefended and unoccupied hill that dominated the city.

Anton turned his attention from the slumbering city to the sound of creaking timber wheels and the crack of a teamster's whip.

The hint of a smile softened his stern, uncompromising expression—one of a professional soldier worn all night as he observed the flurry of activities around him that continued unabated. With dawn but a few short hours away, scores of Washington's soldiers worked to put the finishing touches on an ingenious series of earthworks constructed to protect the guns Colonel Knox had dragged three hundred miles over frozen lakes and along snow-covered trails.

Upon seeing the way Anton eyed his men, a captain of militia who commanded the detachment tasked with protecting the guns called out to him.

"We'll be ready," he declared before turning his attention back to a young teamster guiding a pair of oxen hauling a 24-pounder to its assigned position. "Liven 'em up, lad. Just a little further and you'll be done for the night."

The teamster, a boy Anton guessed was no more than fourteen, and the hundreds of soldiers who had labored through the night would be ready. He would not. Completion of the two earthen forts was only the first half of the plan Anton had helped design. Ensuring the guns brought an end to the year-long siege was the other half of that plan and, by far, most important. As he took to surveying the hive of activity all around him, Anton admitted it was also the easiest.

With the ground frozen eighteen inches deep, all involved agreed it was impossible to erect in a single night the traditional earthworks that could withstand a counter-bombardment. In lieu of the fortifications on which Anton had relied in the past, Colonel Rufus Putnam—a Massachusetts millwright and veteran of the French and Indian War—had designed breastworks consisting of heavy timber frames to hold gabions, fascines, and hay bales. These were covered with a layer of earth. The guns would be placed within them and protected by felled trees carefully placed with the upswept trunk and branches pointed downhill. Slowed by this tangled line of improvised abatis, an assaulting force would be exposed to a devastating hail of grapeshot and musket fire as they labored to hack their way through it. A bit further downhill, the Americans had also placed a line of soil-filled barrels. The barrels not only made the earthworks appear more formidable, but if the British attempted to storm the heights, the soldiers could roll the barrels downhill into the tightly packed ranks of infantry as they formed their battle lines. *"It'll be like playing ninepin,"* one American had informed Anton as he positioned a barrel.

After watching the 24-pounder gun roll past him along a straw-covered path meant to muffle the sound of wheels and ox hoofs, Anton left the cluster of officers and followed. Long before he saw his son, he heard his him issue a sting of commands to the young teamster.

"Alright, boy, bring your team about to the right. Easy now. It wouldn't do to spook those oxen of yours and have them run off with the gun, not after all we went through to get it here."

Anton shook his head in disbelief at the mere thought that a boy not yet seventeen had been entrusted with such responsibilities as his son had been. In the French Army, it took years of instruction under the watchful eye of a master gunner and countless hours of drill to become a gun captain. But this, this was not the French Army he reminded himself as he watched his son and the men wrestle the 24-pounder—once the property of King George III—into position. The Americans had no sergeants who had spent their lifetimes mastering the fine art of gunnery by rote. They also did not have the luxury of time to perfect the necessary skills to properly load and lay guns such as the one his son commanded, much less study the mathematics of ballistics. At best, Anton reckoned, they had two—maybe three—hours before being forced to put whatever knowledge to the test that he had gleaned and other men to whom gunnery was more than theory had managed to impart.

"Not long now."

The sound of his son's voice caused Anton to startle. Lost in thought, he had not noticed Anthony had finished placing the gun he commanded and had made his way over to where his father stood.

"You are ready?" Anton asked after momentarily surveying the gun's positioning.

"Oh yes, quite ready, sir. All we need now is enough light and a suitable target."

The temptation to inform his son they would need a great deal more than that was set aside. The boy, Anton told himself, would come to appreciate just how much he and his companions needed to learn. He listened instead as Anthony hastened to fill the silence as men often did to hid their nervous excitement and fear preluding battle.

"Last June, before the British discovered what we'd been up to all night, I thought I was ready for what the day would bring," Anthony stated in a low voice as he took a step forward toward the parapet protecting his gun and placed a hand on it.

"I too believed myself ready just before my first action," Anton informed his son as he moved to his side.

Anthony slowly looked away from the slumbering city across the bay and studied Anton before asking a question that had been troubling him all night.

"Is it always like this?"

Having no idea what his son meant, Anton glanced over to see if the boy's expression could provide any clue as to what he was asking. At this moment, though, he realized Anthony bore a striking resemblance to his mother in his ability to mask his feelings with an expression betraying nothing. This trick, if it could be called that, did not mean Anton was completely clueless as to what he was being asked.

"It has been my experience that each battle is different," Anton began cautiously. "And yet, they are the same. Some, like the one we are about to engage in, are the result of meticulous planning and careful preparation. Others are nothing more than chance encounters between two forces that blunder into each other."

Anthony slowly nodded as he paused to reflect upon the two engagements of which he had been a part thus far.

"When we were chasing the British back to Boston last April, there were times I couldn't keep from laughing to myself at the sight of the redcoats stumbling and bumbling along the road back to Boston in an effort to get away from us." Pausing, Anthony took in a deep breath and held it for a second before letting it out. "No one laughed last June. I was… I was…"

When he did not continue, Anton turned to face his son, saying, "Only fools, liars, and madmen claim they are not terrified by the prospect of battle."

Sheepishly, Anthony returned the Frenchman's steady gaze with one that matched it before the hint of a smile softened his expression.

"I expect if Mother were perfectly honest with me, she'd call me a fool for running off like I did to join the Army."

Taking advantage of the lighthearted nature of the boy's statement, Anton reached out and placed a gentle, reassuring hand on his son's shoulder in a manner his father had never done.

"I would not wish to go into battle with men who were not a little afraid."

The relief Anthony felt on hearing his father's words was reflected in his expression.

Deciding the boy had managed to overcome the same trepidation and self-doubt he always felt before an engagement, Anton pulled his hand away, straightened up, and assumed a more martial posture.

"Your gun crew awaits your orders and, no doubt, Colonel Knox is wondering where I have wandered off to. So, to our duties."

"Yes," Anthony declared crisply as he, too, drew himself up, mirroring his father's demeanor in every way imaginable. "To our duties."

Boston
5 March 1776

Having listened to all he cared to hear concerning how to best deal with the threat of the rebel earthworks on Dorchester Heights, James Keating made his way to the Long Wharf. There, he found the first of five regiments under the command of Brigadier Valentine Jones waiting to be ferried across the bay to Castle William. Within minutes, his hopes of losing himself in the swirl of activities that always accompanied the movement of a large body of troops were dashed as junior officers—who knew him to be one of General Howe's aide-de-camps—wasted no time in accosting him in an effort to find out if all they had been hearing was true. Having no idea what their colonel had told them and appreciating the rebels had no need to guess what Jones's force was up to, James realized there was no harm in sharing what would be expected of these officers who would be leading their men into battle in a few short hours.

In a manner he hoped conveyed more confidence than he felt, James presented the broad outline of the plan on which General Howe's council of war had settled.

"Once General Jones has assembled his command on Castle Island, he will wait until nightfall before crossing over to the eastern tip of the peninsula on which Dorchester Heights is located. When you are ashore, your regiment and the others under his command will seize the rebel works on the low ground."

Unable to help himself, an anxious young lieutenant James did not recognize interrupted, "I heard we're to go in with muskets unloaded."

Despite sharing his fellow officer's concern for this aspect of the operation, James tilted his head back and sniffed.

"I expect that is true. We don't want the attack to break down as it did last June when the men stopped before closing with the enemy to trade shots with them."

"We?" a captain spat out.

At the last second, James stifled the urge to remind the captain that General Howe's aides had suffered casualties just as staggering as the rest of his command had endured the previous June. Instead, he simply shot the offending officer a withering glare before continuing.

"Once the earthworks on the low ground have been taken, two more regiments and battalions of light infantry and grenadiers will land on the north shore of the peninsula. When ready to advance, the entire force will storm the heights under the cover of darkness. Once they have been secured, General Jones will press the attack as far as Roxbury."

"That's assuming any of us are still alive to do so," the captain asserted under his breath but loud enough for all who were gathered around James to hear.

Were it not for the timely appearance of the regimental sergeant major, James would have confronted the cynic and informed him this was neither the time nor place for such talk. Instead, he stepped aside as the sergeant major entered and took to addressing the assembled officers.

"If you gentlemen are quite finished, I suggest you ensure your men haven't emptied their canteens of the rum and water they've filled them with and still have a full day's rations in their haversacks. I wouldn't want to have to explain to the colonel why they're complaining of having nothing to drink or eat on the morrow."

In a manner that put James in mind of a flock of sheep that had been set upon by a wolf, the line officers scattered, leaving the sergeant major to turn his full attention to James.

"May I be of assistance to you, sir?"

James understood the sergeant major's question was rhetorical. Both men knew he had no business there. Besides, the near confrontation with the captain who mirrored the attitude of many of his men had dashed James's quest to escape the dread he felt over the prospect of once more going up against a well-entrenched foe. With a feigned smile and a quick shake of his head, he bade the sergeant major an appropriately respectful goodbye and left.

⸻

The calm, almost serene mood James found on returning to headquarters struck him as being at odds with what he had expected. It did not take but a minute to discover the reason.

"Where in the bloody hell have you been?" Thomas Shields thundered from his desk set just outside the door leading to General Howe's private office.

Having grown used to Shields's behavior that tended to be abrupt to the point of being abrasive when dealing with officers of lesser rank, James explained as he was pulling his cloak off.

"Down at the Long Wharf, seeing to it that all was in order. By and by, all does seem to be going well, though there is something of a storm coming up from the south."

"Don't bother taking off your cloak," Shields snapped as he picked up a sheet of paper and held it out to James. "You're to take this to General Jones."

As he made his way to Shields's desk, James was sure the carefully folded and sealed sheet was an order. Once in hand, he took a second to inspect it before asking the obvious.

"A delay of the attack?"

"An order to stand down."

"For how long?"

Unable to hide his disappointment over the turn of events that had led General Howe to make a decision he had been putting off, Shields slumped down in his seat after releasing his grip on the sealed orders.

"The attack has been canceled."

Whereas Thomas Shields disagreed with his commanding general's decision, James greeted it with relief—a feeling he expected the men who would have made the assault on Dorchester Heights would share.

"Thank God," James breathed.

Taken aback, Shields frowned and spat, "Thank God? What do you mean, thank God? I do hope you appreciate that our failure to seize those heights means we now have no choice but to evacuate this city."

Unfazed by the sharpness of the major's rebuke, James tilted his head back and stared at him down the bridge of his nose.

"You weren't with us last June when we stormed the rebel works above Charlestown," he stated evenly. "You didn't have to step over the bodies of your own dead or ignore the pitiful cries of the wounded as I did not once, but twice, in our efforts to dislodge an enemy who was not even as well-entrenched as those men are over on Dorchester Heights."

"Are you telling me you are afraid to face that rabble?"

"Yes!" James replied without hesitation. "Any sane man would be who had seen what those rebels can do when they have a mind to and who are well led. Only a madman would wish to go up against such men armed with cannon and, I expect, enough shot and powder to blow this whole army all the way back to England."

Before Thomas Shields could stand or respond to what he considered an insult, James walked out the door and into the teeth of a growing storm. He knew General Howe would use the storm to justify his decision to cancel an attack he, like James, had no wish to make.

Dorchester Heights

For two anxiety-riddled nights, Anthony Carter stood by his gun with his crew and waited for the British to cross over from Castle William and launch an assault. When none materialized, Anthony began to wonder if the British were ever going to attack. It was a question he put to Anton when he and Colonel Knox came by, as they did each morning, to assess the readiness and condition of the guns and the men assigned to them.

Taking his leave of Knox, who continued on with his daily tour of inspection, Anton stepped up to the parapet protecting his son's 24-pounder and took to studying the activities along Boston's waterfront.

Wishing to find out what it was the Frenchman was looking for, Anthony joined him.

"They are preparing to evacuate the city," Anton muttered without taking his eyes off the flurry of activities along the entire length of Long Wharf.

"I almost wish they had made a fight of it," Anthony complained as he watched wagons loaded with boxes, crates, and furniture being led onto the wharf.

On hearing this, Anton looked over at his son, cocking a brow in surprise.

Letting out a nervous chuckle, Anthony returned the Frenchman's quizzical gaze. "Almost."

"Do not trouble yourself," Anton replied as he continued to observe the activities across the bay. "I can assure you, the English will afford you ample opportunities to test your newfound skills."

"When?"

"Soon," Anton replied under his breath. "All too soon."

FIFTEEN

"Those who expect to reap the blessings of freedom must, like men, undergo the fatigue of supporting it."
Thomas Paine

New York
29 June 1776

THE NAME THE Bean in the Pot, which was neatly painted on a sign shaped like a black kettle, was one few people used. Most everyone, especially patrons, referred to the coffeehouse as Tuck Inn—a witty little nickname someone had thought up one day that made light of the name of its proprietress, Elizabeth Tuck. Despite its moniker's lewd connotation, there was nothing uncultivated or bawdy about the establishment, least of all the widow who ran it. Even before Brian Keating had relinquished ownership of the inn to Kat Trent, Elizabeth strove to maintain the same high standards on which her husband had insisted when he had been alive. By doing so, Elizabeth was able to attract a very discerning clientele. Among its chief patrons were speculators, factors, merchants, ship captains, and shopkeepers, if they had a clerk who could be trusted to keep from stealing them blind in their absence. Kat made it a habit of stopping at the Bean in the Pot on the days she made her rounds of the city, paying a visit to each of the businesses and properties she owned and meeting with the merchants, tradesmen, and agents with whom she dealt.

From time to time, newcomers to the city who used the coffee house to discuss business with local merchants raised dubious eyebrows at the sight of Kat seated alone at the table set against the bay window overlooking the street outside, sipping hot chocolate, and nibbling on lemon drop biscuits or warm scones as she perused her ledgers. Self-important men who had the temerity to accost her in an effort to discern why she was not at home tending to more womanly pursuits were always met with a smile so at odds with the pugnacious stare with which she held them. Those who were foolish enough to ignore her less than subtle warning were subjected to an artful dressing down delivered in a well-measured, conversational tone that left the recipient unable to do little more than mutter a brief apology for their rudeness before beating a precipitous retreat.

Kat's reasons for tending to her ledgers in such a public setting provided her with more than a pleasant afternoon respite. Had any of the other patrons taken the time to pay any attention to her, they would have noticed her attention was not solely focused on the ledgers before her. Between sips of chocolate and nibbles of biscuits, she would surreptitiously listen in on exchanges between men seated at adjoining tables. It was a habit that allowed her to keep abreast of events of the day few men would discuss in the presence of a woman.

On this day, she was particularly interested in an animated exchange in which a group of newly arrived militia officers seated at an adjoining table were engaged.

"A lot of good the fortifications General Lee has thrown up all around the city will do us," an outspoken young officer declared. "All Howe will need to do is sail up the Hudson to a place where we're not and land his troops."

"It's not as easy as that," another officer intoned. "Ferrying troops ashore is not the problem. Landing cannon, munitions, stores, and the horse needed to haul them is. Have you ever attempted to hoist a horse up out of the hull of a ship and into an open boat?"

Before the first officer could respond, an older and superior officer grunted, "Don't go selling the Royal Navy short, laddie. If anyone can put an army ashore over open beaches, they can. I saw them do it at Louisburg in '58."

The senior officer's comment effectively ended the matter, but not their discussion.

"If they can land troops anywhere they wish, anytime they wish, then why haven't they done so? I mean, what's Howe waiting for?" another young officer asked plaintively. Kat guessed he was not much older than she was.

"More troops," the veteran officer replied without hesitation.

"If reports concerning the number of ships and transports riding at anchor off Sandy Hook are anywhere near accurate, I dare say they have more than enough men," the young man countered.

The senior officer replied with a humorless laugh before saying, "They've no need to hurry, laddie. This city isn't going anywhere, and neither are we. Only a fool goes riding off to battle with only one boot on. With the troops coming from England and the German mercenaries the King's been gathering, Howe will hold the whip hand and we..." The senior officer paused to take a sip of his coffee as he debated on how best to finish his statement in an appropriate manner. "Well," he finally continued grimly, "we'll have little choice but to do the best we can to show Howe and his King we're not theirs to command—not anymore."

This assessment resulted in another protracted silence the young officer was unable to bear. "I, for one, do not relish the idea of going up against German grenadiers."

The senior officer at the table mirthlessly chuckled at this then asked, "And what, pray tell, difference will it make whether the big bastard wielding an eighteen-inch bayonet affixed to the end of his musket is an Englishman who's taken the King's shilling, or a Hessian his prince hired out to German George for thirty pieces of silver?"

Unable to think of an intelligent response, the young officer lapsed into silence, as did the others. They sat in silence and all took to sipping their coffee.

As much as Kat wanted to wait and see if the animated exchange among the militia officers resumed, the tolling of a church bell warned her she had already tarried too long. Closing her ledger with an audible snap, she prepared to leave and slipped the ledger into the plain canvas satchel made from sailcloth she used to carry items needed when making her rounds. Her sudden flurry of movement caused the militia officers to take notice of her for the first time. She, in turn, repaid their curiosity with a smile and amiable bob of her head. As Kat's eyes darted from one face to another, she could not help but wonder which of the men seated around their table would survive the coming storm that was about to break over the city that was her home.

-⋘⋄⋙-

In the time it took Kat to shut the door of Minden Hall and set her canvas satchel down, Emma Peel, her housekeeper, had appeared before her.

"You're late," the woman declared, in a tone more befitting a mother addressing an errant daughter.

"It couldn't be helped," Kat groused as she struggled to undo the knot she had hastily tied in the ribbon of her hat. "Everywhere you turn these days, you run into General Washington's troops. They're either throwing up fortifications that block the streets or tromping about and making a nuisance of themselves by parading back and forth along the ones they have not yet had time to dig up."

Without asking or waiting to be asked, Mrs. Peel stepped up to Kat, brushed her hands away from the unruly knot, and took to picking at it.

"It will take nothing short of a miracle for Peggy to have you ready by the time your dinner guests arrive," Mrs. Peel huffed.

Kat offered no resistance to her housekeeper's efforts as she dropped her hands to her sides and obediently tilted her head back. She never resisted Mrs. Peel's attentions. Were it not for the way

Mrs. Peel and Peggy, Kat's personal maid, fussed over her appearance, she would have presided at the head of Minden Hall's dining room table that night in the same ill-fitting, work-a-day caraco gown with an unruly mass of red hair tumbling down her shoulders. Kat did not bother to ask if all was ready for later that evening as Mrs. Peel ran Minden Hall with the same firm, uncompromising attention to detail on which Kat relied upon to keep her business concerns prospering at a time when many of her competitors were succumbing to the troubled times they and their city were facing.

Having succeeded in undoing the knotted ribbon, Mrs. Peel took a step back and clasped her hands before her as she inspected her young charge's disheveled appearance.

"Peggy is waiting for you in your room."

A quick glance at the tall case clock in Minden Hall's entrance hall told Kat she had no time to slip into her combination library and office to dash out the notes she had not had time to finish at the Bean in the Pot. Not that she would have been able to as, when Mrs. Peel saw where Kat was looking, she stepped away from her young mistress and placed herself squarely in front of the double doors leading to the study. Resigned to being trussed in a corset and the ostentatious gown selected for her—in happier times—by her cousin's wife, Kat sighed as she took to waving a hand at the canvas satchel she had tossed aside.

"Would you see to it Gwyn puts my things where I can find them?"

"I will see to it myself," Mrs. Peel replied crisply. "Now, off with you."

Bedecked and bejeweled in a manner more fitting the title she took little pride in, Kat Trent stopped by Sarah's room to ask, once more, if she would join them before heading downstairs to greet the guests David Gray had invited for dinner. Even as she was rapping softly on the bedroom door, she knew her efforts were an exercise in futility. Bit by bit, melancholy over James's absence and an abhorrence over the political and social turmoil that had upended the neat, well-ordered world she so loved had taken its toll on Sarah. The vibrant young woman had evolved into a recluse fearful for her own safety and that of her children. Not that Kat could blame her cousin's wife.

The accommodation that had allowed the Royal Governor and New York's Provincial Assembly to coexist in an awkward, if sometimes tense, accord ended abruptly when the Continental Congress, in the guise of its army, all but usurped control of day-to-day affairs from local officials and the moderates in the Colony's Assembly. So too did New York's efforts to remain aloof from the spreading conflict between the colonies as represented by the Congress in Philadelphia and the Crown and Parliament in England.

The imposition of martial law and preparations to defend the city and the harbor that made it the commercial hub of the American colonies exacerbated this upheaval, turning New York into an armed camp. Citizens like Kat who had chosen to remain found they had little choice but to support the rebel cause, or at least create the illusion they did. Those who did not suffered accordingly and were often publicly scorned, ridiculed, and physically abused. Men suspected of being loyalists who refused to take an oath of loyalty to the Congress in Philadelphia when challenged were arrested, or worse.

As the wife of a British officer serving on the staff of the man personally selected by the King to lead the attack on New York and the daughter of an avowed Tory who had made his sympathies known before fleeing to England, Sarah was subjected to public humiliation and ridicule. Not even her brother's commission with an artillery company now serving Washington spared her from verbal abuse and, on more than one occasion, the threat of physical violence. One incident in particular underscored the hazards Sarah faced in a city now governed by men determined to purge it of all who opposed them.

After hours of coaxing, Kat had managed to convince Sarah into accompanying her as she paid a quick visit to her scattered business concerns. *"It's a beautiful day,"* Kat had declared brightly. *"It will do you a world of good to be out and among people. Besides, it will allow Gwyn to tidy up,"* she added as she made a show of surveying Sarah's cluttered and unkempt room.

Despite a chorus of howls unleashed by the twins when they realized their mother was leaving, Kat managed to hustle Sarah out of her room, down the stairs, and out the door. Believing the worst to be over, Kat breathed a sigh of relief as they descended the wide, well-scrubbed steps. Sarah did not, which was why she was the first to notice half a dozen men standing just up the street from Minden Hall. The sight of the men alone was enough to convince Sarah it would be best if they turned around.

"You'll do no such thing," Kat snapped sharply after sizing up the situation and coming to a decision. She grabbed Sarah by the arm and all but dragged her along as she hissed, "I'll be damned if I'm going to allow anyone, man or woman, to stand between me and my freedom to come and go as I please."

Shocked as much by the anger in Kat's voice as by her language, Sarah allowed herself to be hustled along. That proved to be a mistake. When they were but a few paces from the men, the one Kat assumed was their leader boldly stepped in front of Sarah.

"And where do you think you're going?" he snarled.

Before Sarah could answer, Kat released her and slipped between Sarah and the man. Drawing herself up to her full height, which fell well short of her desire to meet the man eye-to-eye, Kat nonetheless endeavored to prove she had no intention of allowing him to cow them.

"You will step aside and let us pass," she growled menacingly.

Turning his full attention on her, the man did his best to warn Kat off as he said, "We've no issue with you, Lady Trent. But, there's no place in this city for a tory strumpet like her—not anymore. She should have left when her father did."

"And you, sir, should have thought twice before you and your friends dared to stand in my way."

With that, Kat took a step back, reached into her canvas satchel, and fished about in it until her fingers touched upon the object for which she was searching. With a steadiness that belied the nervous trepidation she felt, Kat withdrew the small Queen Anne pistol. David Gray had given her the pistol along with the suggestion she keep it close at hand when out and about.

Though far from being an imposing weapon, the drawn gun and the look in Kat's eyes were enough to cause the man before her to take a quick step back.

"I told you, we've no argument with you," he stammered as his eyes darted back and forth from Kat's own to the pistol, as he attempted to gauge whether she had the nerve to actually pull the trigger.

Having gained the upper hand by behaving in a manner so at odds with what was expected of a woman of her standing, Kat pressed her advantage with the same élan and brashness upon which she relied when dealing with business rivals and detractors. Stepping forward, she shoved the muzzle of her pistol against the man's gut and leaned forward until her face was but inches from his.

"Will you yield the sidewalk to us, sir? Or, must I make an example of you and all who chose to replace the King's tyranny with mob rule?"

Any doubt that the fiery, red-haired woman before him would make good on her threat was erased when the man heard the distinctive click of the pistol's hammer being cocked. Without taking his eyes off hers, he ever so slowly backpedaled, raised his hands, and held his palm out at shoulder height as he did so.

"I yield the street to you, Lady Trent—today," he added menacingly before rejoining his compatriots and leading them away.

Kat had little opportunity to savor her victory as she turned to where Sarah had been standing and realized her cousin's wife had fled back to Minden Hall. Kat suspected she locked herself and her children away in her room.

Thus, it was foolish to think Sarah Keating would willingly break bread with the very men responsible for turning her entire world upside down. Still, Kat felt she needed to make the offer if for no other reason than to do everything within her power to keep her dearest friend from withdrawing any further into the same darkness into which she, herself, had once sunk after her beloved sister's death.

Upon recognizing Kat's soft knock, Sarah called out for her to enter. Despite the maid's best efforts every morning to organize and clean Sarah's room, by early evening, chaos, clutter, and the pungent odor of messy diapers had undone the Welsh maid's efforts. Doing her best to ignore the manner with which her friend now lived, Kat approached Sarah where she sat, tightly clutching a disheveled and very messy young James who was perched on her lap. Both were watching little Kitty seated on the floor at their feet. The girl paid her mother and sibling no mind as she tugged at the few remaining strands of yarn that served as hair for the rag doll she was playing with.

After pausing in search of a place to sit and finding nothing free of rumpled cloths, children's toys, or dirty dishes with half-eaten food, Kat had little choice but to remain standing as she implored her friend to join her and David at dinner.

"It will do you some good to be with people."

Without giving the matter the least bit of thought, Sarah looked up at Kat and regarded her with a wan smile.

"It's kind of you to think of me," Sarah whispered in a small, almost lifeless voice while reaching out and latching on to Kat's arm with a free hand. "But I must look after the children. They need me. You have always been so generous and thoughtful when it came to James, the children, and me," Sarah added mournfully. "It is a kindness for which I shall always be grateful."

It was more than the weak, almost detached tone of Sarah's answer that bothered Kat. The manner in which she couched her comments sent a chill down her spine, for it reflected the same fatalistic mood that left the city all but paralyzed. The presence of the Rebel army in the city itself and the appearance of General Howe's British warships had all but brought commerce to a standstill. That and word troops dispatched from England and mercenaries hired in Germany would soon be arriving left no doubt in anyone's mind war was coming to New York. With General Washington determined to fight this mighty host in New York City itself, all expected a cataclysm the likes of which not even the men responsible for setting it in motion were able to predict.

As bad as the actual battle would be when it came, it was the aftermath Kat feared most. If the unchecked passions that were now the order of the day had descended to a level that left the city's citizenry in fear of their very lives even before battle was joined, Kat could not help but wonder what it would be like after blood had been spilled. The penalty for taking up arms against the King was death by hanging. Though she imagined even the most sanguine loyalist would shy away from lynching every soldier who had done so. Stories of the devastation Cumberland's army had left in its wake after the Jacobite Rebellion of '45 left no doubt of the dreadful price to be paid by those who had supported the rebel cause.

Not wishing to dwell on such grim speculation, lest she follow Sarah into a bottomless pit of despair she seemed incapable of escaping, Kat turned her attention to doing what she could to hold things together as best she could until the coming storm had passed. On hearing the babble of voices coming from her guests as they waited for her to make her entrance, Kat stopped at the head of the stairs, closed her eyes, and took a deep breath. Only when she felt ready to greet the rebel officers in a manner befitting a woman of her standing did Kat open her eyes, place her hand on the banister, and prepare to descend the stairs with a grace that belied the uneasiness she felt for the future that had come to haunt her every waking hour.

-⋘⋘•⋙⋙-

Having no wish to spend the entire evening discussing the science of ballistics with the young, very inexperienced officer who had invited him along, Anton took the first opportunity to change the subject as they waited on their hostess to make her appearance.

"As impertinent as it may be, may I ask how it is you gentlemen, good republicans all, are able to set aside your grievances with your King and dine with a royalist?"

"Oh, Kat is no royalist," David Gray replied without hesitation.

Perplexed by what he saw as a contradiction, Anton cocked a brow. "It was my understanding she is the daughter of an earl, which in France would make her a member of the aristocracy. Has she forsaken her heritage?"

Before answering, David turned from the Frenchman and toward the stairs he expected their hostess would soon be descending.

"I don't know," David whispered as his face took an expression with which Anton was quite familiar and wore whenever his thoughts turned to Sarah Carter.

It took a moment for David to catch himself. With a quick shake of his head, he forced himself to set aside his thoughts of their hostess and return to the topic at hand.

"I imagine you'll find Kat Trent to be a woman unlike any a gentleman such as yourself has ever had the occasion to come across."

Anton felt a rueful smile creep across his lips as he silently disagreed. Both the Frenchman's silence and his expression led David to believe his comment had given him the wrong impression.

"Let me assure you, sir, Kat Trent is very much a lady," he hastened to explain. "She's just…" Pausing, David could not help but once more turn his gaze to the stairs before wistfully finishing his comment. "She's just different."

-<<<•>>>-

The guests David Gray had asked Kat to entertain that evening were an eclectic lot, united only in their opposition to the crown. Arriving early with David was Alexander Hamilton, the commander of his artillery company. At five foot seven, the slender young man was only slightly taller than Kat. Even in age he was a near match, being no more than twenty years old. Like David, Hamilton had been a student at King's College and had abandoned his studies to take up arms against the King.

Kat was still standing in the foyer, exchanging pleasantries with Hamilton and Anton when Henry Knox was ushered in. The most impressive thing about the colonel of Washington's artillery, at least to Kat, was Knox's age. At twenty-six, he held both a rank and position she imagined an older, more experienced man would have attained had he been dressed in coat of red rather than the dark blue Colonel Knox wore. Unlike David's friend and commanding officer, Knox was heavyset with a round face and a quick smile. He had met Kat while browsing in her bookstore and had engaged her in a most enjoyable chat long before he was aware of her family connections. Thus, Knox was able to set aside whatever reservations he had concerning her loyalties and enjoy the company of an intelligent and delightful young woman.

Another prominent dinner guest that Phillip Parkman, Kat's factor, had insisted upon was Stephen Moylan, who seemed unable to forget that, even in a city now governed by a Provincial Assembly of freemen, Kat was still referred to as Lady Katherine. Stephen was an Irishman who had recently been appointed to the post of quartermaster general for Washington's Army. Without needing to ask, Kat understood he was there solely to see for himself if, despite her title and the fact that her cousin served on General Howe's staff, she was reasonable and open-minded when it came to the complex politics of the day. These qualities were critical if she were to be allowed to continue to carry on as she had before the arrival of the Continental Army.

Parkman's concern was not simply about keeping Kat in the good graces of men like Moylan—it was essential if he was going to use her connections to supply everything from rations to uniform material. A single word from Parkman, or anyone else on Washington's staff who took a disliking to Kat, would not just bar her from doing business in the city but could see all her holdings confiscated—or worse. Henry Knox himself had watched as the bookshop he had owned in Boston before the war was pillaged and destroyed after word had spread that he had taken up the patriot cause. It did not matter whether Knox's presence and his sad story served as a warning as to what might befall her if she did not accommodate the material needs of Washington's army. Kat had no doubt her every action, innocent or otherwise, was being judged by those who now held sway over the streets of New York.

Once all the remaining guests had arrived and introductions had been made, Kat led the gaggle of officers into the dining room she had once thought to be far too large for her needs. As often occurred when men were introduced to Lady Katherine Trent, those seated around the table who thought of themselves as gentlemen attempted to engage her in conversations most were accustomed to sharing when in the presence of a socially prominent woman. And, as was her wont, Kat quickly disabused them of their preconceived notions of polite chitchat by delving into discussions on subjects in which she was interested—practical matters of importance to her and her business affairs.

Having already managed to gain a measure of their hostess, Knox was more than willing to indulge what others took to be her most unnatural curiosity into the technical aspects of military affairs. For her part, Kat ignored the questioning expressions with which the other guests regarded her as the portly colonel recounted in great detail how he had moved fifty-nine pieces of artillery and their munitions from Fort Ticonderoga to Boston in the dead of winter. Kat had witnessed the effort Hamilton and his men had to expend just to haul eleven guns up Broadway from the Battery to the Common near St. Paul's and found herself in awe and more than a little envious. She envied what a handful of determined, well-led men could achieve.

When she expressed this view, Moylan snorted, "Any animal can be driven to do just about anything. Men need more than the sting of a whip if they're to rise above their mean existence and achieve great things. They need to believe what they are doing matters. They need an ideal, a cause, a tangible goal to aspire to."

Realizing she was being challenged, Kat graced the Irishman with a smile that was neither warm nor inviting.

"I expect what you say is very true. Men, and forgive me for saying so, women, are the most gifted creatures God put on this earth. Not only are we blessed with opportunities to decide what we shall make of ourselves, we have the capacity to decide what is right and what is wrong. I expect this is particularly true of our times, for each of us must make a stand now that we are confronted by the crisis that is not of our choosing."

Whether their hostess had intentionally broached a subject they all had been avoiding, or had accidently swerved into it, did not matter to Moylan. Locking eyes with her, his lip curled upward ever so slightly, for he was determined to draw out his hostess and discover just where she stood on the most significant issue of the day, the only one that mattered to him.

"Tell me, *Lady* Katherine, when it comes to independence, just where do you stand?"

Parkman had forewarned Kat of Moylan's unflinching support of those who called for breaking away from England, allowing her to fashion a response for just such a question long before she had taken her seat at the table. Taking a moment to enjoy a sip of wine, she ignored the surly manner in which Moylan had accentuated the word *lady* and chose to pretend as if she were giving the Irishman's question some thought. When she sensed she had allowed the tension in the room to build long enough, she set her glass aside, clasped her hands together in her lap, and smiled.

"Please understand, gentlemen, my title is but an heirloom my father bequeathed to me," she stated softly as she took a moment to glance from face to face. "If you are to believe in the arguments Mr. Paine so eloquently puts forth in his pamphlets and support the proposition Mr. Adam is fighting for in Philadelphia, it has no place in these colonies."

"If Mr. Adam has his way, these will no longer be colonies," Moylan stated brusquely.

When their eyes met, she hesitated but a second. "To answer your question, *sir*, I stand with those who took me into their hearts when no one else would have me."

"Does that include your cousin, an officer serving the general who is at this very moment is preparing to seize this city by force?" Moylan snapped, making no effort to rein in the contempt he felt for anyone even remotely connected to the English king.

"Yes," Kat answered calmly as she titled her head to one side, forcing herself to keep her lips set in a deceptively inviting smile. "It does indeed, just as I stand by David."

Suddenly thrust into the middle of a contentious confrontation he had wanted to stay clear of, David glanced nervously about the table at the other guests, pleading with his eyes for salvation. His captain came to the rescue by taking up his wine glass, coming to his feet, and raising it in Kat's direction.

"Gentlemen, I expect you can all agree it is for the ladies, women such as our lovely hostess, that we take on the burdens men are expected to shoulder in order to provide them a safe and secure home in which to raise the children they bear us—children who represent our future."

Eager to keep his fellow colonel from ruining the meal he was enjoying, Knox took up his glass as well and joined Hamilton.

"To the ladies."

One by one the others followed suit, leaving Moylan little choice but to join them in Hamilton's toast.

Though thankful for Hamilton's timely intervention, Kat was not at all sure how to deal with the emotions his salutation brought to the fore. Her anger at being depicted as if she were a forlorn waif in need of protection, which even she could not deny, and being reminded once more she could never fulfill the most basic function expected of a woman left Kat struggling to keep her troubled feelings from showing. At the moment, she had little choice but to muster up something of a smile with which to acknowledge the toast.

Most of her guests took Kat's response to their toast as a demonstration of her deference to her betters and in appreciation to Hamilton's gracious gesture. Only Anton saw past Kat's brittle smile, and he suspected the fetching young woman with coppery red hair was troubled by an internal struggle she shared with no one. It was the pair of sapphire blue eyes darting about from face to face as if seeking salvation that led him to respond in a manner he hoped would reel her back from the darkness Hamilton's toast had taken her to. Before anyone had an opportunity to resume their seats, he raised his wine glass in a salute to his hostess.

"Gentlemen, if we are to achieve what Monsieur Hamilton set forth, then our duty is clear," he declared. "We shall have to win."

Seizing upon the Frenchman's response as a way to put an end to what he, too, had perceived to be an awkward moment for Kat, David hoisted his wine glass high above his head.

"Gentlemen," he declared gustily in a manner that startled some of the others around the table. "To victory!"

It was a toast Kat was quick to join, though her enthusiasm was not near as keen as that of her guests.

David's action was more than an act of kindness. He appreciated there was a depth to Lady Katherine Trent that all but defied understanding. His desire to discern her most intimate secrets, deepest felt fears, and fondest dreams was motivated by more than a natural curiously to better know what lay behind the enigmatic smile with which she thanked the Frenchman. Like so many other men who crossed Kat's path, he entertained the hope that one day he could become more than just an acquaintance. It was something he was prepared to fight for, no matter how long it took him. But before he would be free to engage in such a personal campaign, other battles needed to be fought and won—battles being waged with words in a stuffy meeting hall in Philadelphia between men beginning to think of themselves as Americans and those who were equally determined to remind their troublesome subjects who had the whip hand, regardless of the cost.

❖

As Kat stood in the center of Minden Hall's foyer bidding each of her guests a goodnight, David let it be known there was an issue he needed discuss with her in private. Only after she had discharged the last of her duties as a hostess did she set out to find to where he had disappeared.

Kat found Sarah's brother in her study, absentmindedly leafing through a book he had found on a small side table. Pausing as she prepared to close the study's doors, Kat instructed Mrs. Peel she was not to be disturbed. On the surface, it was a simple enough request—the kind any person would make when the presumed subject concerned family matters. Kat, however, suspected David wished to address a subject that had nothing to do with his sister's pitiful state or the well-being of her children—conversations she did not wish those outside a few select individuals to hear. This was especially true of Gwyn Jones, a most annoying young woman who took every opportunity to eavesdrop on her mistress. This caused both Kat and Mrs. Peel to wonder if there was more than simple curiosity to Gwyn's clumsy efforts to listen in on conversations she had no need to be privy to.

Eager to pass on a message he had been asked to convey to Kat and be done with it, David wasted little time engaging in pleasantries and pitched right into a matter everyone had been skirting around all evening as Kat served him a glass of Madeira before pouring one for herself.

"There are a number of influential men who feel you should not be allowed to carry on as if nothing has changed," David announced once Kat had settled into a chair and enjoyed a sip of her wine.

Before answering, Kat glared at Sarah's brother. "I see our dear friends, Colonel McDougall and Mister Sears, have finally gotten around to me."

Unable to help himself, David winced. "Well, yes, they have been expressing their displeasure with the way men like Jay and others in the Provincial Assembly have gone out of their way to protect you," he admitted.

"What are the charges this time?" Kat asked, making no effort to moderate her ire as she had earlier in the evening. "Is McDougall still in search of a scapegoat for the slaughter of the regiment he raised and sent off to conquer Canada with winter coming on?"

David felt compelled to avert his gaze as he recalled how Alexander McDougall had once sat in the very chair he was occupying, graciously thanking Kat for her support in outfitting the 1st New York. Yet the moment he stepped out of earshot, he had begun grouse loudly of his disappointment at how meager her contribution had been—never mind that Kat had given without any thought of recompense. Unable to mount any sort of defense to justify McDougall's behavior, David did not even try but, instead, turned to the matter he had been asked to address with Kat.

"Your efforts on behalf of our cause have not gone unnoticed by those who matter the most, in particular General Washington himself. Others see your generosity as little more than a bribe, an effort to carry on as if nothing has changed."

"Men like McDougall?" Kat asked sharply.

Again, David cringed. Ignoring her interruption, he pressed on, "The general is a good man—a true gentlemen who is dedicated to the cause of independence."

"A matter that has yet to be agreed upon," Kat pointed out crisply as she was raising her glass to her lips.

David did not hesitate as he met Kat's eyes and declared with certainty, "Oh, it has been."

His assured tone struck Kat as being at odds with what she had been hearing about the pathetic state of Washington's army and the heated debate over independence that threatened to shatter the tenuous unity that had so far held the Continental Congress together.

Ignoring the skepticism Kat made no effort to mask, David drew himself up and leaned forward before continuing.

"We've come too far, and too much blood has been spilled, to even imagine we could go back to the way things were. The army King George is sending is not coming here to placate us. They're being dispatched to punish us as a parent would an unruly child. Well, we're not children," he snapped as he eased back in his seat. "The days of being dictated to by a King who has never cast his gaze on this land and a parliament in which we have no voice are over."

It was only then, as she held David's steady, uncompromising gaze that Kat realized the motto *liberty or death* was more than a pithy saying bantered about. If an intelligent, levelheaded man like David Gray was now taking up the call radicals such as Sears had been espousing, all hope of charting a middle course and of finding a compromise that would spare New York and all who called it home from the coming storm was little more than an illusion—one someone in Kat's position could not afford to indulge in. Setting aside her glass of Madeira, she settled back in her chair, calmly folded her hands in her lap, and looked over at David with the penetrating gaze she had come to rely on when negotiating with merchants, business owners, ship's captains, and provincial officials.

"What is it your general wishes of me?"

Whether the fetching red-haired woman seated across from him was merely guessing or if the tight-knit web of shopkeepers, innkeepers, and laborers Kat relied on had already caught wind of his meeting with the gentleman from Virginia and had forewarned her of its purpose did not matter. Washington's wish to tap into her impressive network of informers, as well as Kat's willingness to hear him out, promised to make what he was about to propose far easier than he had originally thought. It also allowed him to pretend he was an innocent messenger boy, for the last thing he wished to do was to jeopardize his chances of becoming something more than just the brother of his sister's best friend and guardian.

SIXTEEN

"Let us therefore animate and encourage each other, and show the whole world that a Freeman, contending for liberty on his own ground, is superior to any slavish mercenary on earth."

George Washington,
2 July 1776

The Battery, New York City
12 August 1776

WORD THAT THE long-awaited fleet bearing troops from England and German mercenaries had been sighted passing Sandy Hook and advancing into the lower bay sent Anthony Carter and the other members of his gun crew rushing to their post on the very southern tip of Manhattan. The relief he felt on finding they had managed to reach the massive 24-pounder they crewed before the British had an opportunity to launch their assault on the city was short-lived.

Only as the hours wore on without seeing a single warship or transport make its way through the Narrows and into New York's upper bay did Anthony begin to wonder if the rumor the city was about to be attacked was no different than countless other rumors that passed through the city like shiftless vagrants. Even the commander of his battery was at a loss as to what to do, for he was no better informed than Anthony. Not knowing what to expect, all he could do was to instruct his gun captains to stand by their pieces and await further orders. It was not until late in the morning that an accurate account of what the British were up to reached the Grand Battery in the form of the French major Anthony had befriended.

After attending a meeting at Mortier's house on Richmond Hill just north of the city, Anton made his way to the Grand Battery as he often did whenever the opportunity arose. He took a moment to chat with the commander of that post, passing on the latest news to which he was privy and receiving the commander's report on the readiness of his gun crews. The latter exchange was a courtesy only, for officially Anton was nothing more than an advisor—a volunteer attached to Knox's staff with a rank many viewed as little more than symbolic. Only when proper military etiquette had been satisfied did Anton make his way over to where Anthony was eagerly waiting to greet him.

With the bravado of a novice, Anthony greeted Anton as he affectionately patted his gun as if it were a cherished pet and not a cold, unfeeling instrument of war.

"We'll be ready for them when they come," his son proudly boasted.

Anton was of two minds when he finally stopped but an arm's reach in front of his son. The urge to give in to his desire to chuckle at Anthony's behavior was dismissed out of hand. The boy was not only doing his best to put on a brave front, but his comportment and his very words bore a striking resemblance to those he, himself, had used as a young man in the throes of war. The need to disabuse Anthony of his foolish naivety in the most strident manner possible was also rejected. Scornful admonishments delivered in a gruff, parade ground tone had no place at a time like this. Men going into battle needed to be reassured and encouraged, not mocked or chastised. Even he needed his resolve steeled at such times, especially when his professional judgment told him the coming fight was as good as lost before the first shot was fired.

With an expression that betrayed nothing, Anton made his way past Anthony to the battlement protecting his son's gun. There he placed a hand upon it as he took to looking out over the upper bay toward the Narrows.

"They will not be coming today or, I expect, tomorrow," he opined casually. "It will take some time to ferry the newly arrived troops and stores ashore."

When he glanced over his shoulder and saw a quizzical look darken Anthony's face, Anton once more had to fight a smile. His son's expression reminded him so much of the expression his mother wore whenever he had used a French word she did not understand.

"The troops in the transports that arrived this morning will need time to recover from their crossing," Anton explained patiently. "Under the best of conditions, a sea voyage is an ordeal. Aboard a crowded transport, subsisting on nothing but salted pork and crackers, it is as near to spending time in purgatory as one wishes to go while still drawing breath."

Stepping up next to Anton, Anthony nodded as he, too, took to staring at the many bare masts marking the anchorage of the British fleet just beyond the Narrows.

"Until we left Cambridge for Ticonderoga, I'd never traveled any further from home than to Boston and back," Anthony replied. "As a child I often dreamed of going to sea, if only to see what it was like. But if it is that bad, I'm glad I didn't."

The hint of a smile lightened Anton's expression as he said, "Not necessarily bad, just arduous—like a long walk over difficult terrain. Naturally there are certain charms to being aboard a ship on the open ocean," Anton quickly added as he lifted his gaze from the Narrows to the puffy white clouds lazily drifting across a pale blue sky. "On days when the seas are calm and there is a stiff breeze filling the sails you can almost imagine you are flying. And, in the evening, the sunsets are…"

Unable to find a word to adequately convey the beauty he sought to describe, Anton hesitated. A quick glance over at his son out of the corner of his eye, however, told him he had no need to find one. The boy's apprehensions over the coming battle no assumed bravado could hide were, for the moment, gone. In its place was a faraway gaze that told Anton his son's thoughts had turned to other, less sanguine adventures, adventures Anton hoped he would live long enough to enjoy.

Staten Island
14 August 1776

With nothing better to do while General Howe and his quartermaster general discussed problems with the rations being issued to the newly arrived troops with a German colonel, the gaggle of aides who swarmed about him like a school of porpoises following a mighty man-of-war under sail used the opportunity to study their new allies.

James Keating was of two minds on the issue of hiring foreign mercenaries instead of raising new regiments in England and Ireland. On one hand, it was eminently practical. The Germans were already fully trained professionals led by officers who had served during the Seven Years' War—the counterpart to the conflict known as the French and Indian War in the colonies. This avoided the problems that always accompanied recruiting the men who would be needed to fill out new regiments, men who were all too often drawn from the dregs of society or culled from overcrowded prisons. Once they had taken the King's schilling, those men would need to be fitted out with everything from muskets to cook pots and then trained. That took time, time in which the rebel leaders could use to train their own men, solicit aid from countries such as France who wished to see England humbled, and, most frightening of all to James, throw up more fortifications like those that had proven so costly to James's regiment in June of '75.

Warring with the practicality of relying on foreign mercenaries was the impact those men would have on the colonies. Other than their reputation, James knew little about the men with whom they would be going into battle. But what he did know was enough. Like his fellow officers who had served in Boston before fighting broke out and during the siege, he had had his hands full keeping his men in check. Few of them were able, much less willing, to discriminate between a colonist who stoutly maintained their loyalty to the crown and one who sympathized with the rebels. They looked upon all Americans with the same disdain ordinarily reserved for enemy combatants. The very thought of unleashing hired soldiers who were as foreign to the citizens of New York as the colonists were to them was terrifying. Before the war, New York had been a proud, prosperous city, just as Boston had been. Having seen how English soldiers behaved when circumstances threw them in among civilians, James had no doubt it would be difficult, if not impossible, to keep soldiers who owed no loyalty to an English king from doing what soldiers all too often did whenever they were far from home and free of an officer's watchful eye.

"Well, we can finally get on with it," Thomas Shields declared crisply to no one in particular among the gaggle of aides and strap hangers as he surveyed the smartly turned-out German soldiers gathered about cook fires or tending to other chores. "We've tarried on this pathetic island long enough. The time has come to put an end to this rebellion—the sooner, the better."

"I expect it will be some time before these men will fit for active campaigning," said a German-speaking captain who had served as a translator for the Germans during the Atlantic crossing and was retained for the same purpose by General Howe.

"Nonsense," Thomas sniffed dismissively. "If they're half as good as we've been led to believe, they'll be able to shake off whatever ails them in a day or two. It didn't even take that long for the troops who'd sailed from Halifax to sort themselves out once they were ashore."

The German captain had been forewarned that Major Shields was not a man who looked kindly upon anyone who had the temerity to argue with him. He did not bother to point out the journey from Halifax took no more than a week and paled in comparison to the eight-week trans-Atlantic voyage the Germans had endured aboard transports overcrowded with the converted merchantmen. Instead of voice this, he turned away from Major Shields and, like the others, looked about the well-ordered encampment they were passing through. On spotting a German captain he had befriended during their passage to the colonies, the German captain tipped his hat in greeting, a gesture that was returned in kind.

On noticing the exchange, Thomas nodded his head in the direction of the German and asked, “That officer there—the one who’s looking this way—he’s what the Germans call a jäger, is he not?”

“Yes, he is a captain in the Hesse-Kassel Feld Jäger Corps.”

Taking an interest in this exchange, James Keating studied the German man as he asked, “They’re not at all like our light infantry, are they?”

The gaggle of staff officers all turned their attention toward the officer in question.

“No, not at all. They’re more like what you call rangers,” the German captain replied.

On hearing this, Thomas grunted, “I hope they’re better than that scruffy lot of provincials Rogers recruited in the last war. Dirty, insufferable, ill-disciplined louts—every one of them.”

“I can personally assure you, Major, Captain Kleist and his jägers are first rate.”

For the briefest of moments, James and the captain of jägers locked eyes as each took the measure of the other. The dour-faced German, attired in a green coat faced in red, had the look of a predator.

“Most of them are hunters or foresters,” the German captain next to Thomas explained. “Every one is a crack shot with the short-barreled rifle they carry. They can hit a man-sized target at more than twice the range of the muskets our grenadiers and fusiliers are armed with.”

Thomas, not in the least bit impressed, shrugged saying, "I suppose that sort of thing would be useful if you were lurking in the woods hunting rabbits. On the battlefield, however, it wouldn't make a bit of difference. You need battalions of well-led men armed with muskets and bayonets—men who are willing to close with the enemy to win battles."

But at a cost, James thought to himself as he and the German officer continued to stare at each other. *A terrible cost.*

Captain Gustav Kleist maintained the martial pose he had assumed until the British general, having finished his discussion with his own colonel, moved on, followed by his entourage. Only when they were gone, did he drop the impassionate expression he had struggled to sustain while they had been watching him, double over, and grip his stomach with both hands. *Why*, he asked himself as a fresh spasm of stomach cramps caused him to wince, *hadn't anyone told them it was not wise to gorge themselves on the fresh food they'd been issued after subsiding for weeks on nothing but salted pork and hard crackers?* A full half of his company was laid low with severe bouts of diarrhea or, like him, crippling stomach cramps. Were it not for the need to carry out his duties in a manner befitting an officer in the service of Landgraf Friedrich II von Hessen-Kassel, Kleist would have staggered off to his tent, pulled the tent flap down behind him, thrown himself onto his cot, and curled up into a ball.

But he was an officer, a jäger officer. He was also the son of a forstmeister. Unlike his fellow officers, Kleist owed his commission to his skill with a rifle, a mastery of field craft, and tactical acumen—attributes he had learned as a child and honed during the Seven Years' War. In an army commanded by men whose surnames were preceded with the aristocratic von, his humble birth was a difference he never allowed himself to forget. He was also a soldier by choice. To him, the profession of arms was more than a way of life.

It defined him. Like his rifle, he was an instrument of war, obedient to his master's every wish.

With more effort than such an action ordinarily required, Kleist straightened up. After allowing the discomfort this otherwise simple gesture demanded to pass, he took a moment to look about. Anyone watching would have thought he was inspecting his company's street. In truth, he was trying to determine if his men, or worse, his colonel, had caught him giving into his malaise like a woman suffering from her monthly menses. Satisfied they had not, or if they had they were going out of their way to pretend they had not, he set about preparing his company for a battle he expected would not be much of a battle. The rebels they would be going against, he had heard, were ill-trained militia, amateurs who would soon learn war was a calling best left to professionals.

New York City
16 August 1776

No one would have thought of calling Kat Trent an opportunist, at least not when she was within earshot. But that was what she was, unabashedly so. For her the social, political, and economic upheaval brought on by the colonies' bids for independence and the crown's response provided her with innumerable opportunities to add to an already extraordinarily diverse collection of enterprises at a cost that would have been prohibitive otherwise. Most, like the print shop she had purchased at a fraction of its true value, had been sold to her by a loyalist who had fallen afoul of Isaac Sears and his Liberty Boys. Other men, like her uncle, had signed over their interests to her to oversee for the duration of the rebellion before fleeing the city with the understanding she would be entitled to all profits derived from them during her tenure—profits that could be used to purchase additional distressed, abandoned, or at-risk properties. In doing so, Kat ran the risk of being the object of scorn by vengeful men seeking to recoup their losses when peace, in whatever form that took, returned to New York.

Lady Katherine Trent, however, was also a gambler used to taking risks. Having arrived in New York City with nothing but her title, three chests filled with books and clothing suitable for the West Indies, and the hope an uncle she had never laid eyes on would take her in, she had little choice but to take chances another woman would have never contemplated, much less acted on.

Katherine Shields, on the other hand, prepared to weather the coming storm by tightening her grip on a mercantile empire her Dutch ancestors had bequeathed to her. Whereas Kat Trent was bold to the point of recklessness, Katherine was cautious, calculating, and quite conventional. She sought to preserve and protect the business interests inherited from her father until her son was ready to take his place as the patriarch of the Van der Hoff commercial empire. That he was not yet willing to assume those duties was disappointing. Edward's decision to reenlist was alarming.

The temptation to forbid Edward from availing himself of the amenities her home afforded him whenever rations in camp were short or if he needed his laundry done as punishment for his decision to defy her was countered by the opportunities his frequent visits afforded her to convince him remaining with the rebels went beyond foolish.

"You know what they will do to you when this is over," Katherine repeated her dire prediction midway through a meal he had been enjoying. "Those who are not hung will rot in prison or, if you are fortunate, be transported to some godforsaken, disease-ridden tropical colony. Your only chance of avoiding such a fate is to make your way to Staten Island, find your father, and declare your loyalty to the King now, before it's too late."

Edward was unmoved by his mother's efforts to dissuade him from his chosen path. Looking up from his plate, he greeted her words with a smile.

"That, Mother, would be the height of folly. We will win this war, and with it, our independence," he declared with a calm assuredness that astonished Katherine. "I would have suspected you, of all people, would have welcomed the opportunity to free yourself of the ball and chain you have been shackled to all these years."

Unable to keep from doing so, Katherine reared up. "That is no way to speak of your father."

"I was referring to Farmer George, our erstwhile King."

"He is still your King."

Edward harrumphed disdainfully, "I think not."

"Have you not seen the British ships in the harbor—ships that have brought the largest army England has ever amassed?" she countered sharply. "They will attack this city, a city the rabble you insist on associating with cannot possibly defend."

After pretending to give her last point a moment of serious thought, Edward nodded before saying, "I expect you're right. Despite all the digging we've been doing, the British and their Hessian mercenaries will take the city. Why they haven't done so yet is what puzzles me. But then what?"

Taken aback by Edward's response, and unsure how to answer, Katherine frowned. "What do you mean, 'then what?'"

"As important as this city is to interests such as yours, it is but a city. It is not America."

Katherine ignored the way her son had referred to the Van der Hoff mercantile empire as *yours* and not ours. Instead, she rose to the challenge, just as he had expected she would.

"This city is the very heart of what you and your rebel friends have come to call the United States. Without it, the colonies will be nothing more than a scattered collection of farms and frontier settlements without a heart feeding it the life blood they need to exist."

Having traveled past the farms and through the settlements she spoke of so disdainfully as his regiment had marched north to Quebec, Edward knew the opposite was true. He had come to appreciate New York City was but a conduit through which the riches flowed from America to fill the ravenous needs of an uncaring mother country that lay across the sea. That the scattered farms and frontier settlements his mother derided could survive on their own with little problem had been amply proven during the Stamp Act embargo. The city of which she was so proud—a city his ancestors had helped found—on the other hand, would wither on the vine without the America he had come to know through the men with whom he served.

So rather than attempting to explain how he could be so confident the colonies would win their independence from Great Britain to a woman whose understanding of the world was limited to that which could be quantified and neatly recorded in a ledger, Edward rose from his seat, reached out across the table, and took to cutting a small slice of meat from the plump suckling pig they had been feasting on, holding it up as he spoke.

"The English and their German mercenaries will take a slice out of us, that much is certain." Easing back in his seat, he continued to hold the freshly cut piece of meat before him on the end of his fork as he returned his mother's steady, unflinching gaze. "What isn't, Mother, is whether they will be able to digest the whole of a carcass that is no longer theirs," he concluded as he turned his full attention to enjoying the extravagant meal she had had set out before him in an effort to lure him away from what she considered to be foolishness.

It was a feast the likes of which he expected he would not see again for some time.

SEVENTEEN

"I have but a moment of time to rite as the boat is waiting. The two armies are entrenched on Long Island and very near to each other. Both lines are constantly reinforcing, and by all appearances a general action can't be far off."

Colonel William Douglas,
Connecticut Levies
To his wife, August 1776

Gravesend Bay, Long Island 22 August 1776

THE FIRING OF a single cannon aboard the HMS *Phoenix*, followed by the hoisting of a blue and white flag to the top of that ship's mizzen topmast, served as signal for the sailors manning transports, barges, and flat-bottomed boats to begin the task of ferrying General William Howe's army across the bay from Staten Island to Long Island. Aboard the *Phoenix*, James Keating and other officers attending Howe stood along the frigate's gunwales, watching as the armada of seventy-five flatboats carrying the first wave of troops made their way toward the hostile shore. It was an impressive sight, James admitted to himself, but then so too had been the small fleet of boats that had carried his company from Boston's long wharf to the Charlestown Peninsula little more than a year ago.

That thought caused him to shift his gaze from the crowded flatboats to the wooded shoreline they were making for. A young lieutenant, newly arrived from England and assigned to General Howe's staff as a favor to a prominent member of the House of Lords, took note of James's worried expression as he warily scanned the far horizon, causing him to look up as well.

"I, for one, think it would have been better if we'd simply sailed up the Hudson and landed on the island of Manhattan just above the city rather than wasting our time hopping about from one island populated by colonial bumpkins and cows to another," he mused.

"And give the rebel gun batteries on the southern tip of that island a chance to learn their trade?" a captain who had endured the bombardment of Boston scoffed. "No thank you, sir."

The captain's retort, while sufficient to silence the young lieutenant, heightened the apprehension that haunted James and others who had been with Howe's army since the first days of the rebellion. James found himself wondering what the troops under the command of General Sir Henry Clinton and General Charles Cornwallis would find when they waded ashore. He, like every officer on General Howe's staff, was well aware the rebels had had months to fortify the island of Manhattan. As daunting as the idea of facing those fortifications had been, it was what would follow that caused James to cheerfully greet their general's decision to seize Long Island before moving against Manhattan.

Turning his attention away from the armada of flatboats and barges that were about to touch shore, James fixed the young and militarily naïve lieutenant in a steady gaze.

"The city of New York, in of itself, is nothing," he declared in a low, measured tone of voice he tended to use when addressing newly arrived officers who assumed to know more than those who had already seen service in the colonies. "It is the harbor, and the land that dominates it, that matters. To allow the rebels to remain unmolested atop the Brooklyn Heights to the east, the Narrows and Governors Island to the south, and Paulus Hook to the west would be nothing short of sheer folly. Even more important than controlling the harbor is that, without the grain, livestock, and firewood farmers on that island send to the city's markets, this army and the city's populace would be reduced to subsisting on little more than cold salt pork and hard crackers," he declared sharply while pointing at Long Island without taking his eyes at the lieutenant he was addressing. "I, for one, have no wish to spend another winter cooped up in a city unable to draw the wood it needs to feed its hearths."

James's well-reasoned admonishment fell on the deft ears of an officer who had yet to wear out his first pair of boots. The lieutenant, the son of a prominent earl, was not accustomed to being talked down to by the son of a merchant, much less one who was a provincial. He did, however, know enough to not argue with a man wearing sun-faded regimentals marred by a poorly mended bullet hole.

Only when the young lieutenant made it clear he had no intention of challenging his point by doing nothing more than a lowering of his gaze did James turn his attention back to the landing force. James knew he should have been there, with them. Hanging back, waiting for his general to send him scurrying about on some meaningless errand, was not in the least bit glamorous or heroic. Nor did it do anything to hasten the hour when he would once more be with his beloved wife and children—children he had yet to lay eyes on. As he watched the first wave of soldiers swarm on the shore, James found himself thinking there might be a young fool no different than the earl's son among them—a callow pup so eager to demonstrate his military prowess to his superiors and peers—who took more chances than the Fates were willing to grant him. That his cousin Kat would use her beguiling charm, influence, and financial backing to see to it he was selected to fill such a vacancy was without question. All he needed to do was wait and, as he was doing at the moment, watch.

-⋘•⋙-

Thomas Shields had been unwilling to wait for happenstance or the good offices of his wife to secure him a posting more to his liking. By exaggerating his knowledge of Long Island, a place he knew only by reputation, he had managed to convince General Cornwallis he would be indispensable to him during the forthcoming campaign. As the crowded boat took him closer to shore, Thomas had not counted on the memories that experience evoked.

The swishing sound of the bay's placid surface being stirred by oars, the muted grunts of sailors pulling on those oars in unison, and the creak of the heavily laden boat carrying him ever closer to the hostile shore were all chillingly familiar to Thomas. Twice before, he had participated in a campaign that had begun with the army for which he served being transported in vessels little different than the one he was in. Both had ended badly. The first occasion had been General James Abercrombie's 1758 campaign against the French fortress guarding the southern reaches of Lake Champlain. It had come to a quick and bloody end after repeated attacks on breastworks thrown up before Fort Carillon were thrown back. The second ended just as abruptly for Thomas when he was severely wounded at Niagara the following year.

It was not fear that caused him to warily eye the beach as the first wave of light infantrymen vaulted over the gunwales of their boats, into the surf, and splashed ashore with their muskets and cartridge boxes held high above their heads. He knew the taste of fear—a sickly, roiling illness of the mind that caused men to drop to their knees and surrender putrid vile dredged up from the depths of their stomachs or left them paralyzed. Thomas reflexively shook his head as if to banish that unwelcomed possibility. The slight quivering of his muscles as they steeled themselves for the effort he was about to demand of them, the quickening of his pulse, and the deep, measured breaths he drew were nothing more than the reflexive preparations all soldiers worthy of that title experienced when battle was near at hand.

A sudden shutter that caused all aboard Thomas's boat to lurch forward told him it had gone as far as it could. Without hesitation, and without reservation, he came to his feet.

"Right lads! Over the side and to it," he shouted to the men around him as he laid his hand upon the boat's gunwale to steady himself and led the way.

Disappointment was all Hauptman Kleist felt as he and his company of jägers cautiously made their way across the flat farmland that lay just beyond the beach. Save for a few random shots aimed at the first wave of boats loosed by concealed riflemen, the American rebels had offered no resistance to their landing. Nor did the American rebels do anything to impede the cautious advancement of his company deeper into the heart of the island. Were it not for the stacks of burning hay and the scattered bodies of livestock that littered seemingly deserted farmsteads, he would have sworn the island was uninhabited.

It was not, of course.

Without having to see them, Kleist knew the owners of the scattered farms his men were passing through were watching them from the illusionary safety of their homes. He had been told the people of this island were loyal to England's King. Whether they were or not was of no interest to him. At the moment, all he was concerned with was sweeping away the scattered bands of rebels who drew back from the beaches without offering any notable resistance. Save for the destruction they left in their wake, the rebels seemed uninterested in contesting the advancement of his company. In time, Kleist expected, they would turn and fight. This was, after all, their country. To willingly surrender it to the cruel mercies of foreign soldiers, be they English or German, was, in Kleist's mind, unthinkable. Having witnessed the devastation French and

Russian armies had visited upon his homeland and by the men he commanded upon lands belonging to other princes, he knew he would not let an enemy go unpunished if they dared tread upon soil he held sacred.

The creak of a farmhouse door caused a pair of jägers he was following to turn sharply. Instinctively, they aimed their short-barreled rifles at the narrow crack in the doorway. On seeing this, the unseen occupant of the house slammed the door shut. Without lowering his rifle, one of the jägers glanced back over his shoulder to where Kleist was standing, asking with his eyes whether he and his comrade should advance on the house and investigate, or continue on.

Suspecting the person behind the door was a curious colonial, with little more than a nod of his head Kleist signaled the pair of jägers to continue on. A foe, even an ill-trained partisan, would have fired by now. Still, as he drew even with the house, he could not help but give it a closer look. They were afraid, Kleist told himself as he did so. That was good. He wanted the Americans to fear him and his men. Fear inspired by the uniforms his men wore, their thick black mustaches, and their fearsome reputations was a weapon no different than their rifles, short swords, and bayonets. An enemy who feared you, Kleist had learned, was an enemy that need not be feared. So, he did all he could to see to it his men cultivated fear in their enemies and those who supported them using every opportunity that came their way. In time, he would unleash his men on the timid foe fleeing before him, allowing them to do what they pleased to give credence to the fear the people of this land had for them. Now, however, he and his company needed to remain focused on the task at hand. As an officer, it was his responsibility to ensure his jägers carried out their duties. There would be time for them to enjoy themselves at the expense of the conquered populace. Soldiers such as his always managed to.

New York City
22 August 1776

The sound of drums beating companies to arms echoed throughout encampments, sending soldiers rushing to fetch their muskets. Civilians were no less alarmed by the sudden flurry of activities. Scurrying this way and that, all wondered if the day of reckoning they had long feared was finally at hand. One harried shopkeeper recognized Edward Shields as he was making his way to where his company was quartered and grabbed him by the arm.

"How long will it be before they are here?" the shopkeeper stammered.

Having been with a fatigue party sent north of the city to gather firewood, Edward was no more informed as to the reason for the sudden flurry of activity set off by the sudden call to arms than the shopkeeper.

"Soon, I expect," he blurted even as he was pulling his arm free of the shopkeeper's grasp.

"What are we to do?" the man called after Edward as he turned away and hurried to catch up to Kevin Farrell.

"Pray!" Edward shouted back over his shoulder. "And bury your silverware," he added as he lengthened his stride.

Abraham Mortier's House, Manhattan

The moods of the senior officers crowded around Washington were somber as they discussed the British's arrival on the shores of Long Island and how best to respond. What little information Colonel Edward Hand's Pennsylvania rifleman had thus far passed to Washington's headquarters struck Anton as being woefully lacking in detail. He knew from personal experience initial reports were more often than not inaccurate. This was especially true when the soldiers who made initial contact with the enemy were either raw recruits who had yet to see their first battle or had been taken by surprise. In the case of Hand's men, both were true.

The temptation to caution the gathered generals to wait until one of their own number went over to Long Island to assess the situation for themselves and reported back before settling on a course of action was checked by Anton's appreciation that he was still very much an outsider. The coming battle, despite the coat of blue he wore, was not his. His reason for violating the charter with which he had been charged by the Comte de Vergennes had nothing to do with the cause for which the men around him were prepared to fight, and if necessary, die. His sole interest in aligning himself with the American rebels was to do all he could to ensure his son survived the coming battle. That and seeing if the love he had for the boy's mother was still as true and passionate as he remembered.

So he did what he often did at times such as these. He hung back with the aides and lesser staff officers who managed to squeeze into the crowded room and listened to their generals discuss and debate how best to deploy poorly equipped troops—men deficient in in every way imaginable in the profession of arms against what many considered to be the finest army in the world.

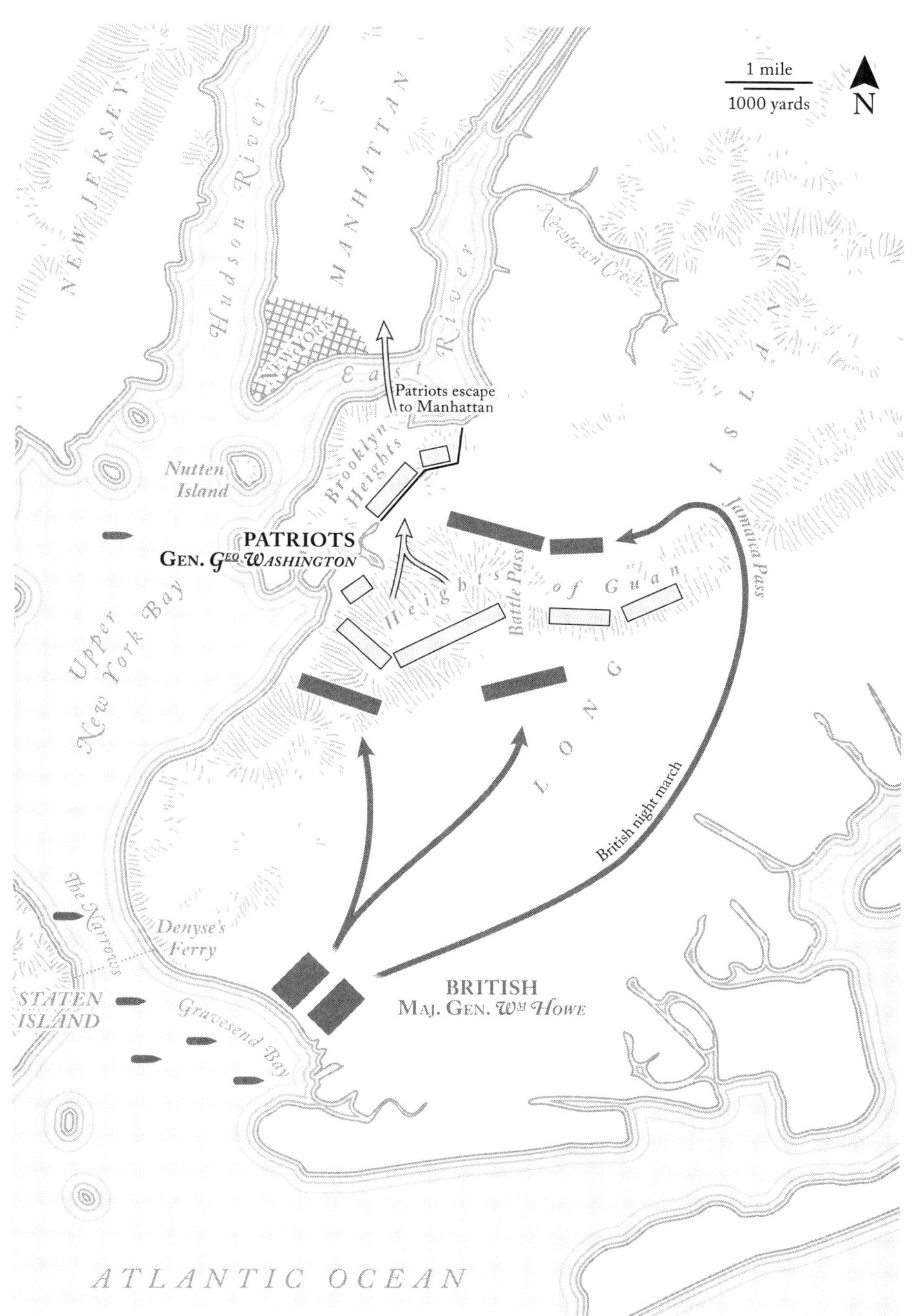
1 mile
1000 yards
N
NEW JERSEY
Hudson River
MANHATTAN
NEW YORK
East River
Newtown Creek
Patriots escape
to Manhattan
Brooklyn Heights
Nutten Island
PATRIOTS
GEN. GEO WASHINGTON
Heights of Guan
Battle Pass
Jamaica Pass
Upper New York Bay
LONG ISLAND
British night march
The Narrows
Denyse's Ferry
STATEN ISLAND
Gravesend Bay
BRITISH
MAJ. GEN. WM HOWE
ATLANTIC OCEAN

EIGHTEEN

"I was very uneasy about a road through which I had often foretold the enemy would come, but could not persuade others to be of my opinion."

General John Sullivan

Long Island
27 August 1776

JAMES WELCOMED the coming of a quiet, uneventful dawn. Not only did it put an end to the foreboding night marches tended to foster in soldiers, but it also told him the light battalions commanded by General Sir Henry Clinton had succeeded in reaching Jamaica Pass undetected and securing it without a fight. Turning in his saddle, he placed his left hand upon the rump of his horse to steady himself as he took to surveying what he could see of the column. James had no need to see the faces of the men following in tightly packed ranks to know all was in order. Both to ahead and behind him, there were no gaps or signs of straggling despite the burdens of their muskets, cartridge boxes, canteens, and knapsacks. This was, in large part, thanks to the vigilant sergeants and corporals able to set aside their own exhaustion and drive their charges on with a steady, unfaltering pace. He also knew all it would take to snap them out of the stupor into which they had fallen during their long march through the early fall darkness would be the sharp crack of a musket and the whiff of burned gunpowder. They were, after all, professionals—soldiers drilled until they were able to respond to the beat of a drum instantly and instinctively.

Satisfied all was as it should be, James turned in his saddle and faced front. In doing so, he caught sight of a familiar landmark—one he and his friends often relied on when afforded the opportunity to set aside their studies at King's College and explore the wilds of Long Island. Not far ahead was Howard's Tavern. If all continued as planned, from there, the army would follow a trail few knew of that led to Bedford, a small farm community between the Gowanus Heights and the East River. On this morning, the rebel forces arrayed along those heights would be the ones who would awaken to find they had been outfoxed. The only thing James regretted as the column continued to plod along at a steady, unrelenting pace was he would not be with his regiment when the moment came to put the rebels to the sword.

Glancing up, he caught a patch of pale blue sky through the tree branches and mused aloud to himself, "James Keating, you've no one to blame for that but yourself."

A passing soldier who thought James was addressing him straightened, took his eyes off the road he had been following all night, and looked up at James.

"Excuse me, sir?"

Realizing he had put words to his thoughts, James shook his head to clear it before returning the man's expectant gaze.

"Nothing, nothing at all," he muttered.

Then, without feeling the need to say anything more by way of excuse or explanation, he spurred his mount and rode on.

"Are all generals' aides barmy?" the soldier asked his messmate as he watched James carefully nudge his way forward between the trees to one side of the narrow dirt track and the endless column on the other.

"I expect they are," the other man grumbled. "If the rebel marksmen are as good as they say, I'd be damned if I'd go prancing about the battlefield mounted on a great lumbering beast."

The first soldier grunted by way of response as he took to rolling his shoulders in a vain effort to shift the weight of his knapsack and musket from one to the other.

"I don't know about that. Given half a chance, I'd gladly run the risk of being sniped if it meant having a horse to haul me and this bloody pack."

From somewhere behind them, the gravelly voice of a sergeant major interrupted their exchange, "Quiet in the ranks."

Without another word, the two soldiers turned their attention back to staring vacantly at the heels of the men to their front as they trudged on.

There was no need for Thomas Shields to look back over his shoulder to know the muffled clip-clop of hoof beats coming up fast belonged to Lieutenant Dale Thatcher's mount. A newly arrived officer who'd been plucked from his regiment by Howe's quartermaster general to serve as one of his assistants, Thatcher had inexplicably taken a liking to him despite Thomas's best efforts to make it known he had no interest associating with the young man. It was not the man's rank that caused Thomas to shun Thatcher when circumstances permitted. By any measure, the cheerful young man was as bright and engaging as an adventurous puppy. Rather, it was his background: Dale Thatcher's father was a London merchant who had neither title nor standing outside his circle of associates.

Thomas Shields was no snob. At least he did not think himself to be one. Having served with men who were unabashedly stiff-necked when it came to their ancestral titles and the prerogatives birth had bestowed upon them, he had always done his best to moderate his own tone and manner when necessity left him no choice but to deal with officers drawn from the middling class. His marriage to Katherine Van der Hoff went far to further an appreciation of how foolish it was to base a man's worth solely on the mere happenstance of his birth. After all, the shrewd, sometimes loutish businessmen who comprised what passed as high society in the colonies were also the bedrock on which his wife's prosperity and his prominence in the colonies had been built. That did not mean he needed to associate with them. As he pointed out when he shared his thoughts on the subject with officers new to the colonies, "*The author needs the printer. That does not make the two equals, obliged to spend time with each other outside the course of their shared commercial interests. I mean, what gentleman worthy of that title would even consider sharing his table with his scullery maid?*"

In Thomas's eyes, Thatcher was no different than the spirited sons of tradesmen, jobbers, and shopkeepers he had come across in the past while serving with the colors. Like countless other young men who sought adventure and social advancement by securing a commission through the hard work and good fortunes of their fathers, Thatcher strove mightily to adopt the mannerisms and attitudes of his betters in an attempt to be gain their acceptance. In doing so, he made already nettlesome circumstances all the more annoying to officers who had been bred from birth to be gentlemen. His only saving grace, at least in the eyes of Howe's quartermaster general, was an analytical mind needed to grasp the minutiae for which an officer was responsible in keeping an army on campaign supplied with the rations, munitions, transport, and quarters. Having served as an assistant quartermaster himself in the French and Indian War for General James Abercrombie, Thomas appreciated the demands of that position placed upon the unfortunate soul plucked from his regiment picked to fill it. That did little, however, to endear him to Thatcher. If anything, it exacerbated the antipathy he felt for him. What little sympathy Thomas had for the daunting responsibilities Thatcher was burdened with day in and day out, whether the army was on the march or simply lying about camp, was negated by the manner with which the young officer badgered him with questions in an effort to draw upon his experiences and knowledge of the colonies and colonials.

Even before he was abreast of Thomas, Thatcher was chattering away.

"Sir Henry has done it!" he exclaimed brightly as he was nudging his horse up alongside Thomas's, never once paying any attention to the scowls exhausted soldiers showered upon him as they were forced to give way to make room for him on the narrow dirt track they had been following for hours. "It would seem we've caught those damnable rebels on the back foot!"

Having been in the saddle since just after midnight, Thomas was in no mood to revisit the debate that had raged between General Howe, the army's commander, and Sir Henry Clinton, his most senior subordinate and, by far, the most irritating one.

Without bothering to look over at Thatcher, Thomas all but growled, "All this stumbling about in the dark has been a waste of time. A volley or two, followed by a bayonet charge, was all that would have been needed to put the rabble holding the Heights of Gowanus to flight."

"I expect that is true," Thatcher muttered in agreement. "But that would have been costly. I hear tell the rebels are all crack shots."

"Some are, yes," Thomas reluctantly agreed. Then, snapping his head around to face Thatcher, he continued. "That does not make them Prussian grenadiers. The lot of them are base, cowardly traitors who've been whipped up into a frenzy by a handful of unprincipled men who seem to believe they are our equals. Well they're not—not now, not ever. The quicker we put them to the sword, the better."

Caught off guard by the sharpness of Thomas' retort, Thatcher drew back, but only for a moment. Unwilling to yield his point, he held Thomas' scathing glare as he straightened up in his saddle.

"We will thrash them," he declared with the confidence of a novice who had not yet fought his first battle. "Not only will Sir Henry's stratagem all but assure that, I expect the cost to this army will be far less than had we simply attempted to bull our way ahead."

Having no wish to revisit an issue their march around the rebel's left flank had made moot with an officer raised by a man whose narrow world view did not go beyond the figures enumerated in a ledger, Thomas spurred his mount on without another word. Ignoring Thatcher and the scathing glances of soldiers forced to yield a portion of the track to him, he made his way toward the head of the column.

What made Thatcher's argument all the more irksome to Thomas was that he was right. Having led men in assaults that claimed half their number, Thomas had no doubt attacking the motley collection of half trained militia deployed along Gowanus Heights would have cost the army trained soldiers who were not easily replaced. Still, that did not mean he needed to concede the argument to Thatcher. To do so would only make the insufferable pup even more annoying.

Gowanus Heights, Long Island
8:30 AM, 27 August 1776

The sight of British regiments executing the intricate evolutions required to transform a lengthy road-bound march into a line of battle was an all too familiar sight to Anton. The same could not be said of the troops belonging to Brigadier General William Alexander, known to his troops as Lord Sterling. Even the handful of officers who had fought the French and their Indian allies in the last war had never beheld a host as massive, or as intimidating, as the one now assembled before them.

No one had ordered Anton to accompany Sterling's brigade that morning when it was sent forward to contest the British advance up the road running along the southeastern shore of Long Island. The commander of a pair of six pounders sited just off the road the British had been following had no need for his advice. Neither did a captain belonging to the 5th Maryland, the regiment anchoring the right of the line. The only reason that officer bothered to strike up a conversation with an officer he knew to be a member of General

Washington's staff was to discover if Washington intended to hold the British at Gowanus Heights, or merely delay them long enough to reinforce the fortifications on Brooklyn Heights.

When Anton informed the Marylander he was not privy to their commanding general's future plans, the captain took to surveying the British line of battle before thanking Anton for his time and returning to his own post. As he watched the captain go, Anton wondered how he and the men he commanded would perform in their first battle against troops belonging to their former King. How it played out, he expected, would go far in predicting whether the newly independent United States of America would be able to elbow its way onto the world stage or, like the rebellion against French rule he had had helped suppress in Corsica, die in the cradle.

That question caused Anton to step back several paces to where he could study the American line of battle. To either side of the guns to which he had attached himself were arguably the two best regiments in the entire army Washington had assembled to defend New York. Both were far better drilled and equipped than most. Like the captain he had just spoken to, the Marylanders, attired in tan hunting shirts, were doing their best to hide whatever apprehensions they had over the coming battle. The same was true of 1st Delaware, the regiment drawn up to the left of the guns. Uniformed entirely in blue coats with red facings worn over white waistcoats, breeches, and black half-gaiters, they were one of the few regiments that bore any resemblance to a regiment belonging to a European army. Whether they would be able to perform on par with one was another matter altogether.

It was a thought Anton chose not to share with an American officer from that regiment who, with nothing better to do as his men waited for an assault they expected the British to deliver, sidled up to him and stuck up a halting conversation.

"They certainly are taking their time," the American mused without taking his eyes off a spectacle that elicited awe and dread in equal measure.

"These things cannot be rushed," Anton replied calmly. "As in chess, the opening moves are often the most critical. A decision made in haste or an ill-timed move is difficult to undo once battle has been joined."

Unable to conjure up a reasonable response, the American simply nodded, leaving Anton to focus on the deliberate, almost laborious manner with which the British were carrying out their initial deployments. *What,* he wondered to himself, *were they about?* The battle, such as it was, had begun shortly after dawn when men belonging to the British vanguard came across American soldiers belonging to a forward outpost in, of all places, a watermelon patch. The resulting skirmish had been short-lived, for the Americans beat a hasty retreat to Gowanus Heights where they fell in with Lord Sterling's brigade. What followed was predictable. A brace of British six pounders wheeled into position opposite the pair of guns near Anton engaged in a lively exchange with the American guns. The casualties resulting from this were negligible for all but the soldiers unfortunate enough to be eviscerated by one of the cannonballs the opposing gun crews were hurling at the stationary line of troops across from them.

The willingness of the American line to stand and take the punishment it was suffering was, to Anton, understandable. Not only did Lord Sterling's brigade hold the high ground, but it also blocked one of the few roads leading to the Brooklyn Heights. If the British wished to seize the high ground that dominated Manhattan in preparation for an assault on that island, they would need to go through the Americans holding Gowanus Heights.

The village of Bedford, Long Island
North of Gowanus Heights
9:00 AM, 27 August 1776

Having reached the small farming community of Bedford, James was confident Clinton's much maligned flanking maneuver had succeeded. Not even a spat of gunfire emanating from the column's baggage train trailing the column did more than cause a momentary flurry of concern among Howe and his senior aides. The ten thousand soldiers who had spent the night snaking their way along a narrow track and through Jamaica Pass before turning west to gain the rebel's rear promised to put an end to a war that had kept him from his dear Sarah and children. If there was anything James was sure of, it was victory was theirs for the taking.

What he and the other officers gathered about their general could not be sure of was just how serious the clash at the rear of the column was. Already keyed up, when ordered to ride back along the length of the column to assess the situation, James did not hesitate. With a sharp tug on his mount's reins that caused the chestnut bay to rear up, he came about, dug his spurs into the horse's flank, and broke into as near a gallop as the crowded track and forests flanking it permitted. Soldiers who had settled along the side of the narrow woodland track the column had been following to enjoy a cold breakfast and rest were forced to leap to their feet or simply rolled over on their side to avoid being trampled. Ducking to keep from being unhorsed by low branches jutting out over the track, James paid little heed to the shouts of angry regimental officers he passed. He was on a mission tasked by the army's commander himself to assess the situation and report back. He only reined in his mount when he came upon a cornet belonging to the 17th Dragoons sitting astride his horse, calmly watching dismounted troopers under his command exchanging fire with rebels half hidden by the woods and clouds of gun smoke.

"Report," James barked in a manner meant to communicate both his seniority and position as a representative of the army's commanding general.

"It would seem the rebels were making their way east along a trail we were not aware of that runs parallel to the one we're on when they came across the rear of the column," the cornet replied calmly without bothering to take his eyes off the line of dismounted troopers slowly advancing.

James was not at all put off by the casualness with which the young officer replied, for it served to reassure him the situation was well in hand. Having no wish to go back where the soldiers who comprised the bulk of column were doing nothing more than enjoying a cold breakfast before pressing home the advantage a long night of marching had bestowed upon them, he nudged his mount closer to the cornet's.

"Ride to the head of the column, find General Howe, and inform him of the situation," James ordered with a crispness he hoped would keep the cornet from challenging his authority.

Unsure of an order delivered to him at a most inopportune moment by an officer on whom he had never laid eyes, the cornet looked over at James and hesitated.

Having no wish to debate the issue with the dragoon who was, he assumed, wondering how best to tell a general's aide to bugger off, James drew himself up in the saddle and took to staring the cornet down.

"Be quick about it, man," James snapped. "Then, report back to me."

Taken aback by the sharpness of James's tone and the steady, unflinching glare with which he was eyeing him, the cornet hesitated but a moment longer. With a quick jerk of his mount's reins, he turned away from James and took to scanning the dismounted troopers closest to him, calling out to the first noncommissioned officer he spotted.

"Corporal, take charge here until I return."

With nothing more than a quick nod after tearing the end of a fresh cartridge off with his teeth, the corporal of dragoons acknowledged the cornet's order.

Once the cornet was well away, James took to slowly picking his way along the rear of a skirmish line made up of dismounted dragoons and soldiers belonging to the light infantry battalions that had earlier been part of the column's vanguard. All were pressing forward, pausing only to reload carbines and muskets as they went. If all had gone as it should have, he calculated, the rebels to his front, and those on Gowanus Heights, were now sandwiched between the divisions that made up the army's left and center and those belonging to the main body, now firmly established in their rear in and around Bedford. With nowhere to flee, the treasonous curs who had authored his long separation from his beloved Sarah would have no choice but to surrender or, if they were foolish enough to stand their ground, die.

Drawing his saber, he took to carefully guiding his mount through the smoke-filled forest flanking the road as the line of light bobs and dragoons continued to make their way forward, firing, reloading, and firing again as they did so.

"Press them," he yelled to soldiers deafened by the discharge of their own weapons. "Press the bastards."

Flatbush Pass, Long Island
South of Gowanus Heights
9:00 AM, 27 August 1776

The distant echo of two cannons fired by gunners with Howe's column were welcomed by Hauptman Kleist. They signaled the main body had reached the village of Bedford and the rear of the American's he and his men had been doing their utmost to distract. They were now free to put an end to the charade in which they had been engaged and close with the rabble they had been sparring with since dawn.

Above the clatter of gunfire and shouted orders, shrilled tunes played by pipers belonging to a highland regiment could be heard as Kleist led his jägers forward. His company was charged with covering the left flank of Lieutenant General Leopold Philip von Heister's division. Just off the Kleist's left were British troops under the command of Major General James Grant. Like Heister's Germans, they had spent the morning demonstrating before the rebels arrayed along the Gowanus Heights. And, like the Germans, they were just as eager to go forward.

To Kleist's great surprise, the rebels did not flee as he had expected. Instead, they met the advance of his company with an accurate and telling fire that impressed him. Even when his jägers closed with them, rebel rifleman and musketeers without bayonets twirled their weapons around, wrapped their bare hands about the hot barrels, and took to swinging them like clubs.

Most, Kleist suspected, knew they were no match for professional soldiers such as his—men hardened by fierce, uncompromising drillmasters. Why they did not turn and run at the mere sight of his men was puzzling but welcomed. To a soldier as dedicated to his chosen profession as he was, there was no joy in dispatching a foe that meekly submitted to its fate. Glory cheaply won had little meaning to Kleist. A hunter such as he took special pride in killing a boar that turned on him and fought to the last. Their heads were the ones he graced his hall with. And while the idea of returning to Germany with the head of a dead American rebel never crossed his mind, even in the midst of the desperate struggle his company was engaged in, Gustav Kleist looked forward to the day when he would be able to regale his prince with glorious tales this day's efforts would yield.

Gowanus Heights
11:00 AM, 27 August 1776

After holding their ground with a tenacity that far surpassed Anton's expectations, the American line to the left of Sterling's brigade began to unravel with the terrifying rapidity of a ship's sail being shredded by a winter gale once it became clear their position had been outflanked. A few chose to sell their lives dearly, meeting their tormentors with clubbed muskets, knives, or their bare hands. Others fell to their knees and begged for clemency from a foe that had little inclination to grant any. Most, however, sought salvation in flight, dooming efforts by their officers to organize an orderly retreat. All knew the day, which had started out so promising, was irreparably lost.

Realizing there was not enough time to bring up the draft horses and limbers needed to haul the pair of six pounders away, Anton turned to Captain Carpenter, the commander of the small battery.

"Leave them!" he implored Carpenter as he took to waving his hand about to indicate his gunners. "Save your men."

Neither Carpenter nor his gun crews bothered to question the French officer's authority to issue such an order. Nor did they hesitate to obey it. After setting aside ramrods, sponges, worms, and buckets, they joined the retreat that was well on its way to becoming a rout. Having done what little he could, Anton took one last look at the advancing British line of battle the American six pounders had been pounding all morning. They would be in no mood to show mercy, not after suffering the punishment Carpenter's gunner had meted out. Turning, Anton began to make his way back to the fortifications on Brooklyn Heights where he and Carpenter's gunners would find safety, provided they were lucky enough to escape the trap closing in behind them.

The Vechte House
Long Island
11:30 AM, 27 August 1776

At Bedford, Thomas found himself on ground he was quite familiar with. He had often forsaken the dubious pleasures of New York City and the company of his wife's friends and associates by traveling the roads and trails of eastern Long Island in search of sport.

"Just up ahead on the road running from Gowanus Heights to Brooklyn, there's an old stone house that was built by a Dutch farmer at the end of last century," he informed an officer belonging to Fraser's 71st Regiment of Foot as the two made their way out of Bedford, riding along with the highlander's regiment and a battalion of grenadiers. "The owner of the house and surrounding farmlands are more than simply a distant relative to my wife. The oysters his slaves harvest along Gowanus Creek are transported down to Gowanus Bay and across the harbor to Manhattan where a good many are bought up by our purchasing agent. Those that do not find their way onto our table are resold at market where they earned us a handsome profit."

At another time, the highlander would have found Thomas's running narrative o[f his wife's affairs interesting. Now, however, his sole concern was reaching the creek Thomas was talking about and seeing to it the rebels fleeing Grant's and Heister's troops did not escape to Brooklyn Heights. That, Thomas reassured the highlander, would not take much.

"I've never been impressed by provincials," he explained. "They make poor soldiers. Even the best of them are unreliable, ill-disciplined, and slovenly."

Distracted by a spat of gunfire just up ahead, the highlander rose up in the stirrups of his mount in an effort to see above the heads of soldiers belonging to his regiment. Low hanging branches and drifting clouds of smoke kept him from seeing what, exactly was going on. Easing back down into the saddle, he turned to Thomas.

"It would seem we're about to see if what you say of your fellow countrymen is true."

Irked at being reminded he was now more American than English in the eyes of many of his peers, Thomas was about to disabuse the highlander of that notion when a thunderous volley, followed by a roll of drums and shouting, caused him and the highlander to once more turn their full attention toward the head of the column. As one, they spurred their mounts on, picking their way forward, past the troops to their front as quickly as they could.

The chaotic scene the two officers came upon when they reached the crossroads just short of the Vechte farm caught Thomas by surprise. Sharply reining his mount in, he was about to ask a wounded grenadier who was making his way to the rear why the advance had come to a halt when a gust of wind blew away a rolling cloud of gun smoke, revealing the well-ordered line of battle that had unleashed the volley were not Fraser's Highlanders or grenadiers, but rebels attired in tan hunting shirts. Even more disconcerting to Thomas was that they were advancing to the steady beat of drums.

After taking in the scene before them, the highlander officer drew his sword as he prepared go forward. But before he did, he turned to Thomas.

"You were saying, Major?"

Dumbfounded, Thomas said nothing as he watched the highlander dig his spurs into the flank of his mount and gallop off. Beyond the soldiers of the 71st and the advancing line of rebels, he could see hundreds of rebel soldiers splashing their way through the marsh bordering Gowanus creek as they fled toward Brooklyn Heights. Anger and a determination to see to it few of those bastards made it to safety fueled Thomas as he drew his own sword and rode toward the stone farmhouse where the grenadiers who had been sent to prevent the rebels' escape had taken refuge.

-«««•»»»-

The sight of the soldiers belonging to the 1st Delaware and Colonel Smallwood's Marylanders holding open the last avenue of escape for their fellow Americans caused Anton pause. Just as they had earlier that morning when they had stood their ground in the face of a superior foe, the men of those regiments did not waver. As hundreds of fleeing Americans plunged into the marsh that barred their escape, they were but two regiments—a mere fraction of the army Washington had collected to defend New York City—but, if they could check the advance of the best troops Howe had at his disposal, then perhaps others, properly equipped and trained as the Marylanders were, could do more than simply discomfort his King's traditional foe. Perhaps their dream of throwing off the English rule could be realized.

A gunner from Carpenter's battery who recognized Anton stopped when he saw the Frenchman standing there, watching the Marylanders reform after a failed charge.

"We've done all we can this day," he stated calmly. "Best we go while we can."

"Yes," Anton agreed without taking his eyes off the Marylanders as they prepared to go forward again.

There were fewer of them now, far fewer. That, however, did not stop those who were left from advancing on a stone farmhouse bristling with muskets belonging to British grenadiers when drummers took up beating the advance.

"Yes," Anton repeated as he turned to join the gunner. "This day is lost, but only this day."

NINETEEN

"Our situation is truly distressing. Till of late I had no doubt in my mind of defending this place, nor should I had yet if the men would do their duty, but this I despair of."

George Washington,
Letter to Congress
September 1776

New York City
28 August 1776

NO ONE NEEDED to tell Kat that Washington's army had been thoroughly thrashed. She could see it in the eyes of the men who drifted back into the city, either assisting wounded comrades or seeking escape from a vengeful foe who had managed to corner the rebel army in a trap of their own making. When she came across an officer she knew who had been on General Sterling's staff seated alone in the Bean in the Pot, she could not keep from marching up to him and asking what had happened.

"It was a rout," the officer growled contemptuously. Either due to shame or disgust, he made no effort to meet Kat's gaze. Instead, he continued to stare intently down at cup of coffee held between hands that looked as if they had not been washed in days. "They came through Jamaica Pass during the night and took us in the flank. All they needed were a few good volleys to scatter the militia.

Most of those worthless scoundrels threw down their muskets and took to their heels like a flock of panicked geese. If it weren't for the British stopping just when they were about to finish the job, none of us would have gotten away."

When Kat asked the bedraggled rebel officer why the King's troops had not pressed their advantage, he slowly lifted his bloodshot eyes, flashing her a wry smile as he did so.

"I guess because Howe saw those of us who still had our heads about us take up position in the redoubts General Lee had thrown up on Brooklyn Heights and remembered the bloody drubbing we gave the bastard the last time he tried to storm our entrenchments. The only problem is Washington has let himself be pinned against the East River," he added as his expression clouded over before once more staring down at the cup he continued to clutch. "All the British have to do now is sail a few warships up the East River behind our army and wait until the poor lads still over there have eaten their way through whatever rations they have in their haversacks."

"Then it's over," Kat sighed, surprising herself at how disappointed she was by the failure of the rebels to turn back an army she now thought of as foreign invaders.

"Yes, it's over," the rebel officer muttered sadly. "Once Washington surrenders, all that'll be left for the bloody red-coated bastards to do is round up those of us who made good our escape and hang us from the nearest tree. Provided, of course, they can catch us," he added before draining his cup and rising to his feet.

With that the officer bowed, bid Kat a good day, and headed out of the coffee shop to continue his flight.

After watching him leave, Kat drifted over to her favorite table where she sat for the longest time, staring vacantly out the bay window and wondering what would become of her and all those she had come to think of as her family. While Sarah and the children would be safe because of James, Kat knew she would be called upon to answer for the way she had supported the rebels. Having entertained their officers in her home and all but emptied her storehouses and shops equipping and provisioning their army, there was no way of hiding what she had done. Men who had succeeded in keeping their preference for the King a closely guarded secret and rival merchants sensing an opportunity to eliminate an annoying competitor would fall over each other in their rush rushed to betray her to the Royal Governor. No doubt, she mused grimly as she absentmindedly took a sip of hot chocolate that had appeared before her as if by magic, in time they would even find out about her clandestine activities which included, of all things, the ownership of a privateer.

It was in the midst of her deliberations of how best to deal with the King's men when the city once more fell under their sway that a saying attributed to the Prussian King came to mind. Ever so slowly a smile lit up her face.

"L'audace, toujours l'audace," she whispered to herself.

"Excuse me, Lady Katherine?"

Having been thoroughly lost in her own thoughts, Kat had not noticed Linda Tuck standing before her table holding a freshly baked plate of lemon biscuits. Flashing the young girl a beguiling smile, Kat reached out and snatched a warm biscuit off the plate.

"It's French," she proclaimed in a cheerful tone so very much at odds with the somber mood that had overcome her after talking to the rebel officer. "Translated it means 'audacity, always audacity.'"

Having no idea what Kat was talking about, Linda simply stood there until Kat gave her head a quick shake, tilted it to one side, and winked.

"We've not had a chance to practice your letters these past few days," Kat declared. "Why don't you leave that plate of biscuits here and go fetch your hornbook and primer so we can pick up where we last left off?"

Having come to enjoy the time she spent with Kat learning to read and write, Linda beamed. After setting the plate down and executing a quick curtsey, she retreated to the coffee shop's backroom to fetch the materials. Kat had been saving them for Sarah's children at first, but recently gave them to Linda, believing she would be able to replace them with more modern, less religious based texts when it came time to introduce her niece and nephew to the wondrous world of books and reading.

While she waited for the girl to return, Kat used the time to firm up her ideas on how she would extract herself from the tight corner her actions and those who worked for her would find themselves in once the ragged troops filling the streets beyond the window were replaced by those of the King. And while she was unable to settle on any specifics before Linda returned, she knew only audacity bordering on the outrageous and unexpected would save her, much as it had not so very long ago.

Brooklyn Heights
Night, 29 August 1776

"If you asked me, that general of ours is making a mistake," Kevin Farrell muttered contemptuously as he and the others belonging to the 1st New York made their way from the fortifications they had held for three days down to a ferry landing on the East River.

"No one asked you, thank God," Edward Shields shot back without taking his eyes off the muddy track they were following.

"Sneakin' off in the middle of the night without firing a shot don't make a lick of sense!" Farrell countered. "As I see it, the way we were tucked in nice and snug behind those earthworks, we could have given those red-coated blackguards a good thrashing they wouldn't have forgotten any time soon."

Edward was not swayed by Farrell's argument and said as much, "Staying where we were, waiting for them to haul their cannons up to those trenches they've been digging in front of our works doesn't make any sense either. I doubt there's an Englishman who wants to be part of another pyrrhic victory like the one they enjoyed at Bunker Hill."

"A pyrrhic victory!" Farrell exclaimed mockingly. "Will ya listen to him?" he asked the man to his left. "And where did you pick up that little gem?" he asked turning his attention back to Edward. "From that bloody thick book of yours you carry around in your haversack?"

Before Edward could respond, an officer they were passing hissed out a stern warning, "Quiet men, or you'll wake up every Englishman and Hessian on Long Island."

In silence, Edward thanked the officer for cutting Farrell's argument short. The man was a good soldier and an even better friend, the kind Edward would need if he were to weather what was turning out to be a war that would go on for God knew how long. Besides, he needed to pay attention to where he was stepping as they snaked their way through the darkness down off the high ground they had been holding and to the ferry landing across from Manhattan and salvation.

Retreats did not win wars. Having been a party to more than he cared to remember, Anton knew this. He also knew holding a position as untenable as the one the Americans had backed their way into was foolish. The British had no intention of launching an assault on the fortifications lining Brooklyn Heights. They had no need to. With their warships free to sail up the East River whenever the tide and winds were favorable, they could carry out a formal siege the Americans had little chance of countering.

"In the end, they will prevail," he informed a captain of artillery as the two stood next to one of the captain's guns. "I assure you, my friend, it is a mathematical certainty."

Fortunately, Washington understood this as well, appreciating that if his army died here, the cause he and the men who followed him would die with it.

The decision to transport the army back to the island of Manhattan had been met with little dissent during a council of war convened by Washington to discuss the matter. Only one man, a New York lawyer and firebrand dedicate to the cause of independence by the name of John Morin Scott, objected to yielding Brooklyn without a fight. Wisely, Washington paid little heed to the man's argument—a decision Anton greeted in silence. The members of the war council turned their attention to the practical matter of how to move 9,500 men, along with all their cannons, equipment, supplies, and horses across the East River in a single night without the enemy discovering what they were up to. They would need more than resolve and the skilled New England fisherman belonging to Colonel John Glover's regiment to succeed. They would need luck.

That luck came in three distinct and timely waves. A storm that blew up shortly after sundown proved to be a mixed blessing, for the ebbing tide and wind coming from the northeast that kept British warships out of the East River also threatened to sweep the boats and barges moving the army across to Manhattan into the bay. The second spot of luck that came their way occurred just before midnight when the winds died down, calming the roiling waters of the East River. The final bit of good fortune rolled in just before dawn in the form of a dense fog that kept the British from noticing the American earthworks along Brooklyn Heights had been abandoned.

It was not in Anton's nature to simply stand off to one side and watch the field guns being loaded onto barges. Whenever an extra pair of hands were needed, he did not hesitate to step forward and help roll the piece up onto the barge and secure it. In addition to making the time pass quicker, it left him little opportunity to speculate on what the British would do once they found out the Americans had managed to give them the slip. Seizing Manhattan Island was a given. What Washington and his most trusted commanders needed to know was when and where—questions made all the more difficult to answer given the length of Manhattan and the ability of the Royal Navy to land Howe's army anywhere he wanted, whenever he wanted.

Worrying about that would have to wait. After satisfying himself the knots in a rope used to secure a six pounder to a barge would be sufficient to secure the gun during the crossing, Anton made his way back ashore to wait for the barge he had just helped load to pull away and another capable of holding a gun to take its place. As he watched the heavily laden barge with precious little freeboard to spare disappear into the shroud of darkness that was blinding the British to their escape, Anton realized deciding what he would do next would also have to wait. It would not occur to him until days later and after he had had an opportunity to sleep, bathe, and don a clean uniform that he had already made that decision. He had made it months before—at a rustic New England inn when the only woman he loved reached out and took his hand in hers.

New York City
29 August 1776

It was not long after she had turned in for the night when a knock on Kat's bedroom door caught her just as she was drifting off to sleep. It was a hasty, anxious sort of knock, the kind that alerted her something was amiss. After easing out of bed and slipping on a robe she kept close at hand, she made her way over to the door, unlatched it, and opened it but a crack. In her usual, no-nonsense manner, Mrs. Peel informed her there were soldiers in the street out in front of the house. Without waiting to hear more, Kat threw open the door and headed toward the stairs, casting a wary eye in the direction of Sarah's room as she did so.

Only when they finally reached the front door of the house and Mrs. Peel saw Kat reach for the doorknob did the housekeeper try to stop her young charge's advance.

"Lady Katherine, you cannot go out wearing nothing but a dressing gown."

As she often did, Kat ignored her housekeeper's effort to rein her in. As far she was concerned, there were times when propriety and decorum were of little concern and this, in her mind, was one of them. Throwing open the door, she stepped out onto the top step of the main entrance to Minden Hall.

It was not the rain that kept her from venturing out any further. Nor was it her concern over modesty. In truth she had no need to do so. Even in the darkness, she could clearly see a steady stream of bedraggled soldiers, hunched over and either staring down at the road beneath their feet or at the back of the man in front of him as they trudged north along Broadway. As wretched as those who had fled in the immediate aftermath of the battle had been, the endless parade of misery passing before her very door, made all the more piteous by the rain pelting them, caused Kat to toss aside all thought of decorum or what might or might not be in her best interest and instead, do what she could to alleviate some of the suffering she was witnessing.

Pivoting about on her heels, Kat found herself confronted not only by Mrs. Peel, but Mary O'Donnell, Gwyn Jones, Peggy Anders, and Steven. Upon hearing the commotion, they too had gathered in the darkened entry hall behind their mistress to see what was going on. Drawing herself up, Kat took in a deep breath as she prepared to address her small staff.

"I do not know where your sympathies lay in this great matter, one that has overtaken us and set our world upside down. Nor do I care at this moment. Those men out there, they are ours," she proclaimed while pointing a finger out through the open doorway toward the street without ever taking her eyes off the small gathering before her. "I for one intend to do all I can to ease their suffering as best I can. If you wish to join me, I would be most appreciative. If not, return to your warm bed, quench your candle, and enjoy your sleep."

Kat, of course, knew she was not giving them a choice, not really. It was a point Mrs. Peel acknowledged by giving her mistress a sly little smile, one Kat replied to with nothing more than a flick of her eyes.

With that, the housekeeper turned about and faced the others saying, "Well then, let's be to it. Steven, you're to run down to the Bean in the Pot and rouse Mrs. Tuck. Tell her we'll need all the soup, bread, coffee, and tea she can spare. Mary, stoke up the fire in the hearth and put on water for tea, coffee, and whatever we've got that will warm those poor lads' inners. Gwyn, gather up cups, bowls, and spoons. When you've done that, help Mrs. O'Donnell, Peggy. By the looks of 'em, I expect some of the lads will need some mending, so gather up whatever is about we can use for bandages. Now off with you."

When the others were gone, Mrs. Peel turned to face Kat. "And what would you have me do?" Kat asked with a mischievous little grin.

Taking a moment to eye her young mistress from head to toe, the no-nonsense housekeeper grunted, "You, young lady, are to go back to your room and put something decent on if you've a mind to step out of this house and help us."

Despite the grimness of the task before them, Kat could not help but snicker as she gave Mrs. Peel a wink before dipping in the same manner Gwyn and Peggy always did when being ordered about by the no-nonsense housekeeper.

"As you wish, Mrs. Peel."

It was well after dawn before the last of the rebel army was passing by Minden Hall. While Mrs. Peel was directing the others who were serving up bowls of soup or hot coffee with all the adroitness of a field marshal, Kat was kept busy cleaning and dressing wounds that had been neglected for days. She was bent over, in the midst of wrapping a bandage about a Marylander's head who was seated on the top step of her house when someone tapped her on the shoulder. Without bothering to look behind her, Kat tilted her head toward the only vacant spot on the steps not already occupied by a soldier enjoying a break and a warm bowl of soup.

"If you take a seat, I'll be with you as soon as I am finished here."

"Oh, I don't need that sort of help, girl," the man replied. "We were told this was the home of Lady Katherine Trent. Is that true?"

"It is," Kat answered without looking behind at the man addressing her.

"Well then, would you be so kind as to run off and fetch her?"

For the first time, Kat stopped what she had been doing and glanced over her shoulder. The man was a young officer. He was, she imagined, an aide to a tall, grim-faced general who remained mounted upon his horse in the center of the street surveying the hive of activity swirling about her.

"And what would you be wanting with her?" Kat asked when she realized the young officer had no idea who she was.

Not that she could blame him. She was dressed in a plain high-necked chemise dress with a kerchief she had hastily draped about her. It, like the unkempt hair cascading down about her shoulders, was soaked and bedraggled after standing in the rain for hours and tending to the needs of men who had stopped their retreat long enough to take advantage of her hospitality and assistance.

Now that he had her attention, the young officer drew himself up in a most officious manner, one that was sadly out of place under the circumstances, and informed Kat his general wished to thank her for all she had done for his men.

"Well, tell your general I appreciate the gesture," she said simply before returning to finish what she had been doing.

"*You're* Lady Katherine?"

Having tied off the ends of the bandage, Kat was finally free to stand upright, turn, and face the pompous young man square on. Placing her hands flat against the small of her back, Kat arched over backwards and stretched her sore aching muscles.

"At your service, sir," she muttered distractedly.

After eyeing Kat up and down as if trying to determine if the her claim could possibly be true, the officer gave his head a quick shake. Then, stepping aside, he turned to his general.

"Sir, I present Lady Katherine Trent," he proclaimed in a tone more fitting a ballroom than a street cluttered with the remnants of a defeated army.

Drawing himself up, the general doffed his hat and bowed deeply. In response, Kat straightened up before acknowledging his gesture with a low, formal curtsey. After holding their respective poses but for a moment, without a word the general replaced his hat, gave his horse's reins a tug to one side, and gently spurred it on.

Only after he and his young aide were gone did Kat ask the Marylander she had been bandaging who the general was.

"Why, that was General Washington," he said.

Realizing she had been the fool, Kat snapped her head about and watched as the tall Virginian rode up Broadway in the wake of his army.

Brooklyn Heights
Morning, 30 August 1776

"Incredible!" Dale Thatcher muttered in sheer astonishment for the third time in as many minutes as he and Thomas picked their way past watchfires that had been kept burning all night by the rebel rear guard to lull British pickets into complacency. "It's simply incredible they were able to pick up, cross the river to their backs, and escape without anyone being the wiser."

Thomas resisted an urge to tell Thatcher to shut up as they neared the landing the rebels had used. Reining in his mount, he took to scanning across the river, now empty of the boats that the rebels had used to make good their escape.

"We should have pressed the attack when we had them on the run," Thomas growled. "We had them. We had damned near the whole lot of them. And we let them slip away."

Startled by the sharpness of Thomas' sudden outburst, Thatcher gave his reins a slight tug, causing his mount to back away. Slowly, almost hesitantly, he then took to surveying the now abandoned fortifications above them. Only when he had managed to formulate what he thought to be a suitable response did he turn his attention back to Thomas.

"Even a successful assault would have been costly," he pointed out. "Why throw away the lives of good men when you can achieve the same result through other means?"

Thomas was in no mood to listen to the argument of a novice and said in clipped tones, "Not everything can be measured as neatly or precisely as a bolt of cloth in your father's shop. This is war, boy. You've got to do more than simply chase your enemy from one position to another. You've got to crush him," Thomas intoned gruffly as he was raising his right hand, palm up, and slowly curled his fingers in as if crumbling an invisible orb. "The hunt will not be over until we've run the fox to ground and it's been torn limb from limb."

Without waiting for a response, Thomas turned his attention back toward the distant shore and its familiar skyline. Having been party to an assault against fortifications such as those behind him, he knew storming the rebel works on Brooklyn Heights would have been a costly undertaking. It would have been worth it, though, if that assault had put an end to this rebellion. General Howe, for reasons he had not bothered to share with anyone, had chosen not to press the rebels. Whether it was out of fear that he would be the author of another ghastly bloodletting, or he wished to try, once more, to treat with the rebels before too much blood had been spilled did not matter. The rebel army, such as it was, had escaped.

"This fox we're hunting is dangerous," he continued in a more subdued tone of voice. "He's chased us from Boston and somehow managed to save his army from certain defeat. Don't fool yourself, lieutenant. He and the rabble that's following him are far from beaten."

The temptation to point out it did not matter whether the rebel commander was beaten today or on another was set aside. It was clear to Thatcher the enraged major was in no mood to listen to logic. With the city of New York and its harbor all but theirs, this war was, in his opinion, as good as won. Of that, he was sure.

TWENTY

"With no other loss we joined the army after dark on the heights of Harlem. Before our brigades came in we were given up for lost by all our friends. So critical indeed was our situation, and so narrow the gap by which we escaped, that the instant we passed the enemy closed it by extending their line from river to river."

Colonel David Humphrey,
aide to General Putnam
on the retreat of Putnam's division from New York City
September 1776

New York City
15 September 1776

LIKE MANY, Kat Trent believed Washington's defeat on Long Island would quickly be followed by a direct assault on the island of Manhattan and the occupation of New York City by Howe's victorious army. That the British did not more than puzzled the person who did not believe in giving a business rival who was in desperate straits the opportunity to collect his wits and rally. Turning away from a letter of instruction to Keith Mathis she had been struggling to finish for the better part of an hour, Kat took to staring out the window of her study.

"A week ago I could have seized the city with nothing more than a corporal's guard," she muttered derisively.

Accustomed to the way her young mistress gave free rein to her thoughts on matters a lady of her standing had no need to trouble herself with, Emma Peel listened attentively, but said nothing as she cleared a stack of books from a side table to make room for the tray of hot chocolate and biscuits Gwyn Jones would soon be bringing.

"What possibly could the Howe brothers be thinking?" Kat snapped as she watched a ragged column of New England militiamen belonging to General Israel Putnam's division make their way up Broadway.

"Perhaps you can ask them when they arrive?" Mrs. Peel offered as she stepped back from the table and looked for a clear, flat surface where she could set the books she was holding.

Turning away from the window, Kat came to her feet. "Oh, I can assure you, I will," she sniffed.

Unable to help herself, Mrs. Peel chuckled. "I've no doubt you will." Abandoning her futile search for somewhere to set the books, the housekeep hit upon a solution. "Perhaps it would be best if I had Gwyn serve you in the parlor where you can join Mrs. Keating."

Baffled by her housekeeper's suggestion, Kat was about to ask why she thought that, but stopped when Mrs. Peel glanced down at the books she was still holding and then, in a very deliberate manner, took to looking about the room. Following her gaze, Kat's eyes darted from tabletop to tabletop, and book shelf to book shelf, all of which were, like her desk, haphazardly cluttered with books, ledgers, stacks of letters, receipts, and bills of lading.

The room was more than a study, library, and office to Kat. To her, it was a sanctuary—a place where she could lose herself between the covers of books that took her to places she would never see, or on adventures a person such as she could only dream about when not otherwise occupied with the task of managing her eclectic collection of businesses. It was also the one room in Minden

Hall where she could conduct her business affairs without the fear of unwanted eyes from happening upon a letter such as the one she had been laboring over. Keith Mathis was the captain of the *Swallow*, the privateer Kat owned. When not waylaying English merchantmen and selling off ship and cargo in Holland, Captain Mathis engaged in smuggling the goods and wares from France and Spain she relied on to keep her shopkeepers, print shop, and coffee house well-stocked.

From the very first day on which Kat had laid claim to Minden Hall, the one hard and fast rule she insisted on was no one, not even Mrs. Peel, was to enter the study unless she was present. Even then, the maids sent in to sweep the floor and dust were under orders not to touch anything unless they had Kat's permission. The rational she used to justify her decree was easy to understand. *"Surely you appreciate my need to be able to put a hand on whatever document or missive I require without the need to waste my precious free time running off to ask Gwyn where she put the book I was in the middle of reading or what she did with a recently arrived letter I've not yet read,"* Kat had explained to Mrs. Peel.

There was much Mrs. Peel did not understand about the peculiar young woman she worked for and, she expected, never would. She did, however, understand an order. To ensure none of the other household staff ignored their mistress's dictate, she saw to it all knew the penalty for entering the study without Kat's permission was immediate dismissal from her service. It was a threat they had no doubt the indomitable housekeeper would carry out without hesitation or regret. She was as ruthless and uncompromising when it came overseeing the running of Minden Hall as was her mistress in her dealings with the hardnosed merchants and businessmen she was in competition with.

The coming of war and Kat's growing involvement in it forced the need to keep curious servants, be their interest in her activities innocent or otherwise, from delving into her affairs. Smuggling was one thing. It was a practice that was officially frowned upon but tolerated, for there was not a single merchant, shopkeeper, ship captain, or public official that did business in the city who did not engage in the practice themselves or profit from it. Supporting armed rebellion against the King, on the other hand, was an entirely different matter, one that required Kat, like all New Yorkers, to walk a fine line between the rebels who controlled the streets and Royal Governor who had taken refuge aboard the HMS *Asia* anchored in the city's upper bay. While women were not required to swear their allegiance to the committee of public safety, they were not entirely safe from the likes of Isaac Sears and Alexander McDougal who aggressively sought out and punished anyone who was even suspected of remaining loyal to the crown. Yet open support to the rebellion would leave Kat vulnerable to retribution when Governor Tyron's pleas for the troops needed to reclaim New York for the crown was finally answered. At best, Kat would lose the mercantile empire she had worked so hard to build. The possibility she would be branded a traitor and hung as others had been could not be discounted.

As grim as those prospects were, the idea of fleeing to England as her uncle had was never really an option. So she took to playing the same dangerous game other New York merchants were engaged in. On one hand, she provided Alexander McDougal the funds and material he needed to raise and equip a regiment. On the other, she had kept the crew and governor's entourage aboard the HMS *Asia* well-stocked with farm fresh food and other necessities up until the very day the Howe brothers sailed into New York harbor at the head of an army charged with reclaiming the colonies for their King.

Well aware of the way her mistress was courting both sides, Mrs. Peel went to extremes to protect her. When asked why she was risking her own life, she drew herself up, tilted her head back, and regarded her mistress with a steady, unflinching gaze.

"The great issues of the day that threaten this city are not my concern. I leave matters I do not understand to those who do. My sole loyalty is to this house and its mistress, a young woman who is as dear to me as my own daughter."

The housekeeper's explanation, like her suggestion that she take her hot chocolate in the parlor, was accepted without hesitation. Frowning, Kat waved her hands about, gesturing at the clutter.

"It seems I've let things get a wee bit out of hand as of late. I so need to spend a day in here sorting through all of this."

"You've no need to apologize, Lady Trent," Mrs. Peel offered. "With everything that's been going on lately, we've all been preoccupied."

Giving her housekeeper a knowing glance, Kat smiled. "That, Mrs. Peel, is an understatement if ever I heard one."

After returning her mistress's smile, Mrs. Peel cocked a brow. "Shall I inform Gwyn you will be joining Mrs. Keating in the parlor then?"

Kat nodded. "Yes, please."

Satisfied with her mistress's decision, Mrs. Peel set the books she had been holding back on the table and left. When she was gone, Kat took a moment to assess the daunting task of bringing some semblance of order to her business affairs. Only when she concluded that would not be possible until the battle raging just outside her very front door had been decided did she make her way out of her study, pausing only long enough to lock the door behind her.

"Finding material such as this is becoming something of a challenge as of late," the seamstress opined as she and Sarah made their way through bolts of cloth Thomas McBride had personally brought to Minden Hall. "It will be a joy to work with it."

Coming upon a bolt of Persian blue silk, Sarah pulled it out from the pile. "This is exactly what I am looking for!" Turning to the seamstress, she held the material out to her. "Do you think you can fashion a robe à la française trimmed with robings of ruched fabric with this?"

Even from where she was sitting across the room, sipping on her hot chocolate, Kat could not miss the glint in the semester's eye.

"But of course, madam," the seamstress purred. "If you like, I can finish it off with a lace fichu about the neckline."

"With lace ruffles about the ends of the sleeves, it will be the perfect dress with which to greet James," Sarah proclaimed eagerly before turning to Kat and held the bolt of cloth up. "What do you think, Kat?"

Lowering her cup, Kat silently eyed the material as if studying its suitability. In point of fact, she was using this pause to frame a suitable answer. As much as she wanted to point out James might not take kindly to seeing his wife dressed in blue, she had no wish to spoil Sarah's cheerfulness. To keep from doing so, Kat did what she expected other women would do. Setting aside her cup, she leaned forward and reached out with her right hand. After running the tips of her fingers across the material Captain Mathis had procured in Cherbourg as an afterthought during his most recent visit to that port, Kat smiled.

"It will be perfect."

Pleased, Sarah turned back toward the seamstress. "When can you have this ready?"

The seamstress was still weighing her answer when Gwyn Jones slipped into the room. As she was making her way round the chair Kat was seated in, she shot Sarah a quick glance before turning to face Kat.

"Lady Trent, there is a gentleman who wishes to speak with you."

With a pot of tea untouched by Sarah and the seamstress engaged in an animated discussion of fashions and the quality of the material they were rummaging through, Kat saw no harm in inviting whoever it was at the door to join her there in the parlor. If the visitor did have matters he needed to discuss with her in private, they could adjourn to her study after she had fulfilled her duties as a hostess by affording him an opportunity to enjoy a cup of tea while she finished her hot chocolate. She therefore asked the maid to show the gentleman in as she was turning to refill her cup, paying little heed to the way the maid hesitated, casting a quick, nervous glance over to where Sarah was seated before withdrawing from the room to carry out her mistress's order.

An abrupt cession of chatter, followed by the nervous shuffling of booted feet behind her caused Kat to look up from her cup as she was about to take a sip and over to where Sarah was seated. The gleeful smile she had been wearing but a moment before was gone, replaced by a black, unflinching glare directed past Kat and toward the doorway. Taken aback, Kat twisted about in her seat and leaned over its arm to discover what had caused such a sudden change Sarah's demeanor.

From where he stood just inside the room, David Gray was unable to do little more than return his sister's stare as each attempted to determine how best to deal with the other. For his part, he was just as surprised by the sight of his sister as she was of him, though for entirely different reasons. Not having seen her in months, he was shocked by Sarah's drawn, pallid complexion and the amount of weight she had lost. She, on the other hand, was doing her best to sort through her own conflicting emotions. While glad her brother alive and well, the color of his coat reminded her he, and men like him, were the cause of her separation from James.

Fearing the two were on the verge of going at each other and eager to find out what the rebel army was going to do now that it had managed to escape the trap it had been in by retreating across the East River under the cover of night, Kat sprang to her feet.

"Sarah, why don't you and Dotty finish here while David and I withdraw to my study and chat. If you wish, you can join us when you're finished."

Whether she would was a question Kat did not wait to have answered. Instead, she hustled David out of the room, asking Mrs.

Peel if she would be so kind as to have Gwyn bring tea for her guest as she passed the housekeeper standing in the doorway of the parlor, ready to bodily place herself between brother and sister should the need arise.

-«««•»»»-

David waited until he and Kat were settled in the study before asking after his sister. Suspecting it was pointless to fudge the truth, especially since David was family, Kat sighed.

"It took me the better part of two days to drag your sister out of her room and another two before Peggy was able to make her presentable enough to pass Mrs. Peel's inspection before she would allow me take her out in public," Kat informed David as she used this opportunity to carefully study Sarah's brother.

Like so many of the soldiers who had returned from Long Island and were now busily preparing their men for what came next, David looked haggard and worn. Gone was his quick, boyish grin. In its place was an expression made all the more disheartening by the sadness Kat saw in his eyes.

"Well, I expect she'll be happy to learn James will be here in a few days," David finally muttered as if to himself.

"So you're leaving," Kat stated flatly. "Washington is abandoning the city."

David did not answer Kat's question at first, waiting to do so until Gwyn Jones had finished serving them and had withdrawn from the study and closed the double doors behind her as she went.

"We've no choice," he finally admitted after taking a sip of tea. "A strong force of British and Hessian troops landed at Kips Bay this morning. Rather than hold their ground, Douglas's militia fled. For General Putnam's division to remain here in the city and allow it to be trapped as we were on Brooklyn Heights would be the height of folly. Only this time, there'd be no escape, not with British warships prowling up and down the Hudson."

On hearing this, Kat placed her cup of hot chocolate on a side table, folded her hands in her lap, dropped her gaze, and sighed.

"Then it's over. We've lost."

Setting aside the beguiling young red head's use of the word *we* for the moment, David set his cup and saucer aside as well. Leaning forward, he regarded Kat with a steady, determined gaze.

"We lost a battle, Kat. Soon we'll lose this city. But that's all."

Drawing herself up, she returned his stare. "Remember who you're talking to. I'm not an empty-headed twit. I saw the rabble of an army that came back from Long Island, an army that has lost more to desertion these past few days then it did to the musketry of the King's soldiers. I've heard the grumblings of both officers and men alike who have lost faith in their cause and those leading it. In a few more weeks, Washington's army will be gone and with it, the free and independent country Mr. Jay and the others in Philadelphia proclaimed in July."

Making no effort to hide the disgust he felt over those who had given up all hope of victory, David huffed.

"Yes, many have turned their backs on our cause and gone home," he admitted bitterly. "But those of us who believe in what we're doing, those who are willing to dedicate their lives to the cause of independence are not about to let a single setback dissuade us from our chosen course."

She was tempted to point out the loss of New York would be crippling, perhaps even fatal, to a country made up of thirteen colonies with little in common and stitched together by men belonging to a congress whose authority over those former colonies was, at best, questionable. But she did not, not after peering into David's eyes and seeing that the sadness she had seen in them earlier had been replaced by a fierce determination. Once more dropping her gaze, she took up her cup of hot chocolate, using the time as she savored the warm, comforting taste of her favorite beverage to collect her thoughts while David did likewise. When they were finally able to continue, Kat asked him if this was just a social visit, or if he had been sent to inquire as to her willingness to extend additional credit to the army in order to replace the material and stores it had lost on Long Island.

"Both, I guess," he admitted sheepishly. "That and something else, something more important."

"Such as?"

Before answering, David cast a quick, leery glance over at the closed doors, then back at Kat. Leaning forward, he placed his elbows upon his knees, clasped his hands together, and began to explain why he had sought her out in a low whisper.

"General Washington intends to leave behind a small group of people here in the city who will be able to supply him with information concerning British plans and activities. As I'm familiar with who can be trusted, as well as who'll be in a position to gather the sort of information he will be interested in, I was asked to sound out those who might be willing to help."

Unable to help herself, Kat pulled away. Again, she had no need to ask her dearest friend's brother, a man who stood ready to continue the fight against her own cousin, to explain any further.

"We've already gone over this," Kat muttered as she looked away. "To jeopardize all I have for a cause in which few believe will last out the year would be the height of folly."

Unable to help himself, David allowed his emotions to get the better of him. Rearing up, he regarded Kat with a cool, contemptuous glare.

"Our cause is far from lost," he declared sharply. "I am asking you to make a stand. I am asking you to help us create something new—a nation where all men, and women, are free, free of the dictates of a king who's never laid eyes on this vast, untamed continent. Free to use their natural talents and ambitions to do what you have done in an astonishingly short period of time."

Setting her cup aside, Kat came to her feet, causing David to do likewise. "You ask too much of me," she repeated. "I am but a…"

Once more Kat found herself unable to finish a statement that was so simple, so natural for anyone else. As had occurred on the day Sarah had given birth to little James and Kitty, when confronted by a terrible truth she could hide but never dare forget, Kat had to leave the room least David see the tears this cruel dilemma never failed to evoke.

New York City
16 September 1776

The day Katherine Shields had been dreading was upon her. With the last of the rebel troops gone from the city, and those of the King firmly established on Manhattan, it was only matter of time before her husband would cross the threshold of a house her great-grandfather had built. Her apprehensions had nothing to do with the fear Thomas would call on her to fulfill her duties as a wife. She expected time not spent gadding about serving his King would be taken up with gambling, hunting, and drinking with his fellow officers. What did concern her, what drove her to ceaselessly pace to and fro in the front parlor, was the inquisition convened by representatives of the King who would demand she, and all who had lent support to the rebel cause during their occupation of the city, justify their treasonous behavior.

The idea of begging for mercy was dismissed out of hand. She was a Van der Hoff, the sole inheritor of a proud tradition that was as old as the city her Dutch ancestors had helped found. To her, representatives of the English King were no better than the men the rebel congress in Philadelphia had sent to milk all they could from the richest city in all the colonies. All of them were little more than intruders, meddling outsiders who passed through New York with little interest in it other than a desire to further their personal fortunes. Prostrating herself before such churlish ingrates was simply out of the question.

On reaching a window set furthest from the parlor's doorway, she stopped. Looking out onto the street, she watched a woman across the way scurrying along as if being chased by a demon. With one hand she clutched a sack to her chest that Katherine imagined contained flour she had somehow managed to worm from a shopkeeper's precious hoard. In the other, she gripped the small hand of a young girl who had to run to keep up with her mother's frantic pace.

Coming about, Katherine once more took up her pacing. Unlike the woman she'd been watching, she would not use her sex to justify her actions. While she was not above drawing upon the well-honed skills and charms others belonging to her gender relied on to achieve their ends, twittering gaily, batting her lashes, and carrying on like an empty-headed coquette was beneath her. In her eyes, such behavior only served to reinforce the low opinion men held to of a woman's ability to do little more than tend to domestic chores, look after the little bastards they had sired, and satisfy their carnal needs.

On reaching the closed door of the parlor, the only barrier she imagined that now lay between her and those who would hold her to account—men that would include her own husband—Katherine stopped. Hiding in the parlor of her home, wasting her time fretting over what was to come, was accomplishing nothing. In her wildest dreams, she could not picture her Dutch ancestors locking themselves away in the parlors of their homes when the English first came to New Amsterdam and claimed it as their own. They, and not the English, had been the victors. Through sheer force of will and an inherent stubbornness that allowed them to overcome obstacles that stood in their way, they had continued on as they always had and prospered.

Drawing in a deep breath, Katherine reached out and grasped the handles of the parlor's double doors. In the absence of her factor, she had needed to assume roles her father had done little to prepare her for. That she had been able to successfully navigate the tumultuous world of commerce and trade during the upheaval the war had created thus far had come as a pleasant surprise to her. Yet as astonishing as that realization was in retrospect, the sense of empowerment and freedom she had discovered while filling such an unconventional role had been illuminating.

Only now, when the old order was on the verge of reestablishing itself, returning the city to the way things had been, did the idea of giving up her new found independence by stepping away from the responsibilities circumstances had hoisted upon her did she realize doing so was more than unthinkable. How she would manage to keep from being stuffed back into a role she no longer wished to assume now that the status quo antebellum was in the offing was a challenge she would have to overcome—one she was ready to take on as she gave the doorknobs she was holding a quick turn and threw the doors open. Drawing herself up to her full height, she sallied forth, determined to make it clear to those who thought they were conquerors they were but guests in *her* city.

Harlem Heights
16 September 1776

The march up from Virginia had been far more wearing on Ezra Shaw than he had expected.

"I'm getting too old for this," he muttered to himself as he carefully slipped the shoe off his right foot.

On hearing this, other men gathered around the same fire he was seated at chuckled.

"You're not old, just well broken in, like those shoes of yours," James McPike quipped.

Shaw made something of a show of carefully inspecting the shoe before holding it up so the others about him could see the hole in its sole.

"In my book, laddie, this is what old looks like."

"I suppose next you'll be telling us we'll be needing to carry you in a sedan chair like they say old Ben Franklin is, carted about from place to place," another ventured.

Lowering the shoe he had been holding aloft, Shaw rested his elbows on his knees, leaned forward, and stared contemptuously at the speaker.

"The only time you, or any of these other miscreants here, will ever need to haul this wretched carcass of mine about is the day you carry me away to my grave."

"From the way you're griping, I expect that'll be any day now," a third declared to the delight of his companions.

Offended, Shaw glared at everyone gathered around the campfire as he spoke. "I'll march the lot of you into the ground long before that."

A sudden flurry of activity in the encampment occupied by the 3rd Virginia put an end to the lighthearted banter Shaw and the men with him had been enjoying. Not having heard the drummers belonging to their regiment tap out the long roll, none paid any attention to what their fellow Virginians were doing until Shaw saw Ian McPherson, musket in hand, rushing by.

"And where, may I ask, are you going in such a hell-fire hurry?" he asked as he continued to massage his foot.

"Major Leitch of the 3rd has been ordered to take three of his companies forward. They're going to outflank the redcoats some New Englanders have been trading shots with."

"So why in blue blazes are you going?"

"I didn't come all the way from Virginia to sit about a fire, moaning and groaning while rubbing my feet," Ian shot back without slowing his pace.

Shaw snorted scornfully, "If Colonel Washington wanted us to go off and join the 3rd, he'd have ordered us to."

Morgan McPherson, seated across the fire from Shaw, could not help but chuckle, as he did every time either he or his father referred to the man who commanded their army as Colonel Washington instead of General Washington.

Looking away from his animated lieutenant to Morgan, Shaw scowled. "If ya feel that way, take this boy of yours with you. I'm growing tired of listening to him complain about never having a chance to do anything but run errands for the adjutant."

Coming to a stop, Ian took to regarding Shaw with a hard, uncompromising glare. "No!"

"Yes," Morgan snapped as he took up his musket and rose to his feet. "I didn't come all this way just to go blind copying orders and filling out reports no one ever reads."

Ian turned his withering glare away from Shaw and over to the boy he and Megan had raised. He did not flinch, returning his father's cold, uncompromising stare. Shaw, seated between them, looked at one, then the other.

"If the two of you two damned fools are so hell-bent on running off and getting yourselves shot, you'd best get going before the lads in the 3rd get all the glory."

The faint rattle of musketry and an irresistible urge to have at soldiers of a King who had been the author of so much misfortune in his life put an end to Ian's efforts to keep his son from following.

"You're as stubborn as your mother," he growled bitterly. "If you're coming, then come. But stay close to me boy, you hear?"

"Like a tick on a hound," Morgan replied as he raced forward.

Shaw watched them go, wishing he was ten years younger and not as worn out by their march north as the soles of his shoes.

Staying to the left and a little behind the man who'd found him wandering in the forest of Virginia's western frontier was not a problem for Morgan. As a child he would scurry behind the man he called father whenever a stranger approached or if he heard a sound that evoked fearful memories he never spoke of. Later, when Ian took him hunting, or called on him to help mend a wheel, Morgan clung to him like a second shadow, carefully watching his father's every move—a habit that allowed him to master the skills he would need when it came time for him to venture forth into the world on his own. On this day, his reasons for keeping up with Ian as they made their way south along a wooded path that ran along the western shore of an island he had been told was named Manhattan was altogether different. Having no idea of what they were up to, he wanted to listen in as a New England ranger explained to his father, as best he could without slowing his pace, his commander's instructions. After thanking the ranger with nothing more than a quick nod, the two separated.

Eager to learn what the ranger had said, Morgan drew closer to his father. "Well?"

"Well what?" Ian shot back without looking back at his son or breaking stride.

"What did he say?"

This time Ian gave Morgan a quick, quizzical glance over his shoulder before once more facing front and taking care to watch where he stepped.

"Did you not hear what the man said?"

The hurried pace Colonel Thomas Knowlton was setting for his rangers caused Ian and Morgan to pause midsentence and gasp for breath as they carried on their exchange.

"I did… but I could not understand… a single word… he said," Morgan replied plaintively as he quickened his pace to keep up with his father.

The boy's response caused Ian to chuckle. Having grown up on the fringes of civilization, Morgan had not found the need to work alongside men and women from other colonies who spoke the King's English with accents the untutored ear could easily mistake for a foreign language.

"Ya can whisper sweet nothings in German to the Richter girl and yet ya can't understand what a New Englander is saying?"

Angered by his father's reminder of how he carried on when he was with Gretchen Richter, Morgan's cheeks, already tinted crimson by their exertions, burned brighter.

"What did the man say?" he snapped in a single, quick breath.

Deciding this was not the time to have fun at his son's expense, Ian passed on what he had been able to understand during his exchange with the New Englander.

"Knowlton and his rangers traded shots with the English vanguard just after dawn. After a while, when they'd had enough, they retreated across a hollow near Harlem Heights where we're encamped."

Coming upon a tangle of brambles he needed to carefully pick his way through, Ian ceased his narrative, continuing only when he was clear of the obstruction and Morgan had caught up to him. "Colonel Washington ordered some troops to draw..." A low branch caused Ian to duck when he was in midsentence. "He's ordered some troops to draw the redcoats off the high ground they're on," he continued once clear of the branch. "That's the shooting you're hearing off to our left."

Ian paused as he cocked an ear and listened for a moment to the sporadic outbursts of musketry that managed to drift its way through the forest they were moving through.

"The rangers and three companies of the 3rd are to come up around behind the redcoats and trap 'em between us."

Satisfied he understood what they were up to, Morgan gave his father a quick nod even though Ian could not see it. He was focused on keeping up with the men belonging to the company he had attached himself to as they sought out the English rear.

As so often happens in war, Washington's plan did not play out exactly as he had hoped. The British advance guard, consisting of a battalion of light infantry and highlanders belonging to the 42nd Regiment of Foot, did accept the challenge from troops from Nixon's brigade of continentals and moved forward into an open hollow between Bloomingdale Heights and Harlem Heights. They pulled back, however, when Washington reinforced Nixon's line. Unaware of this, when Colonel Knowlton reached the western edge of Bloomingdale Heights, instead of finding himself in the enemy's rear, he fell upon their left flank. This brought the advance of his rangers and the Virginians under Major Leitch to a precipitous halt. Without needing to pull back and assess the situation, the two commanders ordered their men to fan out to the left and right and fire on their startled foe.

With his attention riveted to the broken ground they were traversing, least he stumble over a stump or become entangled in vines, Morgan did not notice his father had stopped until he plowed into him. The sharp reprimand he expected as he was taking a step back did not come. Only when he took the time to look past Ian did Morgan see a gaggle of highlanders backing away from a stone wall they had been using as cover and face about in an effort to meet the new threat looming large and at close quarters to their left.

Never having laid eyes on kilted highlanders before, Morgan exclaimed in awe, "Those are Scots, like you."

"Aye, they're Scots," Ian growled bitterly at the sight of men who had once been his fellow countrymen. "But don't ever think they're like me," he continued even as he was cocking his musket and raising it to his shoulder. "They're no better than the Campbell's who murdered the MacDonalds of Glencoe. Feckless curs, the lot of 'em."

With that, Ian took aim and fired.

In a quick, easy motion, Ian brought his weapon down, reached behind his back with his right hand to fish a fresh round from his cartridge box, and began the intricate task of reloading. He was halfway finished doing so when he noticed Morgan was standing motionless next to him, staring wide-eyed at the fearsome warriors in kilts and feathered bonnets who, but a generation ago, had been England's fiercest foe.

"Are ya just going to stand there and gawk, ya wee fool?" Ian barked in an effort to be heard above the growing din of battle.

By way of response, Morgan brought his musket up to the ready, jerked the hammer back to full cock with his thumb, and checked the pan to make sure the priming powder had not spilled during their flanking march. Satisfied all was in order, he tucked the musket firmly into his shoulder and took aim at the first red-coated Scot the front blade of his weapon's sight fell on. Caught up in the excitement of the moment and hurried on by the rapid pounding of his heart, he gave no thought to the realization he was about to kill a man. He simply squeezed the trigger as he had been taught and fired.

TWENTY-ONE

"The Hessians are continually plundering and are countenanced by their general; and General Howe dares not punish them for fear of producing a general mutiny."

Letter from an American officer
Harlem Heights
25 September 1776

New York
17 September 1776

BEFORE SHE SAW James, before he had a chance to even rein his horse in just outside the window of her study, Kat knew he had returned. All but tossing aside the book she had been struggling to read in a vain effort to keep herself occupied, she sprang to her feet. By the time she'd reached the study's doors and threw them open, James was standing in the middle of the foyer, his eyes darting about like a lost child desperately seeking his mother.

When he saw Kat standing in the open doorway, he rushed over to her. Both tossed aside all decorum and pretense as he scooped her up in a crushing embrace and twirled her about.

"Dear God, Kat, I cannot tell you how pleased I am to see you."

Kat held nothing back as she returned his fierce hug with all the strength she could muster. Pulling her head back as far as she could, she returned his beaming smile.

"Not near as glad as I am to see you return healthy and whole."

Following a second hug that was no less enthusiastic than the first, James set her down but held onto her forearms as if fearful she was but an apparition that would vanish the second he let go.

"Sarah! How is she? Where is she?"

From the top of the staircase, Sarah cried out in a small voice, "I'm here, James. I'm here."

She was breathless as she all but flew down the stairs and into her husband's waiting arms. For a long, lingering minute, the two were inseparable, greedily drinking in the frenzied flurry of kisses each showered upon the other. Not knowing what else to do, Kat averted her gaze as she stepped away. In doing so, a sudden and totally unexpected chill caused her to shiver as a bout of melancholy crowded out the joy of the moment.

Clasping her hands before her, Kat peeked up at the scene before her. James, resplendent in his scarlet and gold trimmed uniform coat, was all but engulfing Sarah who was attired in a blue gown gaily trimmed with white lace about the bodice and three-quarter sleeves. Each held nothing back, freely giving themselves over to their passions in a manner Kat knew she would never be able to give herself over to. In a world in which the ebb and flow of events had all but banished any certainty, the only thing Kat found she could be sure of was that she would never be free to enjoy an embrace such as the one playing out between two people she dearly cared for. Not even in a city where men like John Jay claimed all things were possible if a person had the courage to put forth the effort needed to realize their fondest dreams, Kat knew the freedom he and David Gray were fighting for had its limits. They were simply rebelling against a king. She, on the other hand, was defying the very society both Englishmen and Americans sought to govern.

In an effort to keep the melancholy she felt over this awful truth from casting a shadow upon her cousin's joyous homecoming, Kat withdrew unnoticed back into her study. There, she did as she always did whenever dark thoughts threatened to overwhelm her: she kept herself busy.

-⋘⋄⋙-

It was not until later that evening, after Sarah had excused herself to help Mrs. Wren settle the children in for the night, that James was able to speak to Kat in private. He wasted no time getting to the nub of the concerns he had managed to keep to himself throughout the day.

"She's not been well, has she?" James asked as he stared down at the glass of Madeira he was holding.

Having expected this moment to come, Kat set aside the glass of wine she had been nursing and clasped her hands in her lap, staring down at them as she took a second to reflect on how best to answer her cousin. The whole truth would not do, she decided as she peeked up at him.

"As you can well imagine, from the minute you left for Boston, Sarah has worried about you. At first she was able to muddle along after a fashion. But, then, the children came and, well, things became difficult for her."

"Is not the nurse you hired doing a proper job of looking after their needs?" James asked pointedly.

"She is," Kat responded crisply. "Do you think she would still be in our employ if things were otherwise?"

"No, of course not," James muttered sheepishly when he realized just how foolish his question had been. Pausing, he took a sip of his Madeira in an effort to allow Kat's pique to fade. "I imagine the rebels have been quite cruel to her," he ventured cautiously as if unsure if his cousin was ready to continue their discussion. "She wrote to me of her fears after they had ransacked the shop you so generously gave her."

The flurry of anger that had overcome her was replaced by a somber, almost sorrowful grimace.

"She was not the only person who suffered at the hands of those who sought to punish anyone who did not embrace their cause. If the person himself was not within their reach, miscreants and ruffians who fancied themselves patriots sought vengeance upon those who remained loyal to the King by destroying the property they left behind. Though I tried to protect all of your father's business concerns here in the city, some fell prey to the mob."

"But none of yours, or so I've been informed."

Despite being careful to couch his observation in a non-accusatory manner, Kat could not help but appreciate James was alluding to the manner with which her various concerns had escaped retribution and reprisal. Doing her best to keep her mounting apprehensions in check, she rose from her seat, took up her glass, and made her way to the side table where the decanter of Madeira was.

"I was more fortunate than most," she responded without bothering to look over to where James was watching as she refilled her glass even though it was far from empty.

"Rumors abound, dear cousin. Rumors that claim your good fortune involved more than luck."

With a calmness that belied the mounting concern she was struggling to keep in check, Kat ever so slowly made her way back to her seat. Only when was once more settled and had taken a long, lingering sip of Madeira did she bother to look over at James who had been watching her every move.

"Am I being accused of being in league with the rebels?" she asked smoothly as a wisp of a smile tugged at the corners of her lips.

"Are you?"

"Cousin James, even if I were, I'd be a fool to admit to such a thing."

"Umm, quite right."

"Do you believe these rumors?" Kat asked, doing her best to make her question sound as if she were trying to make light of the accusations James was putting forth.

Unable, or perhaps unwilling to, he did not answer. Setting his glass aside, he came to his feet.

"It's been a long and tiring day," he declared. "I expect tomorrow will be no less demanding."

Seizing upon this opportunity to change the topic, Kat gave her cousin a sly little grin as she regarded him out of the corner of her eye.

"I do hope it's not been too tiring for you. I expect at this very minute Sarah is… um, how should I put this… preparing herself to show you just how happy she is that you have returned."

Unable to keep his eagerness to rush upstairs and into the embrace of his wife contained, James winked. "Yes, well, I think the time has come to find out just how happy she is. And you?" he asked before turning away. "Are you happy to once more have me back?"

"Of course I am," Kat replied in truth despite the conversation they had just shared.

As she had anticipated, the manner in which Major Jonathan Lowe III questioned Kat the following day about her dealings with the rebels during their occupation of the city was far more direct than James's had been. Whether the imperious little prig was attempting to intimidate her by conducting himself as if he were the Inquisitor General of Spain, or he was, by nature, little more than an insufferable toady did not matter to Kat. All that did was her ability to convince him her behavior and business dealings over the last few months had been above reproach. Failing that, she needed to do what she could to deflect attention away from her sympathies for the rebel cause—leanings that were at odds with the city's new masters.

This was not easy, for the questions he peppered her with were quite detailed and shockingly so. Within minutes, Kat realized whoever had supplied the major with information about her business affairs was intimately familiar with them. She felt relieved she had taken the precaution of using the Bank of Amsterdam to underwrite the activities of Captain Mathis and the privateer she was sole owner of and he, Dutch merchants to take whatever English goods he seized off his hands. That, and the rich pickings he found just off the Thames Estuary brought a smile to Kat's face, one that caused Major Lowe to pause in the middle of a question.

"Excuse me, Lady Trent, but may I ask what you find so amusing about my questions?" Lowe asked, making no effort to curb the ire he felt at the manner with which she had been treating him all morning.

Realizing she had allowed her thoughts to stray onto dangerous territory, Kat hastened to catch herself on. In doing so, she seized upon Lowe's tone of voice to turn the tables on him and hopefully bring an end to his insufferable questioning. Drawing herself up, she tilted her head back ever so slightly until she was peering at the King's dutifully appointed representative down the bridge of her nose.

"Well, if you must know, I find this farce of yours rather ridiculous, not to mention a waste of my time and yours," she declared haughtily.

"I hardly think questioning the possibility of conspiring with rebels to be a waste of time."

Rising off her chair, Kat drew herself up to her full height as she took to glaring down at Lowe through angry, narrow slits.

"How dare you," she hissed. "How dare you come into this house and accuse me of treason against the King. Other than rumors and lies spread by those who might find my success as a merchant to be an affront to them, or competitors who are seeking to drive me out of business, what proof do you have that I have been disloyal to the crown? I demand you provide me with evidence—real evidence—as well as the names of those who are accusing me of treason this instant."

Startled, and thoroughly unhinged by the way Kat went from behaving in a manner expected of a woman of her standing to lashing out at him as if he were an errant subaltern, Lowe was reduced to stammering as he sprang to his feet.

"Lady Trent, I… I mean no offense. Nor am I accusing you of treason. It's just that I… ah… I am trying to…"

"Yes?" Kat snapped with as much indignation in her voice as she could manage.

Flustered, Lowe dropped his gaze as his eyes took to madly darting about the statements laid out on the table before him as if searching for a suitable answer.

"It's just that your business agent, this Mr. Parkman, a man who handled your day-to-day affairs, seems to have been in league with the rebels."

"Seems to be?" Kat snapped. "Seems to be?" she repeated sharply for emphasis. "Are you telling me you are basing these scurrilous accusations against me on nothing more than fanciful suppositions fabricated by my detractors?"

When the flustered major did not respond, Kat leaned over, planting her fists on the table separating her and Major Lowe.

"Hear me and hear me well, *Major*. I have every intention of taking this matter up with General Howe. And if he is unable to provide me with a satisfactory explanation as to why I'm being treated like this, I shall write to the King himself and ask how it is one of his officers—a rather common one at that, with neither title or property other than what he carries about in his saddlebags with his dirty linen—assumes to have the right to insult a member of the peerage and the child of an officer who gave his life in the service of the crown."

With that Kat straightened up, threw her head back, sniffed, spun about, and stormed out of the room.

James, who had been watching from a corner of the room, found it difficult to keep his laughter in check. Once his cousin was gone, he looked over to where Major Lowe stood. He was clearly stunned and totally flummoxed by the sudden turn of events. When he saw that the man was not at all sure what to do, James cleared his throat.

"I think it might be best if I saw what I could do to mollify my cousin. Though I am not at all sure if I will succeed in placating her after the way you behaved, I will do my best to see if she will accept your apologies and allow this matter to be forgotten." Then, hesitating just as he was turning to leave, James looked back at Lowe. "That is assuming you wish to apologize."

Still rather rattled, Lowe shooed James along with a dismissive wave of his hand. "Yes, yes, of course. Go. Do what you can."

Though he still had his doubts about his cousin and where her loyalties really did lie, James could not help but chuckle to himself once he had left the room. If nothing else, Cousin Kat was still as fiery as her red hair and just as devilishly fun in her own unique way as she had been before the war. And if there was something James needed now more than anything else, it was something to smile about. For while many of his fellow officers took comfort in the belief the rebels were all but whipped, he understood the American character. They, like Kat, were not easily brushed aside or cowered by a little adversity. If anything, their stiff-necked pride and tenacity allowed them to draw strength from hardship. They had a knack of finding opportunity in the challenges that were part of their daily lives. Like his cousin's determination to fashion a life for herself on her own terms, this war—a war that would once more tear him away from his beloved Sarah—was far from over.

"Kat?" he called out as he knocked on the door of her study. "Kat, could I have a word with you?"

Opening the door a crack, Kat peeked out. "Has that disgusting little toady gone yet?" she asked in a whisper as she attempted to look out and into the foyer past her cousin.

"No, not yet, but only because he's still doing his best to collect his wits." Pausing, James did his best to make his next comment come across as being serious, but failed miserably. "I fear Major Lowe is rather shaken. It seems he's not at all used to being talked to like that, especially by a woman."

"Well, if he intends to stay in New York, he had best get used to it."

Unable to help himself, James chuckled. "Has anyone told you you're a wicked little minx?"

"Yes, you," Kat replied as her expression finally gave way to a broad grin. "Now, march on in here like a good officer of grenadiers and tell me everything that little weasel said after I left the room."

Hessian Encampment, New York
17 September 1776

Hauptmann Kleist was in the middle of inspecting the picket line his company was deployed along when a messenger dispatched from brigade informed him he was to report to his colonel. Such a summons, delivered to an officer whose company was in close proximity to the enemy was never a good thing. Kleist carefully mentally reviewed the activities of his men since they had disembarked on the island of Manhattan as he made his way back to camp.

He arrived at his colonel's tent without being able to divine the nature of the infraction he or his company was guilty of. Coming to a halt before the open flap of the tent, he waited for his colonel to look up from the letter he was writing. To Kleist's surprise, when his colonel finally did take notice of him, he winked.

"Good, good," the colonel muttered by way of greeting. "I shall be with you in a moment."

Confusion replaced the concern the captain of jägers had been troubled by as he watched his colonel scratch out a few more words before setting the quill aside. Coming to his feet, the colonel lifted the letter and blew away the excess dust. When he finally turned his attention to Kleist, he did do so without taking his eyes off the missive on which he had been working.

"A report to our prince," he declared when he finally looked over to where Kleist was still standing just outside the entrance to his tent. "I mentioned you by name in it twice," he declared proudly as he held the letter up. "Once for the élan and skill you demonstrated on Long Island, and again for the alacrity your men displayed in rushing to the aid of the British vanguard yesterday."

"I thank you, Herr Colonel," Kleist replied cautiously, for he knew he would not have been called away from his duties simply to listen to his colonel sing his praises.

Taking note of Kleist's guarded demeanor, the colonel decided it would be best if he disposed of the annoying matter he had been charged with tending to without further ado. After setting the letter back down on his field desk, he took up his hat and donned it.

"If you would be so kind as to accompany me, Herr Hauptmann, there is another subject I find I need to discuss with you."

"Yes, of course, Herr Colonel," Kleist replied glumly as he prepared himself as best he could to be reprimanded for an indiscretion or failure on his part that he had unwittingly committed.

The two officers slowly walked in silence for several long minutes, weaving between the well-ordered rows of vacant tents belonging to the brigade. During that time, the colonel attempted to discover how best to broach a subject that the British found to be vexing, but one he, himself, would have hesitated to burden one of his officers with had they been on campaign in Germany.

"I expect some of your men are finding the English and their ways to be… oh, how can I put this… strange."

"They are not alone, Herr Colonel. I, myself, am having some difficulties understanding why the English are behaving as they are, particularly in regard to their treatment of subjects who have taken up arms against their sovereign lord."

"I must remind you, not all the American colonists are rebels, Kleist. I have been told most are unfalteringly loyal to their sovereign lord—men who have no wish to be separated from him."

Though still unsure where this exchange was going, Kleist sensed his colonel was open to hearing his thoughts on the matter.

"If that is true, then these American colonists have a strange way of showing their gratitude to soldiers belonging to an army that has rid them of the troublemakers and miscreants who brought this war to their doorstep. I have seen the way they hold back when English soldiers march by. There is no joy in their faces, no indication that they are relieved to be free of men who fancy themselves patriots."

"I have been reminded more than once by officers on General Howe's staff these colonists are not used to seeing soldiers parading past their doorstep. They are ignorant of war, in particular our manner of waging it. Which brings me to my reason for calling you away from your duties."

Relieved to be putting an end to the verbal sparring they had been engaged in, Kleist prepared himself as best he could for what was about to befall him.

"I am listening, Herr Colonel."

"It seems some of your men forced themselves upon a young woman before you were called away yesterday to deal with the rebel attack on the English vanguard."

"Is this woman positive they were my men?"

"I was told by the officer sent by the English provost marshal all she could say for sure was that the three men who took her were Germans attired in green."

"My men are not the only jägers, Herr Colonel," Kleist was quick to point out.

"No, they are not. But the reason I am sure they were your men is due to the fact the alleged incident took place in an area where a detachment of your men had been foraging."

His colonel's certainty and snippets of conversations he had overheard while making his way among the campfires of his company the night before caused Kleist to cringe.

"I shall look into the matter at once, Herr Colonel."

By way of response, the colonel waved off Kleist's offer with an airy wave of his hand, "There is no need. I expect the matter will be forgotten as soon as the English general decides the time has come to stop treating these Americans as if they were naughty children and begins to suppress this insurrection with the vigor and ruthlessness it deserves."

Pleased to hear this, Kleist nodded. His men, after all, were soldiers who expected to be free to avail themselves of the spoils all soldiers are entitled to enjoy in the wake of a victory. That the English somehow did not understand this was their problem. His was keeping his men in hand, after a fashion, and ready to follow him into battle without question or hesitation.

New York
17 September 1776

Despite an overwhelming desire to make it clear to her husband she was not at all pleased he had invited his fellow officers to dine with them without first consulting her, Katherine Shields went out of her way to play the attentive and gracious hostess. There was, of course, more to her decision not to make an issue of what was, in retrospect, nothing more than an inconvenience. Having engaged in commerce with representatives of the rebel army during its occupation of New York, she needed to do all she could to demonstrate she never wavered from her loyalty to the King. The one time the subject was brought up by a very self-righteous major who was aware of her activities, Katherine responded in a manner she had spent a full hour rehearsing.

"What, may I ask, would you have had me do, major?" she countered in a soft, dulcet tone as she gently placed the tips of the fingers on her left hand lightly against the bare flesh just above her bosom in an effort to draw the major's eyes, and with them his thoughts, away from a subject she wished to avoid. "It was either treat with those scurrilous scoundrels on terms that were nothing short of thievery or lose all I had." Bringing her hand down, she lowered her chin a smidge so that she was now looking at the officer she was addressing through her lashes. "No doubt you've seen for yourself what they did to the homes and shops of those who fled rather than forsake their King."

"Yes. Yes, I have, madam," the major replied thoughtfully without taking his eyes off the spot where Katherine had moments before rested her hand.

"And woe be to the rascals responsible for despoiling this fair city," a captain at the far end of the table proclaimed lustily.

"Here, here," another captain across from him chimed in as he all but jumped to his feet and raised his wine glass high in salute to his fellow officer's declaration.

Eager to add their voices, the other officers, resplendently attired from head to toe in their finest uniforms, took up their glasses and joined the spontaneous toast. By the time they had resumed their places and turned their attention back to the feast Katherine's cook had spent the entire day preparing, the subject that had led to the outburst had been all but forgotten.

What was not forgotten by Katherine was her husband's behavior earlier that day when, on entering the home that had been in her family for generations, he had conducted himself as if he was her master and not simply a man who was her husband in name only. Determined to remind him he, like the armies vying for possession of the city were, in her eyes, little more than annoying travelers passing through it, after the main course was over and as the table was being cleared, she looked down the length of the table at Thomas and cleared her throat in an effort to gain his full attention.

"The presence of the rebel army did afford me one blessing," she declared brightly. "It allowed me to spend time with our son when he wasn't otherwise occupied by his duties."

"*Your* son," Thomas shot back as the color rose in his cheeks. "That treasonous wretch is no son of mine."

Acutely aware the mention of their host's only son was a subject no one dare mention in his presence, the room was gripped by a deathly silence. Wearing expressions that reminded one officer of men staring at the burning fuse of a mortar shell, all seated at the table warily eyed their host and hostess. For her part, Katherine paid no attention to them as she busied herself delicately rearranging the few pieces of silverware that remained before her. Thomas, on the other hand, was perched on the edge of his seat, glaring at his wife as he waited for her to continue.

"As distasteful as you find Edward's politics, he is your son—your only son," she added as she peeked up at him.

"I will not suffer to hear that name mentioned in my presence."

"He is your son!"

"He is a traitor!"

"This war will not last forever," Katherine informed her husband in a dismissive tone. "Like all wars before it, it will end. When it does, I expect you will lay aside your sword, and Edward his musket, and I the responsibilities I have been forced to take on, leaving us free to find a way of making things right between us."

Slowly, in a manner that reminded Katherine of a stubborn mule shaking its head to shoo away annoying flies, Thomas shook his head.

"Treason against our King cannot be swept aside and forgotten."

"Would you put loyalty to *your* King above your duty as a father?"

Tiring of this exchange, Thomas pushed away from the table and came to his feet. Throwing his head back, he fixed his wife in a steady, unflinching stare.

"Yes!" he nearly yelled before pivoting about on his heels and leaving the room before Katherine had an opportunity to respond.

Katherine was unruffled by her husband's behavior. She had, in fact, counted on it. She reasoned to have done otherwise in the presence of his fellow officers would have left them wondering if they could trust his judgment when it came to dealing with the rebels.

After waiting for her guests to recover from the shock of seeing their host storm out of the room, Katherine took to looking about the table at them.

"My cook has prepared a marvelous cherry tart for dessert," she declared brightly. "Would you gentlemen care for some?"

Encampment of the 1st New York, Harlem Heights 17 September 1776

On returning from picket duty just after sunset, Edward Shields made his way from campfire to campfire looking for his messmates. When he found them, he settled on the ground next to Kevin Farrell, lay aside his musket, and, with a whispered "thank you," accepted a steaming bowl of stew they had been saving for him.

Instinctively, Edward brought the bowl up to his nose and sniffed it. Unable to identify the aroma, he looked over at Joshua Cooper. As he had worked in an inn and tavern down by the city's docks that catered to sailors and stevedores, Cooper did all the cooking for the men gathered about the fire.

"What is it?" Edward asked as he tipped the bowl slightly in an effort to examine its content using the light thrown off by the fire.

"Supper," Cooper informed him gruffly.

"I know that," Edward declared peevishly as he gave his friend a dirty look. "What's in it?"

"This and that," the cook replied as he rose up on his haunches, took up a wooden spoon, and stirred the contents of a blackened cook pot hanging over the fire.

Concluding Cooper was not going to give him a straight answer and guessing it was probably best if he did not know the contents of the stew, Edward dropped the subject and fished about in his haversack with one hand for his spoon. Pulling it out, he wiped the hand-carved horn spoon on his pant leg and took to enjoying his meal as best he could.

"Have you heard?" a boy named Collins seated across the fire asked Edward as he was blowing on a spoon full of stew to cool it.

"Heard what?"

"Archie's gone for sure," the boy replied. "Took his musket and blanket and snuck out of camp while you were gone."

"No loss there," Farrell grumbled as he jabbed a stick into the center of the fire, causing a flurry of sparks to rise up into the chilly night sky. "The man was worthless. Did nothin' but gripe."

"He wasn't a total slouch," Collins countered. "There was no one better than Archie at finding food when there was none to be had."

"A good thing too, since he ate most of what he brought in," Cooper growled contemptuously as he resumed his seat.

Unfazed by his messmates' less than charitable remarks about the latest member of their company to desert, Collins continued. "Where do you suppose he'll go?"

"To hell, I hope—provided the devil will have him," another man ventured.

Feeling sorry for the abuse the others were piling on Collins who had been Archibald Cole's only friend in the regiment, Edward looked over at Collins after enjoying a few spoons full of stew as best he could.

"I can tell you where he's not going. He'd be a fool if he tried to sneak back into the city. From where I was posted, I could see a line of redcoat watch fires stretching from the East River to the Hudson."

"If I was him, I'd head for the Mohawk Valley," Collins mused as he held his empty bowl out to Cooper.

"This will be your second helping, boy," the cook grumbled even as he was taking the bowl to refill it.

"Enjoy while you can," Farrell added. "If this plays out the way things did when we were in Canada, we've many a hungry day to look forward to."

The memory of that misbegotten campaign and an appreciation they would be fighting the British well into the fall and perhaps even the winter caused Edward to shiver. Determined to eat all he could while there was something still to eat, he turned his full attention to the stew in his bowl. There would be another battle before the year was out. That much he was certain. What he, or anyone else in his small circle of friends could never be sure of was whether there would be food for them to share.

TWENTY-TWO

"Had I been left to the dictates of my own judgment, New York should have been laid to ashes before I quit it... Providence, or some good honest Fellow, has done more for us than we were disposed to do for ourselves, as near One fourth of the City is supposed to be consumed."

George Washington,
A letter to his cousin, Lund Washington III
6 October 1776

New York

Just after midnight, 21 September 1776

THE NIGHT ABOARD the *Swallow* and the terrible events that led up to the death of her sister were the first things in Kat's mind just before the sound of someone pounding on her bedroom door catapulted her from a fitful sleep. The pungent smell of smoke was the second.

"Lady Katherine! You must wake up. Lady Katherine!"

In the dim light of a single candle, Kat slipped out of bed, grabbed the robe she always kept near at hand, and wrapped herself in it as she made for the door. Unlocking it, she threw it open.

"Is the house afire?"

Wide-eyed and trembling from head to toe, Peggy Andrews gave her head a quick shake. "No ma'am. The city is."

-«««•»»»-

The sound of booted feet pounding up the stairs and down the hall, followed by someone hammering on the door of her husband's room, woke Katherine Shields from a sound sleep. Rolling over onto her side, she grabbed her pillow to cover her head in the hopes it would muffle the racket of the officers Thomas had been carousing with earlier that evening. Entertaining such men in an appropriate manner was one thing—an annoying necessity she expected she would need to endure if she and her interests were to survive during the troubled times that had befallen her beloved city. Putting up with a house full of drunkards who carried on well past midnight as if her home were a dockside tavern was quite another—a matter she was determined to address with Thomas in the morning.

A loud, excited exchange between two men in the hall just outside her door, one of whom Katherine identified as her husband, was the last straw. Tossing aside the pillow she had been using in a vain to muffle revelry that only seemed to be mounting, Katherine threw off her quilt.

"I'll not stand for this!" she spat as she slipped out of bed and made ready to go out into the hall where she intended to have it out with Thomas.

Before she was able to reach the chair where her robe was draped, the door of her bedroom flew open, and Thomas, dressed in only his breeches and shirt, rushed in.

Assuming the worst, Katherine drew back. She was about to warn him to stop right where he was when, of his own accord, he did. For a brief, terrifying moment, she watched as he swept aside his unbound hair from his face. When he finally did speak, his words tumbled out between quick gulps of breath.

"Get dressed as quick as you can, then come down."

Confusion replaced the fear Thomas's abrupt intrusion had evoked. Staring at him as he stood in the open doorway across the room from her, Katherine at first thought she was imagining things. Rather than being dressed in a snowy white linen shirt and breeches that were as much a part of a British officer's uniform as was his distinctive, eye-catching coat, her husband was attired, from head to toe, in red. Even his face was illuminated with ominous tones of crimson. Then, with the suddenness of a thunderclap, Katherine realized it was the flickering of light pouring through the window behind her, bathing him and all in the room in an unnatural hue. Spinning about, she gasped when she saw the stately home just across from hers was totally engulfed in flames.

"Katherine, please hurry," Thomas called out to her. "We must be away before the fire spreads to this side of the street."

Quickly coming about, she saw her husband was holding his hand out to her.

"No!" she responded impulsively.

"You must," Thomas shot back. "The whole west side of the city is being consumed."

"I refuse to abandon this house."

"Katherine, don't be foolish. It's only a house."

"Not to me. If you must, go."

Realizing his wife would never leave a home that was, to her, the very symbol of her proud heritage caused Thomas to slowly lower his proffered hand. He knew something about pride and the power it had over a person who placed more value on something that was intrinsically more important to them than life itself. For him, it was King and country. For her, a city her ancestors had founded and a heritage of achievement she would one day pass onto her son—their son, he reminded himself—come what may.

"If that be the case, get dressed," he ordered in the calmest voice circumstances and the need for haste permitted. "I shall gather the staff and anyone I can dragoon to fight for this house for as long as we can." He made ready to turn but stopped when he was halfway out the door. "I cannot promise you we can save it, but I will do my best."

Caught off guard by Thomas's unexpected commitment to stand with her, Katherine made to thank him but was too late, for he was already gone. He was, she reminded herself, a soldier, a unique breed of men who did not waste time dithering, debating, and squabbling as her father and his cronies had been in the habit of doing before deciding any matter—no matter how trivial. Thomas did what he believed needed to be done and did it. For the first time since they had married, she realized that it was a commendable attribute, one for which she was grateful at times such as these.

After seeing to it his wife, their children, and Kat were up and ready to flee at a moment's notice if the fire jumped Broadway, James headed out into the chaotic night. He was in search of a way to help save a city that was more than a prize to the King's forces and a key in controlling the American colonies; it was his home.

On reaching the sidewalk in front of Minden Hall, he paused before going any further. Charging off willy-nilly without a firm grasp of the situation would have been beyond foolish. As in battle, he understood he needed to take the time to assess the situation confronting him, as quickly and completely as circumstances permitted before acting. So, he stood there, looking up and down the length of Broadway. The entire southern ward of the city, or most of it, was burning, as was much of the western ward. Driven by a wind coming from the south, the fire was making its way from house to house. As if to confirm this, the windows of a house on the west side of the street not far from where he was standing blew out into the street in a shower of shards that twinkled and glittered in the light of the roaring flames now spewing from the doomed structure. If he was going to have any hope of keeping that from happening to Minden Hall, he would need help. For that, he headed to where the docks and wharfs were located. If there were men who could be bribed, cajoled, or shammed into joining him in what could very well be a hopeless endeavor, he would find them there.

New York
22 September 1776

Standing before the charred, tumbled down remains of The Curious Mind, Kat found it took every bit of effort she could muster to keep her tears in check. It was gone. More than simply a building and its contents had been lost to the fire that had swept through the city, consuming a full quarter of all its buildings in a single night. For Kat, the loss of her beloved bookstore and all it contained was a tragedy. In her mind, the flames had carried away more than simple paper and print, both of which she knew could be replaced. What pained her and reduced her to despair was the loss of the collective wisdom contained within those books, along with the tales of high adventure explorers. She wondered if this was this how the Ancients had felt when the Great Library of Alexandria had been destroyed.

She was still standing there, lost in her thoughts, when she felt a gentle hand upon her shoulder.

"When I heard the news, I knew I'd find you here," James murmured sympathetically as he came up beside her.

Kat did not bother to look over at her cousin as he drew her into him and she laid her head upon his shoulder. "I know I should drop to my knees and thank the Lord on high that this is all I lost. But I can't. I…"

The trickle of tears she had grudgingly permitted gave way to a torrent, cutting short her efforts to express her feelings in words. Appreciating it was up to him to help his cousin move on, James ever so gently brought her around and led her away from the ruins of her most prized possession. He knew she would rebound from this tragedy. At least he hoped she would. The news he had to share with her would be almost as difficult for Kat as had the loss of her bookstore, the jewel in her crown that was Minden Hall.

In a manner that separated those innkeepers who simply tended to the needs of their clientele and the ones who were cherished, Elizabeth Tuck saw to it there was a fresh carafe of hot chocolate, freshly baked scones, and a pot of apple butter sitting on Kat's favorite table even before she and James had taken a seat. None of that would do a thing to mitigate the loss of her bookshop. They, and the slavish attention Linda Tuck lavished upon her at the expense of the other patrons did, however, go a long way in reviving Kat's spirits. Accordingly, James hoped Kat would be more amenable to a decision he had made earlier that morning. But, before he had an opportunity to inform her of it, Kat had asked James how her uncle's property had faired.

"Rather well, I am pleased to say," he responded as he set his cup of tea down. "All of his commercial interests were untouched by the fire. Though one of his warehouses was broken into and robbed of everything that could be carried away during the ensuing chaos. Like you, he's luckier than many."

"Hmmm. Do I detect a 'but' neatly tucked away somewhere in your assessment?" Kat ventured as she slathered globs of apple butter all over a scone she was delicately holding up on the tips of her fingers.

"Well, yes," James replied glumly. "I am afraid Keating Manor is no more."

As much as she detested her uncle, it pained her to hear the man had lost his home.

"It would seem Fate, for once, is on our side," she declared as brightly as she could in an effort to mollify James. "I did manage to save your mother's harpsichord and the portrait of my mother from your father's home before the rebels who captured it had tossed everything into the hearth."

After pausing to savor a very unladylike bite out of her scone, Kat continued, "Like all of the homes used by General Washington's army, Keating Manor did not fare well. While I can appreciate the need to house their soldiers, I cannot understand why those who allow the occupation of private homes could not find it within themselves to ensure the property of the home's owner was looked after. It was almost as if they wanted their soldiers to conduct themselves as if they were little more than common ruffians."

Rather than easing what little grief he felt over the loss of Keating Manor, Kat's efforts to console him caused James to grimace—a response she was quick to notice.

Ever so slowly, Kat set her half-eaten scone down on the plate before her, took up a napkin, and began to dab the melted apple butter off her fingers.

"Why do I have a feeling your efforts to seek me out on a day like today—a day when every man spared by your general is running about searching for some mythical rebel who supposedly started the fire—are not entirely altruistic?"

Taken aback by his cousin's comment, James pulled away and said, "You think what happened the night before was nothing more than an unfortunate accident?"

"I do."

"Yes, I expect you would, wouldn't you," James replied dryly.

Now it was Kat's turn to draw away from her cousin as she snipped, "And what, exactly, do you mean by that?"

Amused, James took up his tea. "As clever as you are when it comes to commerce and financial dealings, there's no escaping the fact you are a woman."

Stunned by his comment, Kat took to staring at her cousin wide-eyed. James, in turn, could not help but wonder why Kat was behaving so. Like everyone he knew, he was sure women—not even one as gifted his cousin—simply did not have the capacity to deal with the cold, hard logic such topics demanded when it came to politics and military matters. Sensing he was on the verge of being drawn into an argument in which he had no wish to engage and before he was able to inform her of the true purpose of his visit, James set his cup aside and took to staring down at it as he hurriedly gathered his thoughts. Only when he was ready did he peek up at her.

"I must confess there is more to my need to seek you out and talk to you. You see, the fire has created something of a problem for us. The solution to it is one I am afraid you will not like."

Setting aside the ire she felt over the dismissive manner with which her own cousin was treating her, Kat drew herself up as she prepared for the worse. Unfortunately, what she thought was the worst turned out to be wide of the mark.

-««•»»-

Sporting a self-satisfied smirk, Colonel Robert Rawlings, the Earl of Monmouth, once more looked about the room that was, for Kat, as much a sanctuary as a place of business.

"Yes, this is more than adequate," Lord Robert murmured as if to himself before glancing over at James in the open doorway. "Of course, it's not at all comparable to my library back at Monmouth Manor, but then what is?" Taking his time, Lord Robert made his way over to Kat's well-ordered desk and took a seat. "Well, I suppose one must make do with what one can find when on campaign," he sighed as he began to brush aside the ledgers and files Mrs. Peel had not had time to clear away before James had appeared with Lord Robert and his covey of aides, orderlies, and military servants.

The sound of a sudden intake of breath behind James served as a warning that his cousin was on the verge of losing what little self-control she had managed as Lord Robert had wandered through Minden Hall, inspecting each and every room, including her bed chamber.

Clearing his throat, James captured the earl's attention and said, "If you would excuse me, sir, I need to speak to Lady Trent about the arrangements we will need to make."

"Yes, yes, of course," Lord Robert replied offhandedly. "We mustn't keep her Ladyship waiting while I dawdle about your home like a beggar in search of a place to rest my head."

Realizing Lord Robert's comment would, in all likelihood, send Kat over the edge, James spun about, snatched her by the arm, and hustled her away as quickly as he could into the parlor across from the library. Once there, he closed the door behind him. By the time he had turned around to face his infuriated cousin, she was already across the room clutching her fists at her sides as she paced to and fro like an enraged panther.

"You do realize you have little choice in the matter," James declared evenly without leaving his post at the parlor door.

Pausing, Kat glared at him. "Little choice? It would seem I have no choice."

"Surely you appreciate my position, Kat."

"Your position? What about mine? Did you even take a moment to consider *my* position before you offered up my home to that… that…"

Unable to find a suitable word to describe Lord Robert, she turned, stormed across the room, pivoted about sharply, and marched back to where her cousin was standing.

"I've been reduced to being little more than a guest in my own house. *My* house, Captain Keating, not yours."

Growing tired of what was fast becoming a pointless argument, James decided it was time he made it clear to Kat her position was not a particularly strong one. Drawing himself up, he made his way over to a chair and took a seat. Stretching out, he crossed his ankles and clasped his hands before him as he took a moment to study his cousin.

"Must I remind you of our conversation the other night? You are in no position to make demands," he stated flatly. "While you were able to chase Major Lowe away like a naughty boy and avoid answering for your activities during the rebel occupation of the city, Lord Robert is not easily intimidated. Besides, things here in the city have changed."

Throwing her head back, Kat sniffed. "You have no need to remind me of *that*, sir."

"Kat, had Lord Robert wished, he could have turned you out without so much as a word," James pointed out, doing his best to be as patient as he could while at the same time making it clear to his cousin she was in no position to argue. "As a result of the fire, the city is under martial law. Those responsible for provisioning the army, officers like Lord Robert, have been given the right to confiscate whatever property or stores required to ensure our forces in the field are able to continue their pursuit of the rebel army and those left here in the city are sheltered and provided for."

"Are the goods in my warehouses and shops to be taken from me as well as my home?" Kat snapped.

"First off, your home is not being taken from you," James explained slowly. "A few officers and their servants are simply being quartered here. Second, I expect if you had allowed Lord Robert to explain things instead of going off in a huff like a spoiled child, you would have understood his purchasing agents and representatives have every intention of procuring the needs of the army—and the navy I might add—at fair market value. Only those military stores abandoned by the rebels and clearly identified as such are to be confiscated."

For the first time that morning, Kat took a moment to reflect upon her situation. Crossing her arms tightly against her chest, she once more took up her pacing, though this time it was not to work off her anger, but rather to think. After several minutes during which time James watched her from where he was seated, she stopped.

"Tell me, dear cousin, just how did his lordship come to pick Minden Hall?"

"Lord Robert, like everyone else on General Howe's staff, knows I was born and raised here. Naturally when it came to finding suitable quarters they sought my advice and recommendations. Had the fire not destroyed Keating Manor I expect his lordship and his staff would be there right this very minute, cleaning up the mess the rebels who had occupied it during our absence left and settling in."

"May I ask how he came to think you, and not I, own this house?"

"Colonel Robert is not at all familiar with our arrangement Kat. The idea of dealing with a woman as if she were an equal is foreign to him. I imagine he and his fellow officers unfamiliar with our ways see you as no different than their mothers and wives back in England—delicate creatures who spend their entire lives cloistered away in stately country manors or richly appointed townhouses."

James waited to see the effect his comments had on his cousin, and when he was sure Kat was not going to go off on him again, he continued.

"If you're to weather this storm and profit from it, I recommend you swallow your pride and allow him to believe what he wishes. You know what the truth is, as do I. Were I you, I would leave it at that."

For the longest time Kat regarded her cousin, wondering if they would have been holding this conversation if he really did know the truth—the real truth about her as well as her sympathies for the rebel cause she could no longer deny.

Believing he had mollified his cousin, James decided to attend to the Earl before he left to oversee the transfer of his personal kit from the cramped quarters he had been occupying.

"Besides," James added in a more conciliatory tone as he rose to his feet. "I do not expect we'll be staying in New York very long. Once we've managed to secure our footing here, we'll be off after General Washington and his ragtag army. It may take us awhile to run him to ground, but do not fear, we will. And when we do, we'll tear him and every traitor who's still with him to pieces."

"I wouldn't be so sure of that," Kat cautioned.

In no mood to argue the point with her on matters beyond the comprehension of a woman, even one as intelligent as his cousin, James decided to let the matter drop. Eager to get back to see what Colonel Robert was up to, he excused himself. Besides, he could not help but think Kat just might be right and that the rebels were far from beaten. As he left the room, James felt beyond grateful she was not on their side. Otherwise, he imagined, the war would drag on far longer than even he feared.

TWENTY-THREE

"Many plans for our further proceedings became now and again the subject of deliberation. Mine, still inclining for Rochelle, was at last adopted."

Sir Henry Clinton
October 1776

Springfield, Massachusetts
October 1776

RELIABLE NEWS of the momentous events playing out in and around New York was as rare as a warm New England day in February. What news did find its way to the inn where Sarah Carter worked was colored by the experience of the person passing through who willingly shared with local patrons or in the political leanings of the broadsheet in which it was published. The only undisputed fact all the stories had in common was that Washington's Army had been soundly whipped and was now, according to some, on the verge of collapse. That the most vocal naysayers were deserters—men who had left the ranks rather than weather the coming winter fighting for what they considered a lost cause—made little difference. Just as church bells had once echoed across Massachusetts when the last of the King's soldiers had sailed from Boston harbor, the heady days of spring were now nothing more than memories—swept away by a seemingly endless tide of defeat.

As scarce as news was, the odd letter Anthony Carter found time to send to his mother amounted to little more than a terse narrative of his mundane, day-to-day activities. Nothing in them cast any meaningful light on either his circumstances or feelings for a cause many now saw as being all but lost. So, when he called out to his mother from the doorway of the inn's cook house, she had to fight the urge to drop to her knees then and there to thank God he had returned to her whole and safe. She believed he had come to his senses and had turned his back on the war that had taken him away from her.

Rushing to her mud-spattered son, Sarah gathered him up in her arms and wrapped him up in a fierce embrace that took Anthony by surprise. Unprepared for such a reception, he took to looking about and noticed as he did the other women his mother worked with were going about their chores in a half-hearted effort, pretending as they did so they were not watching. Embarrassed by the quick, fleeting glances at him out of the corner of their eyes and the little smiles they made no effort to hide, he gave himself over to the emotions of the moment. Dropping his chin, he wrapped his arms about his mother and lightly kissed her forehead, just as Anton had done so many years before when he had bid Sarah what both thought would be their last farewell.

For her part, Sarah rested her head upon his shoulder as she clutched him. She was hoping upon hope he had seen enough of the world beyond the orderly confines of the small New England village they called home to satisfy the same restless curiosity that had led her dead husband to venture into an untamed wilderness.

That he intended to remain in Springfield with her was a notion he quickly disabused her of later that night. He was in the midst of wolfing down a second helping of the stew she had served him as if he had not eaten in weeks when he announced he would be leaving in the morning.

"If truth be known, I shouldn't even tarry here that long," he confessed sheepishly.

Taken aback by this unwelcomed non sequitur, Sarah straightened up in her seat and gave her head a quick shake as she blinked furiously.

Taking no notice of his mother's response to this most unwelcomed news, he went on, telling her between mouthfuls how, after having to spike his gun when the army abandoned New York City, Major Chevalier had once more taken him on as his orderly until he could find a position with another gun crew. Anthony's reason for traveling north to Boston was, he explained, one of his duties.

"It seems the owner of the home where Major Chevalier stayed before we left Cambridge last May agreed to hold any letters from France addressed to him. In addition to returning to New York with whatever mail he has received, I have been asked to find a way of posting his letters to France, either through the same gentleman in Cambridge or with a ship's captain willing to run the blockade out of Boston."

The revelation that her son had done more than stay in touch with Anton after Washington's army had marched off to New York caused Sarah to blanch. On seeing this, Anthony hesitated just as he was about to devour a spoonful of stew. Believing she was worried he had allowed himself to be drawn into some sort of nefarious conspiracy that involved Major Chevalier and the French government, he lowered the spoon he was holding and hastened to assure his mother the letters were quite harmless.

"I can assure you, mother, there is nothing untoward or treasonous with what he's asked of me. He even let me read this one before he sealed it," he told her as he set aside his spoon and fished about in a leather haversack he kept at his side. Pulling out a thick letter, he held it out to show her. "It's a report on conditions here addressed to the Comte de Vergennes, King Louis's foreign minister. In it, the major takes great pains to point out that, despite the recent reverses we've suffered, he believes we can beat the English, though he does call attention to our many deficiencies, informing the Comte de Vergennes we're going to need help by way of weapons, munitions, and, most important of all, money."

Her son's words washed over Sarah as she focused on the red seal depicting a unicorn with a broken chain about its neck rearing up in a fighting stance Anton had affixed to the letter using his signet ring. It was a ring with which she was quite familiar. She first took notice of it one morning many years before as she lay beside him in the small Quebec inn where they often met. The sight of the red wax seal resurrected the memory of the shared passion she had enjoyed with a man unlike any other she had ever known before or since.

In the quiet predawn darkness of their secluded sanctuary on a morning long ago during another war, she had taken Anton's hand in hers as he lay asleep beside her to study the ring. Roused by the touch of his lover's hand, Anton opened his eyes, hoping the woman at his side was not a dream and as real as the passion she aroused. The sight of Sarah gazing down at his hand brought a smile to his lips.

"My father presented that ring to me by way of acknowledging his paternity," he explained in quiet, hushed tones so as not to startle her as he watched Sarah run a delicate finger across the face of the engraved gemstone. "The unicorn has been part of his family's coat of arms for centuries."

"Why the broken chain?" she whispered as if fearful speaking louder would shatter the solemnity of the moment.

Moving his head closer to hers on the pillow they were sharing until his forehead touched hers, he looked down at the hand she was holding.

"I asked him that very question when he gave it to me, for the unicorn on his ring didn't have a chain about its neck. At the time I couldn't understand why he wouldn't tell me. It wasn't until I had been here, in Canada, for almost a year that I understood."

Sarah gazed up into his eyes but inches from her own. "And?"

"I would like to think he was trying to tell me that I was free of the bonds that held him and his forefathers to a way of life that was moribund, a past that held little promise for me. He claimed me as his son but made it clear my future lay elsewhere."

"Is that what you believe?" she had asked shyly as she returned his steady, unflinching gaze. "Does your future belong elsewhere?"

Anton had not answered her question, at least not with words. By way of response, he had pulled away the hand she was holding. Reaching up, he placed it on the back of her neck and, ever so gently, drew her head closer to his until their lips met.

"Mother? Are you not feeling well?"

Startled by the sound of her son's voice piercing the shadow of a memory she had become lost in, Sarah gave her head a quick shake as the memories of that day—memories that still had the power to evoke the shared passions that had consumed her and Anton—vanished.

"Yes. Yes, I'm fine," she blurted hastily in a vain effort to push past the embarrassment she felt at having allowed herself to become so caught up in a waking dream. "It's just that I thought you were going to stay and that you were through with the army," she stammered in the hope her response would explain away cheeks as red as a fresh cooked lobster.

Pulling back, Anthony stared at his mother as if her question was the daftest thing he had ever heard. "Why would you think that?"

"The English are winning, are they not?"

"They've won a few battles, yes. But that's all," Anthony countered with a jaunty nonchalance. "The war, according to Major Chevalier, is far from over."

"Does Anton believe Washington and his army can beat the English?"

"He does," Anthony declared with the unshakable certainty of a zealot, overlooking entirely the familiarity with which his mother referred to the Frenchman. "I must admit, it pained me to spike my gun when the army was forced to abandon the city of New York," Anthony informed his mother as he took up his spoon and resumed eating as fast as he could as if fearful the bounty laid out before him would be snatched away at any moment. "'Cannons can be replaced,' the major reminded me after he had plucked me from the ranks of the militia regiment I had fallen in with during our retreat from the city. A good orderly who can speak French like a native, can ride reasonably well, and knows the way to Boston, it seems is not replaceable, or so Major Chevalier claimed before sending me off to see his letter to Louis's foreign minister finds its way back to France."

Sarah dismissed, as nothing more than foolish, youthful enthusiasm, her son's dedication to the cause of independence and his decision to continue the fight regardless of the hazards he would face. He was not the same boy on the cusp of his sixteenth year who had rushed off into the predawn darkness more than a year ago when the men of Springfield were called to arms. The naïve youth who had kissed her on the check and bade her a hasty farewell on that chilly April morning was no more. He was a man now, one who had stood his ground on Breed's Hill and ventured deep into the heart of the savage wilderness that had claimed her husband and the siblings he knew little about in the dead of winter to retrieve guns from the shores of Lake Champlain. Sarah was saddened as she realized nothing she said could possibly compete with the unwavering conviction his demeanor betrayed for the cause he was dedicated to. Like his father, a man who placed his loyalty to his King above all else, her son was wed to a cause few believed would survive the coming winter. The only comfort to which she latched as she sat watching Anthony enjoy his meal was knowing Anton—the other man in her life who held a place in her heart—would do all he could to keep their son as safe as the capricious and deadly nature of war allowed.

White Plains, New York
28 October 1776

The sight of fleeing militiamen panicked by British cannonade being checked by New York regiments belonging to McDougall's brigade did little to allay Anton's concern for the position that anchored the American right. Collapsing his telescope between the palms of his hands, he shifted his attention away from the mélange of American units holding Chatterton's Hill to one just south where British and Hessian troops stood in silent readiness. Having failed to dislodge the Americans with cannon fire alone, if it was General Howe's intention to turn the American right, he would need to order them forward. Anton was sure of that, just as he was sure the presence of steadfast continentals belonging to Haslet's Marylanders, the 1st Delaware, and McDougall's New Yorkers would not be enough to keep raw militiamen, already shaken by the cannonade they were being subjected to, from breaking long before ranks of resolute British musketeers and fierce Hessian grenadiers closed with them. When they did, the American line would shred like a rotting ship's sail in a winter gale.

The position, in of itself, was a good one. To seize it, the troops carrying out the assault would have to ford a freshwater river called the Bronx that emptied into the East River. Crossing would be difficult but not impossible. The marsh on either side formed by the low-lying ground at the foot of Chatterton's Hill was another matter. Maintaining order in the ranks as their soldiers waded through waist deep water while under fire would require unwavering courage and determination on the part of the officers leading them. Once those natural obstacles had been overcome, the combined British and Hessian force would then need to ascend a steep incline in the face of enemy fire delivered by troops protected by numerous stonewalls enclosing farm fields that covered the forward sloop and crest of the hill. No doubt, Anton concluded, the British and their

German mercenaries would pay dearly for every foot of ground they gained.

That position, as formidable as it was, however, was not a place Anton would have chosen to anchor the army's flank. In addition to a nearly mile long gap between it and the rest of Washington's army, the same river that would be an impediment to an assault by the British and Hessians would make it difficult for Haslet's and McDougall's troops to withdraw when, not if, that became necessary.

Turning his attention away from the growing threat facing those troops, Anton took to studying their commanding general. As he often did at times like this, Anton stood apart from the small knot of officers who were General Washington's most trusted aides. He wondered if the American general understood just how precarious his position was. Although Anton was a veteran of the French and Indian War, the enemy he had faced then—and the tactics he had relied on to fight them—bore no resemblance to the foe he now faced. In Anton's opinion, luck, an uncanny sense of timing, and General Howe's half-hearted prosecution of the campaign to date were the only things that had thus far kept the imposing Virginian from suffering a catastrophic defeat. Even so, the losses suffered from desertion by men who had given up all hope in their cause had resulted in far greater losses than British and Hessian shot and shell. No one dared ask how much longer those who remained with the colors would stay, but Anton suspected it was a question weighing heavily on the minds of the many men gathered about Washington as each day wreaked yet another setback to the fledgling American cause.

The pounding of drums in the distance sounding the advance caused Anton to return his attention to Chatterton's Hill where a mix of resolute continentals and rattled militiamen stood ready to receive an attack by some of the finest infantry in the world.

-«««•»»»-

"Here they come," a raw recruit muttered to no one in particular as he and the other men belonging to McDougall's brigade watched British troops step off.

"It's about time," Kevin Farrell growled contemptuously as he brought his musket up and inspected its lock's frizzen and pan. "A man could grow old waiting for the regulars to up and do something other than parade about."

Casting a quick glance over at his friend out of the corner of his eye, Joshua Cooper snickered. "Why so impatient?" he asked, doing his best to sound as if his question was serious. "It's not as if we had anything better to do."

"It's all well and good for those bloody, red-coated bastards over there to stand about all day," Farrell shot back. "*They've* nothing better to do. Me? I've a farm and wife in desperate need of my attention."

On hearing this, Hiram Blair leaned forward. He was a gregarious barkeep at a tavern Edward had often frequented with his college friends and one of the few who, like Farrell, Cooper, and Edward, had been with the regiment from the beginning. He took to eyeing Farrell up and down with a deliberateness Farrell could not help but notice.

"What are you looking at, ya mangy runt?" Farrell snarled as he returned his companion's thoughtful perusal with a contemptuous glare.

"I was just wonderin' what any woman would want from the likes of you," Blair replied dryly.

After casting a quick glance to where the British were exchanging fire with skirmishers McDougall had thrown out and determining it would be some time before they would be in musket range of them, Farrell returned Blair's steady gaze and replied in a whisper meant to be heard by all around them.

"Well now, I'd tell ya if it weren't for fear of offending young Master Shields's delicate ears."

On hearing this, Blair let out a loud, derisive snort. "Delicate ears? In case you don't remember, that fine young gentleman on the other side of you spent the whole time during the march south from Canada cursing up a storm that would have made a sailor blush."

"Aye, he does have a way with words," Farrell snickered.

From somewhere behind them an officer who had been nervously pacing to and fro barked, "Quiet in the ranks."

"Why bother?" Farrell shot back without hesitation. "I expect the bastards know we're here."

A Marylander who had been listing to the exchange between the pair of New Yorkers wryly eyed the solid ranks of red clad regulars who had begun to make their way up the hill toward them.

"Aye," he muttered grimly. "They know we're here. And, in another minute or two, the whole lot of them will be here as well," he added even as he was tightening his grip on his musket.

Throughout the exchange between his friend and others who paid no heed to their officers' admonishments to settle down, Edward's full and undivided attention was riveted on the spectacle playing out before them with an odd mix of admiration, awe, and trepidation. Save for when the British soldiers marched out from behind their works to surrender the previous year at Saint John's, he had seldom caught but a glimpse of his foe. During their ill-fated New Year's Eve assault on Quebec, an effort that had cost the regiment dearly, he had not seen any.

If General Howe's intention over the past few days was intended to impress Washington's army with a display of England's martial might, Edward concluded he was succeeding brilliantly. Throughout the morning he and his companions had watched as regiment after regiment of red clad English soldiers and Hessians in dark blue coats were drawn up just south of the line of hills where Washington had chosen to make a stand. The most impressive aspect of the English preparations for their assault was the crisp, almost mechanical manner with which they went about it. The detachment sent forward to throw a bridge across the Bronx River approached the task with a deliberate, businesslike manner as if the well-fortified American troops on the hill above them were a hundred miles away. Not even Smallwood's Marylanders and Haslett's Delaware regiment—reputed to be the best drill units in the Continental Army—could match the enemy's methodical approach to the attack that, in a few brief moments, would be unleashed upon them.

"Don't go and let those lobsters worry you," Farrell whispered in Edward's ear when he noticed the way Edward was eyeing the solid ranks of British infantry advancing. "They're no different than you and me. A well-placed ball fired by a man who keeps his wits about him will go through those fancy coats of theirs just as easily as what we're wearing."

Having been unaware his expression had been betraying his thoughts, Edward cut a quick glance over at Farrell out of the corner of his eye. On seeing this, the gruff farmer winked.

"Just remember to take your time and aim low before you shoot. And, if things look like they're about to go to hell in a handbasket, do your best to keep up with me."

Try as hard as he could, Edward found he could not do anything more than respond with a quick, jerky nod before turning his attention back to the line of British troops that continued to close on their position with a steady, unfaltering pace that matched the *tap tap tap* of drums.

-«««•»»»-

The long, maddening hours waiting for General Howe to maneuver his troops about with a thoughtful deliberateness that reminded David Gray of a chess player moving his pieces about a board were at an end. Within minutes, the issue would be decided in a brief, chaotic storm of fire and blood. With the Hessians now firmly established north of the Bronx River and well within range, David ordered the crew of the only gun for which he was responsible to switch from round shot to canister.

In a somber, businesslike manner, the gun's crew quickened their pace as they went about their duties. David's choice of munitions meant the Hessians advancing on their position were on the verge of entering the deadliest portion of the battlefield—the last one hundred yards or so would allow them to finally bring into play the smooth bore muskets they were armed with.

The gun captain, a man who had been a fellow classmate of David's at King's College, acknowledged David's order with nothing more than a curt nod before relaying the command to the powder handler, a fair-haired lad of seventeen posted well to the rear of the gun. Like many of his fellow Americans stationed along the forward crest of Chatterton's Hill, the former printer's devil met the enemy approach with an odd mix of relief and dread. The relief he felt now that the hours of waiting were over was counterbalanced by the fear of what would happen once the Hessians struggling through the tall meadow grass at the foot of the hill reached his gun. Bending over without taking his eyes off the line of blue-clad Hessians, he withdrew the round called for from the powder box, straightened himself up, and stepped off, making his way past his gun captain and to the loader whose eyes, like everyone else up and down the line, were fixed on the Hessians as they drew closer with each passing second.

A hooper turned artilleryman posted to the left of the gun's muzzle accepted the round of canister from the powder handler before turning his back to the approaching enemy and loading it into the gun's warm maw. Only after glancing to the rear of the piece to ensure the vent tender had his leather-clad thumb firmly pressed down over the vent to prevent air from entering into the bore of the gun did he continue, easing the round carefully into place until it was fully seated. Stepping back, he made way for his fellow crewman, a stout, muscular man wheeling a ramrod that was as long as he was tall.

Years of working on the docks of New York City, loading and unloading cargo day in, day out, allowed the former stevedore to twirl his ramrod about with ease as he brought the plunger to the gun's muzzle. Using all his strength, he rammed the round of canister down the full length of the gun's bore with a single, full-bodied thrust, stopping only when it came to rest against the breech end. This step in the gun crew's intricate drill was the most hazardous part of preparing their gun to be fired. A single unquenched ember from a previous round catching a whiff of air that entered the bore through an unattended vent could ignite the powder of the round being loaded and discharge the new round together with the ramrod in front of it before the man on the other end of the ramrod would have a chance to release his grip and step out of harm's way. Not even the heavy leather gloves worn by the crewman handling the ramrod would save him from serious injury or a quick, violent death. Even so, the former stevedore gave the newly loaded round a second, quick tamp to ensure it was fully seated before withdrawing his ramrod.

Once he was sure his fellow crewmen at the front of their piece were well clear of the bore, the vent tender removed his thumb from the vent at the gun's breech end and, using a thin metal priming iron suspended from a lanyard about his neck, inserted it into the vent and pricked the round's powder bag just as he had done nineteen years before when he had been a young man fighting with the British during the siege of Fort William Henry. Satisfied the powder bag had been pierced, he took hold of the powder horn dangling at his side, pulled the stopper from it, and carefully poured loose powder into the vent until a bit spilled out and filled a small indenture surrounding the vent.

Only when he was satisfied his crew had performed their duties properly, were clear of the piece, and had checked the gun's lay did the gun captain give the crewman responsible for tending the linstock a quick nod. Stepping forward, a man who had been a farmer a scant twelve months before blew on the end of the lit, slow burning match wrapped about the linstock, extended his arm, and touched its glowing ember to the small pile of powder the vent tender had left.

A flash, followed by a brief sizzle as the powder in the vent caught, preceded a deafening boom as the round's powder ignited and propelled the canister packed with fifty-six one-and-a-half ounce balls down the length of the bore and whizzing like a swam of angry bees toward the advancing Hessians. At point blank range, a round of cluster could reduce a line of troops to a heap of shredded corpses in the twinkling of an eye. Not that the round shot the British gunners had been hurling their way in return was any less deadly. A single well-aimed cannonball could bowl through the ranks as cleanly as a ball in a game of nine pin, leaving a swath of dismembered and disemboweled men in its wake. A cannonball, however, could be ignored by a man who had the grit to keep his wits about him and stand his ground even when he could see one skipping along the ground, provided of course it was not bouncing its way directly toward him. The carnage created by canister was an entirely different matter.

Momentarily blinded by the cloud of smoke the discharge of their piece created, the gun crew was not able to witness the havoc their efforts caused among the Hessians. David, having positioned himself upwind of the gun, could. What he saw both pleased and appalled him. From a professional standpoint, the gun captain's aim could not have been any better, for it struck down a number of men who made up Fusilier Regiment Von Lossberg's party. The red flag bearing the crest of the Landgrave Frederick II of Hesse-Kassel would be taken up by other members of the color party and advanced. But their fallen comrades would be left behind to fend for themselves until after the issue had been decided, one way or the other. Those who had been wounded and could do so would crawl away to safety. Those who could not would lay where they fell, lost and, for the moment, forgotten amid the tall marsh grass set ablaze by Hessian jägers sent ahead to clear away skirmishers American commanders had thrown out to contest the regiment's crossing of the Bronx. How officers such as those leading the Hessians and British soldiers up the hill were able to accept the cruel nature of their chosen profession was a question David often wondered but had neither the answer or time for.

Without waiting for further orders, David's gun crew set about preparing their piece for the next round, starting with the stevedore turned gunner who had taken up a ramrod topped with a sponge made of lambswool dipped in a bucket of water. This, he used to swab out the full length of gun's hot bore, quenching burning fragments of the previous round's powder bag that had not been spit out.

With nothing more than a quick shake of his head, David banished all concern for the men his gunners had struck down. Drawing himself up, he turned his full attention to the issue at hand.

"Reduce elevation," he ordered. "Concentrate your fire on the front rank."

As before, the gun captain acknowledged David's command with little more than a nod as he watched the powder handler making his way forward with a fresh round of canister.

Brigadier General Alexander Leslie did not wait for the Hessian regiments to his left struggling through the tall marsh grass to pull abreast of his troops before driving up the forward slope of Chatterton's Hill. Whether it was nothing more than impatience or the customary contempt the British had for the men awaiting their attack did not matter to Edward. In those final moments—before the unnatural silence that had fallen upon the American line shattered with the crack of gunfire—only one thing mattered: making his shot count when the order came to fire.

The biblical commandment, *thou shall not kill*, had never been taken seriously by him. As a boy of ten, he had asked his family's minister why God, who had passed that commandment down to his chosen people, would anoint a boy no different than him as a King simply because he had killed a giant with a stone. After an awkward silence, the minister had pointed out David had had no choice and explained that if David's people were to be free of the Philistines, he had to strike down Goliath.

There were no giants among the men clambering up the hill toward Edward and his fellow New Yorkers. Nor did Edward consider himself to be like Goliath's David. He did, however, know that if he and the men around him did not stand their ground and slay the agents of a King who wished to enslave them, no one would. He scanned the ranks of the red-clad Philistines making their way toward him as he waited for the order to fire, searching for his personal Goliath as he nervously flicked the hammer of his musket with his right thumb.

His choice of target proved to be surprisingly easy. A veteran who had fought along the shores of Lake Champaign with Robert Rogers once told Edward in a fight, it was the quiet ones you needed to mind. "*The men who whoop and holler loudest when going into a fight are the ones who will be the first to turn tail and run when they think the fight's going against them. It's the quiet ones, the ones who keep coming on, slow and steady, staring straight at ya with a look that tells ya he'll not stop until one of ya is dead.*"

The British soldier on which Edward set his sights was not particularly imposing. Like most Englishmen, he was rather small. But, what he lacked in stature, he more than compensated with an expression that told Edward he would keep coming, the devil be damned. Without shifting his eyes from his chosen target, Edward mechanically raised his musket when the command was given to poise firelocks.

The next command his officer gave to cock firelock, when executed smartly, resulted in a loud, ominous metallic click that resounded across the dead space between the unit announcing the imminent release of a volley to the ones about to receive it. That there were no American units on Chatterton's Hill able to match the crisp, intimidating snap a British line regiment could generate when doing so did not matter. The sound of hundreds of hammers being jerked back into the full cocked position was enough to cause some of the soldiers struggling their way up the hill to flinch. Seeing that the man he had been eyeing made no effort to hold back brought a small, self-satisfied smile to Edward's lips. He had chosen well.

The final command to take aim and fire were shouted out by Edward's captain with a single, hurried breath, resulting in a disjointed, rippling volley instead of a single, thunderous clap. Again it did not matter that the fusillade McDougall's brigade loosed was decidedly discordant. A thousand individual musket balls striking home at different times were no less deadly than they would have been had they all been fired together.

It did not matter to Edward that a vale of dirty white smoke kept him from seeing if his aim had been true. In the immediate aftermath of firing, most important was reloading his musket, for even if his shot had been true, countless others had not found their mark. This would allow the majority of British soldiers unscathed and able to continue on—driven either by fear of their officers or a bloody-minded determination stronger even than the inherent predilection for survival even the most ardent warrior possessed.

Edward was in the process of ramming home a fresh round, the third of the day, when someone off to his right cried out in utter amazement that they had stopped the British. Taken aback by this most welcomed turn of events, he looked up and through the wisps of drifting smoke filling the void between him and where the line of British troops had been. As best he could tell, the enemy was in the process of drawing back and away from them. It was not a rout or even a retreat, not like any in which he had taken part. There was a noticeable reluctance on the part of the red-coated soldiers as they backpedaled, taking great care to keep from exposing their backs to their foe. The attack, Edward concluded, had been checked, but not stopped. They would try again whenever their generals decided the piece of ground held by Edward and his fellow New Yorkers was more valuable than the lives of the men they sent to seize it.

Edward was in the middle of taking a sip of water from his canteen during the lull that followed the first attack when his attention was caught by the sound of gunfire and shouted orders to his right. He barely had enough time to recork his canteen and turn his full attention in the direction of the commotion when he heard Kevin Farrell cry out to him.

"I told you those damned New Englanders wouldn't hold."

Startled by the sight of militiamen sprinting for their lives behind the line, it took Edward several seconds to grasp the grim reality. Their position on Chatterton's Hill had been flanked and was unraveling with a rapidity reminiscent to the rout on Long Island.

A hand grasping his arm caused Edward to look away from the harried gaggle of New Englanders and over at Farrell who shouted out to him as soon as he was sure he had Edward's full attention.

"There are days when ya need to stand your ground, baring your teeth and growling like a cornered badger. Today isn't one of them. If ya want to live long enough to show that mother of yours you're a better man than she deserves to call *son*, ya best flee like a rabbit hounded by a pack of angry dogs 'cause Hessians are comin' on fast, and it looks like they don't mean to stop anytime soon."

Without waiting for a response, Farrell released his grip on Edward's arm and took to his heels. Edward did not bother looking back to where Hessian soldiers and mounted British dragoons were slashing their way through the panicked mob of fleeing troops. Having done all that was expected of him, he felt no shame in running. There would be another battle, on another day, one he intended to be part of and, God willing, help win.

-<<<•>>>-

From his vantage point in the center of the American line, Anton watched as Hessian troops on Chatterton's Hill swept before them. He took no pleasure in being proven right in his earlier assessment, for even an aspirant new to the profession would have been able to spot so glaring a flaw in Washington's dispositions. Which is why the American general had taken such care in ensuring a second line of fortifications be prepared along a string of hills just to the rear of the ones his army currently occupied. He knew even before the first shot of this battle was fired there would be another retreat, if not straight away, then later. When he could do so, Washington would move his army away unhindered by General Howe, a man who had, to date, been inexplicably reluctant to press home every advantage provided him by the overwhelming superiority of his superbly trained and equipped army.

This retreat, like the one before it, would lead to another battle fought on the ground of Washington's choosing and, if the past performance was any predictor of the future, another retreat. Anton wondered at Washington's purpose in following a strategy that yielded nothing but defeat. The Virginian had to appreciate the men he commanded were rapidly becoming disheartened by being chased from pillar to post by their foe with nothing to show for their sacrifice. *Just how long did he imagine they would continue to follow him?*

It was a question Anton was determined to see answered but not out of professional curiosity. His reason for staying with the Americans was quite personal. If he could not convince the Comte de Vergennes France to support the American cause, if for no other reason than to weaken his country's traditional foe, then he could, he hoped, save his son. That would be not be easy. Having listened to the way Anthony spoke of the cause to which he was wed, Anton knew the boy would follow his general to the very end—even to the gallows.

It was an end Anton had no intention of seeing play out, not without doing all he could to whisk his son and Sarah to France and safety and away from the cataclysm that would befall the American colonies. Doing so would be a Herculean task as he watched British dragoons spurring their mounts on as they rode down their fleeing foe. Having donned the coat of an American officer, he expected he would share whatever fate the men he served would fall prey to. For Anton, it was a fate infinitely more preferable than turning his back again on the only woman he had ever loved.

Thus resolved, Anton came about and hurried off to rejoin Washington and his staff making ready to lead an army diminished by defeat and desertions on another retreat.

TWENTY-FOUR

"I am inclined to think it will not be prudent to hazard the men and stores...but... as you are on the spot, I leave it to you to give such orders as to evacuating Mount Washington as you judge best."

Letter from George Washington to
Major General Nathaniel Greene
8 November 1776

On the Eastern Shore of the Harlem River, Manhattan
16 November 1776

TO THOMAS, the order to delay the attack on the last rebel stronghold on Manhattan due to contrary tides did not matter a fig. To him, it was nothing more than further proof General Howe—a known critic of the Prime Minister's policies to suppress the rebellion—had no intention of dealing with the treasonous blackguards the way he and other like-minded officers felt they should be. Three times the general he had attached himself to had held back when he should have used the overwhelming force at his disposal to crush a despaired and disorganized foe. Instead, General Howe left them free to retreat, reorganize, and fortify the ground of their choosing. There was no denying that desertion and disease had substantially thinned the ranks of the rabble that fancied itself an army. Yet, to officers who understood war as Thomas did, the only way to bring this rebellion to a decisive end was to crush the enemy in battle, march on Philadelphia, and hang every scoundrel who had attached his name to that contemptuous declaration of theirs. The thought that today's effort might yield yet another victory that fell well shy of achieving even one of those goals rankled him—though not for reasons tied to grand strategy.

Thomas scoffed at the notion that officers advanced their own fortunes while in the service of King and country solely through conspicuous and superlative success on the battlefield. Having led troops in battle, he appreciated that the risks inherent with being conspicuously heroic far outweighed the gain. All line officers were expected to be courageous and unflinching in the face of danger. It was seniority, patronage, and the wherewithal to purchase a commission superior to the one an officer held that were the real keys to advancement. Having sold the commission his father had secured for him in 1745 and left active service after his marriage to Katherine, Thomas had forfeited the first. Pride precluded him from returning to her and asking for the sum needed to secure the lieutenant colonelcy of a regiment—the highest rank an ambitious officer could secure relying on his personal fortune alone. That left patronage and the reason Thomas had sought a position on General William Howe's staff in the summer of 1775.

At the time, he thought serving an officer with Howe's reputation would be to his advantage. Howe was more than the commander-in-chief of all British forces in America. Prior to the campaign to secure New York, he was known throughout the army to be bold to the point of reckless—an attribute that accounted for some of his greatest successes. In 1759, he had personally led the vanguard of light infantry up the Heights of Abraham that led to the fall of Quebec. The following year, he commanded a brigade during the capture of Montreal which had ended a hundred and fifty years of French rule in Canada. In 1761, his brigade participated in the successful invasion of Belle Île off the coast of Brittany before returning to the Americas where he served as General George Keppel's adjutant general during the successful siege of Havana in 1762. As recently as June of 1775, during the bloody but successful assault on the Charlestown Heights, he had proved once more he was still the same daring and determined officer who had scaled the cliffs below Quebec in the dead of night. When he joined Howe's staff, Thomas had no reason to doubt the reward steadfast and selfless service—during what was expected to be a swift and successful campaign—to a commander such as Howe would yield in the advancement of his own fortunes. Yet, that hope was inexplicably withering away as quickly as the campaign that so many had believed would crush the colonists' desperate bid for independence.

"This should have ended two months ago," Thomas grumbled in frustration as he watched the lead companies of light infantry belonging to Cornwallis's division struggle with musket and kit as they clambered into boats manned by sailors of the Royal Navy.

With little to do until his men were called forward to embark, a major belonging to the 1st Battalion of Guards overheard Thomas's mutterings. Believing those remarks directed at him, the major sidled up next to the man to which Cornwallis had taken a liking and offered his own thoughts on Howe's conduct of the campaign.

"I expect this day's efforts will go far toward that goal," he ventured in a nonchalant manner Thomas had often heard Guards officers affect even in the direst of circumstances. "How many more whippings can the motley collection of militiamen led by an amateur who fancies himself a general endure before they realize their rebellion has failed?"

Already in a combative mood, Thomas rounded on the Guardsman with eyes ablaze and jaw thrust forward, and snapped, "Only a *simpleton* lets the fox run free at the end of a hunt. That general of theirs is no fool. He knows all he need do is keep an army in the field long enough for those in the common governed by merchants and jobbers to demand we reconcile with the rebels. Then what?"

Appalled by what he was hearing, the major took a quick step back.

"Mob rule will replace the King's law," Thomas continued as he stepped forward to close the gap the man had attempted to put between them. "I've seen it. Once the common lot sees they can defy their betters and flout the King's law, there'll be no end to it."

Shock was too mild a word to describe the major's reaction on hearing one of Howe's own aides disparage his commanding general so openly. In desperation, he latched on to the first thought that came to mind in an effort to counter Thomas' outrageous accusation.

"I dare say the scoundrels holed up in that pathetic excuse for a fort over there will not slip away, not today," he countered firmly as he thrust an outstretched arm to point in the direction of the rebel fort on Manhattan.

Caught off guard by the Guardsman's retort, Thomas reined in his anger. What the man said was, in all likelihood, true. Cornwallis' division was but one of three converging on the rebel positions. Coming up from the south, Lieutenant General Lord Percy, commanding one brigade of British and one of Hessians, would sweep a small force of rebels off Harlem Heights and approach Fort Washington from that direction. A division consisting entirely of Hessian troops led by Lieutenant General Wilhelm von Knyphausen would, at the appointed hour, close in from the north, having already crossed over King's Bridge and onto Manhattan following the Post Road. Cornwallis's division, though the smallest of the three columns converging on the rebel stronghold from the east was, in Thomas's opinion, the most impressive. Cornwallis's regiment included two battalions of the King's Guards and two of grenadier companies drawn from other regiments led by a vanguard comprising two battalions of light infantry. Once it was across the Harlem River, Thomas was confident Cornwallis would tolerate the dawdling and hesitation as had been allowed in September following the landing at Kip's Bay and again, earlier that month, at White Plains. The rebels defending Fort Washington—a force made up of

Pennsylvania militia and riflemen from Maryland and Virginia—would be trapped between the converging columns commanded by general officers just as frustrated as he was by Howe's failures to crush the enemy when they were on their back foot.

Still, Thomas was in no mood to concede the point the Guards officer was endeavoring to make. Throwing his head back, he regarded his fellow major with a cold, dispassionate stare.

"Yes, this day will be ours, that much is certain. But it will not be enough to put an end to this war. All we'll have is a city, the island it's on, and a few of the surrounding counties populated by citizens whose loyalty is as fickle as the tides. The fox will still be free to scurry away into the interior where he'll raise a new army and wait."

"Wait for what?" the Guardsman snorted.

Thomas regarded the officer before him with a cold, dispassionate glare. "I've lived among those people. They're a stubborn race. Once they get a notion in their heads, it's all but impossible to beat it out of them. We've got to crush them as we crushed the Scots in '46. Until we've hung their leaders, burned their homes, and scattered them to the four winds, they'll keep at it," he growled with a savageness that caused the Guardsman to cringe.

To a man whose sole experience in dealing with commoners was restricted to the tenant farmers and laborers who worked his father's estates in England, the very idea the rebels would continue to fight on once they had been shown just how futile their efforts were was unimaginable. In his opinion, and those of his fellow officers, another defeat, followed by the prospect of spending a long, hard winter in the wilderness would be more than enough to snuff out whatever hope to which the rebels still clung. With a nonchalance intended to infuriate the unhinged man before him, the Guardsman dropped his gaze for a brief moment before once more looking up into Thomas' eyes.

"I expect you are right. We will need to hang some of the more radical rebels such as Adams, Jefferson, Franklin, and, of course,

Washington, if for no other reason than to set an example for the rest. But as far as laying waste to this land and exiling the entire population, I hardly expect that will be necessary. I mean, only a fool would slaughter a flock of his own sheep simply because the herding dog led them astray. Now," the Guardsman declared crisply before Thomas could respond, "if you will excuse me, there are pressing matters I must tend to."

The Guardsman's reminder that he would have a role to play in this day's action while he, Thomas, was left with nothing of great importance to do was akin to a slap in the face. Unable to come up with an appropriate rejoinder, he simply stood there and watched as the Guardsman made his way down to the riverbank where his regiment was waiting to embark.

North of Fort Washington
16 November 1776

Trying to avoid a bullet that had already been fired was foolish. Still, even an experienced soldier such as Hauptman Gustav Kleist could not keep from flinching whenever a menacingly near miss zinged close to his head and smacked into the tree he had been using for cover or ricocheted off a nearby rock. One such stray bullet peppered him with a cascade of razor-sharp splinters, causing him to throw himself behind a man-sized boulder. Pressing his back up against it, he quickly pulled his leather gauntlet off his right hand, brought it up to his face, and, ever so tenderly used his fingers to probe for any jagged fragments that might be protruding from a particularly nasty cut. Only when he was satisfied there were none did he drop his hand, pull his gauntlet back on, and turn his attention back to assessing his company's tactical situation.

In doing so, he found it hardly odd that the teachings his company commander had so carefully imparted to him as an aspirant now sprang to mind. *"An attack that has faltered is not easily resumed,"* the veteran officer had hammered home to Kleist time and again. *"This is especially true of a unit like ours. Jägers do not go into battle bunched together like children,"* his captain had declared with more than a little pride. *"They do not need officers and NCOs on both flanks and to their rear, ready to push and prod the slow, the hesitant, and the cowardly. As their name implies, our men are hunters, as skilled in the use of the terrain they move through as they are with the rifles they carry. When they go forward, they do not need to be led by the nose or driven with a kick in their backsides. Each and every man can be trusted to aggressively seek out positions from which he can place deadly accurate fire on the prey he is stalking. Still,"* he continued after a short pause during which his expression had darkened, *"they are only human. Once allowed to go to ground, they are difficult to roust out from behind whatever cover they've chanced upon. In the attack, you must keep them moving forward. Otherwise, you will lose them."*

It had not taken Kleist long to realized that his first commanding officer—a man more mentor than taskmaster—knew exactly what he was talking about. Throughout the course of the Seven Years' War, even when pitted against some of the best troops in Europe, soldiers armed with a smoothbore musket were no match for his rifle-armed jägers. The freedom to use the ground they were crossing to their advantage, combined with the range from which they could engage their foes, made them all but immune to effective return fire. On this day, however, the foe they were pitted against were rifleman—Americans who had been raised handling weapons every bit as effective and as deadly as those Kleist's men carried. Were it not for the inordinate amount of time required to load such a weapon and the cover of the tree-studded, rock-strewn hillside his company struggled to ascend, Kleist expected it would have been all but impossible to advance as far as they had, not without suffering crippling losses.

As it was, the cost of closing to within striking distance of their tormentors had been heavy. Far too many of his green-coated jägers lay motionless among the piles of dead leaves. Those who were still struggling to press forward found they, like Kleist, had little time to return the deadly fire they were being pelted with. To order his men to stop and do so would go against all he had been taught. Not only would resuming their advance be difficult, if not impossible, but remaining where they were—trading shots with a foe entrenched in a prepared position on the high ground—would, in time, spell the destruction of his company. Withdrawing was discounted out of hand. The very idea of allowing himself to be humbled by a treasonous rabble of peasants was nothing short of repulsive to an officer like Kleist.

"No," he muttered bitterly as he slowly shook his head even as he returned his attention to his immediate front.

Ever so carefully, he looked around the edge of the boulder behind which he had taken cover. From where he was, the closest rebel works was no more than seventy-five yards further up the hill. A quick, full-blooded charge, pressed home with élan, would bring his men close enough to the enemy to use their swords—a weapon the rebel riflemen lacked. Some of the rebels, he expected, would stand their ground, using their rifles as clubs. Most would not, for he had seen for himself that Americans had no taste for cold steel.

Thus resolved, Kleist took care to remain behind the boulder as he reached across his body with his right hand and grasped the hilt of his sword. Those of his men who had been watching him and waiting to see what their commanding officer would do understood what this meant. One by one they slung their rifles over their shoulders and, like Kleist, drew their short swords.

Only when he was sure his company was ready to pounce did Kleist break cover, bellowing out with every ounce of breath he had in his lungs a loud, full throated, "HURRAH!"

As one, Kleist's jägers sprang forth from behind the trees and rocks they had been using as cover. Echoing their commanding officer's battle cry, they rushed forward as best and as quickly as they could, wearing demonic expressions while brandishing their drawn swords.

Caught off guard, the Virginians and Marylanders who had just a moment before believed they held the upper hand suddenly found themselves confronted with a situation few were prepared to deal with. In the time it took each man to decide what to do, Kleist's jägers were among them.

Like wolves falling on a flock of hapless sheep, men who moments before been subjected to a punishing and deadly fire they had found difficult to return tore through the rebel ranks, hacking and slashing at any man who stood in their way. Few did. Those who found themselves unable to escape the slaughter and sought quarter found none. The screams of the dying and the cries for mercy uttered in a language Kleist's men did not understand only added to the frenzy that had possessed the incensed jägers as their captain looked on.

Kleist made no effort to rein in his men, for the conventions that governed their conduct in battle did not apply to rebels who had taken up arms against their sovereign lord. Death to all traitors, be it at the point of a sword or at the end of a rope, was what was called for if law and order was to be restored. That goal, together with a burning desire to exact vengeance on their tormentors, drove Kleist's men on long after they had driven the Americans out of their forward positions and back into the fort that bore the name of their commanding general.

New York City
18 November 1776

It did not matter in the least to James Keating that the role his grenadiers played in the capture of Fort Washington had been minor, almost trivial. The opportunity to lead troops into battle once more had been exhilarating. Eager to share his accounts of a victory that had resulted in the surrender of over five thousand rebels, as well as spend as much time with his wife before the army took up pursuit of what remained of Washington's army, he slipped away as soon as he could. Spurring his mount on, he rode out of camp at a full gallop to Minden Hall where, he expected, his beloved Sarah was anxiously awaiting him.

James had no need to do anything more than cross Minden Hall's threshold to discover he had been right. Even before he had a chance to throw off his cloak and unbuckle his sword belt, Sarah burst out of the parlor where she and Kat Trent had been keeping each other company. Rushing across the foyer, she threw her arms around his neck.

Caught up in the moment, James paid little heed to Kat Trent's enigmatic expression as she stood in the doorway of the parlor watching them. It was not until dinner later in the evening that he took note of her dour, almost sullen, demeanor. He was in the midst of regaling the officers belonging to Lord Robert's staff seated around the table when she set aside her knife and fork, folded her hands in her lap, and looked up from her plate over to where he was seated.

"Then it's over," she blurted dolefully without preamble.

In an instant, all eyes were on her. For the longest time, no one spoke as each officer quartered in the home James and Sarah shared with Kat found themselves wondering to whom she had addressed her comment. James, realizing it was up to him to break the tense, awkward silence, eased back in his seat as he weighed how best to respond. Both her expression and tone of voice made it clear she did not share the joy he felt over the army's latest victory. Keenly aware some of the officers seated at her table, gorging themselves on her food and enjoying the comforts of her home still questioned her loyalty to the crown, he made a show of shrugging dismissively as he set his glass down.

"Not quite, dear Kat. There's still the matter of the rebel army that's crossed over to New Jersey."

On hearing this Sarah, seated next to him, latched onto his arm. "Then you'll be leaving."

Shifting his attention away from his cousin, James hastened to reassure his wife as he cooed, "It's almost over. Those who haven't already given up and gone home won't last the winter. Come spring I expect Washington will be lucky if he can muster a corporal's guard."

The desperateness in Sarah's voice, James's effort to calm her, and the realization her outburst had raised more than a few eyebrows kept Kat from challenging her cousin's assertion that the American cause was all but lost in the presence of his fellow officers. There would be time, she reasoned, to do so when she was alone with him and both were free to speak their minds.

Despite the lateness of the hour and a promise to his wife that he would be along shortly, James lingered in a corner of the parlor, waiting until the last of the officers belonging to Lord Roberts's staff had made their excuses and retired for the evening. He watched Kat from across the room to where she sat staring down at the dying fire before her and wearing an enigmatic expression with which he was very familiar as she slowly sipped her Madeira. Realizing it was up to him to break the silence, he drew in a deep breath, then slowly let it out as he steeled himself for what he expected would be a most contentious exchange.

Feeling the need to fortify himself before he broached a subject he had put off far too long, James came to his feet and made his way over to a side table where Kat kept her spirits.

"Would you care for another?" he asked offhandedly as he refilled his own glass.

"Will I need it?" she replied dryly without bothering to look over at James.

Sensing his cousin was in a combative mood, rather than resuming his seat, he made his way over to the fireplace. Placing his free hand on the mantel, he leaned forward ever so slightly and, like her, started down at the warm, glowing fire.

"I do hope you appreciate the day of reckoning is nigh at hand."

Kat had no need to ask James to elaborate. Tradesmen, innkeepers, and servants in her employ had already informed her that inquiries continued to be made by representatives of the crown into her dealings with Washington's army when it had still held sway over the city.

"Are you speaking to me as your cousin or an officer of the King?"

Unable to help himself, James chuckled. Of all her many attributes, the one he most admired was her no-nonsense directness. It set her apart from every other woman he had ever known. It was a trait that earned her admirers as well as more than a few detractors. Dropping the hand he had been resting on the mantel, he turned and faced her.

"A little of both, I expect."

"Should I be concerned?" Kat asked airily.

"Should you?" James countered bluntly.

Bristling, she met her cousin's steady, accusatory stare with the same hawkish glare she often relied on to unnerve a competitor.

"Like others caught up in this war, I have done what was needed to survive—no more, no less."

"There are men who will not see things in that light, Kat. They will use your dealings with the rebels to ruin you and all you've worked to build."

Cocking a brow, Kat snickered warily. "I expect you're talking about your father."

"He's but one, though his reasons for doing so have nothing to do with the war. You've humiliated him, twice—something a man like my father is unlikely to forget."

"Twice?"

"Twice. The first instance was when he was all but shamed into paying your ransom."

Kat scoffed. "I don't remember asking him to. Nor can he blame me for being taken captive by those brigands."

"No, he can't," James confessed sheepishly before returning to the matter at hand in a manner he hoped would come across as menacing. "But he can hold you to account for threatening to take him to court if he didn't honor the provisions of our grandfather's will."

"As I recall, dear cousin, it was you who put that idea in my head and egged me on every step of the way," Kat countered sharply. "Had you not broached the subject, I would have remained blissfully ignorant of your father's duplicity."

"True, true," James confessed ruefully as he dropped his gaze. "Still," he resumed after looking back over at Kat and meeting her eyes, "it was you who brought him to account, just as I expect he will do. He will ensure the King's men leave no stone unturned when it comes time to look into your dealings with the rebels."

Drawing herself up, Kat set aside her glass, gracefully clasped her hands in her lap, and put on as brave a face as she could knowing that effort was already well underway.

"Good! I look forward to being afforded the opportunity to embarrass my dear uncle yet again."

James was not at all amused by his cousin's effort to brush his warning aside. "Kat, not everyone shares General Howe's attitude toward the rebels. If some of the King's closest advisors and ministers have their way, the retribution that will follow this war will be worse than '45. Any man found guilty of having taken up arms against our King, as well as anyone who supported their cause, will pay dearly for their treason."

Kat blanched at the very idea that the devastation unleashed on the colonies would be on par with that the Duke of Cumberland had been wreaked upon the Scottish Highlands in the wake of Prince Charles's failed rebellion. The hope that a failure of the American cause would be followed by an easy peace had all but vanished once rumors reached the city of the way Hessian mercenaries slaughtered American soldiers seeking quarter. The punishment meted out by the King's appointed representatives for those accused of aiding the rebels was but one of many threats with which Kat might have to contend. Other consequences of American defeat that would prove to be more damaging to her would come when merchants who had fled the city returned. As James had pointed out, men like his father would not be satisfied with simply seeing property and businesses they had lost returned to them. They would not rest until everyone they suspected of profiting from their absence had been stripped of all their worldly possessions and punished to the full extent of the King's law.

Kat's expression was all James needed to see to know she was ready to listen to reason, or what he hoped was reason. Settling down in a seat next to hers, he took a sip of Madeira.

"I'll be leaving in the morning," he stated off handedly. "I expect once enough boats and barges have been moved up the Hudson to where the army is currently camped, we'll cross over into New Jersey and take Fort Lee, should Washington be foolish enough to try to hold it."

"Will he?" Kat asked hesitantly.

"I doubt it," James shot back without consideration. "I could not fathom any reason to hold one of the two forts meant to deny passage up the Hudson when one of them has fallen. No, I expect he'll move inland, away from the Hudson and the reach of the Royal Navy."

"And you'll follow—you and Howe's army."

"Of course. Even if we don't take Philadelphia before winter makes campaigning impossible, we'll need to occupy all of New Jersey if we are to have any hope of collecting the food stuffs and forage the army will need to last through until spring—not to mention the wood needed to keep you and everyone else in the city warm."

"Forage? Or pillage?"

"Don't be fastidious, Kat," James muttered. "We're at war. General Howe's first responsibility is to see his troops are fed, properly clothed, and adequately quartered. Besides," he added as he glanced down at his glass and swirled its content, "a demonstration of what awaits those who have taken up arms against the crown will go far in keeping anyone who's still thinking about throwing their lot in with the rebels from doing so."

With that, he drained his glass and set it aside. "Now, if you'll excuse me, I expect Sarah is waiting for me."

"I expect she is."

Hesitating in the doorway, James looked again at Kat still seated and staring impassively into the dying fire.

"For your sake, Kat, I hope you give some thought to what I have said."

"Yes," she replied quietly without bothering to look over to where he was standing. "I most definitely will."

"Good night, Kat."

As tired as she was, Kat did not rush off to her room. Unlike her cousin, she had no compelling desire to retreat to a space that had become little more than a place where she slept and dressed. It was her sole enclave of privacy in a house now reduced to a barracks for officers of the crown intent on punishing an insolent people few still considered English. There—and only there—was she free to conduct her affairs without fear of uninvited guests rifling through her ledgers, reading her personal correspondences, or delving into her journal. Instead of retreating to bed, she simply sat before the fire, her half-empty glass in her lap, turning over in her mind what a defeat of the American cause could mean for her.

It was only now, in the stillness of a room lit only by a few flickering flames that she came to appreciate freedom was no small thing. Quite suddenly she realized it was everything—everything, that is, that mattered. Without freedom, she had been exiled once more to a room no different than the one in which she had hidden as a child, with only her books for company, locked away by her uncle in a gilded cage as she had been when first arriving in New York. That is, she grunted, if she was lucky. Having seen the way merchants and tradesmen who had fancied themselves patriots had used the war to crush their rivals in business, Kat had little doubt the men they had run out of town or ruined would demand the King's courts wreak havoc on anyone for whom they took a disliking.

"Well, it seems there's but one path open to me," she muttered as she held her glass out toward the burning embers struggling to remain lit. She smiled warily and said, "It's liberty or death, God help us all."

With that, she drained her glass, set it aside, and came to her feet. She had much to do, and not much time, if she was to carry out what she could to save a cause many believed was all but lost.

TWENTY-FIVE

"You see, my dear sir, that I have not been mistaken in my judgment of this people. The southern people will no more fight than the Yankees. The fact is that their army is broken all to pieces and the spirits of their leaders and their abettors is also broken. One may venture to pronounce that this is well nigh over with them."

Francis Rawdon,
1st Marquess of Hastings and aide
to General Sir Henry Clinton
November 1776

New Brunswick, New Jersey
29 November 1776

EZRA SHAW found Ian off to one side at the southern end of the bridge over the Raritan. His grim-faced lieutenant was hunched forward, leaning on his musket for support as he watched the bedraggled army they belonged to making its way down Albany Street. Coming up beside Ian, Shaw said nothing for the longest time as he joined in assessing the ranks of continentals and militiamen filing past them.

"It's a waste of time counting them, if that's what you're doing," Shaw finally stated flatly. "I've been told there's a number of units that'll be leaving in two days when their terms of enlistment are up."

"Like ours will, come the first of the new year," Ian replied glumly without taking his eyes off the ragged procession passing before them.

Unsure how he would convince men like Ian to stay, Shaw quickly changed the subject, "Your boy was lookin' for ya. Seems there's something he needs to discuss with you."

For the first time since Shaw had joined Ian, he looked over at his company commander but said nothing before turning his attention back toward the road just as a downcast civilian passed leading a jaded horse harnessed to an overloaded cart. The cart behind the man carried his wife, their two small children bundled in blankets, and—Ian imagined—all the worldly possessions the man had managed to cram into it before fleeing their home.

"I wasn't taken after Culloden—not right off," Ian stated in a low, almost mournful tone as he continued to watch the destitute family make their way past. "If I had, I expect I would have been put to the sword like so many of my kinsmen were that didn't—or couldn't—run as fast as I did from that wretched place."

Ian's sudden non sequitur caught Shaw off guard. The dour Scotsman standing beside him had never uttered a single word concerning Prince Charles's failed rebellion, let alone his own role in it. Unsure of what to say—or if he should say anything—Shaw remained silent.

"I hid as best I could during the day as I made my way home," Ian continued without taking his eyes off the family he expected would find no safe haven. "By the time I managed to reach the small croft that had been home to my family for as long as anyone could remember, the English were there."

Ian paused, silently replaying the sights, sounds, and smells he had beheld that day in his mind. Twenty years that had passed since that wretched day but had done little to diminish his anguish. When he spoke again, Ian did so in a doleful tone as sorrowful as the memory.

"Like Morgan, I watched as a red-coated bastard—no different than the ones chasing us now—dragged my mother from our home while two others laughed and set it alight."

Only when the refugee family had passed from sight did Ian abruptly grasp his musket by the forestock, hoist it onto his shoulder, and turn to face Shaw.

"I did nothing to stop them," he lamented. "Nothing. I just lay there, cowering in the heather, as I watched the King's soldiers take everything I cherished—everything I knew—from me and mine."

Leaning forward and wearing an expression of uncompromising rage that knew no bounds, Ian made ready to turn his back on sights that bore a striking resemblance to those he had witnessed as a boy.

"I ran, Ezra. Ran for all I was worth. But I'll tell you this—I'll be *damned* if I'm going to run again," he declared with a palpable bitterness.

Without explaining any further—not that he needed to—Ian pivoted sharply about and headed off to find his son.

Ian found Morgan holding the reins of several horses while the officers they belonged to stood on the riverbank, facing north and quietly conferring. Among them was Brigadier General Lord Sterling—Ian's brigade command. When he had learnt Sterling was in need of a courier, Ian had offered up Morgan's name, hoping to keep the lad out of the firing line. Ian knew couriers were often sent galloping about the battlefield with orders and reports, but that seemed a far better fate than seeing the boy in the ranks—where sooner, rather than later, he would be on the receiving end of a British volley loosed at point-blank range.

"It would seem you've grown a wee too big for your breeches," Ian remarked glibly as he approached his son. "In most armies, it's the officer who sends for a soldier when he wants a word, not the other way 'round."

Morgan ignored his adopted father's effort to inject a bit of humor into the bleak circumstances that grew bleaker with each mile they marched away from New York City. The enemy now had complete and undisputed control of the city, its harbor, and, according to a French officer on Colonel Knox's staff, a central position that would allow them to strike out in any direction whenever they pleased.

"Will we be making a stand here?" Morgan asked without taking his eyes off the gaggle of generals.

"Is that what you called me all the way over here to discuss?" Ian asked incredulously. "You sent a captain off to find me just to ask me a question even the fine gentlemen running this army don't yet have an answer to?"

Morgan shrugged off Ian's retort. "I thought you might have heard something." Pausing, the boy drew in a deep breath as if needing to steel himself before continuing. "Some of the officers I overheard think we will. They say this is the only place between here and the Delaware that offers us a decent chance of stopping the English."

Ian gave Morgan's question some thought as he searched the expressions of the gathered officers. "There's always talk among those who don't know what's going on—rumors, wild speculations, all sorts of nonsense. I expect we'll just have to wait and see."

Snapping his head about, Morgan glowered bitterly. "Wait for what? Wait to see if there's enough of an army left to make a stand? Have you not heard? A whole brigade of Jersey militia will be leaving in two days." Then, after dropping his gaze, he sighed. "I expect most of the regiment will as well when our term of enlistment is up at the end of the year."

"Aye, that they will," Ian asserted grimly. "General Washington knows as well as we do if he doesn't do something soon, he'll not have much of an army left."

"Will you go? Will you head back to Winchester when the time comes?" Morgan asked hesitantly.

"I will not," Ian declared crisply as he brought his musket down off his shoulder, planting its butt end on the ground. "English soldiers took my home from me once. I'm too old and too ornery to let them do it again. Besides," he added wistfully, "the idea of giving up just because we've had a run of bad luck just doesn't seem right."

On hearing this, Morgan gave his head a quick shake and blinked. "A run of bad luck?"

"The way I see it, this isn't all that different than the way things went in the last war. Almost to the very end, things never seemed to go our way for one reason or another. And yet, we still won."

"Things were different back then, weren't they?"

"True, true," Ian nodded thoughtfully before stepping around in front of Morgan and drawing himself up as he often did when he was in a combative mood. "Things were different," he growled menacingly. "For one, we were fighting for the English and whatever it was they wanted. This time we're fighting for what we want. And what I want is to be free of those bastards—now and forever."

Taken aback by the way his father had rounded on him as much as by the fierce defiance he saw in his eyes, Morgan took a step back, causing one of the horses he was holding to rear up. Ian used the time his son needed to settle the skittish animal to steady his rising ire—anger that grew harder to continue with each passing day. The army and its cause drew ever nearer to an abyss much like the one that had destroyed his childhood home and crushed another cause to which he, and so many others, had given their all.

"When the time comes, I want you to go," he stated quietly once Morgan had managed to calm the steeds in his charge. "Marry that German girl who's taken a liking to you and head west. Settle in Kentucky and start a family of your own." Pausing, Ian took to looking about at the quiet New Jersey village he imagined would soon fall victim to the ravages of a vengeful foe. "With luck, you'll escape the worst of the wrath the English and Tories are sure to exact once this is over," he added quietly. As always, when his guard slipped, the memory of the home and family he had lost as a young man played out in his mind.

To Ian's surprise, his son—a quiet lad who had always listened attentively to his advice—turned on him with a vengeance the likes of which he had never seen.

"I will do no such thing!" Morgan snapped as he met Ian's stare with a fiery gaze. "I will marry Gretchen, that I promise. And together, we will start a family, but in Virginia—a free and independent Virginia."

Not knowing what to say, Ian simply blinked as Morgan continued in a low, ominous tone. "My parents ventured into the wilderness with me and my sister in the hope of starting a new life for us. All they found was death. I'll be damned if I'm going to let that happen to Gretchen."

Morgan's response left Ian speechless. Just as Ian never spoke of Culloden and the devastation he had witnessed in the Highlands, Morgan had locked away the memories of his family and their deaths at the hands of a French-led war party. For the first time, Ian realized they shared a common experience that transcended the ties that normally bound a father and son. For them, "victory or death" was more than a trite saying. Without a word, Ian accepted Morgan's resolve—just as Megan had again accepted his own decision to take up arms to fight for something he believed in. Without another word, he reached up, placed a hand on Morgan's shoulder and gave it a firm but gentle shake before turning away and heading off to where the regiment was encamped.

He had no idea where their retreat would end or how the generals gathered on the riverbank would manage to turn their fortune around. All he could count on was that when that happened—if it did happen—Morgan would be there with him. And, for that, he was glad.

New Brunswick, New Jersey
1 December 1776

The appearance of British dragoons belonging to a vanguard of Cornwallis's division caused the alarm to be raised throughout the American camps. Within minutes of this first sighting, companies of light infantry and Hessian jägers began to fan out along the north bank of the Raritan, triggering a hurried, last-minute attempt to burn the bridge over the river by the Americans guarding it. Failure to destroy the bridge put the burden of keeping the enemy at arm's length on the shoulders of Colonel Knox's cannoneers and riflemen. They fired from houses along the southern riverbank while what was left of the army prepared to continue their retreat.

Having spent most of the previous night standing watch, Edward Shields was not roused from his deep, peaceful sleep even by the beating of drums rippling throughout the camp. Even when Kevin Farrell pulled off the blanket in which he had wrapped himself, Edward did little more than roll over onto his side and pry one eye open in an effort to determine what loathsome miscreant had the unmitigated gall to disturb his well-earned rest.

"What?" Edward demanded.

"Are ya deaf? Do you not hear the drums?"

Blinking, Edward propped himself up on an elbow, cocked his head to one side, and took a second to listen. Above the frenzied tune being tapped out on the drums calling his comrades to arms, the sound of cannon and musket fire slowly gained purchase in his sleep addled brain.

"So, they're here," he muttered.

"Aye, they're here," Farrell responded grimly as he dropped down on one knee and began to roll up his own blanket.

On seeing this, Edward heaved a great sigh. "We're retreating?"

"That's what all the fuss is about. Captain says we're to take only our haversacks and blankets. Everything else is to be burned."

On hearing this, Edward jolted fully awake. "The tents?" he asked, praying even as he did so the answer would be the one he hoped for, and not the one he expected.

"The captain says we've neither the time to strike them or the wagons needed to haul them away. The tents, and everything we can't stuff into out haversacks, are to be burned."

Reflexively, Edward looked up at the thin layer of canvas that protected him and his messmates from weather that seemed to grow worse with each passing day. Having no wish to dwell on how they would manage without it in the coming days, he turned his attention to more immediate matters.

"Did the captain say where we'll be going?"

"No, but I expect it'll be west."

As the land his mother had inherited from her Dutch ancestors lay north of New York City along the Hudson, Edward had never found the need to venture into the interior of New Jersey. He was, thus, woefully ignorant of what lay ahead.

"What's west of here?" he asked groggily.

"Not much," Farrell ventured without bothering to give the question much thought. "Other than a few villages and farmsteads, there's nothing until we reach the Delaware."

"And what's on the other side of the Delaware?"

Only after he had finished securing his rolled-up blanket with a leather strap did Farrell look over at Edward who had managed to gather himself up into a seated position.

"Safety," was all he said before rising to his feet, gathering up his pitifully few belongings, and heading off to where the company was forming up.

Left on his own once more, Edward set about gathering up his musket, cartridge box, haversack, and blanket as he prepared for another retreat that would take him further from a home where he felt he was no longer welcomed and a family that was as cold as the wind rippling across the canvas about him. The only comforts he and his comrades would be able to count on would be their blankets, a campfire, and hope that, as long as they held together, the faith they had in their cause, and each other, would see them through.

⁂

From a hill located on the ground of Queen's College, David Gray and the gun crews belonging to Hamilton's battery traded fire with British artillery throughout the afternoon. Other than keeping troops belonging to each side from venturing out into the open, neither David's gun nor those of the British were doing much damage. Not that his guns needed to do anything more than keep the British at bay until what was left of the army had broken camp, destroyed whatever stores and equipment they could not take with them, and marched off toward Princeton.

At the moment, David was finding it difficult to focus on seeking out targets worthy of wasting valuable powder and shot on. Even as he held his spyglass to his eye, scanning the opposite riverbank, he was unable to ignore the French officer who had attached himself to Colonel Knox's small staff standing just behind the battery's gun line as he often did at times like this. The Frenchman was no doubt waiting for the most inopportune moment to step forward and offer unsolicited advice David felt he had no need of.

Like Hamilton, David looked upon the Frenchman as little more than an adventurer, a sellsword who was, in their eyes, no better than the Hessians. The need to draw upon the expertise and experience of professional soldiers like the clashed with an idea held by David and others that, by relying on men who were drawn from the ranks of the Old World, they somehow sullied the cause for which he and his fellow Americans were fighting.

Had David bothered to take the time to ask the Frenchman why he was taking such an interest in what his gun crews were doing, he would have found Anton's reason had nothing to do with the manner with which David's gunners were going about their duties, or the effect British return fire was having on them. If truth be known, Anton was all but ignoring everything save for the one person he was watching—the only person he cared about in an army that was slowly bleeding to death. Anton was wondering as he stood just behind the American gun line how he was going to pry his son away to safety when the last vestige of the cause the boy believed in was stamped out by the same enemy that had brought an end to French rule in Canada.

The signs of imminent collapse were beginning to become all too clear to Anton—a man who had served with the Troupe de la Marine during the entire course of the French and Indian War. He could not help but compare the way civilians and militiamen alike were backing away from a cause many had once embraced. The Indians and the French-Canadian colonists behaved in much the same manner when France's fortunes in the New World had begun to ebb. And while it was true there would always be a determined core of men who refused to yield—just as French regulars and officers like him had stoically soldiered on long after any hope of victory had vanished—there would be no formal surrender such as the one he had been part of in 1760.

Having witnessed the manner with which Corsican independence had been crushed in 1770, Anton had no doubt the end of this rebellion would be followed by retribution meted out by agents of a vengeful King. Officers denied a noble death in the final battle as the Marquis de Montcalm had at Quebec would be hung while soldiers taken under arms would be imprisoned or transported as slaves to the West Indies, if they were lucky. Members of the Continental Congress who had sought to establish a free and independent country would be executed. Even merchants, members of the landed gentry, and farmers who had supported the rebellion would be stripped of all they possessed, if not by agents of the King, then by their former friends, neighbors, and competitors—men who had suffered during the war for the crime of remaining loyal to the English crown. Those rebels who sought to escape into the vast western wilderness beyond the Appalachians would find little peace, for they would be hunted down like animals, provided they did not fall prey to Indians intent on protecting land that was rightfully theirs.

Unwilling to wait until all avenues of flight were closed, in an ill-timed effort to keep his son from falling victim to the vengeance that would follow a collapse of the American cause, Anton had opened a rift between himself and Anthony. It began the day Anthony had returned from Boston. Unable to keep his disappointment in seeing the boy return from showing, Anton did nothing to keep the anger he felt over his son's foolishness in check. Rounding on him, he asked why he had returned.

Anthony was no fool. Having been with the army when it had been nothing more than an ad hoc collection of militia companies called to arms by the cries of men like William Dawes and Paul Revere, he could read the mood of an army as well as any man. In his wanderings through camp in search of Anton, he could not help but notice officers and men alike were on edge—and with good reason. Most of Westchester County and everything south of it, including New York City and its harbor, had been lost to the British. This was a state of affairs that had left Anthony no choice but to follow a long, circuitous route during his return journey. Even more worrisome to the soldiers and militiamen he encountered during his travels was the growing number of men giving up on the cause. In the words of one man making his way home with whom Anthony had shared a meal one night at a backcountry inn, *"We've given it our best, but it just wasn't good enough."* It was a sentiment to which Anthony did not subscribe.

So, when the Frenchman snapped at him asking why he had returned, Anthony replied with a jauntiness he and others used to mask their apprehensions.

"To fight," he had chirped with a nonchalance that caused Anton to shudder.

"Do you not see what is happening?" Anton had shot back brusquely.

Taken aback by the Frenchman's attitude, Anthony had hesitated before responding, looking about as if trying to discover the reason he was being subjected to such an odd line of questioning. Seeing no appreciable difference in the condition of the army he had rejoined—other than it was now in New Jersey and New York was irretrievably lost to the British—Anthony had blinked at a loss momentarily. He had then given his head a quick shake and drawn himself up. *"I am well aware things have not gone well these past few months,"* he had stated ever so carefully.

"Not gone well?" Anton had all but shrieked as he stepped ever closer to Anthony. *"Washington has lost more than a few battles. He's lost a most important city—one the British will use as a base from which they will finish the task of crushing your rebellion come spring."*

It was more than the Frenchman's manner that caused Anthony to rear up. His use of the word *your*, clearly referring to Washington's army for the first time in many months as if he were not part of it. This struck Anthony as being incongruous with the sentiments the Frenchman had laid out in the dispatches he had had him forward to the French minister of foreign affairs. That the words Anton had penned had been a ruse—intended to keep rebel officials from delaying his dispatches—was a secret known only to Anton and the Comte de Vergennes. Only once his messages had reached France and were in the Comte's hands would the paper be exposed to the heat of a candle revealing the hidden caveats Anton secretly included.

Suspecting the Frenchman was losing faith in the American cause, Anthony met Anton's ire with a sharpness that caused his father to recoil.

"You forget, sir, I am from Massachusetts. I've seen firsthand how easily a tyrant and his minions are able to casually set aside the rule of law when it suits their needs, treating those they presume to govern little better than chattel." Warming to the subject, Anthony fixed Anton in a steady, unflinching glare and growled in a low, menacing voice the likes of which Anton had never before heard the boy use. "We have a chance to rid this land of English rule and govern ourselves. I've no intention of letting that opportunity slip away—consequences be damned."

Dumbfounded, Anton was unable to muster up a suitable response before Anthony pivoted about on his heels and trooped away. By the time he was able to discover where the boy had gone off to, it was too late to make amends. He had attached himself to Hamilton's battery, stepping in to replace a gun crew member who had fallen ill.

Standing back, behind the piece his son was serving, Anton watched as Anthony used the gun's worm to scour the bore for embers left by the powder bag of the round just fired. With his attention fully focused on the task at hand, Anthony paid no heed to Anton's presence. That suited Anton, for he was at a loss as to how he would repair the rift between them and convince the boy to flee to France with him when, not if, the enemy—currently engaged in a lively exchange with Hamilton's guns—smashed each and every one of those guns, and with them, the cause they were fighting for.

TWENTY-SIX

"We continued our retreat; our regiment in the rear and I with thirty men, in the rear of the regiment, and General Washington in my rear with pioneers tearing up bridges and cutting down trees to impede the march of the enemy. I was to go no faster than General Washington and his pioneers."

Enoch Anderson
Haslet's Delaware Regiment
December 1776

"It became clearly evident that the march took place so slowly for no other reason than to permit Washington to cross the Delaware safely and peacefully."

Captain Johann Ewald
Hesse-Cassel Jägers
December 1776

Princeton, New Jersey
7 December 1776

BOOKS NEVER held much appeal to James Keating. To his mind, the boys his father allowed him to associate with wasted their time studying subjects that had no practical application to the world they would one day govern. To his knowledge, there wasn't a single merchant in New York City who conducted his affairs in ancient Greek—a language his tutor had taken great pains to all but beat into him. Nor, he suspected, would a study of Marcus Aurelius's *Mediations* have any practical use when it came to dealing with gruff sea captains and the stevedores who unloaded cargo brought into New York from all parts of the world. Besides, for as long as he could remember, James dreamed of being a soldier. One did not need to have a command of Tacitus to lead men into battle. Courage and coolness under fire were the qualities soldiers admired in an officer. In James's opinion, all else was little more than useless foppishness.

Still, the sight of a soldier belonging to the 64th Regiment of Foot hauling away an armful of books from the library belonging to the college housed in Nassau Hall out into the early evening darkness was distressing to him. When James asked the man what he intended to do with the books, the soldier gave James a most peculiar look.

"It'll be cold tonight, sir," the soldier replied. "Colder than last night, I suspect."

Any thought of admonishing the man was dismissed without a second thought. There were precious few houses, barns, and structures worthy of that name in this part of New Jersey. Even he had to make do with nothing more substantial than a hastily erected tent shared with another officer. If the rank and file were to be fit to fight when the army finally caught up with what was left of the rebel army, they needed to be well-rested and in good spirits. On a night like the one they would be facing, that meant having a good fire to cook with and huddle around as they slept. With a curt nod, James sent the soldier on his way.

"The man's right," James muttered to himself as a gust of icy wind caused him to gather the collar of his cloak about his neck. "It is going to be cold tonight."

Too cold to be standing about asking silly questions, he thought as he turned to head off to where his orderly was busy preparing a meal for him over a fire James hoped would keep him warm until morning.

Trenton, New Jersey
8 December 1776

A near miss by a cannonball loosed by rebel guns on the far shore peppered Thomas Shields and his mount with great clods of dirt and mud. With General Howe and Lord Cornwallis calmly discussing the situation but a few yards away, he paid no heed to the way the jägers and light infantrymen who had pushed down to the banks of the Delaware were scattering for cover as he struggled to keep his skittish horse from bolting. Like his superiors, he understood it would not do to be seen scampering away from the contemptible rabble they'd chased across the breadth of New Jersey. Officers were expected to set an example for the men they commanded if they had any hope of keeping them from giving into their fears and fleeing at the first sign of trouble.

Hauptmann Kleist, on the other hand, saw no point in standing about in the open. Like Thomas, he knew there were times when an officer needed to boldly place himself in harm's way if he expected his men to follow. This, however, was not one of them. Having assessed the situation before him and deciding there was little to be gained by providing a rebel cannoneer with an opportunity to take his head off, he swallowed his pride and sought cover behind a dockside shed where several of his men were huddled in hope the enemy would focus their attention on a far more lucrative target, such as the pair of mounted generals who were making no attempt to withdraw to safety.

⊰⊱

As had occurred at Brooklyn, the last boat ferrying Washington's army touched the western bank of the Delaware just as the vanguard of the British army pursuing it appeared. Unlike that occasion, the British had no way of following, for the Americans had taken the precaution of taking every boat and barge along the river for miles with them. Deprived of support from the Royal Navy, it would be some time before the British could collect enough boats to mount a serious crossing, provided they wanted to.

With winter all but upon them, Anton expected the British would follow convention and curtail full-scale operations. With New York well in hand and the whole of New Jersey's bountiful resources to draw from, there was no need to push any further. Whatever was left of the American army could be dealt with come spring by troops who were well-rested and reinforced by fresh levies sent from England to replace soldiers lost during a campaign that had, by any measure, been a resounding success.

Unconcerned with what the gunners he was with were doing, Anton turned his attention to what he would do now. The lateness of the season and the relative safety the Delaware provided him and Washington's army was an opportunity to collect itself. Paying no heed to the desultory cannonading Knox's gunners were engaged in, Anton cast his gaze south, toward the road that led to Philadelphia. If he left now, he reasoned, he would be there by the following afternoon. With the Royal Navy settling in at Newport, Rhode Island for the winter, he expected it would not be difficult to book passage on a vessel headed for either the Spanish or French West Indies. From there he would be free to travel on to France. The only flaw in that plan was his unwavering determination to see to it his son also escaped the retribution all would suffer who had taken up arms against their King.

Turning his attention back to the gun line Knox had established across from Trenton landing, Anton watched Anthony as he went about his duties. *How long,* he wondered, *would the boy stay with the colors once it became clear all hope for their glorious cause was gone? Would he leave on the first of January when the terms of enlistment for many of the American regiments expired?* He knew asking Anthony such a question would have been more than a wasted effort. Anton suspected it would only deepen the rift that had opened between him and his son. He would need to wait until the boy himself came to appreciate the cause he was fighting for had been but a dream. *A noble dream, yes,* Anton admitted, *but a dream nonetheless that, like all dreams, evaporated in the harsh light of reality.*

⋘⋙

"How long do *you* think it'll be before they find a way across?" Ian McPherson asked as soon as Ezra Shaw was near enough to hear him.

Stopping as he entered the small circle of men gathered about Ian, Ezra leaned on his musket for support as he took a moment to study Ian's expression. Only after had gauged the expression of a man who was more than his lieutenant did he slowly settle down in front of a small fire Ian had started using wood collected as what was left of the regiment made its way from the banks of the Delaware to where they hoped they would be spending the night. Ian's grim demeanor and tone of voice told Ezra Ian's spirits were about as low as they could be. In an effort to keep from dragging them down any further, he shrugged.

"Why are ya asking me?" he grumbled offhandedly in an effort to keep from adding to Ian's already cynical outlook. "Your boy probably knows more about what's going on than either one of us."

"I doubt that, not unless the general's horse has begun to talk."

Ian had not meant his comment to be funny, but Ezra, seeing an opportunity to lighten the mood of the men around them, chuckled.

"If it has, I hope it's making more sense than the general. In case you haven't noticed, we're running out of places to retreat to."

"There's always Virginia," Angus Brodie offered as he held his hands out toward the fledgling fire in an effort to warm them. "I wouldn't mind it if we kept going until we were back where we should be."

Before marching off to war, Brodie had spent much of his free time seated before the great hearth in the wayside inn Ian and his wife owned telling stories. Brodie's comment earned dirty looks from both Ian and Shaw.

"I'll be damned if I'm going back to Virginia dragging an army of vengeful Englishmen and their German mercenaries behind me," Ian snapped before Shaw had a chance to offer up a more moderate response. "The red-coated bastards took one home from me. They'll not take another, not as long as I draw breath."

For the longest time no one spoke for fear of evoking Ian's ire as Brodie had. Determined to dispel the hushed tension that had befallen the little group gathered about the fire in the fading light of day, Ezra look over at Ian.

"Say, Ian, have you something in that haversack of yours to eat?"

Just as eager to set aside the bitterness he felt, Ian turned his attention to something other than their wretched plight. After conjuring up something of a smile, he nodded.

"Aye, I do. Would you care for some of it?"

Shaw made a show of straightening up as if he were taken aback by Ian's question. "Well, I wouldn't have asked you if I didn't," he exclaimed.

As one, the others about the fire broke out into a chorus of nervous laughter. They were just as relieved as their captain and Ian were to find a way of setting aside their concerns over what the next day would bring as they prepared to pass a night all suspected would be miserable as amiably as their circumstances, and that of their army's, allowed.

TWENTY-SEVEN

"What we obtain too cheap, we esteem too lightly: it is dearness only that gives everything its value. Heaven knows how to put a proper price upon its goods; and it would be strange indeed if so celestial an article as freedom should not be highly rated."

Thomas Paine,
The American Crisis

New York City
21 December 1776

WHEN WORD THAT General Howe was declaring an end to active campaigning for the year and returning to New York, officers who had little taste for the rustic charms of New Jersey followed their commanding general's example. This sudden influx of the British Army's leadership, fresh from the field, provided Kat Trent with an opportunity too good to pass up. Drawing upon every resource at her command, she all but threw the doors of Minden Hall open to men who had spent the last three months pursuing a foe they had beaten time and again, but had yet to vanquish.

"We had all hoped to draw the rebel army into the open and crush them in a fight worthy of being called a battle, just as we did to the Scots in '46," a colonel opined as Kat was refilling his wine glass. "I expect we'll never get that chance."

"Whatever do you mean?" Kat asked innocently as she met the colonel's lascivious gaze with a look of pure innocence, one she knew men found captivating.

"The winter," a major replied before the colonel could. It was a supposition every officer in the room greeted with nods and knowing smiles without hesitation.

Having captured their comely young hostess's attention, Thomas Shields held out his empty glass toward Kat as he explained.

"You see, Lady Katherine, the terms of enlistment for most of the rebels still in the field expire at the end of this month. I mean, what fool would suffer through a winter such as the one we're facing to fight for a cause anyone with the slightest jot of common sense knows is all but lost?" he added as Kat was filling his glass.

A fool who was fighting for their freedom, Kat found herself thinking as she topped off Thomas' glass. Naturally she did not put her thoughts to words. To have done so, particularly at this point in the evening, would have been counterproductive. After treating this evening's guests to a lavish meal, the kind she imagined they had not enjoyed for months, she had led them to her parlor where she invited them to help themselves to a stock of wines and spirits she kept for such occasions. It was there, in the warm glow of a fire, the men sipped their drinks of choice and freely discussed the events of the past four months, debated the wisdom of decisions made by their betters, and speculated on what the army would do come spring.

Kat was quick to appreciate Major Shields was a particularly harsh critic of how General Howe conducted the campaign that had won them New York and New Jersey but had fallen short of ending the rebellion he and his brother, Admiral Lord Richard Howe, had been sent to crush.

"Had General Howe followed Sir Henry Clinton's advice, this war would have been over months ago," Thomas ventured.

Straightening up after filling Thomas's glass, Kat titled her head to one side as she quizzically gazed down at Thomas. "Am I mistaken, or were not the Howe brothers charged by the King with the responsibility of finding a peaceful solution to this terrible war?"

"Peace comes when the foe has been defeated," another major behind Kat interjected. "We are soldiers, not diplomats—a point some seem to have forgotten."

"Well, if what you say is true about the rebel army, then you will achieve that purpose without the need for further bloodshed," Kat offered as she slowly made her way about the room, filling the glasses of other officers as she went.

"But where would the glory in that be?" Thomas offered, recalling the praise his actions on the field of Culloden had earned him as he took a sip of wine.

Those who agreed with the notion Thomas had put forth raised their glasses and toasted him with a gusty round of slurred "Here, here." Others, like the colonel, eyed the younger officers in the room with a look that did little to hide the contempt he felt for those who were too quick to rush toward the sound of the guns. Had they had to step over the corpses of their fellow officers as he had at Charlestown in April of 1775, he expected they would not be so damned sanguine in their quest for glory—a fleeting commodity purchased at a terrible price.

-⋘•⋙-

Seeing the last of her guests off at the conclusion of each night's festivities and retiring to her room did not put an end to Kat's nocturnal activities. Relying solely on the flickering illumination provided by the fire in the hearth, she pushed aside the ledgers and tally sheets and set about engaging in high treason. She had no idea if the information she gleaned from the officers she entertained nightly and forwarded to David Gray was of any use. For all she knew the chatter that flowed as freely as the wine she served her guests was nothing more than idle gossip—speculation on what should be, rather than what was.

The only thing she was sure of was that doing nothing and remaining aloof of the great events playing out all around her was unacceptable. Having tasted the fruits of freedom, she had no intention of allowing men who were little different than her stepfather to govern her as she had been when she had been but a child.

For her, Patrick Henry's declaration of "Give me liberty, or give me death" was more than a pithy saying intended to rouse his fellow Americans to follow him into open rebellion. Kat had come to believe life without the freedom she had grown to enjoy would be akin to death. She did not imagine it would be a physical death, not like the punishment Patrick Henry and his fellow patriots would be subjected to. Death for her would come in the form of subjugation to a social order she wanted no part of. While some women like Sarah were content to be looked after and live within the traditional boundaries of home, hearth, and children, Kat was a wolf, not a sheep.

Following the same methodical methodology she used to organize her day-to-day activities, Kat quickly scribbled down everything of importance she could recall hearing. When she was finished with her first rough draft, she read it through, amending each item as was necessary, or crossing it out if it struck her as being of little importance. Once done, she prioritized the list and encrypted her notes using a cypher John Jay had developed that used numbers to refer to a page and line where a plain text word could be found in a dictionary both parties had. It was a tedious undertaking that demanded her full attention as she triple checked each piece of information she was passing on. She suspected bad information could be just as harmful to the cause as no information.

From time to time, she found herself working through the night. This was particularly true on evenings when the wine she served had loosened the tongue of even her most taciturn guest. No one, save her ever loyal housekeeper, saw the late hours Kat had taken to keeping as anything out of the ordinary. Had her cousin been present, he might have asked her why she was always so tired. But James, ever the dedicated officer, remained with his battalion in New Brunswick where two battalions of grenadiers and three troops of dragoons were posted—information she knew to be accurate based on James's letters to her.

That her activities could result in a fight that took James's life was a possibility that haunted her. The rationale she drew upon that allowed her to risk the loss of one so dear to her was that freedom was no different than the commodities she dealt in. It came at a price.

Comparing a man's life to a bolt of cloth is cold, she wrote in her journal just before dawn one night after sealing a letter containing her latest collection of information. *Were it not for the discussions I have been privy to these past few weeks, I suspect I would have been unable to make the choice I have regarding James's welfare. But war, I have come to appreciate, is a cruel business. If one is to win, their heart must be as cold as a stone on a winter morn. So, I will soldier on, in my own way, just as the men who have remained with General Washington these past few months—consequences be damned.*

Eastern Pennsylvania
23 December 1776

"You're an educated man," Kevin Farrell declared as he and Edward Shields took their watch along the eastern bank of the Delaware. "Do you think what that fella said is true—that what we're doin' here is gonna make a difference to anyone other than us?"

That fella, Edward knew without needing to ask, was Thomas Paine, a man who frequently traveled with the army and wrote pamphlets extoling the virtue of their cause. His latest missive, entitled *The Crisis*, had been read to the entire regiment just before Edward and Farrell had left camp. They had gone to relieve the corporal's guard watching for any activities by the Hessian garrison at Trenton. At first Edward had dismissed many of the sentiments Paine had put to words as little more than hyperbole—an emotional appeal intended to quicken the pulse and egg on the faint of heart in much the same way fife and drum were used to encourage men going forward into battle.

It was only later, as he and Farrell maintained their silent watch, that Edward gave the meaning of those words the thought they demanded. These were, indeed, the times that tried a man's soul. The fifty odd men belonging to the 1st New York who listened to their regimental commander had long ago seen the backsides of what Paine called sunshine patriots. All that was left were men such as he and Farrell—men willing to soldier on as long as there were others, like them, willing to fight.

"I expect Mr. Paine did get a wee bit carried away with the imagery he used," Edward offered.

"His what?"

"The comparison he made referring to King George as Satan and America as Eve," Edward patiently explained as he always did whenever he used words the farmer did not quite understand. "I mean, I doubt if King George is all evil. He is, after all, human, even if he is a tyrant. And America isn't near as innocent as Eve was. Anyone who's spent time on the docks of New York knows an American can be as intemperate and wicked as the saltiest sailor alive."

"I expect so," Farrell admitted as he scanned the far shore for any sign of the Hessian pickets. "But that wasn't the part I was talkin' about. It's the way he says we have a natural right to be independent of King George. How can he, or anyone else, be so sure of such a thing? I mean, everyone needs to have someone in charge."

Edward did not need to give his response much thought. Drawing upon his own experience and a line Paine had mentioned in his latest pamphlet, he put a question to Farrell.

"Do you not wish to see your son strike out on his own when he's old enough—either taking over your farm or heading west to start his own?"

"He better," Farrell replied gruffly. "I may love the lad with all my heart, but I'll not sit idly by and watch him carry on at my expense like some foppish gentleman."

"That's because you're a good father and willing to endure the anguish you'll feel when the day comes for him to bid you and your wife farewell. King George is not a good father."

"You can't compare what a father does with the way a King runs his country," Farrell countered.

"Can't I?" Edward asked. "And before you answer that, give the matter some thought," he added quickly.

Knowing Edward wouldn't explain any further, Farrell harrumphed loudly. "Serves me right to ask someone who's book-learned a question."

Still, as the day came to an end, ushering in Christmas Eve, the New York farmer gave Edward's explanation and Paine's admonishments the thought they deserved.

TWENTY-EIGHT

"Shit upon shit! Let them come. We will go at them with the bayonet."

Colonel Johann Rall
to Major von Dechow

Bordentown Road, South of Trenton
25 December 1776

A SPATTERING OF musket fire unleashed on the tail end of the small escort he was leading catapulted Hauptmann Kleist out of the lethargic stupor he had fallen into. Having no need to assess the situation, he quickly came about and rushed toward the sound of the gunfire.

"After them," he yelled as he shoved the soldiers he came across to where he suspected the rebels ambushing them were. "Do not let the scoundrels escape."

Eager to reach Trenton before nightfall, the lieutenant who Kleist's small detachment had been escorting countermanded that order.

"Hold to the road," he yelled out to be heard above the tumult caused by the rebel fire and Kleist's response to it.

Confused by the contradictory orders, the soldiers around Kleist hesitated as they took to glancing back and forth between the captain of jägers who was obstinately in charge and the officer they were escorting. On seeing this, Kleist came about on his heels and trooped up to the lieutenant who was the son of a minor nobleman and a member of Colonel von Donop's staff.

"We must run the villainous curs down," Kleist barked angrily as he glared up at the lieutenant mounted upon a mare that had been spooked by the sudden burst of gunfire.

"To what end?" the lieutenant replied once he had managed to regain control of his horse. "Even if your men did manage to catch them, by tomorrow, there'll be twice as many taking their place."

Dumbfounded by what he was hearing, Kleist could do nothing more than stand there before the lieutenant and stare up at him. *Did the fool not understand the only way they had any hope of stopping attacks on foraging parties, couriers, and supply columns by local militiamen was to hunt them down and kill every armed partisan they found?* To simply let them go and to march on without responding would only encourage the treasonous scoundrels that had just fired on them to try again.

The lieutenant did not need to be clairvoyant to know what was going through Kleist's mind. He understood there was a need to make examples of rebels whose attacks on the scattered garrisons were growing bolder with each passing day. On this day, however, that was not his responsibility. Charged with delivering his commander's response to Rall's latest dispatches, the lieutenant returned Kleist's contemptuously glare.

"Reform your men and continue on, captain."

Appreciating there was no point in arguing with an arrogant prig, for the American rebels were, by now, long gone, Kleist snapped curtly, "As you wish."

The lieutenant could not help but take note of the surly manner with which the jäger captain had acknowledged his order. The man had also failed to end his response with the honorific "my lordship"—a courtesy he expected a social inferior such as Kleist to render despite their difference in rank. The lieutenant concluded it did not matter so long as they reached Trenton before dark and he completed his mission. He did not much care what the captain of jägers thought of him.

On reaching Trenton, Kleist wasted little time releasing his men as quickly as he could. Though it was Christmas, he expected they, like he, were in no mood to celebrate. The need to respond to incessant attacks on outposts around Trenton—attacks that grew at an alarming frequency and scale—was wearing on officer and soldier alike. Far from being cowered by the defeats they had suffered during the previous months and the occupation of much of the colony, the people of New Jersey gave every indication that they intended to carry on with a war British generals believed was all but won. As Kleist unbuckled his sword belt and threw himself onto his camp bed—still wearing his frock coat and boots—it never occurred to the German officer that his troops' conduct during the conquest of New Jersey was largely responsible for the growing insurgency now threatening their hold on the colony. He was much too tired to dwell on that—or any other concern. All he wanted was to sleep for a full night undisturbed by the beating of alarm drums. Everything else was of no importance.

New York City
25 December 1776

All through the Christmas service at Trinity Church, Kat Trent could not help but notice the way the two officers she was sandwiched between eyed each other. Each, she suspected, was wondering who would win the right to escort her home after the service. So, it came as no great surprise to her the captain of Guards, seated to her right, turned to her as the last notes of the recessional hymn was fading and bowed.

"Lady Trent, would you do me the honor of allowing me to see you home?"

Kat waited until after they had made their way out of the church before responding. Stepping off the path leading to Church Street, she graced him with a chaste little smile that would have brightened the day of even the glummest man.

"Captain Wilford, I do appreciate the offer. I really do," she replied huskily. "But I am afraid I am obliged to make a number of stops along the way to pay my respects to friends and business associates on this festive holiday."

"I would be more than happy to wait for you as you did so," Wilford offered in a desperate bid to gain Kat's consent.

Canting her head to one side, Kat grinned shyly as she peered up at him through her lashes. "That is most gallant of you. As much as I would enjoy your company, I fear you would soon grow bored. I have been accused of engaging in the sort of discourse a gentleman such as yourself would find dreadfully tedious."

"What gentleman worthy of that title could ever grow bored when in your company?"

In an effort to put an end to this foolishness she was quickly growing bored with, Kat tightened her grip on the captain's hand. It was an action that caused Wilford's pulse to quicken.

"May I suggest that, rather than waste your precious time following me about, you join me for dinner later this evening. I am hosting a Christmas dinner for several of General Howe's officers."

Delighted, Wilford took Kat's hand, brought it to his lips, and kissed it. "I am, as always, Lady Trent, your most humble servant." With that, he bowed, to which Kat answered with a graceful curtsey.

Wilford tarried only long enough after Kat had left his company to give the lieutenant who had been seated to her left a look that warned him it would be against his best interests to step in and attempt to poach the prize he had been denied. That officer, belonging to one of the line regiments that had remained in New York during the army's pursuit of Washington across New Jersey, dutifully averted his gaze, pivoted sharply about, and beat a hasty retreat up Church Street.

With her would-be gallants neatly disposed of, Kat headed off to the Bean in the Pot. There, she collected a basket of parcels containing small cakes and sweets. After chatting with the widow who ran the inn for her and wishing her and the inn's staff a happy Christmas, Kat set off on her rounds.

With this being Christmas, most of the businesses she owned were closed. Her stated purpose for visiting the proprietor of each shop and their families was, for the most part, social. Still, being the kind of person she was, after giving them a parcel from her basket and wishing each member of their families a happy Christmas, she made a point to note their immediate needs as well as collecting any information that might be of use to the American army.

Having spent far longer than she had intended during each of her visits, it was late afternoon before Kat returned to Minden Hall. On entering Sarah Keating's room, she endured a sharply delivered harangue from Sarah for behaving like a silly coquet during her first season.

"Honestly, you would think a woman many believe to be intelligent would have enough common sense to keep her priorities in order." When Kat said nothing, answering with little more than a knowing smile as a maid put the final touches on Sarah's hair, she sighed. "You are incorrigible."

Glancing at Sarah's reflection in the mirror, Kat winked. "Oh, to be sure, I am many things," she replied cryptically. "Now," she continued as she drew herself up. "We must not keep our guests waiting."

"Are you not going to change into something more fitting?" Sarah asked as she eyed Kat's reflected image.

Kat made of show of glancing down at her gown. "And what is wrong with what I am wearing?" she asked innocently. "If it was good enough to enter into the presence of our Lord, it should be more than acceptable to wear while dinning with officers of his Britannic Majesty."

Rolling her eyes, Sarah gave her head a shake. After dismissing the maid tending to her with a wave of her hand, she came to her feet and, facing her dearest friend, heaved a great sigh.

"There's not a day that passes that I do not pray one morning you will wake up and start behaving in a manner fitting your position in society."

Rather than be offended, Kat replied with nothing more than an enigmatic little grin, for she *had* come to accept her responsibilities. They simply were not those associated with the society Sarah was referring to.

"Shall we go?"

Seeing no point in belaboring this oft repeated discussion, Sarah followed Kat from the room and down the stairs where officers invited to enjoy a Christmas dinner with them were anxiously awaiting their hostesses. After a round of greetings and small talk, all took their places at the dining room to enjoy a festive evening of fine dining, pleasant conversation, and unending glasses of wine and spirits.

Even as they were delving into their meal, little more than sixty miles away, an American general stood on a windswept dock jutting into the Delaware River lit by flickering touches. He ignored the cold night air as he watched armed men clothed in little more than rags carefully climb into boats manned by spirited fishermen who hailed from Marblehead, Massachusetts, led by a colonel who was as gruff and hearty as his men. There would be no warm meal waiting for them on the other side of the river. Nor would they be celebrating this Christmas with their families. The task before them was as grim as the password their commander had selected for the enterprise upon which they were embarking.

On this night, "Victory or death" would be more than a way of identifying friend from foe in the darkness of the distant shore. It was a commitment.

-⋘⋙-

On reaching the stately mansion his wife's ancestors had built, Thomas Shields reached out with one hand and placed it on the ornate wrought iron gate to steady himself, but did not open it. Instead, he took to studying the cold, dark edifice before him. Katherine Shields, he expected, was not at home. She seldom was these days. No doubt, he ventured, she was out making merry with her chosen circle of friends, just as he had been. Even if she were home, she would not bother to greet him if he bothered to go in. She had become as cold and lifeless as the wrought iron fence surrounding the house before him.

The catalyst for her behavior was not difficult to fathom. Just as Kat Trent had done, Katherine Shields had taken on the burden of overseeing the various enterprises bequeathed to her and would, he expected, be passed on to their son—a mutinous cur he had no doubt Katherine would manage to save from the hangman's noose. *Why,* he asked himself as he stared at the unopened door before him, *could his Katherine not be more like Lady Trent?* The latter was lively, enticing, and beguiling despite her need to engage in affairs no woman worthy of that title had any business dabbling in. The only rational answer to that riddle in Thomas's mind was that Lady Trent was English. She was from a breed of women who, unlike the dour Dutch witch he was married to, were like swans—graceful creatures gliding serenely along the water while paddling furiously below the surface as they navigated their way through the sophisticated labyrinth of England's social order.

This last thought brought a smile to Thomas's lips. In a few days he would take ship with Lord Cornwallis and head off for England. There, he would be free to spend the winter months in the arms of his mistress—a woman with no need to fill her head with ledger entries and other such foolishness. That it would be weeks before he would lay his head on her warm, inviting bosom caused Thomas to shiver. Until then, he would have to make do with a woman who made her living by selling her company to the highest bidder. With that goal in mind, he turned his back on his wife's mansion and staggered off in search of a bed warmed by a woman who expected nothing more from him other than a few shillings and a pat on the bum when he was finished.

New Brunswick, New Jersey
25 December 1776

Long after his fellow officers had retired for the evening, James Keating remained comfortably sprawled out in a chair before the warm glow from the hearth's fire. With drink in hand, he did his best to picture in his mind the image of his wife and beloved cousin as they celebrated the day's festivities. He had no doubt Kat would go all out as she so often did on such occasions, pilling Minden Hall's dining room table with delicacies until it groaned under their weight. He could all but hear Kat's clear, dulcet voice as she went from engaging her guests in sharp-witted exchanges to no-nonsense discussion on important events of the day, inviting each of them to share their thoughts with her.

The ease with which his cousin was able to entice men into discussions no woman had a need to trouble herself with caused James to raise his glass.

"To you, dear Kat," he muttered to himself as he held out his glass in a toast to his cousin before finishing his drink. With that, he set aside his empty glass, rose to his feet, and retired for the evening.

McConkey's Ferry, Pennsylvania
25 December 1776

Orders to ensure each man had sixty rounds in his cartridge box and three days rations tucked away in his haversack had been enough to alert Ian their general intended to lead them into battle. Instructions that all officers and drummers were to be armed with muskets and the night's chosen password told him the coming fight was to going to be a daring gamble—a desperate roll of the dice no different than the charge of the Highland clans at Culloden had been. For a man who had been part of that wild, frenzied onslaught, the comparisons of that long ago day and the preparations they had been engaged in throughout the day were all too real to ignore.

Like an unwelcome specter, memories of that day haunted Ian as he prepared for the coming ordeal. Then, a ragged army that had rallied to Prince Charles Stuart's banner had set out on a night march with the intent of falling upon the English army asleep in their tents. Stuart's generals had failed him that night, turning back at the last minute. What had followed was a standoff between a well-rested, well-trained, and smartly turned-out foe and a desperate army near the end of their tether.

The sight of Morgan joining the ranks of the 1st Virginia earlier in the day as it was preparing to march off toward the Delaware only served to heighten Ian's unease. He had not been much older than Ian when he had joined the men of his clan in 1745. The difference was, unlike him, Morgan was no wide-eyed innocent. After two years with the regiment, he knew what awaited them on the far shore. He also knew what he was fighting for, just as Ian did. So rather than waste what few precious moments they had before the order to move out was given, Ian made his way over to his son to bid him luck.

On seeing his father drawing near, Morgan drew himself up. "You'll not be telling me to stand aside—not tonight," he declared. "I've the general's permission to go with the regiment."

To Morgan's surprise, in the flickering light of a nearby campfire, he saw a smile slowly tug at the corner of Ian's lips. On stopping before the befuddled boy, Ian reached out with his free hand and rested it on Morgan's shoulder. When he spoke, he did so in a manner he hoped came across as being sincere and heartfelt.

"What I want to tell you—what I need to tell you—is that I am proud to have had the privilege of calling you son."

Though the sentiment his father was sharing with him was one he shared, Morgan was at a loss as how to respond. On seeing this, Ian gave the shoulder he was holding a slight, fatherly pat before bringing his hand away again.

"In the morning, when we go forward, I want you at my side."

Morgan made no effort to hold back the tears welling up in his eyes. "I will be," he replied solemnly. "I will be."

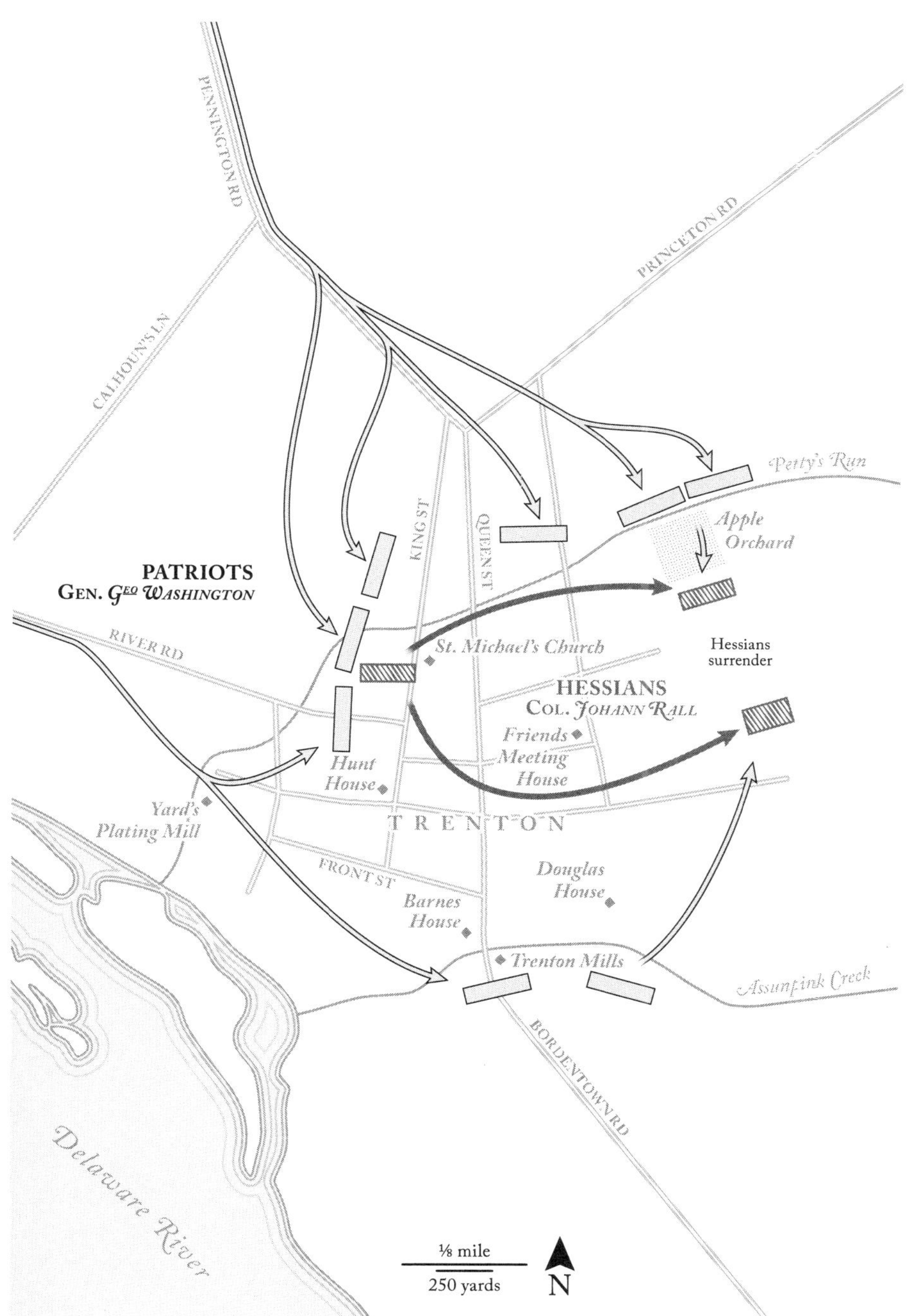
PENNINGTON RD
PRINCETON RD
CALHOUN'S LN
Petty's Run
KING ST
QUEEN ST
Apple Orchard
PATRIOTS
GEN. GEO WASHINGTON
RIVER RD
St. Michael's Church
Hessians surrender
HESSIANS
COL. JOHANN RALL
Friends Meeting House
Hunt House
Yard's Plating Mill
TRENTON
FRONT ST
Douglas House
Barnes House
Trenton Mills
Assunpink Creek
BORDENTOWN RD
Delaware River
⅛ mile
250 yards
N

TWENTY-NINE

"It was broad daylight now, and the storm beat in our faces. The attack commenced on the left, and was immediately answered by Colonel Stark to our front, who forced the enemy's picket."

Major James Wilkerson

On the Delaware, North of Trenton
Just past midnight, 26 December 1776

OVER THE STEADY howl of wind that cut like a knife, the rhythmic swish of oars manned by Colonel Glover's Marbleheaders, and the chattering of his own teeth, Edward Shields could barely hear Kevin Farrell mumbling to himself.

"I hate boats," Farrell grumbled in a voice that was barely audible.

"That's a hell of a thing for a man who lives on an island to say," someone seated behind Edward muttered in a desperate attempt to take his mind off his own misery. "What's so frightening about a boat?"

"Didn't say I was afraid of the damned things," Farrell shot back as he clutched his arms tighter about himself in a vain effort to keep what warmth the ragged blanket he had draped over his shoulders provided. "Said I hated them, them and men who wander about like forlorn souls belonging to the lost tribe of Israel seeking out the Promised Land."

This comment earned Farrell a dirty look from the Marbleheader seated on the bench next to him, one he returned with interest.

"Farming may be hard, but at least ya know what's underneath you and where you are when you wake each morning."

"Have ya any idea where we're gonna be come tomorrow morning?" the gruff fisherman next to him asked as he was pulling back on his oar.

Before answering, Farrell wrapped his arms even tighter against his chest as a gust of wind showered him with a spat of freezing rain.

"I know where I'm not gonna be, and that's here in this boat with you."

As much as he enjoyed listening to the spirited exchange between his friend and the Massachusetts fisherman, if for no other reason than to distract him from his own misery, Edward could not help but dwell on what the morrow would bring. They had been told they would be going up against Hessians—fierce mercenaries who granted no quarter. Surprised or not, the coming fight was not going to be easy. He did not imagine men who made a living hiring themselves out as soldiers would sell their lives cheap.

Even more disconcerting to Edward was they, and not the Hessians, would be the ones pressing home the attack. There would be no earthworks providing cover as there had been on Long Island, or stone walls to protect them from enemy fire as had been the case at White Plains. The regiment would go forward at an unnervingly slow pace, held back by its officers until they were within a musket shot away from the fearsome German mercenaries. What would happen then was anyone's guess. *Would they be brought to a halt in order to unleash a volley? Or would their officers simply call on those who were still with them to charge home with the bayonet—an instrument Edward had yet to use as it was intended?*

Such questions swirled about in Edward's head like the eddies left by each stroke of the oars manned by Glover's New Englanders. All Edward could be sure of was that he would be there, on Farrell's left, when they were answered.

On the Jersey Shore of the Delaware, North of Trenton
Just past midnight, 26 December 1776

For the third time in less than an hour, the lieutenant standing next to Anton held a pocket watch out before him, flipped open the cover with his thumb, and tilted it in the palm of his gloved hand, this way, then that, until he could read the watch's face in the glow of a nearby fire. After drawing in a deep breath, the lieutenant looked up, snapped the watch closed, and muttered something to himself Anton expected was a colorful oath, for Washington's army, which should have been fully assembled and ready to move on Trenton by now, was far from achieving that goal.

Turning his attention back to the spot where a cannon was being unloaded from a barge, Anton watched as his son tugged on a rope attached to the gun. At the moment, he was shifting his weight about in an effort to gain better footing on the frozen riverbank before giving it another go. The boy, Anton realized, was just as determined to fight on as he was to do whatever was in his power to save him from the hangman's noose. Having failed to wrestle his son away from the cause he was wed to, Anton decided the best he could do on this night and, during the coming battle, was to do all in his power to ensure he survived both.

To that end, Anton carefully made his way down to where Anthony and the other members of the gun crew he belonged to were pushing and pulling their six pounder off the barge. On reaching them, he grabbed the dangling end of the rope his son was tugging and began to pull.

The added heft on the rope he was gripping caused Anthony to cast a quick glance over his shoulder in an effort to see who was behind him. The sight of the French major heaving away brought a smile to his face—one Anton returned despite the freezing rain pelting his face. Though their purposes for pulling on the same rope were poles apart, on this day, father and son would meet whatever challenge awaited them together.

The sight of the French major pulling on the end of a rope also brought a wry smile to David Gray's lips. "Welcome to the party," he muttered derisively.

Thinking David's comment had been directed at him, a captain whose regiment was providing security for the landing site glared. "Excuse me?"

Unaware someone had come up next to him from behind and was had overheard him, David blinked as he looked over to see who it was.

Realizing he had taken the young lieutenant of artillery by surprise, Ezra Shaw turned his attention back to where the gun crew had finally managed to haul their piece off the barge and up onto the riverbank.

"We're running late, aren't we?"

Without needing to check the pocket watch he was holding in the palm of his hand, David nodded. "More than an hour. And the army's nowhere near finished crossing."

On hearing this, Shaw grunted as he tightened his grip about the musket he was cradling tightly against his chest as if to protect it from the freezing rain that now beginning to mix with snow flurries.

"With a ten-mile march ahead of us, it'll be well past dawn before we reach Trenton."

"I expect so," David replied grimly.

Neither man said anything more. There was no need to. Both understood what that meant. The surprise General Washington had been counting on to give his army an edge in the coming battle would be lost. The Hessian garrison in Trenton, alerted by their outposts, would be drawn up in battle lines and ready to receive the American attack. Still, there was no turning back—not now. David and Shaw, as well as the men they would soon be leading into battle, were committed.

Along the Pennington Road, Northwest of Trenton Just after dawn, 26 December 1776

The only way Morgan was able to avoid being blinded by snow and rain being buffeted about his face by the howling gusts of wind was to keep bent. He leaned over with his shoulders hunched forward and his head bowed as he trudged along, following the bloody footsteps of the men who had gone before him. With each step he took, he whispered a silent prayer of thanks to Gretchen Richter. Without needing to be asked, the daughter of German immigrants had thoughtfully included a pair of stockings she had knitted for him in a package Morgan's mother had sent to Ian by way of a peddler she often dealt with whenever he was passing through Winchester on his way from Philadelphia. Unlike the poor bastard ahead of him, Morgan was well shod and clothed thanks to her and a father who had an uncanny knack for finding whatever they needed before it was needed.

On this night, however, warm stockings and shoes were not near enough to protect him from the storm that had blown up not long after they had left their Pennsylvania encampment. Numbed by the bitter cold and exhausted by a harrowing night bereft of sleep, Morgan's mind flitted from one random thought to the next. He found it odd that he could picture every detail of the German girl with whom he had grown up with as if she were there before him. But, for the life of him, no matter how hard he tried, he could not conjure up a single memory of the woman who had given him life. He supposed that was to be expected as he had been but a toddler when she had been taken from him. Still, he imagined someone as important as his mother should have left a more lasting impression on him.

Perhaps that was the way of things, he reasoned as he clutched the musket he held in the crock of his arm tightly against his side. His mother—his birth mother—had once been important to him, but was no more. She was a relic of the past, a person who had nurtured him when he had been a helpless babe, but was no longer needed now that he had matured into a full-grown man able to make his own way in the world. Maybe England and its King were no different. His future, and that of Virginia, did not belong to them, not anymore. They belonged to Gretchen and the family he expected they would one day have.

"Sections break off from company!"

Ezra's Shaw's order, shouted out above the howling wind in a single breath, caught Morgan by surprise. Snapping his head up, he suddenly realized the man who had been in front of him a moment ago was no longer there. Like those before him, he left the road, following his officers as they signaled for the men to form into lines of battle. After giving his head a quick shake, clearing it of the mental fog he had been lost in, Morgan picked up his pace and rushed to catch up.

Without stopping, the regiment pressed forward through the barren forest they had been moving through as best they could, deploying into lines of battle as they went. Once they were clear of the woods and in the open, Morgan took to looking around. Like the 1st Virginia, the other regiments belonging to Sterling's Brigade were moving forward under leaden grey skies and across snow-covered farm fields just north of the town of Trenton. Save for a single, unarmed blue-clad figure standing in the doorway of a house two hundred yards or so from where they were, there was no sign of the enemy.

Gone was the debilitating exhaustion he had been fighting through but a minute before. Forgotten too was the bitter cold that had all but numbed both his body and mind.

"We've caught them asleep," Morgan gasped in utter amazement as he went forward, jostling with the men to his left and right as they struggled to keep their place in the ranks.

In the distance, the blue-clad figure began to yell in German.

"What's he saying?" Ian asked without taking his eyes off the doorway of the distant house as other Hessians began to tumble out of it.

"The enemy, the enemy," Morgan replied as he watched the first figure, who was clearly an officer, frantically push and shove his men into a line stretching across the road before the house.

"Now there's a brave fellow," someone off to Morgan's left muttered as they watched soldiers who were clearly part of an outpost prepare to receive them.

"He's a damned fool," another added.

"If that's so, he'll soon be a dead one," Ian snapped. "Now quiet in the ranks and listen up for orders."

After coming to a halt, an officer began to issue a now familiar series of orders Morgan responded to without hesitation.

"Pose firelocks!"

Even though he instinctively knew they were too far from the small detachment of Hessians, Morgan obediently brought his musket up until it was perpendicular to the ground and its lock was level with his eyes.

"Cock firelock!"

With a twist to the left, Morgan turned his musket so that the lock was now turned away from his him while, at the same time, sharply bringing his right elbow up until his arm was horizontal to the ground. He momentarily rested his right thumb on the lock's cock. Then, without any need for further prompting, in near unison with the other men belonging to Sterling's Brigade, he smartly jerked the hammer back into the fully cocked position. This action did more than prepare the weapon to be fired. The sharp, metallic click of hundreds of hammers being locked into position was galvanizing to the soldiers performing the drill and intimidating to those who were about to receive their volley.

"Take aim!"

"We're too far," someone muttered loudly.

That revelation, as far as Morgan could tell, did not stop the man who had made that observation or anyone else from bringing their muskets up, tucking the butts into their right shoulder, and taking aim at the small detachment of Hessians.

"FIRE!"

On the River Road, Trenton
A few minutes past 8:00 AM, 26 December 1776

The soldiers belonging to Major General John Sullivan's division were bearing down on Trenton from the west when the sound of distant gunfire off to the left told them the battle had been joined. To a man, the men of the 1st New York quickened their pace. Eager to close with the enemy before they found themselves facing more than the handful of jägers spilling out of an isolated house off to one side of the road they were on, Edward used his musket to push the man in front him along.

"Come on!" he implored sharply through clenched teeth. "Come on!"

The soldier he was shoving did not turn on him. He was just as caught up in the rush to fall upon the Hessians before they had a chance to recover from their surprise and defend themselves.

"Come on!"

The Military Barracks at the head of Front Street, Trenton
A few minutes past 8:00 AM, 26 December 1776

Kleist did not need someone to tell him they were, once more, under attack. The sound of men shouting, the pounding of feet on the wooden stoop outside his door, and the faint echo of gunfire in the distance were sufficient to rouse him from his deep slumber. It was not until he was reaching for his sword and sword belt that he noticed the light of a new day streaming through the window of his room.

By the time his excited orderly threw open the door to wake him, Kleist was on his feet and ready to sally forth. In an effort to calm the jangled nerves of the man before him, Kleist made a show of adjusting his hat in a small mirror hanging on one of the room's walls.

"I see the rascals have grown bold," he declared in the same deliberate manner he relied on to steady his men when on the verge of losing their heads. "A raid in broad daylight, on a day like this?" Turning, he greeted his orderly with a well-crafted little smile. "Well, let us see what this is all about."

Having caught a quick glimpse of the mass columns of rebels making their way down the River Road and into town, the orderly was tempted to warn his captain this was more than a raid. But the orderly was but a private—a common soldier who knew better than correcting an officer. So, he dutifully stepped aside, away from the open doorway, and allowed Kleist to pass him.

The sight of his NCOs hastily assembling his company pleased Kleist. These men were professional soldiers who knew what needed to be done without his needing to tell them. A single glimpse of the rebel columns bearing down on them, though, horrified him. This was no raid. It was a full-scale attack. Dropping all pretenses, Kleist hastened to join his company. Without pausing before it to assume command from his senior sergeant as custom dictated, he yelled out to his company to follow as he ran past them and toward the house just outside of town where a small corporal's guard of jägers was posted. He gave no thought to the fact that even if he did reach the outpost before the rebels did, his forty odd men would be woefully inadequate to stop the American attack. They were, after all, rebels, contemptuous vermin who, in the past, always fled before them like so many frightened children. Kleist was sure a determined show of defiance and a well-delivered volley—maybe two—would be enough to bring them to heel. His men were professionals.

Efforts by the Hessians posted along the River Road to buy their fellow soldiers time to assemble, valiant as it was, did nothing to impede the forward momentum of Sullivan's division. An attempt by Hessian commanders to collect their men as they tumbled out of the houses, stables, and barns and form a line of battle along the western edge of the town was quickly undone by a devastating barrage loosed by American cannons and howitzers arrayed along the Pennsylvania bank of the Delaware. In danger of being overwhelmed by Sullivan's division closing in from the west and the enfilading artillery, Hessian officers had no choice but to withdraw and abandon the lower part of the town to the Americans. In doing so, they opened the way for the rebels to continue their advance toward Assunpink Creek south of Trenton and the only bridge that crossed it.

At the forefront of this advance were Edward Shields and Kevin Farrell. Discovering that every round in their cartridge boxes was wet did nothing to slow them as they made their way along Front Street. Both were following on the heels of their company commander and jostling with the men around them when a Hessian soldier came charging out of an alley between two houses.

Farrell was the first to catch sight of their assailant out of the corner of his eyes. Wheeling about to his right, he lunged at the Hessian who used his musket to parry Farrell's wild attack. Coming up on Farrell's left, Edward took advantage of the opening the Hessian's desperate move had created.

Animated by an all-consuming rage, Edward tightened the grip on his musket as he drove the tip of his bayonet into the Hessian's exposed midsection. Shocked, the Hessian turned his attention away from Farrell, locking eyes with Edward as he released the grip he had on his own weapons and grabbed the barrel of Edward's. Ever so briefly he struggled to keep Edward from driving his bayonet further into his body—a last desperate act of a dying man that failed.

For the longest time the two of them just stood there, staring at each other as if neither could believe what had just happened or knew what to do. Wishing to put an end to this grizzly standoff and be free of the Hessian, Edward brought his left foot up, planted it squarely against the Hessian's chest, and pushed the dying man off his bayonet.

Mesmerized by sight of the dying Hessian writhing in the throes of death on the ground at his feet and clutching the bloody gash he had made, Edward did not move until Farrell, satisfied the Hessian was finished, grabbed him by the arm and gave it a quick jerk.

"Come on, boy!"

Snapping his head about, he met Farrell's steady, unflinching gaze. "He's done." With that, the farmer turned soldier nudged the former student along. Together they rushed off to rejoin their company that had continued to make its way down Front Street, yelling like fiends as they went.

What shocked Edward as he pushed his way forward in an effort to keep up with Farrell was how easy it had all been. There had been no need to think, no need to weigh the morality of taking a life. The Hessian was his enemy—a foreign mercenary sent by an English King to whom Edward felt no allegiance. The sooner he rid this land of both, the sooner Edward would be free to live his life as he, and not others, saw fit. It was that shockingly simple.

THIRTY

"We presently saw their main body formed. But from their motions they seemed undetermined how to act."

George Washington
on seeing the Hessians
in Trenton respond to
the American attack

High Ground, North of Trenton
26 December 1776

IN MAKING HIS way forward to where he needed to position his gun, David Gray could not help but notice men who had, just a short time ago, been consumed by their own misery, were now alert and animated. The grim determination that had driven them to push on throughout a night of unimaginable suffering was still there but now that indefatigable resolve was focused on driving home the attack. Whatever doubts David had entertained concerning the wisdom of embarking on an enterprise that had struck him as being little more than a desperate gamble were gone. It would be victory for them, and death to the Hessians.

On reaching a spot that gave him a clear, unobstructed view of the unfolding scene before him, David stopped. Ahead, at a distance of less than a mile, he could see the entire town of Trenton laid out before him like a map.

The road they had traveled from McConkey's Ferry continued down into the town where it met the one leading to Princeton at the northern edge of the town. There, the two roads bifurcated, forming a pair of streets running north to south, diverging further apart as they went. At their foot, a creek ran and was spanned by a single stone bridge. In the center of town, David caught glimpses of the men belonging to the Hessian garrison rushing to form up on their regimental colors. Without needing to be told, he knew they would not be the first target he would fire on. That honor belonged to a small battery of regimental guns that had taken up a position at the juncture of the two north-south streets. Those Hessians who had managed to fall in on their colors were firing on the American line as it slowly wrapped its way around the town to the left.

The sound of the limber horses huffing and the jingling of their harnesses as they struggled to pull his gun forward caused David to glance over his shoulder.

"Here," he yelled to be heard over the howl of the bitter winter wind that whipped past him unabated.

The gun captain, on spotting his officer, gave the lead limber horse's bridle a tug to one side as he led the animal and the gun it was pulling to the spot David was pointing at.

Like the other members of his gun crew, Anthony Carter was eager to bring their gun up and engage the enemy. So too was Anton—only his response was purely visceral. Like all veteran soldiers, it took but a single whiff of gunpowder to quicken his pulse. To him the smell of battle was more intoxicating than the most exotic perfume imaginable. Caught up in the moment and unable to hold back as he had in past battles, he put his back into helping the gun crew his son was part of to lift the piece up off the limber and wheel it around. Though he was tempted to usurp the authority of the young American lieutenant standing off to one side, Anton knew it was not his place to point out targets to the gun captain. Not that he needed to, for the obvious choice was a pair of enemy guns that were already being taken under fire by a Pennsylvania battery.

"There," David Gray called out to his gun captain as he thrust his arm out toward the same Hessian guns Anton had been eyeing. "Solid shot."

He expected that last command had been unnecessary, for the gun captain was just as savvy as to what type of ammunition was best used in a counter battery duel. Still, he had given it. There was a set drill he needed to adhere to and the gun crew, fast becoming proficient at their trade, were expected to follow.

With the gun in place and its crew going about their duties with an adroitness that belied the notion they were, in comparison to the Hessian gunners they were about to fire on, amateurs, Anton once more found himself to be little more than a bystander. Stepping back to keep out of the way of the gun crew, he watched as the batteries Colonel Knox had brought forward began to smother the Hessian guns in a deluge of deadly fire. One by one, the Hessian gunners and the limber horses they would need to move their guns back if they hoped to keep them from being captured by Washington's advancing infantry were being struck down. It was, in that moment and without giving the matter the thought he should have, Anton decided when the time was right, he would go forward and not only help capture those guns but, if he could find enough willing hands, turn them on their previous owners.

It was more than a foolish plan. It was reckless. He had no need to expose himself to the danger a fight for the guns would result in. A gunner fought to save their guns with the same bloody-minded doggedness musketeers fought to keep their regimental colors from being captured by their enemy. This was not his war. He had been charged with the duty of observing and reporting on the American rebellion against their King, not join their fight. That had been the Comte de Vergennes's sole purpose in sending him to America. Vergennes, however, was a politician, but Anton was a soldier. With the acrid smell of gunpowder filling his nostrils and a tantalizing opportunity to do more than simply stand about while others acted, the instincts of the soldier prevailed.

Trenton
Along the western side of Kings Street
26 December 1776

Rushing headlong through the backdoor of the first house he came upon, Ezra Shaw paused but a second. Only when he was satisfied it was unoccupied did he level his musket to his side and, with its bayonet held out before him, make his way through to the front room of the house. There, he threw himself to one side of the doorway leading out to the street beyond before turning about to face the men following him.

"Those of you who have muskets in good working order take up at a window. Those who need to, do what you can to clear your piece."

Ian, who had been following close on Shaw's heels, took up position at the open front door opposite him. Having no need to fiddle with his weapon, for it was one of the few in good working order, he took a quick peek outside. The scene playing out on the street before him was chaotic. To his left, at the north end of the road, a spirited melee was underway around the Hessian guns that had been firing on them earlier. Up and down the street, and on the next one over, Hessian officers were attempting to bring some semblance of order to their shaken commands. For their part, the Hessian soldiers were not at all sure what to do. Some were in ranks, patiently waiting for someone to lead them forward, into the attack. Behind them officers were grabbing any soldier they could lay their hands on in a desperate effort to add to the ragged line of battle. Others were making their way forward to join the melee the Hessian gunners were clearly losing. More than a few were simply standing about, looking up the street to where the fighting was sharpest, then glancing longingly in the opposite direction to where, Ian imagined, they hoped to find safety.

After sizing up the situation, he brought his musket up, jerked the hammer back to full cock with his thumb, took aim at one of the Hessians who seemed hell-bent on joining the fight swirling around the guns, and fired. Expecting to catch a glimpse of Morgan standing at the window closest to him when he stepped back out of the open doorway in order to reload his musket, Ian was momentarily rattled when he saw his son was nowhere in sight.

"Morgan!"

On hearing his lieutenant's plaintive cry, Shaw glanced over at him as he was bringing his musket up to fire.

"I expect the lad's somewhere in the back room with the others, drying his musket."

Shaw's explanation was both welcomed and vexing. Ian had twice asked Morgan if he had taken all necessary precautions to ensure his powder stayed try and his musket's lock was covered. He had done so once as they were preparing to leave camp on the Pennsylvania side of the river and again when they were about to begin the march on Trenton. Morgan had responded the first time Ian had asked with a quick, curt nod of his head. The second time had been abrupt. *"Yes, of course,"* he had snapped. *"You would think I didn't know better."*

Expecting the prospect of battle had his son as keyed up as he was, Ian had said nothing at the time. Nor, he decided as he turned his attention to reloading his musket, would he when this fight was over and they were back in camp, wherever that might be. The boy, he figured, would be sufficiently chastened by the way his self-assuredness and cocky arrogance had betrayed him. No need to rub the lad's nose in it.

In this, Ian was spot on. On discovering his efforts to fire resulted in nothing more than a flash in the pan, the sound of his father's voice muttering the oft repeated *"Did I not tell you!"* echoed in his ears. All the way down the hill from where the regiment had first formed and into the town of Trenton, Morgan's thoughts were not on the dangers he was about to encounter, but rather the stern admonishment he would be subjected to when the battle was over. It was a need to do whatever he could to mitigate the venom he would be subjected to when that time came, as well as join a fight he had made such a fuss over participating in, that Morgan set about clearing his fouled weapons as quickly as he could.

On entering the house Ezra Shaw and his father had ducked into, Morgan ran over to a table in a room he thought to be a kitchen. With a sweep of his arm, he cleared a table sitting in the middle of the room, lay his musket upon it, and, with deliberate haste, set to work.

In addition to the rounds of ammunition neatly stored in his cartridge box, all the tools he needed to care for his weapon were tucked away in a pocket stitched onto the front of it. Since the flint of his musket striking the lock's frizzen had twice managed to ignite the fresh powder he had poured into the pan when he had attempted to fire his musket, Ian knew there wasn't a problem with it. Logic, and a very embarrassing experience Ian never let Morgan live down, told him the cartridge was, in all likelihood, wet. That meant he would need to draw the round out, dry the barrel as best he could, and reload a fresh, dry round.

To this end, Morgan fished a small tool known as a worm from the compartment where it was stored. After attaching the piece that resembled a double corkscrew to the end of his musket's ramrod, he inserted the ramrod down the length of the barrel and, on meeting resistance, carefully twisted. Only when he was sure he had managed to sink the pointy ends of the worm into the ball and wadding at the breech end did Morgan begin to draw them out, taking his time in doing so, least the worm lose the tenuous purchase it had on the soft lead ball. Both his skill in the handling of weapons and his determination to keep his desire to rush the extraction of the ball in check were rewarded. The offending ball, the wadding of paper in front of it, and the damp powder were all cleared in his first attempt.

As eager as he was to join the others in the front room of the house, Morgan took the precaution of running a dry patch of cloth down his musket's bore. Not having a stitch of clothing on him that was dry, he looked about the room for something he could use. Snatching up a cloth among the broken crockery he had swept off the table, he used his teeth to rip off a piece small enough to do the job. After stuffing it down the musket's muzzle, he used his ramrod to drive the patch down the full length of the bore. Extracting the ramrod once it had rammed the patch home, he twirled it over his head and reinserted the end with the worm attached to it. Once more, he gave the ramrod a twist. When he was sure he had managed to latch onto the patch, he pulled it out.

Only when he was satisfied the bore of his weapon was dry did Morgan move on. To be sure all was in order, after unscrewing the worm from his ramrod and returning it to its pocket, he withdrew the vent pick. Resting the musket on his knee, he inserted the pick and drew it out, carefully inspecting the small, sharp wire for any sign of moisture. Satisfied it was dry, he went about loading his musket with a fresh cartridge. Only when he was ready did he make his way into the front smoke-filled room where his father and the others belonging to his company were firing on the mass of Hessians milling out in the street beyond.

Morgan made a point of catching his father's eye as he took up a position at a nearby window.

Looking up from his musket as he was loading, Ian could not help but smile to himself when he caught sight of Morgan. He was proud of the boy. That pride, however, would not save the lad from a good tongue lashing, for negligence as heinous as Morgan's could not be allowed to pass without comment. That, however, would have to wait, Ian reminded himself as he brought his own musket up to the ready, peeked around the corner, and took to searching for a suitable target.

Trenton
North end of town, at the juncture of Kings and Queen Streets
26 December 1776

Having beaten back a determined effort by Hessian grenadiers to recapture their regimental guns, Anton turned his attention to putting them into action against their previous owners. At first, this proved to be difficult. Not only were the soldiers who had help wrestle the guns from the Hessians eager to press home the advantage, but American soldiers in the midst of a vicious fight with foreign soldiers were naturally suspicious of any officer with an accent. Still, despite the hesitation from some of the soldiers he was attempting to dragoon, Anton managed to gather enough men willing to sling their muskets over their shoulder and lend a hand.

As quickly as he could, Anton pushed and shoved men who were now part of his ad hoc gun crew into position, explaining to each as he did so what was expected of them. He himself drew a round of canister from the gun's powder box, carried it to the muzzle end of the cannon, and inserted it, looking down the length of the gun as he did so to make sure the man he had assigned as vent tender was holding his calloused thumb pressed down on the vent. Stepping back, he directed the American to whom he had given the ramrod to drive the round home. At another time, the man's awkward handling of the ramrod would have earned him a sharp reprimand. This, however, was not the time or place for such things. Getting the job done as quickly as possible was all that mattered.

Returning to the gun's breech end, Anton took the powder horn he had stripped from the body of a dead Hessian gunner and motioned for the vent tender to step away.

"You prime the piece like this," he told the attentive vent tender in a calm voice that belied the nervous excitement he felt at being in combat. After handing the powder horn back to the vent tender, Anton motioned to a soldier holding the linstock to step forward. "The piece will recoil quite violently," he told the man. "Stand here." When he was satisfied, he continued, "Reach out and touch the priming powder with the lit end of the match."

Hesitantly, the soldier complied, causing the pile of powder surrounding the vent to ignite. The bright fizzling of powder was followed by a deep-throated roar. Even before the gun had settled and the smoke had cleared, Anton turned to his novice gun crew.

"Again. As I showed you," he barked crisply.

To a man, they responded with an enthusiasm that brought a smile to his face. It was a smile his son mirrored as he waited for the powder handler belonging to his gun to bring up a fresh round. He was glad to see the French major had decided to join their fight. Perhaps, when this battle was over and he had a free moment, he would be able to approach the major and renew the friendship the two had enjoyed in the past. It no did not matter at all if, in doing so, the Frenchman tried, once more, to lure him away to France. The bond he hoped was still there was far too important to let a little thing like that keep them apart.

"Carter!" Anthony's gun captain cried out. "Pay attention."

Pulled back from his wandering thoughts, Anthony brought the wooden end of his ramrod up and drove home the charge the powder handler had inserted into the gun's maw.

Until the order to once more move his gun was given, David Gray had little to do but observe the effectiveness of its fire and keep an eye open in case the situation took an unexpected turn. Not that that seemed likely—not now, he realized as he watched the shattered remains of the Hessian regiments draw back and away from the brutal pounding they were being subjected to by a deadly combination of cannon fire and musketry.

Having gained control of the point where King and Queen Streets met, Knox's batteries were free to fire down their full length, pelting the Hessians with round after round of grapeshot. Soldiers belonging to Mercer's and Sterling's brigades who had taken up positions in and around houses along King Street were adding to the maelstrom. With the sound of fighting to their rear, those Hessian officers who still had their wits about them began to shepherd whatever soldiers they could gather around them eastward—out of town and into an orchard where they hoped they would find an open line of retreat.

They would not find it, David told himself. Even as he was watching, Virginians belonging to Stephen's Brigade and Fermoy's Brigade of continentals and Pennsylvania Germans were rushing to sever the road leading from Trenton toward Princeton. All that remained to be done was to continue pouring shot and canister into the middle of the confused mass of Hessian soldiers and wait until their officers realized they had no choice but surrender.

South of Trenton, along Assunpink Creek 26 December 1776

"They're surrendering."

"Well, wouldn't you?" Kevin Farrell asked caustically as he and Edward Shields watched company after company of Hessian soldiers hoist the butt ends of their muskets upright to signal they were giving up the fight. "With us over here, and all those other fellows over there wrapping their way around them, they've nowhere to go."

Edward, and the soldiers belonging to Sergeant's Brigade who had taken up positions south of Assunpink Creek, blocking the road to Bordentown, could clearly see that. Still, as welcome as the idea was that the hated mercenaries who had hounded them on Long Island and at White Plains had been beaten, it was difficult for him to accept. Only slowly, as the sound of battle died away and the sight of American officers making their way forward to accept the proffered swords of Hessian officers did he finally relax the grip he had had on his musket.

"It's over," he whispered in awed reverence.

"Not hardly," Farrell quickly countered. "I expect, once word gets out we're here, every English soldier and German mercenary in New Jersey will come running with but one thought in their heads."

"What would that be?" Edward asked naively.

Before answering, Farrell turned to face his young friend. "Vengeance."

THIRTY-ONE

"Heard the news a whole brigade of Hessians under Col. Rall being taken prisoners by a large body of Rebels and at nine o'clock in the morning. I was exceedingly concerned on the public account, as it will tend to revive the drooping spirit of the rebels and increase their force."

Ambrose Serle
Private secretary to
Admiral Richard Howe
27 December 1776

Mount Holly, New Jersey
Late afternoon, 26 December 1776

THE DESIRE TO use the minor wound sustained during his company's fighting withdrawal from Trenton as an excuse to hide his face was almost too strong an urge to resist, but it was one Hauptmann Gustav Kleist had no choice but to confront and overcome. He was, after all, an officer. In addition to the duties he was expected to carry out regardless of circumstances, there was the matter of his honor. To shirk in a corner like a frightened child would only add to the humiliation of his company's flight from Trenton.

In his heart, Kleist knew his decision to surrender in the face of overwhelming odds had been more than right. At the time, and in the circumstances under which he had made it, it had been the only choice open to him that made any sense. To have done otherwise and stood his ground until the last of his men had been struck down or taken prisoner as Rall's regiments had been would have been folly. Still, that did not make the panicked flight of camp followers, wagoneers, farriers, and other riff-raff an army relied upon that his company had been caught up in was any less humiliating.

As he was reporting the particulars of the battle as best he could to Colonel Carl von Donop, Kleist found he could not ignore the cold, accusatory stares officers and members of von Donop's staff had held him in as they listened in silence. *How,* Kleist imagined they were asking themselves, *could three regiments of professional soldiers allow themselves to be caught so badly unprepared to meet an attack as Rall's brigade had?* It was unthinkable, even to him. Yet, there was no denying it had happened. Nor could anyone listening to Kleist's candid report ignore that unimaginable feat had been perpetrated by a ragged army all had believed would, in a few months, be no more.

That assumption, now seen in retrospect as more of a hope than an inevitability, was no more. Americans would take heart from Washington's victory. His depleted ranks would be filled with fresh recruits. The militia that had been harassing British and Hessian outposts scattered across New Jersey would be emboldened to redouble their efforts. And a rebellion that should have been crushed months ago had there been a will to bring the full weight of British forces to bear had, in a single day, been given new life.

All who had listened to Kleist's report on the audacious rebel attack, and the ferocity with which it had been carried out, suddenly realized the war was far from over. A new campaign would be launched, the sooner, all agreed when Kleist was finished, the better. The stain on the honor Rall's defeat left on every Hessian officer and soldier in the Americas had to be expunged.

On being dismissed by von Donop, Kleist drew himself up, saluted smartly, and pivoted about. There was much to be done. He needed to gather up the remains of his company and prepare them for the coming battle—one he was determined to win or die trying to win. His honor as an officer would be satisfied by nothing less.

New Brunswick, New Jersey
Evening, 26 December 1776

News that the entire Hessian garrison at Trenton had been captured by an army they had bested on every occasion was, at first, dismissed by James Keating's fellow officers. Even when it was confirmed, they found it difficult to accept a ragtag mob of provincials had somehow managed to cross a major river undetected and take the Hessians completely by surprise. The incredulity, however, did not keep them from taking every conceivable precaution to ensure their commands did not share the same fate that had befallen the hapless Hessians. On the heels of word that Trenton had been attacked came rumors the rebels would follow up their success with a quick strike at other posts. Only the coming of night without any sign of the rebels eased those fears, allowing those officers who were not on duty to retire to their quarters. There, they gathered together and did what officers always did in the wake of an unexpected turn of events; they shared their opinions on how any officer worthy of that title could have allowed his command to be caught so unprepared as Rall apparently had and what their generals would do by way of a response.

"The Hessians may be German, but they're not of the same caliber Frederick the Great demands of his troops," a major who had served with Sackville at Minden during the Seven Years' War opined with an air of authority. "I mean, what king or prince would hire out his best troops?"

A few of the officers gathered before the hearth, sipping wine and listening to the major's assessment nodded languidly in agreement. From the very first day Hessian troops stepped ashore on

Staten Island, there had been an unstated undercurrent of disdain for them among the officers who held the King's commission, a feeling made all the more acute by the inherent distrust Englishmen had of foreigners. James Keating shared this opinion, but was not as ready to place all the blame on Rall's shoulders. Having been born in America, he had a far better grasp of the uniqueness of the American character than did his fellow officers, allowing him to attribute some of the reasons for the rebel success at Trenton to the same tenacity and undaunted courage that had allowed their forefathers to conquer the savage wilderness they found along the shores of North America. Whether those attributes would be enough to see them through the storm that would soon be unleashed upon them once General Howe's army reassembled and it was ready to take the field was a question he found he could not answer.

"If Washington is smart, he'll tuck tail and scurry back across the Delaware," the major asserted as the conversation moved on to what lay ahead. "He's done all he could with what he has. To throw away what is nothing more than a moral victory by risking defeat in open battle with us would be the height of folly."

A captain who was well into his cups raised his glass in a mock toast. "Here's to folly."

Following a round of nervous laughter, speculation as to how Howe would respond took a more serious tone.

"I think it would be wise for all of us to prepare ourselves and our men for hard marching," the major advised. "God willing, the campaign I expect we'll soon be embarking on will see the end of this foolishness."

Unable to help himself, James winced. He knew the men who were following Washington—men like David Gray, his brother-in-law—were no fools. Gray believed in the cause he had dedicated himself to. Like the campaign that had sputtered out along the banks of the Delaware but a few weeks ago, it would take more than the one they were about to embark on to stamp out support for a cause that now seemed to be as alive as ever. Of that, James was sure.

Coming to his feet, he set his empty glass aside and made his excuses. "Gentlemen, the hour is late and, as Major Graham has pointed out, we've hard marching ahead."

James's declaration was greeted with nods and muted agreement. One by one, the other officers finished their drinks, came to their feet, and filed out of the room until only Major Graham remained staring into the dying fire. In the silence of the room, he found himself wondering if even he believed in what he had said. After draining the last of the wine he had been nursing all night, he too rose from his overstuffed chair.

"Well, there's nothing for it but to see what the morrow brings," he muttered before heading off to his own bed.

New York City
26 December 1776

Lord Robert was in the middle of sharing a delightful little story with Kat Trent as they enjoyed their early afternoon tea when a courier was ushered into the parlor by one of Kat's maids. With his free hand, Lord Robert took the message even as he was apologizing for the untimely interruption.

"If you'll be so kind to excuse the interruption, Lady Trent."

"Oh, pay me no mind," Kat replied huskily as she reached out and daintily laid a hand on Lord Robert's arm. "I fully understand the need to tend to one's business."

"Um, yes, of course," Lord Robert muttered distractedly as a crimson hue brightened his cheeks.

Doing his best to ignore her hand on the sleeve of his coat, he turned his full attention the message. Holding it out at arm's length, a frown darkened his expression as he read it.

"Unwelcomed news?" Kat asked coyly as she eased back in her seat and brought her teacup up to her lips.

"Orders," Lord Robert replied flatly without looking over at her. "It seems Lord Cornwallis has been instructed to take to the field and run the rebel army to ground should they be bold enough to recross the Delaware."

"Will they?"

Having been distracted by a second reading of the message, Lord Robert looked over to where Kat was watching him with an intensity that put him in mind of the way a cat watches a mouse hole.

"Will they what?"

"Will the rebels dare to recross the Delaware once word reaches them Lord Cornwallis is headed their way at the head of an army?"

Lord Robert shrugged as he came to his feet. "There's no telling what the scoundrels will do," he grumbled distractedly as he began to mentally tick off the numerous items he would need to tend to before Lord Cornwallis headed off on campaign. "If you'd excuse me, Lady Trent, there are things I need to see to."

"I do hope they will not keep you from joining me for supper tonight," Kat mewed plaintively as she gazed up at Lord Robert through her lashes.

Bending over, he took up Kat's proffered hand and kissed it. "I would not miss it for the world."

"Excellent," Kat murmured as she decided to put off sending word to David that Cornwallis would be taking to the field forthwith.

She would wait until later that evening to do so in the hope she would be able to wean further details of the coming campaign, if not from Lord Robert himself, then from one of the young officers on his staff always willing to share what they knew with what they considered to be one of the most charming and eligible females in the city, if for no other reason than to hold her attention.

Newtown, Pennsylvania
Evening, 26 December 1776

As Ezra Shaw stepped into the light of the campfire, the expression on his face told Ian the news he brought would probably not be welcome. In an effort to cheer him up and help Ezra to work up the nerve to pass on his tidings, Ian used the ladle he had been using to stir the stew to tap the edge of a blackened pot hanging over the fire.

"Hungry?"

"When am I not?" Shaw muttered distractedly as he settled down among the tight little circle of men gathered about the fire.

In silence, he took to fishing out his wooden bowl and horn spoon from his haversack. Reaching over the fire, he held the bowl out for Ian to fill.

"Well?" Ian asked as he was ladling stew into Shaw's bowl.

"They're discussing it now," Shaw replied cryptically as he settled down and took to dipping his spoon into the stew.

Ian had prepared it using vittles he had scrounged from abandoned Hessian stores before leaving Trenton. Out of habit, Shaw stirred his soup, carefully examining the bits and pieces of meat, carrots, and potatoes Ian had thrown into the stew before tasting it.

James McPike, who had been watching Ian and Shaw, could not help but ask the question that was on the minds of all of Shaw's men.

"Will we be going back across the river?"

Shaw did not answer right off. Instead, he took a mouthful of stew, closing his eyes briefly as he savored its warmth and flavor. Only after he had chewed and swallowed the first substantial mouthful of food he had been able to enjoy all day did he look over at McPike.

"If the general was a cautious man, he'd wait until after the New Year to see just how many of us were still here."

Ian, who had first marched with Washington in 1755 as part of Washington's Virginia Regiment, grumbled, "But he's not."

"No," Shaw, who had also been part of that first campaign, agreed as he scooped up another spoonful of stew. "I expect we'll be going back. Word is Washington's already sent orders out to the Pennsylvania and New Jersey militias to assemble and be prepared to march."

"To where?" Angus Brodie asked as he held his empty bowl out toward Ian in the hope he would refill it.

"Don't know," Shaw replied quietly. "But as soon as we get there, I'll let you know."

Shaw's effort to lighten the grim mood that had settled over them with humor was rewarded with a ripple of nervous laughter. Wishing to put an end to any further questions on what the near future held for them for he had no answers, he looked across the fire over at Ian.

"Where's that boy of yours? Off with the general?"

"Last I saw him he was still with the Hessian prisoners, chattering away with them as if they were long lost cousins."

"That girl of his, she's German," Shaw ventured. "Maybe some of them Hessians are related to her?"

The need to fight Hessians had made any mention of Gretchen Richter's heritage a touchy subject for Ian. Frowning, he returned Shaw's stare.

"That girl is as American as you or I."

Shaw, born in Ireland, was tempted to remind a man who had been raised in the wild highlands of Scotland their claim to that distinction was just as tenuous as the young woman Morgan spoke of with a fondness that portended more than mere friendship. But Shaw held his tongue.

After hacking out a place to call their own in the wilderness and spending the last two years fighting to win the right to govern themselves, free of a King neither had ever laid eyes on, Shaw imagined that he, Ian, Morgan, and the German girl had earned the right to call themselves whatever they wished. Be it a Virginian or an American, none of the men seated around the fire with him were what they had once been. They were something new. If what they were to go by was to be *American*, so be it. He could live with that.

ACKNOWLEDGEMENTS

To Kurt. You are a credit to your country, your family, and those you served with.

DON'T MISS THE PREQUEL:

Ambition swells into vengeance and honor stumbles before survival as the 18th century wilderness of North America boils with the French and Indian War.

In *A Savage War of Empire*, New York Times bestselling author Harold Coyle rips open the bloody marrow of a continent in turmoil, plunging readers into a maelstrom of fire, fury, and fate. Soldiers, settlers, and warriors collide in a brutal struggle that will shape the future of nations.

Highlander Ian McPherson charges into the chaos seeking land and redemption. Across enemy lines, French officer Anton de Chevalier commands with deadly precision, fighting a dawning, damning realization. Between them, Native leaders Toolah and Gingego fight for their people's future – and their own souls.

From ambushes in dense forests to sieges of mighty forts, this unflinching triumph of historical fiction delivers relentless action, unforgettable characters, and the raw fury and burning heart of a continent at war.

A SAVAGE WAR OF EMPIRE
ADVANCE PREVIEW:

PROLOGUE

Saint Croix Island
Fall 1604

AS HE HAD EACH morning since the strangers had come, the old warrior stepped out of the forest across from the rocky banks of the island just as darkness gave way to the cold, pale dawn. The only sound that disturbed the stillness surrounding him was that of the swift river before him splashing on nearby rocks. Peering through the early morning mist rising off the turbulent waters and over to where the strangers had made camp, he uttered a silent prayer in the hope the sunrise would find them gone.

Yet even before he could see them, he knew they were still there. He could smell them. It wasn't the smoke from their fires that set them apart from his people and those of other tribes he had come across in the past. Its burning wood smelt no different than that which warmed his own lodge. Rather, it was the stench that rose from the squalid living conditions the strangers seemed to revel in that marked them as being different, as different from his people as the white banner adorned with three yellow emblems of their tribe. Slowly, the warrior squatted down onto a comfortable position on a large, flat rock, from which he could watch the comings and goings of the strangers as they tended to their early morning rituals and tasks.

One of the first stirrings that occurred each morning was the appearance of a handful of men dressed in armor. Once bright and shiny, but now, like the leaves on the trees, dull and lifeless by the passing of time. The stranger at the entrance to their crude log enclosure seldom greeted the group of men as they approached. Instead, with bowed head, the man left the spot where he had stood watch throughout the night and trudged away to join the others. This was done with less enthusiasm than a captive faced with certain death. In his place, another man, similarly dressed and looking equally dejected, took the first man's place at the entrance. Once he had reached the spot that seemed suitable for him, the new guard lowered the wood and metal weapon he bore, eased it down until one end rested on the ground, and leaned against the post that the rickety gate hung on.

It was only after he was comfortable that the new sentinel bothered to lift his gaze from the dirt at his feet. Slowly, more from want of amusement than from attentiveness, the sentinel surveyed the island he and his companions had chosen to occupy. The old warrior wondered if the strangers, with skin as white and as fair as any he had ever seen, and faces covered with hair, saw the same things that he saw. He liked to think that they did, that the strangers shared more than bodies shaped as his was. But the more the old man watched them, the more he came to realize that this breed of man was unlike any other human he, or anyone he knew, had ever come across. Even the shaman, after much contemplation and consultation with the spirits, was at a loss to explain who these men were and what their coming foreshadowed.

Unable to find answers in the legends of his people or in the wisdom of the elders of the tribe, the old warrior decided to do what he always had done when faced with a new situation or challenge. He would study it, as often as he could and as long as he could. It was important, he knew, to be familiar with the land that surrounds you and all the creatures that inhabit it. While this simple prescription had failed to gain him sufficient triumphs to be considered a leader within his tribe, it had permitted him to live to an age none of his boyhood friends had, and to bask in the warmth of a family that honored him as if he were the greatest warrior chief who had ever lived.

When the eyes of the stranger guarding the enclosure of the settlement on the island finally fell upon the old man, the stranger studied the warrior for a moment. There was no surprise in the man's face, for he and his companions had seen the warrior and others of his tribe from afar on many occasions. Only the warrior seemed to show any real interest as the two men stared at each other for several minutes. One question, the same one that always came to mind whenever the old warrior knew he was being watched, was why the strangers, after all these months, still refused to make an effort to contact them. It was foolish, he thought, utterly foolish on the part of the strangers to stand aloof on their isolated island, in the middle of their own stench, and make no attempt to come to terms with the world or the people about them.

Suddenly, the stranger's eyes lifted slightly, so that they were now gazing over the old warrior's head. Seeing something behind the old man that aroused his interest, the stranger pushed away from the post he had been leaning on and straightened up. For a moment, the old warrior perked his ears, but he did not turn around. There was no need to, for even with the noise of the turbulent river before him, his tired ears easily recognized the familiar footfalls.

"Why have you come here, my child, and disturbed me?" the warrior demanded, not taking his eyes from the stranger.

"I come here for the same reason you come, in search of answers," the sweet voice of his granddaughter responded.

"Then you are wasting your time," the old warrior responded gruffly. "Men such as those can provide us with no answers."

With a smile, the young girl came up close to her grandfather and settled down next to him. Without a word, the two eased against each other, both for support and for warmth, as they had done on so many other mornings. Together the old, tired eyes of the warrior, set deeply in the crags of a face that had seen many winters, were joined on their lonely vigil by the wide, eager, bright eyes of a girl on the verge of womanhood.

Across the way, another fair-skinned stranger emerged from the compound with a wooden bucket in each hand. When he came abreast of the sentinel, he stopped and looked across the river at the old warrior and his granddaughter. After a moment, the two strangers exchanged comments. The old man enjoyed listening to them talk. Though he had no idea what they said, their language had a lyrical quality that reminded him of a young woman's song.

"What do you suppose they are talking about?" his granddaughter asked, in the sweet tones that only an innocent maiden could manage.

From the look in the stranger's eyes, the old man knew full well what they were discussing. Yet he did not tell her. Instead, his response reflected his own feelings and beliefs. "It does not matter what they speak of. People who are foolish enough to settle on an island that has no game, no source of fresh water other than the river itself, and will wash away when the floods come in spring should not be listened to. They are like the rainbow, my child, perhaps beautiful to behold, but of no importance. In time, they will be gone."

His granddaughter thought about his words as she watched the man with the buckets move down to the river, fill them halfway with water, then trudge back to the enclosure. Finally, she turned her face toward the old warrior's. "Do you really think that they will be gone soon?"

That was a question that the old man had pondered himself many, many times. His brain told him that they would not, could not, last very long, not if their choice of settlement was any indication of their skill and wisdom. Yet, in his heart, he knew that there was more to be feared from these strangers than their actions to date indicated. As stupid as he liked to make them out to be in his own mind, the old man knew that these strangers had a presence about them that was, for the warrior and his people, ominous. In his dreams, these strangers had come to personify all the faceless fears and demons he had known since childhood. Though they had not done him or his people any harm, the old warrior had lived long enough to know evil when he saw it.

"You fear them, too, don't you?" his granddaughter finally stated as she looked back across the river.

Taking his hand out from under the fur that had been keeping it warm, he grasped the girl's hand. "No, my child, I do not fear these men, for I am an old man that is not long for this life. I believe that my eyes will not see many more winters. But," he said as he squeezed her hand, "I fear these are not men, not as we know. In time we will be allowed to see inside their hearts and learn what it is that brings them here, to our shores. When we do, I fear our people will weep."

The chill that swept across them didn't cut the young girl as deeply as her grandfather's words had. For she, too, had felt the same foreboding the old warrior had put to words. Unable to think of a suitable response, the girl simply squeezed the old man's hand and sat beside him in silence, watching, studying, and waiting.